The House that Jack Built

Catherine Barry lives in Dublin with her two young children. She has had a number of poems and short stories published in the past. *The House that Jack Built* is her first book.

The House that Jack Built

Catherine Barry

POCKET BOOKS

TownHouse

First published in Great Britain and Ireland by
Pocket/Town House, 2001
An imprint of Simon & Schuster UK Ltd, and
TownHouse and CountryHouse Ltd, Dublin

Simon & Schuster UK is a Viacom company

1 3 5 7 9 10 8 6 4 2

Simon & Schuster UK Ltd
Africa House
64–78 Kingsway
London WC2B 6AH

Simon & Schuster Australia
Sydney

TownHouse and CountryHouse Ltd
Trinity House
Charleston Road
Ranelagh
Dublin 6
Ireland

A CIP catalogue record for this book is available from
the British Library

ISBN 1–903650–09–7

Typeset by Palimpsest Book Production Limited,
Polmont, Stirlingshire
Printed and bound in Great Britain by
Bookmarque Ltd, Croydon, Surrey

Acknowledgments

Thanks to John and Maureen Barry for being my parents and loving me unconditionally.

Thanks to Jonathan, Mark, Frances and Damien for keeping the faith when mine was dwindling.

Thanks to Darley Anderson, my agent and friend. You changed my life in a matter of hours.

Thanks to Clare Ledingham and Suzanne Baboneau my editors, for excellent guidance.

Thanks to Treasa Coady of TownHouse Publishing and Ian Chapman from Simon & Schuster for finding me.

Thanks to my truly wonderful and talented friend Peter Sheridan, who believed in this book when I couldn't. You supported and encouraged all that is good in me and I love you for that.

Thanks to Phil Costigan of St Mary's School, Killester who planted the seed all those years ago.

Thanks to all my friends in Killester and Raheny, especially

Dave and Patricia Coyle, for giving me a life beyond my wildest dreams.

Thanks to my children, Davitt and Caítriona, my best critics, my best friends, and my best teachers.

My thanks to Vincent who started all this. You said five years . . . here I am! Thank you for showing me how to live. I will always love you and you are always with me.

Most of all . . . thank you, God.

To Vincent.
Your gift, as promised.

Glossary

1. Grushy: a handful of coins thrown to children, traditionally by the groom, after an Irish wedding ceremony.
2. Ten or five spot: ten or five pounds' worth of dope.
3. Parallels: Parallel trousers worn in the seventies. Trousers that were of equal width and length.
4. The Joy: common Irish abbreviation for Mountjoy Prison.
5. Tayto bag: Tayto are Irish manufacturers of crisps. Tayto crisp bag.
6. Bull Wall: well-known feature of Clontarf seafront, a long wall taking in the Bull Island view.
7. ESB: Electricity Supply Board.
8. Marie Céleste: brand name of cheap sherry.
9. Bowl: pipe-like utensil for smoking dope.
10. FÁS: Irish government training and employment agency.
11. The Hill: well-known Dublin street market, set on a hill in the inner city.

Chapter 1

'Is there anyone here with any Irish in them? Is there any of the girls who would like a little more Irish in them?'
Phil Lynott, Dalymount Stadium, 1978

I lost my virginity on 31 December 1978. I lost my knickers too. When I stepped out of the blue Fiat van, they hula-hooped around my knees, worked their way down my calves and finally crash-landed on the moonlit beach. The whole ordeal had taken exactly three minutes. I, Jacqueline Joyce, of Clontarf, Dublin, had waited fifteen years for this momentous occasion, and I had been saving myself for the right man. My accomplice in crime was my brother's friend Matt. As he was one year older than me, I expected him to be fully experienced in the art of love-making. *Wrong*.

In a hopeless attempt to salvage what remained of his manhood, he savaged my self-esteem on that ill-fated journey home afterwards.

'For fuck's sake!' he spat. 'Haven't you ever heard of foreplay?'

This remark only served to make me feel worse. The sexual fiasco must somehow have been my fault, I thought. I searched my mind for a humorous retort.

'Sure, I've read all his books.' It was a lame effort.

Already my beau was engaging in the serious business of rolling a joint large enough to wipe out armies.

The night in question fell two weeks before my sixteenth birthday. It seemed only fitting. After all, it was New Year's Eve and Matt (abbreviation for Matthew) had presented me with a pre-birthday gift: a pair of dangly silver earrings sporting multi-coloured feathers, and a bottle of Tramp – the quintessential kit for an upwardly mobile amateur hippie of my description.

The evening was off to a good start, despite the fact that Matt had arrived predictably two hours late. I had borrowed a cheesecloth ankle-length dress from a kind friend. She had purchased it from an Indian shop on trendy Grafton Street. The fact that she was a blubbering four-foot nothing, as wide as she was long, who resembled a St Patrick's Day float, did not deter her. On slender little me, the dress was perfect. It was the ideal 1970s sexual aid, buttoned conveniently right down the front; any would-be suitor would be hard-pressed not to manipulate the simple structure to his advantage. A few delicate flickering fingers could have it gaping open in one minute flat. I knew because I had done a dummy run twice, and timed it myself. My attire that evening was very important. With a spray of Tramp in all the right places, and my feathered friends jangling from my ears, I felt like a woman. Not at all the fifteen-year-old girl that I was in reality. I was in love with Matt Howard and tonight was 'the' night. There was no doubt about it.

Earlier on in the pub that evening I was feeling queasy. Partly with excitement about what was to come, but more probably because of the six Bacardi and Cokes I had poured down my throat in a show of bravado. Matt and I linked little fingers under the table. I thought it was cute and I felt really happy.

The fact that Matt was mysteriously disappearing into

the toilet every five minutes did not diminish my enthusiasm. 'The Sea View', a dingy pub that boasted hideous 3D maroon wallpaper, had only one saving grace. It was conveniently situated 100 yards across from the seafront. Glasses clanked noisily, people laughed heartily; bad jokes were standard and vomiting compulsory. Swilling my Bacardi and Coke around the glass like an expert wine-taster, I watched the curious comings and goings.

Matt had disappeared again.

'What's wrong with him?' I asked my friend Karen. 'Is he constipated?'

'Yeah, looks like it,' she laughed. 'Hey, Mick,' she beckoned to the barman. 'Do you serve laxatives?'

'Yeah, we serve anyone,' came the tarty reply.

Matt returned looking sheepish and glassy-eyed. He sat down beside me.

'Where were you?' I asked, already knowing the answer.

'Ah man, the van was giving me trouble.'

Not bad, I thought. I had heard worse. The truth was, of course, that Matt and his cronies were making their ritual rounds of the local chemists, gathering prescribed bottles of cough medicine. None of them had a cough to speak of, and the prescriptions were forged. It was a cheap and effective drug at the time. Failing that, they were crossing the road to the seafront where most of our hash supply was dealt. The peeling green-painted shelters came alive at night. Couples huddled inside them, making use of their over-sized duffel coats to camouflage their adolescent groping. Dutch clogs, red and yellow, scraped the pavement in haste, as five and ten spots were discreetly negotiated. Gangs congregated along the Clontarf Road, and all the way down the causeway. This was New Year's Eve. You were supposed to be drunk, at the least stoned, but preferably both.

I had had a crush on Matt since I was nine and a half. We had enjoyed a turbulent and ever-changing relationship. Of course, Matt wasn't aware of the fact that we had been having this fictitious affair. Most of it had been created in my head. I had obsessed about him for so long that I missed this important tiny detail. We had broken up, made up, had sex, gotten married and divorced. All in my pea-sized immature imagination. My mother had already pointed out my 'blind spot' regarding Matt.

'That boy is trouble,' she would sigh under her breath. She remarked that when he *was* around, he always seemed vaguely incoherent. 'Did he have a head injury or something?' she would ask innocently.

This question wasn't completely without basis, for Matt constantly behaved like a hospital patient who had taken too much ether. He was always taking too much of something. I defended him hotly and refused to acknowledge the fact that he had perfected the art of being in a near-permanent state of coma. That was all he did, get permanently smashed, day in, day out. The rest of his time was spent trying to maintain it.

Matt had been a frequent visitor to our house as far back as I could remember. My younger brother Jason and his friends had one thing in common: they all loved music. They listened to music incessantly, swapping new LPs and exchanging gossip about forthcoming albums and so on. It was not unusual for them to stay in the back room for four or five hours a day, just listening to music. The only lull occurred when my father found a copy of a Black Sabbath record. He found the very title of the band offensive, and music was banned completely for two weeks. Eventually, he gave in and allowed them to play 'morally enhancing and spiritually uplifting' records. Now they played Mike Oldfield's *Tubular Bells* day in day out. My dad found it difficult to admit that it was 'creative'. It was never off the turn-table.

Occasionally, Jason would emerge from the smoke-filled cesspit to make tea and toast (the staple diet of the day). Copious amounts were wolfed savagely, and my father often wondered aloud whether the other boys were ever fed in their own homes. It was during these intermissions that I tried hard to make myself known. The gatherings were sacred and ritualistic. Nobody was allowed in. The best option was to offer to dust the piano (my father's pride and joy), to attend to the gathering ash and fingerprints left by the lads. It came as a welcome suggestion, any day.

Sheepishly I would enter, armed to the teeth with Mr Pledge and any number of old rolled-up vests and knickers, a look of supreme single-mindedness on my freckled face, as if my mission was one of gargantuan importance. For all my acting abilities, they hardly nodded an acknowledgement.

Not surprisingly, as I boasted the most hideous braces across my front teeth, which were prominent enough in themselves without drawing any further attention to them. They were a feature which invited cruel remarks from schoolchildren. They had taken to calling me 'Plug', after a riotous character from the *Bash Street Kids* strip in the *Beano* comic. I made several desperate attempts to 'lose' my braces and to break them, but to no avail. My final attempt ended in tears of frustration; I had buried them in the dog's kennel, and the dog proudly presented them to my father at the dinner table. He wagged his tail furiously, the braces in the grip of his mighty jaws. Dad retrieved them from his drooling mouth, and patted him affectionately.

'Good dog! Good boy!' There was a look of smug satisfaction on his face. 'I'll make her eat them,' he muttered under his breath, and I fled to my bedroom in terror.

Still, the first time I was permitted entrance to the sacred domain it made way for my second encounter with true love. From the orange turntable a variety of throaty vocals poured forth. On this particular day, it was the beautiful velvety voice of John Martyn that made its way into my heart. My first experience of elation, via music, stayed with me for life. I became a slave to music, as had all my family before me. My sister was bopping to the likes of The Real Thing, The Chi-Lites and The Stylistics. In the fog-infested den, I was introduced to such geniuses as Bob Dylan, Bruce Springsteen, Rory Gallagher, Thin Lizzy, Led Zeppelin, Supertramp, Genesis, Joan Armatrading, Fleetwood Mac and James Taylor. I tinkled the odd note on the piano, while I feigned the dusting operation. The boys shouted loudly over the music, exchanging opinions on their idols, breathing in note and lyric as if their very lives depended on it. In an ironic way, it did help to alleviate the boredom and treachery of Intermediate Certificate exams just around the corner. Much better to hang loose with 'Bull Frog Blues' or chill out to 'At Seventeen' by Janis Ian.

The gang were an elite gathering of friends of all ages between thirteen and seventeen. Friends, at that age, were simply the most important thing in your life. They were harmless really. Lazy legs sprawled across the floor. They were the proud owners of a candle, moulded into the shape of a mushroom, which was ignited with religious fervour every time they gathered. The candle represented the quiet rebellion of those who sought inspiration in magic mushrooms, ten spots, oblivious of the inherent danger of such drugs (this wouldn't come to light for another two decades).

A mellow bunch, they would while away those summer afternoons. I, a scrawny thirteen-year-old feeling the first pangs of adolescence, clung lovingly to the piano keys and listened, with pricked ears and clanking braces. In years to come, the boys eventually accepted my presence among them without rancour, as long as I held my tongue. I had formed a slight lisp, which I still have today. This became more pronounced on drinking sprees later on in life, but that's another story. I admired Matt from afar. My head was filled with romantic notions about him. I longed for the day when he would speak to me personally. I had tipped my cap. I was smitten.

Matt had developed the perfect art of laughing at himself. I loved it. He made *me* laugh. His sense of humour was extraordinarily attractive. His impressions and contorted faces kept us all rolling in the aisles. It was probably this quality which kept me hopelessly hanging on, for so many years. I didn't understand why he laughed so much. I had no understanding of drugs and their effects on behaviour. I recall coming home from school, lopsided from a heavy school bag, and on entering the hall, standing still to see if I could hear his voice. When I did, I raced upstairs to get changed. Wild horses could not keep me from the object of my affection.

It was not until some years later, though, that the inevitable happened. He spoke to me. He actually noticed me, and *spoke to me*! I knew he was speaking to me, because he was looking at me, and calling me by name. I tried to appear cool and aloof, and give a devastatingly intelligent response. A hushed silence engulfed the room, leaving only the words from Boston's 'More than a Feeling' taking centre stage. How appropriate. I have no idea to this day what he asked me, nor do I recall what my response was. I only knew that I had been rocketed forth into a new dimension of Nirvana.

I was a more rounded fourteen-year-old, the day Matt first graced me with his personal attention. I had some notches under my belt, so to speak. I had French-kissed a boy that year, for the first time. It was a dare I had consented to, during a game of Spin the Bottle. I didn't want to appear to be 'tight'. The revolting encounter had left me none the wiser, and I pondered the whole 'teenage philandering' thing. Yet, in this very precious moment with Matt, I was bursting to shout the fact out loud. ('I French-kissed a boy, sunshine, so don't act the bollox with me.')

I was a woman of the world now. How I wished that I had a dirty great love-bite on my neck. That would have brought the message home, good and proper. Instead I went for a gleaming grin, which exposed straight, white, brace-free teeth. That ought to have done it, but instead he abruptly turned his attention to my brother, who was wearing headphones so big that he looked like Minnie Mouse taking a growth spurt. Oblivious of the hash-heavy atmos, and mouthing Mick Jagger's 'Brown Sugar', Matt made a second effort. This time I was prepared. A teenage twit, opportunistic to the last. 'Howya,' he said.

My journey had begun.

So, to New Year's Eve, 1978. Now the great night was upon me. I was just about to turn sixteen. I was just about to become a 'woman'. Had Matt passed out in front of me, I would have proceeded alone. Nothing was going to stop us. New Year's Eve seemed an appropriate time to shed my adolescence once and for all.

Without discussion we left the pub and drove in silence to our 'nest'. Searching out seclusion on Dolly-mount Strand was proving difficult. There were more writhing bodies in rocking cars than the bumpers in Bray on a summer's day. The traffic was like Fairview in the rush hour. Was everyone in Ireland losing their virginity?

The most important rule of the night was to appear to be 'cool'. If I had been any cooler, I would have frozen to death. I tried to display a little maturity although I was scared shitless right down to my size 32AA teen bra. If he was afraid he did not show it.

'Are you sure you want to go ahead with this?' he asked softly, his hand cupping mine on the gear stick.

'Of course I'm sure,' I replied, confidence oozing from every petrified pore. 'It's not the first time, you know.' It was a bare-faced lie.

'Me neither,' he smiled.

Fuck. 'Oh. How many times?' I query. Suddenly I have visions of this Casanova who has bedded the entire population. A poster of him with *Most Wanted Lover* captioned underneath is bill-boarded from here to Howth.

'Only one other time,' he said.

That seemed even worse than before. I had wanted him to be the first so badly. However, now that I had convinced myself that he was an accomplished and artful lover, it spurred me on to increase my own fictional romantic exchanges. Another blatant lie unfurled.

'Yeah, I can't remember how many times I've done it, to be honest.'

Pause. No reply.

'I'm not saying I know it all or anything but you're not dealing with a novice here.'

Silent, cringing, self-inflicted humiliation.

We eventually came to a standstill at the end of the strand. We had been driving around in circles for so long, I expected to see the bright lights of Holyhead across the way. Instead the familiar outline of Howth Head lay to my left, and the rosary-beaded lights of the East Wall lay in front. They reminded me of God, and in advance of the penance I would surely get when I went to Confession next week, I tried to say three Hail Marys in succession. I was appalled to find I couldn't remember anything after 'Thy womb, Jesus'. Matt was smoking another joint, the

Bacardi and Cokes were making me sick and I was bursting to go to the toilet.

I got out and squatted in an undignified fashion at the back of the van. A gust of wind and sand whipped around my thighs. I wasn't sure if I'd pissed on my shoes or given the Fiat a free car wash. It was dark and scary and the popping grass was giving me some weird paranoid thoughts. I had begun to appreciate why Matt was always in 'good form'. I had dabbled innocently with drugs only to get closer to him, and wasn't really enjoying their effects. My stomach churned but I didn't want to appear foolish.

I whisked my pants up again, checking that my dress had not become wedged into them as well. I remembered seeing a woman come out of a pub toilet with her dress encased in her knickers and a beautiful trail of pink toilet paper flowing from her arse to the ground. I wondered, should I try to get sick now or after?

Back in the van, Bruce Springsteen is wooing us with 'Darkness from the Edge of Town'. I am wondering how to make the move from the front to the back. Glancing casually behind, it looks so small all of a sudden. How are we both going to fit in there, never mind actually do it? Matt is kissing me. It's not a romantic kiss. In fact it's rather rough and unrhythmic. I try to get into the swing of it, but he is dancing to a different tune altogether. His French-kissing feels more like a mechanically faulted cement-mixer. Round and round he goes; where he stops nobody knows. I know it is par for the course, but it is doing absolutely nothing for my hormones, not to mention my jaws. I am bored and wondering still how we are going to manoeuvre ourselves without awkwardness. He takes the bait. 'C'mon, let's move into the back.'

We scramble over the seats, bumping heads and bruising thighs, and crash on to the floor laughing. I am lying uncomfortably with my head twisted against a spare tyre. I don't care. Any minute now and the deliciousness will begin. I could almost hear the gentle groanings as our bodies twisted and turned in blissful union, and the choirs of angels burst forth in heavenly chorus. What actually happened was that Matt yanked my knickers down to my knees, entered me and it was all over in seconds. The only thing that burst forth was Matt. Prematurely, at that, and not even a hint of Aled Jones.

'Fuck me,' he snorted in my ear.

Yes please, I thought.

Chapter 2

I never fully recovered from that encounter with Matt. It was one massive disappointment. I went home feeling dirty, upset and confused and spent the following week immersed in music and staying quiet, which I was prone to do anyway. Thank God, my parents didn't seem to notice my mood change. It all seemed wrong. I didn't want to feel that way. So I did the second thing that would become a character defect for life. I lied to myself. I did a good job of it too. Perhaps everybody's first sexual experience was like that? Yes. That was the only thing I could think of that made two wrongs a right and brought me some comfort. It never occurred to me that Matt had been vastly inexperienced too. I carried on as normal. Living in my illusions. Isn't that what the 1970s were made of?

Contrary to popular belief, the 1970s held two very different factions. I belonged to the 'freaky hippie' contingent. I was full of brotherly love, peace and Flower Power. My younger sister Rachel belonged to the 'Boot Boys' and 'Skinhead' gangs, who roamed St Anne's Park, and frequently beat the crap out of each other. They expressed their feelings with lethal weapons such as coshes, chains and planks of wood. They sought out confrontation and acted tough.

At the same time, they wore Brüt aftershave and Old

Spice, which was a bit of a contradiction. They venerated Bruce Lee, and anything violent.

As far as fashion goes, they wore parallel trousers, preferably two-toned, with a waistband that could double as a scarf. There were pockets at the bottom of their trousers, and nobody knows why. Numbered T-shirts were also popular, especially 69 ones, as were the comical platform shoes and studded brogues – the more studs the better, as the noise was intimidating. Girls wore the 'Midi' hairstyle – remember Suzi Quatro? And in the height of it, tartan scarves were draped from the wrist, in honour of those wonderful Bay City Rollers. There was an imitation Bray City Rollers but they were beaten to a pulp too.

It was a crime for one gang to be seen with the other. For a long spell, I was in conflict as to where my loyalties lay. I sneaked in to see *Saturday Night Fever* and was wowed by John Travolta, but I never told anyone. I loved some of the 'other' music, and still do to this day, but was loth to admit it. In the end, I decided I was a full-fledged hippie and I never really departed from the beaten track again.

While my sister and her friends frequented discos such as The Blind, The Apartment and Club 74, me and my buddies visited Toners, The Baggot Inn, The Crofton Airport Hotel, McGonagles, The New Morans Hotel and the coolest joint of all, The Limit, in Clontarf. There had previously been an No Limit and, I was told, if you hadn't been a member there, you were nothing.

The Saturday following my disastrous encounter with Matt, I qualified to become a member of The Limit. The lower the membership number, the better your status. I once met a guy who was member 34. All we were short of doing was taking out our prayer mats. I had spent the day doing the usual Saturday things. A typical Saturday always included a trip to The Dandelion Market at the top of Grafton Street. I had tried to forget about Matt but much to my amazement, I found that despite our bad experience, my feelings were still the same for him, and I had begun to blame myself. Another character defect that would bedevil me for the rest of my life.

I wasn't too sure whether I could trust my friends with my secret. In those days, sexual conduct was coded into 'The Seven Stars' system. One, a kiss. Two, a French kiss. Three, a feel outside your bra. Four, a feel inside your bra. Five, outside your knickers. Six, inside your knickers. And Seven . . . well, you can guess the rest.

Nobody did the Seventh Star; if they did they never told me. If you didn't do some of these you were branded 'tight'; if you did you were 'loose'. If you did the Seventh Star, you were nothing less than an out-and-out slut. I wanted badly to talk to someone, but just couldn't summon up the courage.

I wandered around The Dandelion Market with my two best friends at the time, Jill and Karen. I bought a white grandfather shirt, two sizes too big for me, which was the correct size. Then I nipped into one of the Indian shops, my favourites, and bought some incense and patchouli oil, and a little leather sandal dangling from a choker necklace. I wanted to buy a pair of cowboy boots, but my parents refused to give me the money, so I bought a pair of desert boots, which were a perfect second choice.

I had £6 left and carefully perused the hundreds of LP's stacked on table after table. I found *Jailbreak* by Thin Lizzy and carefully held on to the precious object all the way over to St Stephen's Green. It was my first ever album and I was elated. I made sure everybody could see the silver cover, and turned it right side out.

In Stephen's Green, the ducks looked starved. Karen called them like dogs. 'Here, boy!'

We threw in our meagre handful of popcorn. I was reading the credits on the back of the Lizzy album. You had to drop the 'Thin' to be cool. Jill had scored some grass in the market, and wasted no time rolling up. I wasn't really interested, as my experience of dope so far had only brought paranoia and nausea. I declined a blast as they passed it back and forth.

'What's up with you?' Karen asked through clenched teeth.

'Nothing.'

'Are you coming to The Limit tonight?'

'Yep.'

'You should be getting your membership card, right?'

'Yep.'

'Yep,' Jill aped.

'Shut up,' I snapped.

'What the fuck's up with you? You've had a face on you all week.'

'I told you. Nothing.'

Jill lay on the grass, breathing in the smoke deeply. 'Fuck it, this is good stuff.'

'Too right,' Karen agreed. The pair of them were sighing orgasmically. 'Sure you don't want a blast?'

'Yep.'

They were beginning to get on my wick. Jill began to sing Roxy Music's 'Let's Stick Together', one of our favourite songs. Often we would link arms and walk along the road singing it. Today, I didn't want any loving camaraderie. Besides, I was stone cold sober. Jill and Karen were beginning to giggle. They were starting to get their words mixed up.

'Hey. What's that song by Rhyff Clitoris?' Jill asked innocently.

'Don't you mean Cliff Richard?'

'Or that one by Bushy Kate. Oops. I mean Kate Bush.'

I opened a bag of Maltesers and they descended on me like vultures.

'Oh man, I have the munchies. Shit, Jill, go and get some cheese and chocolate quickly.'

They devoured my sweets and went across the street to buy some more.

I lay on the grass, and thought about school. We had been 'mitching' on a regular basis. I had returned on the Monday, dreading it yet almost welcoming it at the same time. Anything to take my mind off Matt. I loved school. We always seemed to be laughing. The Head Nun complained that I laughed too much. She told me it would upset my father if she had to call him to come to the school about it. I never really fathomed the mysterious evil that was inherent in my merriment, for that was all it was, merriment, a sense of fun. The nuns couldn't comprehend it, so they tried a different tack. Now I was 'mentally unstable' because I laughed too much. It was the best they could come up with.

That day, during our break, a gang had congregated in the school oratory, a tiny chapel that guaranteed privacy. The nuns were thrilled to bits to see so many of us go in and out. They had no idea of the ulterior motive behind our gatherings. It certainly wasn't a spiritual quest that kept us coming back, but a rather old worn-out copy of *Playboy*.

'Jesus, did somebody come on this fucking thing?' said Maria Troy, most experienced and mature student in the sexual arena. I had never heard the word 'come' before.

I was dead impressed. Maria had gone all the way to the Seventh Star, and was entitled to use such expletives. She spoke openly about it. The whole school knew about Maria. She wanted it that way. Maria was constantly in trouble with the nuns. Sometimes I think she went out of her way to attract attention. It's possible, of course, that she hadn't had full sex with anyone, but she made a good job of convincing us.

Maria was sitting on the altar with her legs dangling over the side. Jill was lighting candles to beat the band, and Karen was sure she could find a way to get the wine out of the sacristy. Some other girls were huddled in a corner, eagerly lapping up every word from Maria's mouth. She was reading an extract from the *Playboy* magazine's so-called problem page. The problem had something to do with a man using fruit as a sexual aid, and how his partner was having great difficulty 'accommodating' it.

Like the rest of the girls I was perplexed, but too embarrassed to ask a simple question. Why in God's name would anyone want a pineapple up there? Thank God I did not let my ignorance be known. There were plenty of other idiots to make up for my silence.

'Imagine Danny coming up to me with an orange. You have your shite, I'd tell him,' one commented.

'Your Danny's a perv, he'd get up on a cracked plate,' Jill answered.

'What would you know, you wouldn't get a ride in Leopardstown.'

'Ah, you're all fucking thick,' said Maria with authority. 'It's supposed to be *nice*. Honest to God you's know nothing,' she finished, and climbed down from the altar and threw the magazine on the pew. They clamoured like children at a grushy. Maria left the oratory. No sooner had she closed the door than they tore her apart.

'That one's only a whore.'

'Tart.'

'A right slut.'

'A brasser if there ever was one.'

'The fellas have no respect for her. They only use her for the one thing, my ma told me . . .'

I looked out the side window of the oratory and saw the tainted Maria cross the school yard. She reached into her school bag and took out a small tube of Smarties. She

looked lonely and sad and I felt sorry for her. I wanted
to ask her questions about my experience, but I didn't. I
decided to wait until Saturday night, when I would see
Matt myself, before I told anyone anything.

Now Saturday night was before us. On the way back
down Grafton Street, Jill, Karen and I decided to go into
Bruxelles for a pre-Limit drink. We pushed Jill in front
of us first, because she had the roundest arse and the
biggest tits, and always passed for eighteen. The jukebox
was playing Al Stewart's 'Year of the Cat'. We sat sipping
our jug of Sangria, a cheap and effective way to get drunk
fast. By the time I got home, and had dolled myself up
for The Limit, I was well on. I was in full battle dress
for the evening. I wore a pair of faded jeans that used
to be flairs; I had ordered my mother to turn them into
straights. To my disgust, she had also taken it upon
herself to mend the frayed ends, not understanding that
they were supposed to be like that. Embroidered down
the front of the left leg was *Status*, and down the right
leg was *Quo*.

My white over-sized grandfather shirt looked cool, and
I finished it all off with an embroidered sash, gathered
through the loops of my waistband, and hanging groovily
down the side of my hips. A touch of patchouli oil and the
job was complete. I was massive.

It was utterly forbidden to arrive at The Limit any
earlier than 10.30 pm, although the doors actually opened
at 9.30 pm. I arrived at the entrance door, flanked by Jill
and Karen who swayed unsteadily. I had temporarily
sobered up. I *had* to get in there.

'I was told I could join up as a member after six weeks,'
I said matter-of-factly to the big burly bouncer.

The guy was enjoying his momentary power and authority. He was playing with my life, and knew it. After
looking me up and down for what seemed like an eternity,

he motioned to the desk on the right, where other new members were queuing.

'Thanks!' I squealed like a baby, and held up the precious piece of green cardboard displaying the number 4,938. It was official. I had arrived!

Inside the dark smoke-filled hall, everyone had their 'spot', a place where they hung out every week. New members tended to gather at the front, old fogies at the back, and especially reserved for VIP's was the stage. The DJ in The Limit knew exactly what to play, when to play it, and how to keep us screaming for more.

While he was whacking them out, I wonder was he aware of the many innocents who lost their virginity beneath the turntable? My gang hung out on the right-hand side, almost in the centre of the hall. There were up to twenty of us on any given night. I left my duffel coat in the cloakroom, careful to remove the small baby vodka concealed inside. I bought a can of club orange, and disappeared into the toilet. Depositing half the orange down the loo, I topped the rest up with vodka. Karen and Jill were rolling up joints. The toilet stank of patchouli oil, black Moroccan and cider. To this day, I don't know why the bouncers didn't search us girls. Weren't their suspicions ever aroused when we came in perfectly sober and went home legless with vomit matted in our hair?

'Any sign of Matt yet?' Jill asked me, her eyes looking like two UFOs from *Close Encounters of the Third Kind*.

'I don't know, I haven't gone down there yet,' I replied.

'What's the story anyway? Are you two getting it together or not?' she pushed.

'I'll see tonight,' I answered quietly. 'I'm not sure he's into me,' I added, preparing them both just in case.

'Don't be a prick,' Karen slurred, losing her balance on the cistern, and dropping her joint in the toilet.

'Jesus, I'm wasted,' she whispered.

'We're not carrying you out of here, like we did last week, Karen.' Jill tried to sound all grown-up and responsible.

'Jaysus, look at the cut of her, the head on it.'

I lowered the remains of the vodka. Already I could feel the warm glow engulf me, but I wanted more.

'Jaysus, I'm wrecked.' Karen slid down the wall and landed in a crumpled heap on the floor.

'For fuck's sake, get her out of here before the bouncers see her or we'll all be thrown out,' Jill said.

We propped Karen up between the two of us, and managed to pass the bouncers, looking like three very affectionate and amiable friends. Once at our spot, we dumped Karen like a sack of potatoes in a corner on the floor, and threw some coats over her.

Every week, Karen's night began and ended in the same way. She got drunk, she got stoned, and then she got depressed, in exactly that order. The next day she would brag about how 'wrecked' she had been the night before, and how great it was. It must have been great; she couldn't remember any of it. That was the ultimate proof of a good night out.

On the floor, the gang were simultaneously shaking their heads to Deep Purple's 'Smoke on the Water'. The sea of hair was making me dizzy. Together they stood in a circle in their own make-believe band. They played their imaginary instruments with surprising clarity. Our gang grew steadily as the weeks went by. Sometimes there would be twenty-five of us in a circle.

I clobbered the drums, someone else played a ripping guitar solo and Jill played the keyboard, note for note. A gobshite was asking Karen to dance. It didn't seem to matter that she was unconscious.

In the distance, I saw Joe approach me. He had hung around in the gang for as long as I could remember. He

had beautiful wavy fair hair down to his shoulders and
large green eyes. We had taken to calling him 'Jesus'
because of his hair. Secretly, I think Joe wanted to look
like Clifford T. Ward but he couldn't manage the locks.
However, he made up for it all with a wicked sense of
humour. I saw the hair before the face as he lurched
forward wrapping his arms around me. 'What's wrong
with you?' he asked.

Please do not be nice to me. I will cry.

'The usual,' I sighed. I was trying to hold back but it
was pathetic really.

The fast set came to an abrupt halt and the DJ started to
play 'Stairway to Heaven' by Led Zeppelin. Now I had a
genuine reason to cry, so I let rip.

Joe eased me on to the dance floor and I buried my
head in his chest. He pretended we were dancing real
close, while all the time I sobbed uncontrollably.

'Is this about Matt?' he asked matter-of-factly.

'Yes,' I whispered. 'Joe, is he here?' I added.

'He's here all right,' he sighed.

I knew what that meant. I entered negotiations with
God. Please, God, let him see me right now, right here.
Please, God, make him walk past and see me with someone
else, and then he'll get jealous, and push Joe out of
the way, and then he'll tell me he loves me, and then
everything will be back to normal, everything will be OK.
Please, God, make him notice me, *please*?

Joe held me close. I wallowed in his warmth and
protection. I needed him. In truth I was using him, but
it wasn't making a damn bit of difference. As time passed,
I realised that something was really wrong. Matt had not
come looking for me. I would have to attend to the dirty
work myself.

I excused myself, and paid a visit to the ladies toilet.
Looking at my reflection in the mirror, I was surprised

to see how pretty I looked. I had borrowed Barbara Streisand's hair perm from the film *A Star Is Born*. It suited me. My eyes were large and wide from the dope, but my mouth felt dry. I spent a long time at the mirror, mouthing the alphabet. All of a sudden, the letters seemed hilarious. Especially the letter 'O'. I did that one over and over again, until I realised I was completely out of my face. I didn't care. In fact, I was delighted. I wanted to be like him. I wanted to impress him. I wanted him to see how mature I was, by how stoned I was.

Jill burst into the toilet, ran past me and spewed up all over the floor like something out of *The Exorcist*.

'Fuck,' she muttered, and threw up again, only this time it was a perfect hit, a bull's-eye, straight into the toilet bowl. I tried the other toilet but it was locked.

'Excuse me,' I hissed through the hinges. 'Some of us would like to have a piss.'

The door opened and a threesome sheepishly crept past. The floor was littered with empty cans and bits of tobacco. I relieved myself amidst Jill's gagging and groaning next door. She was leaning over the hand basin when I came out, the ends of her long hair dripping from the running water.

'Jaysus, I'll never smoke that Leb again, deadly shit.' Then she rolled up again, lit it, and did just that.

I left her to it, and made my way back through the dense crowd. The DJ was playing 'Dark Side of the Moon' by Pink Floyd. I wandered slowly around the back of the hall, trying to look like I was searching for a friend. Suddenly, I saw him. I ditched behind some longhaired louts. The music had begun to slow down, and cheers from the floor welcomed the familiar first few guitar riffs from 'Still In Love With You' by Thin Lizzy.

My worst fears were realised. There he stood, his arms wrapped tightly around another girl. A beautiful girl, with long blonde hair. As if that wasn't humiliation enough, she was wearing a magnificent hand-knitted mohair jumper. She had breasts too. The bitch.

I wondered, had he already touched them? He hadn't bothered to touch mine. Mine were so small that had I pushed the two of them together, they still wouldn't have made even a half decent tit. I watched them dance slowly, his fingers entwined in her golden mane. My sense of defeat was complete. I had won the battle but lost the war. He never so much as glanced in my direction.

Standing there, listening to that song, watching them, was the single most heartbreaking event in my life. Until a great big whale of a girl wearing stilettos dug her heel into my foot.

'Ooops, sorry,' she offered pathetically.

'No problem, I'll put an earring in it.' You great big fat fuck, I thought, wincing, and returned to the gang.

For the rest of the evening I sat nursing my bruised ego. Karen arose, like Lazarus from the dead, at around 12.50 am. Jill, who had mysteriously disappeared for most of the night, returned around the same time, and confided in me that she had wanked a fella in St Anne's Park, next door. She said her hand was absolutely 'fucked'. It took me years to figure it out.

Chapter 3

Schoolfriends are hard to lose. I tried losing Karen and Jill but we ended up being stuck together like glue. In the summer of 1980 we finished school. Down the back lane beside Karen's house, we started a bonfire and hurled the dull grey uniforms on to it with glee. We did an Indian dance around the fire, war whoops and pow-wows included.

The smoke from the fire was horrific. Karen was furious that the uniforms were taking so long to disintegrate. We wanted to go out, all guns blazing. We wanted to see the uniforms crackle and shrink like a crisps bag. Instead, they filled the lane with smoke, which alarmed the neighbours, who called the fire brigade. Our moment of triumph was short-lived. We abandoned the blaze and legged it to a field nearby, leaving the half-burned clothes smouldering. We were supposed to be mature women by now, not the amateur pyromaniacs of the future generation. We were supposed to know exactly what we wanted from life and how to go about getting it. Towards the end of our final term, we all paid a visit to the school's career guidance teacher.

Jill and Karen had it all figured out. Karen was going to be a beautician. Jill was going to be an architect. I told her I thought that was a great idea. I didn't tell her that I thought she wouldn't have the stomach for it. That would have been ignorant and rude. It never occurred to me to find out what an architect was. I thought it had something to do with the research of bodily organs. That was how I left school. Completely ignorant.

'Well, Jacqueline,' the career guidance teacher started, 'what plans have you for when you leave here? Have you decided on a career yet?' She peered at me through her National Health glasses.

'I'm going fruit picking in Donabate,' I answered.

'Very good,' she said with a resigned sigh. Another one bites the dust, another teenage delinquent in the making. She never tried to *guide* me, as her title would suggest. Career guidance teacher, my arse! I was guided gently to the door and told in polite terms to please fuck off and don't tell anybody that you went to this school.

'Goodbye, Jacqueline,' she smiled, as if I were headed for a long spell in Mountjoy Prison. Nothing else. No suggestions, no encouragement. No exploration of my talents, or even a small inventory to see if there were any.

Jill and Karen were the bright ones. While we lay in the fields, smoking, they discussed their plans with enormous enthusiasm.

'I'm going back to college,' Karen said. 'I need better marks in my Leaving Cert. I think I'll do it again,' she said with serious tones.

'Probably do the same myself,' Jill added.

'Are you both fucking mad?' I shouted at them. 'You want to go back for *more*?'

'Hey! I want to be something,' Karen defended herself.

'So do I,' Jill added. They were rolling joints and counting their pennies to see if they had enough for a few cans. I smirked at the irony.

'What are you going to do, Jack?' they asked together.

'How the fuck should I know,' I answered irritably. Everybody seemed to know everything all of a sudden.

I hadn't the faintest idea what I wanted to do. I was free of school – that was all I could think about. That was all I wanted to think about. Not college, or repeating Leaving Cert. I wanted to have fun. I wanted some money. I wanted to party every night. The three of us sat and smoked and watched the shrieking neighbours as they helped the firemen douse our little fire.

Finally, they put it out. It was symbolic. In many ways, our personal 'fires' were being doused too. We were young women entering the big bad world, poorly equipped with the necessary skills to become anything other than ordinary housewives. Our rebellious days were coming to an end. We were being challenged to open up and take chances. Barely eighteen, we were bordering on being fully grown human beings, but we had the minds of infants. The only things that mattered were sex – where to get, how to get it, how to *not* get pregnant – the best place to score hash, buy cheap booze and where was a safe place to drink it.

The summer of 1980 was still ours. No matter what Karen and Jill thought about their future careers, our childlike minds kept calling us out to play, and we answered that call, enjoying those first months of freedom as adults. We spent long lazy days on the seafront, walking, talking, larking about. It was perfect. Joe and his friends would join us on the bull wall. We were paired off like mating gerbils at an alarming rate. We swapped boyfriends and girlfriends so many times, every day brought juicy new gossip. Jill was with Matt. Matt was with Karen. Karen was with Joe. Joe was with Mary. Mary was with Anne. *With Anne?*

Up from the country, friends of friends. The group expanded; the circle widened. It was all just cavorting camaraderie. Nobody took anything seriously. Matt was always the centre of attention. He was the wild card, the one who made everybody laugh. He did handstands on the wall and cartwheels across the grass.

He could have fallen and broken his neck. He could have toppled over into the sea. He would have done anything to amuse us, and did. His eyes were constantly bloodshot and he disappeared regularly to a house on the front, always returning a bit crazier. No one took any of this seriously, except me. I was worried about Matt. I couldn't understand the others not noticing just how out of control he was. It was impossible to get close to him. First, because there was a queue of girls wanting his attention. Secondly, he rarely seemed able to hold an intelligent conversation. It was funny, but looking back it was sad really. The cards were already being marked for Matt. Somewhere inside, I had a sneaking suspicion that things would go wrong eventually. This was an ironic sixth sense of mine, for I didn't behave any better.

I went through about ten boyfriends, none of whom I felt particular interest in. I still pined for Matt and my sense of inadequacy remained intact. My feeble fumblings with other boys behind the toilets and shelters did nothing to alleviate that sense of failure. I had wanted it to be Matt. It *had* been Matt, but I really wanted to try again and make perfect what had gone wrong. I was sure, given the right opportunity, we would have another chance. Sadly, Matt drifted, becoming more and more withdrawn, sullen and sensitive.

Often we would pile into the back of Matt's van and take off to the dunes.

The dunes was where the serious stuff happened. If you went down there, you had better be prepared. Full sex was imminent. The dunes acted as marvellous camouflage and the weather made full intercourse more than a possibility. I declined any offer to get down to it on the dunes. A hand in my knickers was permissible. Sand in my knickers was not.

On one of these evenings, Joe arrived with a six-pack.

'It's Jesus,' Karen smiled.

'With a perm,' Jill added.

We were knee-deep in the waves with our trousers rolled up. I saw the poodle-like head approach and almost fell over in the water. We could hear voices from Matt's van. Hysterical laughter.

'What the hell are they doing up there?' I asked Joe.

'Matt's locked. The wheel has become embedded in the sand and they can't get the van out. Come on, you lot, give us a helping hand.'

We vaulted up the strand, six-pack under Joe's arm, Karen and Jill squealing as their bare toes scraped against the rough pebbles.

We reached the van and stared in confusion. Peter, a quieter member of the gang, was lying face down in the sand. He was covered from head to toe in brown masking tape. Matt and his cronies thought it was hilarious. It was. Peter mumbled through his gagged mouth. They had done a good job.

'What the fuck have they done to you! You mad bastards!' Jill was trying hard not to laugh. Matt was rolling around the sand, unable to stop laughing. Joe and I picked Peter up and put him in a sitting position. He slid back down, unable to hold himself. He was as drunk as the rest of them. Joe pulled the tape off his mouth.

'Be Jaysus, it's Jaysus,' he slurred.

We laughed until we were sick. Joe and I undid the tape piece by piece. It was getting dark and the van wasn't budging. Jill and Karen pushed from behind. Joe and I dug a hole around the sunken tyre with our hands. The more we dug, the worse we made it. It was stuck fast. It wasn't going anywhere. Matt kept his foot on the accelerator. The wheel sped round and round, moving deeper into the groove. There was nothing for it but to bed down for the night, and face some angry exchanges the following morning.

Karen and Jill rolled up in the back of the van. Joe and I curled up in the passenger seat. I slept on his lap. We were all tired and drunk. I would have slept on a bed of nails.

Joe cuddled me close and kissed me lightly on the neck. I let him. He was warm and soft. Without warning, he fell asleep and snored heavily in my ear. I drifted off to the sound of the lapping waves moving ever closer by the minute. The quarter moon shone through the window, casting a dim light on the bodies in the back. What a mad bunch of lunatics we were; we could have been swept out to sea!

In the morning there was panic. Matt and Joe walked to a telephone kiosk and contacted the police. They gave them a cock and bull story about the van – claimed it had been stolen the previous night. A tow truck arrived and we all went home.

There was murder to face. I was lectured on 'responsibility' again. I realised that I had better get my skates on. The summer was drawing to a close and I had no job. What amazed me was how the others 'suddenly' had jobs. Either through parents, or family connections, everybody seemed to know what they were doing. I bought a newspaper and saw a small ad for an assistant in a jewellery shop in Grafton Street. I went for an interview and to my surprise was offered the job immediately.

Jill and Karen got average results in their Leaving Cert. Both did go back to school to repeat, in the hope of attaining higher grades. Karen never made it past the first year. She went to work for her father in the catering trade. Jill stuck with it. I was surprised.

A new world was opening up to us. Slowly, but surely, in the following years, we gradually turned into adults.

Joe never really took to office jobs, of which he had plenty. He worked for a transport firm as a courier, then he moved to a truck rental company. Then he made a living out of stocking up cigarette machines in pubs. He even wore a suit and tie one day. It just wasn't him. I liked Joe, because he was like me. We didn't know what we wanted, either of us. We were experimenting with different things. I was surprised to find I made a good sales assistant. In the quiet moments, I cleaned the silver and rearranged the display cabinets.

Years passed quickly. We were hitting our twenties and were permitted to drink legally now. We frequented more stylish clubs like Saints and Tamangoes. We were perfecting our social skills as well as our careers.

From 1982, things started to plummet in Ireland. Jobs became scarce. Some of us were lucky, some of us weren't. Money was tight and the climate was explosive. Everybody felt the crunch, mostly at home. Our parents struggled to hold on to their jobs. Those in small companies fared the worst. One collapsed, then another and the domino effect took hold. In truth, the Depression had been building for some years, but as youngsters we didn't take it seriously. Not until it made a personal impact.

Karen was in luck. Her father's trade boomed mysteriously. Some put it down to the fact that the economic Depression whetted people's appetites. The same went for the entertainment business. It, too, was making a profit. People wanted escapism. People wanted to forget. To relax, leave their cares and worries behind.

We met regularly in the evenings to discuss the state of the country. Suddenly we were taking an interest in the economy. We were forced to. Joe's father had taken a redundancy package at the age of fifty-five and he never expected to work again. The redundancy payment was dangled before him, as it was many others, like a carrot. He took it to pay off his mounting debts. Soon it would run out. Joe was annoyed with his father.

'What would you have done?' he challenged Jill.

'I would have taken it,' she said assuredly.

'He'll never work again, he's too old now. Who's going to give him another job? It's hard enough for us and we're young. He hasn't a chance.' He spat on the carpet angrily.

'That's disgusting,' I remarked, not getting the point at all. My father was lucky to work for the railways. There was no chance of *his* job being sliced.

'There has to be food on the table,' Karen said flatly. 'We don't know what it's like to have all those bills. Hey, we just hand up a few bob every week. There's a mortgage and ESB and gas and phone . . .'

'Yeah, yeah,' Joe sneered.

'I'd pay the fucking bills. He did the right thing, Joe,' Jill repeated.

'Since when did you become an economist?' he shouted at her.

'Hey. Calm down,' I intervened.

Silence descended on our group. The pub was packed to capacity. People talking about the state of the nation. People talking about having no money. People spending money on drink and cigarettes that they couldn't afford. Might as well enjoy it. Spend the few pounds talking, instead of doing anything about the situation.

We knew what was wrong with Joe. We knew the real reason for his resentment. It was self-blame. Joe hadn't managed to stay put in an office job for long. If he'd made a better effort at securing a permanent job, he might have been able to give something back. He was feeling partly responsible for his family's financial troubles. It was easy for us to pontificate. We were OK. Our parents looked after us, made sure we were fed, dressed and so on. There were other families bordering on the poverty line.

Joe's family had become another statistic. His father was joining the dole queues along with the other men. We didn't understand the effect this had on the whole family. Joe wanted to do something about it, but he couldn't.

A group had formed in the back of the pub. I noticed Matt standing on the table with a bottle, miming to a very bad rendition of 'Whiskey in the Jar'.

'Look at the state of him,' Karen pointed.

'They couldn't play snakes and ladders, never mind an instrument,' Jill sneered.

I nudged Joe in the chest.

'What?' he said.

'Go on, you know,' I urged him. Joe was a good guitarist. He could also play the *bodhrán* and the flute. 'Go down there and play something.' I smiled at him.

'No, I'm not in the mood,' he said grumpily.

'Go on, for me?' I urged.

He got up reluctantly and joined the group. Matt fell on to the floor singing and clapping out of time. The group members knew Joe. They knew he could play in tune. They clamoured to offer him their instruments. Joe took a guitar and hit the first chord of 'Whiskey in the Jar'.

He played it to perfection and the whole pub joined in singing. When he had finished, a few old men threw some money in a hat and sent it down. Joe played another song. More money was thrown in the hat. The pints were flowing, the money piled up. Unknown to Joe, he had found his niche. Music had chosen him. It would serve him well in the following years.

Chapter 4

On 14 January 1987 I was twenty-four years old. My birthday present came in the form of a 'positive' result from a home pregnancy-testing kit.

I remember sitting on the toilet in a white bathrobe, peering into the pink tube, nauseous with a mixture of terror and excitement. I had stopped taking the pill, due to continuing attacks of migraine, two weeks ago, and was amazed at how quickly I had become pregnant.

I rattled the tube backwards and forwards hoping it would change colour. For a few seconds it did, then it went pink again. I was devastated. I had spent years taking ridiculous risks. Risks that should have seen me pregnant a million times over, but I had always gotten away with it. I had come through my teenage years without getting pregnant and was proud of it. I had seen many friends' lives ruined due to pregnancy. I had witnessed their struggles, their lack of freedom, their youth cut short. I had seen them age before their time.

I had looked into their eyes, which were old from too much responsibility. Young women, with hair streaked yellow and the roots showing, too busy to get them redone. They dressed scruffily and always seemed in a hurry. They clogged the post offices on Thursdays with their benefit books, and got pissed on Family Allowance day. I saw them in pubs, in the evening, their crisp-filled

children running wild, bored, wanting to go home and
have their dinner. I didn't want to belong to that set.
I was above that. How could I have been so foolish?
Sitting on the toilet, I willed my period to come. I had
heard of spontaneous abortions, miscarriages within the
first three months, gin and hot baths, washing-up liquid
and knitting-needles. Horrid thoughts assailed me.

The story of my ill-fated pregnancy began in England. I
was living in Sevenoaks, Kent, a large town with character
and style. Jill and I had emigrated there the previous year,
when the recession in Ireland hit rock bottom. Unemployment levels had soared to astronomical proportions.
It had been an unhappy move, initially. We were leaving
Karen behind; she was the only one of the gang in a stable
job. Although I was sorrowful saying goodbye to Matt,
greener fields beckoned.

The excitement of England and its promised affluence
over-ruled any lingering sadness. Besides, Matt insisted
we had our priorities about-face. He would rather have
died than take on a nine to five job. In fact, he would
rather have died than take on *any* job. No, I found there
was simply too much to do and see in London; there were
things to achieve, places to go. It helped me to forget the
distance between Matt and me.

Jill and I became staunch Nationalists overnight. To be
honest, I didn't know the difference between a Tánaiste
and Taoiseach, let alone who was running what country.
British taxpayers were paying our wages. We were living
in their country, living off their system, but we behaved
as if they were our number one enemy. In the evenings,
we congregated and sang 'The Fields of Athenry'. We
mouthed the lyrics because none of us knew them. We
listened to The Fureys and Foster and Allen. Had we
been in Ireland, we wouldn't have been caught dead

mentioning them, but it seemed the right thing to do. One night, we smashed our glasses against a wall when the resident band (from Ireland) did a rendition of Paul Brady's 'Hard Station'. It was a stroke of luck they didn't do 'The Island' or there might have been fatalities! We clung to our Irish friends, and only drank in Irish bars. A society within a society.

Joe followed us over from Ireland but hated the quiet of Sevenoaks so he went to live in Finchley. He might as well have been in Hawaii. He jumped on the Traditional Irish Music bandwagon too, and was successfully making a living out of it.

Joe was just as convinced as any of us that our fortune lay on English soil. He insisted the music was a temporary pit-stop. He would get a 'real' job soon. Of the three of us, he was making the most money. His musical talents were in great demand. As more and more Irish settled in England, the demand for Irish entertainment grew. Joe was in the right place at the right time. One night a week we made our way to Finchley, where he shared a house with several others. In the local pub (Irish, of course) he played to his heart's content. The 'brickies' piled in to hear his guitar playing. The sessions were wonderful. So was the drinking. We forgot, temporarily at least, that we were away from home.

Our two-bedroom flat was small and our wages were even smaller. I got a sales receptionist position in Otford, a small town not far away. Jill worked as an air hostess from Heathrow. She took the one-and-a-half-hour journey into Central London every day, and then tubed it out to the airport. By the time she came home, she was fit to collapse. We hardly ever cooked. We lived out of The Pizza Hut and the local Indian take-away.

Jill had changed in the last few years. She had begun to show a degree of maturity that scared the life out of me.

She was no longer interested in excessive drug-taking, or consuming enormous quantities of alcohol. She had begun to knuckle down to the hard graft of pursuing a career. It was proving to be a cinch. She was a stunningly beautiful woman. Her popularity soared wherever we went. Sometimes, I tired of living in her shadow, but in truth, it was Jill who received all the interesting party invitations. Our social life kept me alive. I was grateful for her company and her common sense.

One of those invitations was to the opening of a trainee pilots' drinking club in Frith Street, Soho. My journey into premature motherhood started there.

Jill insisted that I go. There would be very interesting people there. Interesting to her, that is. I would rather have watched paint dry. I was dressed up like a dog's dinner. The take-aways had started to take their toll and spare tyres had appeared almost overnight. The 1980s' fashion craze was a leap into faith. I was nearly twenty-four years of age, but grossly immature still. My clothes advertised this fact. I wore 6-inch-heeled court shoes, the most uncomfortable shoe ever invented. I still have the pyramid toes syndrome to prove it. My slinky mauve Latex skirt looked more like a belt, and my white blouse had a million frills dangling from the collar. To top it all off, I wore a pair of diamanté evening gloves and cheap diamanté earrings and necklace.

I looked like a cross between Queen Elizabeth II and Adam Ant.

I knew by the look on Jill's face that she didn't approve. That wasn't surprising. We hardly saw eye to eye on anything any more. Image had become her number one priority, her God. Having a good time had become mine.

At the opening, Jill was awesome, turning her feminine charm on every unsuspecting male in the room. They stared openly at her. I felt like a rag doll, torn and dirty. I had become tired of this shallow life, and the pretence. My homesickness was growing worse and worse. It seemed ironic that I had come to make my fortune and was wasting it all trying to keep in touch with Ireland. A light had gone on, and wouldn't go off. I wanted to go home.

I went to the bar and ordered some drinks. Nobody drank from glasses; they drank from their bottles. No airs and graces – I liked that. The barman's name was Andrew, a tall, slim and dark character who was immediately taken with my Irish brogue.

'I used to have an Irish girlfriend,' he commented.

'Oh yeah?' I drained another bottle. 'Where are you from?' I asked. At least he had bothered to talk to me.

'Southampton,' he smiled, a gleaming white set of teeth unveiled.

I like you. You've a beautiful smile for a barman. 'What the hell are you doing here?' I asked, suddenly very curious.

'I'm a trainee aviation-instructor. I've got to clock up a certain number of hours before I qualify.'

Keep talking, Andrew. 'Why is an aviation instructor serving drinks?'

'I have to, I need the money. I just do it at weekends. Hey, would you like another drink?'

Do bears shit in the woods? I sat drinking with Randy Andy the barman-cum-aviation-instructor and found him thoroughly interesting, especially his teeth. By the end of the evening I could think of nothing nicer than taking a flight with my new friend. To my delight, that was exactly what he suggested.

The following morning, I had a shocking hangover. I jumped into the shower and took two Anadin Extra, my now constant handbag companion. I borrowed Jill's clothes while she was still sleeping, although I knew there would be a price to pay. I couldn't go flying in a pair of jeans, could I?

Andrew was punctual, and looked wonderful in his spruce, freshly ironed uniform. We drove to a small airport and I boarded the tiny two-seater plane. It was not unlike a car. The door didn't close properly, and I had to slam it shut. I was absolutely petrified. Every blast of wind and turn of wing could be felt fifty times more intensely. I sat in silence for the take-off. The plane felt so small and confined. I was impressed with Andrew as he radioed to air traffic control. Composed. Intelligent. Totally in control.

'Where are we going?' I eventually asked him shakily.

'You'll see,' he smiled.

A thrilling half-hour later, we arrived in Alderney, one of the Channel Islands, and 'parked' the plane in a wide-open field.

Alderney was quiet and beautiful. We walked around the island, enjoying the breath-taking scenery. I liked Andrew – he was a good conversationalist. However, I was not planning to have his baby. Yet I never thought of the consequences of unprotected sex. Was I crazy? Yet I really thought that unwanted pregnancies only happened to other people.

The island seemed almost deserted. We ate in a small restaurant; I noticed he did not drink. That was perfectly acceptable – he was 'driving', so to speak. The day was lovely. The perfect date – romantic and unique.

On returning from Alderney that evening, I followed Andrew to the Pilots' Club and sat at the bar while he worked. We chatted. He told me about his Irish ex-girlfriend. He showed me a photograph of her. Long hair, very pretty. He had not been interested in anyone since they had broken up.

My interest was purely sexual. I got the feeling he felt the same. In the small hours when the club had closed, I drove to his flat with a bottle of wine. We made love all night. It was pure, unadulterated, uncomplicated, blissful lust. Andrew and I had a six-week affair. I enjoyed every minute of it. We locked ourselves in his tiny bedsit almost every night. I hardly ever saw Jill, but she was working most of the time and didn't really miss me.

I was enjoying the sensation of sleeping with someone, and we had some fun times together. I never really expected it to last; I don't think he did, either. It finally put to rest any doubts I had about my sexual attractiveness. Andrew was a good lover. He taught me a lot. It was only when I experienced the real thing that I realised what a fumbling bumbling pair of idiots Matt and I had been.

When I discovered I was pregnant, initially I clung stubbornly to self-delusion. I had to. It was momentary denial. I conjured up images of a giggly gurgling infant, complete with one tooth and ponytail consisting of four hairs. My thinking was more on the lines of a 'pet'. I had seen the ads on television for nappies and baby bath oil. Georgeous, pink-skinned, cuddly, laughing babies! This kind of thinking was short-lived.

My mother's face zoomed into view. I began to think about her, and what motherhood had done. I had watched dreams fade from her eyes as the years went by, and we stole those years from her. She had tried hard to disguise her disappointment. Eventually, she gave up any secret wishes to be anything other than a mother. I did not want to be like her. I loved her, but hated what the family had done to her enthusiastic personality.

Reality hit home without wasting another minute. Babies were not pets, they were human beings, and they grew up, just like I had. The truth about my situation made itself painfully obvious. I had visions of Corporation Housing lists, butter vouchers and cheap mince. In truth, I was petrified. I felt my life, as I knew it,

was over. I buried my head in the pillow and cried hard.
How could this be happening to *me*?

When I was all cried out I buffeted the blow by telling
myself it would be exciting. This was pure naivety, not
a true understanding of the enormity of motherhood. If
I had thought about it for too long, God only knows
what I would have done. I walked the roads for most
of the day, waiting. Jill would help me. She would know
what to do.

I told Jill that evening. Her negative reaction was the
last thing I needed.

'What the hell are you going to do?' she barked. 'You
can't stay here. Have you told Andrew? Have you told
your mum and dad?'

'Look, hold on a minute, will you? It's not the end of
the world.'

'Jack, you haven't a fucking clue, have you?'

That really pissed me off. 'What's that supposed to
mean? Since when are you the expert? You might at least
take a breath before you launch into your "responsibility"
lecture.'

'Well, that's just it,' she said smugly. 'I don't think
you know exactly what's involved. You never plan anything, your life seems to be one big party. You won't
be able to keep living the way you are living now,
speaking of which, where you are going to live? What
about finance, and most of all, what about this poor
unfortunate's father?'

'I'm not exactly stupid,' I defended myself angrily; I
was upset and needed her compassion, not this overdose
of reality. 'This is the 1980s, everyone is having kids, not
all of them have a father, either. I don't intend to stay
here, and I've always hated it. The jet-set life doesn't
appeal to me the way it does to you. I'm going home,
so you needn't worry, and thanks for your support, Jill.

You've been a great help.' At which I stormed out of the flat.

That was the first time I thought about having an abortion.

I wandered aimlessly, thinking, thinking, and thinking. Should I phone Andrew? I really didn't want him to know. I wanted to be back home. I couldn't bear to think that my family might reject me too. They couldn't. They wouldn't. They *mustn't*!

In my confusion, I found myself on a train to Central London, and then I got on the tube. I hadn't made a conscious decision to call on Joe; my feet just seemed to be carrying me there. I was still thinking. Thinking. The stifling heat was overwhelming. My head was jammed in the rancid armpit of another passenger. I felt like throwing up but was stuffed like a sardine in a tin can. Thinking, I hate London. I hate London. I took the steps two at a time up to Joe's flat and knocked on the door.

Here I am again. I'm sorry I haven't called you. Please don't give me that look. 'Here she is again, with another problem.' Please don't be with someone. Please don't turn away. Please answer the fucking door. 'That's right, Jack. You only ever turn up when the shit hits the fan.'

No answer.

I knocked again, and peered in the small window. There was nobody in. It had taken me an hour to get there. My disappointment was awesome. I walked slowly back down the steps and started to head for the tube station. The tears were flowing fast and hard now. Too upset to be dignified, I walked along the footpath snivelling and wondering where to go now, and hating myself. Just then, I heard footsteps quickly running up behind me. I turned around.

'Are you fucking deaf?' It was Joe, panting and puffing between words.

'I'm fine, thanks,' I said.

'Did you not hear me screaming up the road after you? What the hell are you doing here, anyway? You know I'm never around in the evenings. I just happened to come back to pick up some lyric sheets for the lads down in the pub.'

'I'm fine, thanks,' I said again, smiling cheekily.

'OK, OK . . . shit, I can't breathe.' He took a deep breath.

'I'm pregnant.' It's out. No point in waiting. There is no right moment or great words that will ease the blow.

He put his hands on his hips and bent down. 'Fuck it, I've a stitch in my side.' He either didn't hear me or wasn't listening.

My nose was running and my face was wet with tears. I started to dig into my pockets for a handkerchief but couldn't find one so I wiped my nose on my coat sleeve. My self-disgust had come full circle. I then realised that Joe was staring very hard at me.

'Are you pissed again?' he demanded.

'Pregnant. *Pregnant.*'

I suddenly felt very, very giddy. An unbearable urge to laugh came over me. I laughed right in his face. He just stood there staring at me, expressionless. I laughed until it occurred to me that I was really crying. It was a mixture of both. I heard him tut-tutting, not in a condescending way, but more like a resigned sadness. We stood there looking at each other. Then he did that thing. The same thing he did at The Limit when we were sweet sixteen. He moved forward, put his arms around me and I dissolved like a Disprin.

We stood on the pavement, swaying to the sound of silence, Joe humming softly in my ear. No words, no nothing. Joe and me. A pair of idiots. After a few minutes, my sobs subsided. But still no words would come.

We walked slowly back to the flat, me sniffing all the way. Inside, I kept hoping that something would happen to make it all go away. Perhaps Joe would have some major plan. Perhaps the test was wrong? Maybe I should do it again! Sinking feeling. I know I'm pregnant. *I know I'm pregnant*. With each passing moment now, the reality is becoming clearer, the baby girl in pink frills image is wearing off. Like a junkie, I need a fix. *Somebody fix this.* I took a chance. I was paying for it now. I was not ready to be a mother.

Joe walked in carrying a cup of tea and a toilet roll. He placed the cup of tea at my feet, and the toilet roll in my lap.

'There's plenty more if you need it,' he whispered in my ear.

We both burst out laughing.

'Firstly, have you a name?' he started.

'Jaysus, how can I think of babies' names right now – are you crazy?'

'The name of the father, you dozy idiot.'

'Of course I have a name. It's not like I've been sleeping around.'

'Does he know?'

'No.'

'Why not?'

'I don't want him to.'

'Why not?'

'I want to go home.'

'How convenient.'

I gave him a cold glare. I wanted the truth, but I wanted it easy. Could nobody see that I knew all this?

'I can't say he'll be exactly over the moon.'

'Well, how did it happen, for God's sake, Jack? I don't understand.'

'I had to come off the pill, I was getting terrible migraine headaches.'

'That's it?' he said angrily. 'This is 1987. You can buy condoms in the garage, for fuck's sake! Please don't tell me you didn't bother.'

'I didn't bother. I thought I would be safe. I was just finished a period. I didn't think it would happen so fast.' There's no better weapon to confuse a man with than to mention periods. It always works.

'Well, what now?'

'I've got two choices,' I said huskily.

'Yeah?'

Wait for it. 'I'm thinking of having an abortion.' I paused. 'Or I go home and hope it works out.'

'What about the third?'

'What?' I asked.

'The third option. You could tell the father. Things might work out between you and him. Who the fuck is he, anyway?'

'There's no third option. He's just a guy. I don't want to be involved with him. It was pure sex, that's all.' Christ, I can't believe this is really happening.

'Christ, when will you ever grow up, Jack?' he sneered.

'I didn't think it would happen to me, OK?' I couldn't believe my friends were turning on me.

'Why not? What's so different about you?' he shouted.

I had no answer for that one. I felt like a fool.

We sat, we smoked and we talked. We sat. We smoked. We talked.

While we were doing that, the notion of an abortion had taken root. I felt unequipped to take on the responsibility of a child. It wasn't that I really didn't want one, it was more like a crippling fear that I would handle it the way I had handled everything else in my life. I would make a complete and utter balls of it. The thoughts of ruining someone else's life were too much to bear. Somehow, I couldn't find a way to explain that to anyone. I couldn't put it into words. Yes. It was not fear, but a genuine belief that I could not do it. I kept these thoughts to myself, however. I felt no urgency to tell anyone what I was planning to do. I played the game. At the end of the day, the decision was mine to make, and mine alone.

When Joe took me home that evening, he was silent for most of the journey. I felt isolated and rejected. I was completely wiped out.

The next morning, I woke up feeling someone nudging me impatiently.

'Hey, Jack! Wake up.' It was Jill.

I sat up in bed, bleary-eyed and exhausted. The previous night's discussions had left me drained.

'I made you a cup of tea,' she said. It was a pathetic effort but I was glad. However, the sight of the warm milky tea made my stomach do a double somersault. I barely made it to the toilet before I threw up. Jill followed me in a panic with a piece of toast.

'Here, try this, they say it settles your stomach.'

She sounded like a midwife. The sight of the toast only sent me reeling again. I threw up twice in succession, but still the queasy sickening sensation would not abate. The smell of burning bread was all of a sudden revolting. I was so sick I could barely talk.

I got back into bed and pulled the covers up around my neck.

'Jack, I'm really sorry. My God, you've gone fifty shades of green.'

'Irish, through and through,' I joked shakily.

Jill had tears in her eyes. I was delighted – served her right. For once in my life I was genuinely sick. I didn't have to fake it. I milked it to the extreme.

'I told you I was homesick,' I whined. 'Jesus, I don't think I can get up,' I eventually managed. It wasn't exactly a lie, but I was going to make her pay.

'Where the hell were you?' she sobbed. 'You could have rung or something. I was out of my mind worrying about you.' She fussed over the pillows like a mother hen. This is brilliant, I thought.

'I went to see Joe,' I sighed.

'Jack – I know you. Now don't go making any rash decisions. This needs to be discussed at length. You know I'll always be there for you, no matter what. I only said all those things because I was worried.'

The last was uttered under muffled tears. I could see Jill was really upset. I felt sorry for her and didn't know why. I was the one with the problem! I hugged her fiercely and had another little cry myself. I realised I needed every single person I knew, especially the ones who knew me the best. Jill had been one of my closest friends since we were kids.

At that moment, I understood how much worse the situation could be. My father had always said, 'The lesser by the greater, is made lesser.' How right he was. I eventually managed to assuage Jill's fears. No, I was not going to get on a plane for Dublin. No, I was not going to phone home yet. No, I was not going to tell Andrew yet. No, I was not going to fling myself in the Thames. No, I was not going to contemplate an abortion. *Pause.*

I did an expert job at persuading her to go to work. It was an Oscar-winning performance. In truth, my stomach was still very sick. I could have stayed in bed all day, but the sickness was a constant reminder of my predicament. As soon as she was gone out the front door, I dragged myself out of bed.

When I located the local Well Woman Clinic, I was

received rather coldly. At first I thought I was imagining things. The nurse hardly passed words with me and carried out the routine checks without any emotion whatsoever. It was a lonely experience. I could almost read her thoughts. *Another Irish slut up the pole. Fuck off home, Paddy. You're taking up valuable space, space for real English people.* I was lying on a hard cold stretcher and she squeezed my nipples to check whether they were introverted or extroverted. By the time she was finished they had practically developed personalities. I wanted to smack her head against the wall, and get her dirty hands off me.

After the probing and prodding operation was complete, I was sent into another room to discuss my options. Again, it was a very straightforward, non-emotional exchange.

'Are you keeping it?' The doctor kept his eyes down and wrote as he talked.

Hello? I'm here, right across the table from you. You can look at me if you wish. I don't have Aids – you can check the blood tests.

'I don't know. I haven't made a decision as yet.'

'You must make a decision, and soon, if you intend to abort it.'

Suddenly, my baby was an *it*. For the first time, I allowed my hand to ramble over my lower abdomen. It felt the same. No bump. No magical movement.

'I am giving you some literature, Miss, Miss . . .'

'Thank you,' I said coldly, getting up from my chair and grabbing the leaflets from his hand.

'Should you wish to consult with a counsellor, I can arrange that too,' he finished solemnly. *Consult with a counsellor? If they're anything like you I would be just as well to put a Band Aid on my head.*

I left the Well Woman Clinic feeling anything but a

well woman. I was panicked, and confused. Time was crucial. I had not thought about that. I was now more pressured than ever to make a decision. At home, in the flat, I made some tea and managed to get two slices of toast into my stomach. Unfortunately, I made the fatal mistake of reading the literature at the same time.

I had gotten as far as the procedure for a 'saline'-type termination. Another trip to the toilet saw me gasping for air. I lay down on the bed with the pamphlet crumpled in my sweating hand. A picture peeped out from between my fingers. A tiny hand was grimly displayed on the front of the leaflet; beside it, a full-sized adult's thumb to illustrate the comparison. I slowly opened the tatty pamphlet, smoothing the creases outwards. I stared long and hard at the picture. I imagined my baby's hands, mutilated, torn and dumped in a black sack. The minute organs dismembered, burnt, hidden and forgotten. Out of sight, out of mind.

The clinic didn't know it, but handing me that infor-mation was the best thing they could have done for me. I didn't need Joe, Jill or anyone else to advise me in that terrible moment. In the dim light of my bedroom, the dark image stapled itself to my brain cells for ever. I made my decision. It was final. This baby was going to live.

I patted my tummy almost instinctively. In this action, I acknowledged the baby's presence. For the first time in my life, I had made a choice that was 'selfless'. A choice based on another's needs, another's welfare, another's life. I never *ever* wanted to have that choice again.

In the following weeks, I prepared to go home. I tied up all the loose ends, my job, my bills, my plane ticket, and my possessions. Joe and Jill helped as best they could. I was almost excited. We had contacted Karen and her longtime boyfriend Mick. They offered their support and begged me to come home. I wanted to. Except that I was more terrified of telling my parents than anything else. I picked up the phone and put it down again, and picked it up again dozens of times. It went on and on. When I had procrastinated to the point of having nothing else to do, there only remained two small jobs. I dreaded them both.

'Hello, Andrew.' I leaned against the inside of the red telephone box.

'Hello, Molly.' Andrew had nicknamed me Molly after Molly Malone. He thought it was an original joke and I hadn't got the heart to tell him it was about as funny as a road accident. Why did every English person believe they were the first to think of calling us 'Paddy', or slag us about leprechauns? Didn't they know they were extinct? What made them think we still had no television? That we had never heard of *EastEnders* or tasted tagliatelle? Will someone please tell them that we stopped living off spuds in the 1900s?

'I'm sorry I haven't called you for a while. I've been really busy lately – how have you been?' I knew quite well he didn't really care whether I had been busy or not, otherwise he would have called me.

The affair was over. There is only so much sex one can have, and the buzz wears off. If there's nothing else between two people, it usually falls apart very quickly after that. Just like we had. I could detect the hesitation in his voice. I wasn't really supposed to be phoning him, I knew that. So I cut straight to the point.

'Hey, Andrew, I just wanted to let you know that I'm returning to Ireland. For good.' I was determined to keep my secret to myself, but somehow I felt I had to make the phone-call anyway.

'Oh? I'm not surprised, really. When are you going? Perhaps we can meet up before you leave.'

'Thanks, but I'm actually going tomorrow. I just didn't

get the time to call you before now.' I could literally hear the physical exhalation on the other end of the phone.

His voice rose an octave with relief. 'Well, will you leave me a forwarding address? You never know when I might be in Dublin.' He sighed, delighted to have escaped all that shite. 'If you ever need anything, Jack, don't hesitate to contact me. I really enjoyed being with you.'

I will never need you. How I wish I could tell you that. It is enough to know it. You great big gobshite. 'Thanks, it was fun for me too,' I told him politely. 'More fun than you can ever imagine. I think I will always remember you.'

He let out a ridiculously feigned laugh. I said goodbye, and hung up. I was right. I *knew* I was right. I was so glad I didn't have to humiliate myself to find out any more. To always be wondering was there an exceptionally talented father inside him, just waiting to get out? I didn't think so. I had heard enough to confirm my suspicions.

The next phone-call I made from the flat. It would be long, and I needed the privacy and the quiet of my bedroom. My mother answered the phone. A mere 'Hello' had me struggling to keep back the tears. Her voice made me forget I was a grown woman. She had the power to take me back to that childlike place. Instantly, I was nine years old again. I wanted to be back there right now. There, in my mother's arms. I wanted to be tucked in with my favourite story and the light on low, the door slightly ajar. I was about to destroy that child with my words. In her eyes, her daughter would be gone for ever. The guilt was overwhelming.

'Mam, guess what?'

'What, love?'

'I'm going to have a baby.'

'Sacred heart of Jesus.' I could hear her drop the phone as she blessed herself.

'Mam?'

'Jack, are you there?' I could hear her sniffling now.

'Mam, it's OK. Honestly.'

'Oh, sweet Jesus, what will the neighbours think?'

'Mam, I'm in London. How will they know?'

'Don't tell me you intend to bring a child up in that place? Suffering Saint Joseph, what will your father say?'

'Mam, I'm not coming home unless it's OK. With you and Dad.'

She was still wailing and calling on the saints. Then, 'Oh darling, how could you do this to us?' she sobbed down the phone.

I was getting angry. Despite knowing it would be like this, I hadn't prepared for the rage I was feeling now.

'Mam, I haven't done anything to *you*, I've done it to myself! Why is everybody behaving like they're pregnant? I'*m* the one who's having the baby!'

'Jack, I can't think straight. You'll have to give me some time to talk it over with your father. Sweet Mother of Divine, his heart will give in.'

'Mam, I'll phone you later. Mam, I love you. I'm sorry.' Somehow, the apology seemed empty, a useless word with no meaning.

'All right, darling, I love you too. We'll work something out.'

The phone-calls kept coming all day. First my father, then my brother, then my sister, then a neighbour, then a distant aunt who I hadn't seen since I was two years old. I had visions of the Neighbourhood Watch committee gathering to discuss the situation. By the end of the day, there had been nineteen calls in all. The decision had been made. I was to come home immediately.

My father was furious. He tried hard to remain calm about the whole thing, but I could read between the lines. At one stage, we had a three-way conversation. My parents both went to separate phones, and spent most of the time arguing with each other.

'You don't know what you're talking about, William. The girl needs our support.'

'Ah, support me arse, a good boot up the hole would be more likely. If you hadn't spent your life working away from the home, she wouldn't have turned out the rotten rip that she is!'

'Don't listen to him, Jack. At least someone brought some money into this house. You make my blood boil, you – you ignoramus!'

I held the phone to my ear as they argued back and forth. It was hilarious. I might as well not have been there. They were talking over me. When had that started? I couldn't remember the last time that they talked *with* me, like a grown adult. They always gathered together to 'talk to me', but it never happened. They wanted to be morally supportive parents, united and strong, pulling together for the sake of their wayward daughter, but they invariably ended up like this, at each other's throats. Talking about their own stuff. Stuff that had nothing to do with me. It was a battle of the most persistent. My mother always won, hands down.

That night I crawled into bed desperately wanting to sleep, but knowing the hideous nausea would be there to greet me when I woke up. I dozed off and dreamed of Matt, my teenage lover. It was the original nightmare. The recurring one I had had since I was a child. The people in it changed from time to time but the content was always the same. He was laughing at me and pointing his finger in my face. It was horrible.

The following day, I collected my aeroplane ticket and packed my meagre belongings. There were several outbursts of tears from Jill. She had gone shopping and handed me some gifts to take home. As practical as ever, they included vitamins, and anti-stretchmark cream. One of them was a small envelope. I opened it up and found a tiny wristband. It was her hospital name-tag from when she was born.

'I want you to have it. It's the most precious thing I have that I could think of to give you.'

'I don't know what to say. Christ, do you really want me to have it?'

'You're my best friend!' She threw herself at me and started to wail.

'I'll cherish it,' I whispered. Again, I was comforting someone else. 'Jill, I'm going to be fine. I'm not being sent to Auschwitz or anything.'

We stood there hugging and laughing and crying. It would be a long time before we saw each other again.

Joe took me to the airport. The journey seemed to take for ever.

He was quiet and withdrawn. I was nervous and excited. A couple of workmates met us at the departure lounge. We said our goodbyes over a few quick drinks. I promised to return with 'red' lemonade and draught Guinness 'in a bottle', both of which they refused to believe existed.

Before I knew it, the last call for boarding was announced over the intercom. Standing at the gate I suddenly felt sad. Joe had his hands behind his back and that smug grin from ear to ear. For a split second, I felt something move in me. Had I imagined it? Perhaps it was the baby. Perhaps it was because I was saying goodbye. Joe took his hand from behind his back and held up a fluffy toy.

'This is Sam,' he said. 'Whenever you are lonely, or feeling rotten, you cuddle him, take him to bed, talk to him. In fact, he does anything you want, really. He even sings – look.'

He handed me the toy. It was a yellow chicken with a

green hat and denim dungarees. 'Squeeze his hand,' he instructed.

I squeezed. 'Nothing's happening,' I laughed.

'Squeeze, girl. Use your imagination, if you must.'

I laughed again and squeezed the hand even harder. '*Old MacDonald had a farm, ee-i, ee-i, o.*'

I started to cry. I felt like an idiot, standing there with a stuffed chicken, playing that ridiculous tune.

Joe held me tight and kissed me gently on the head. 'I will see you soon. I'll visit when I can, I promise. Call me if you need anything, OK?'

'OK,' I answered obediently like a child. I didn't want to go now. The air hostess was urging me to hurry. I squashed Sam under my arm and picked up my bags. It was only when I was seated on the plane and belted in, that I realised I had walked away, not really saying goodbye.

Perhaps it was meant to be that way. I relaxed back on the headrest, and wondered if Matt was still in Dublin.

Chapter 5

I proudly donned my sod of shamrock, and touched down in Dublin on a typically wet and dreary St Patrick's Day. My family were there to greet me, including my sister, who was appropriately dressed entirely in green. I swore there and then I would never go away again. I moved immediately back into my parents' home. My father had painted the spare room. It was his way of acknowledging his acceptance of the baby. It was a beautiful gesture.

However, I was a moody, bad-tempered bitch for the rest of the pregnancy. A sadness descended, so great that I thought I would die. This was not what I had planned. I didn't mind having the baby; I just didn't want to be alone with it. How would I cope? Where would I live? What would I do for money?

I had a long wait ahead of me; it was probably the most boring few months I have ever experienced. I spent my days crying, and dragging my tired swollen body from room to room. I passed the time doing crosswords, baking bread and walking. The summer was ferociously hot, and my ankles swelled to elephantine proportions. I went to Dollymount Beach with my sister but felt like a beached whale on the sand. I was stigmatised and humiliated. I was now an unmarried mother who sponged off the social welfare system. The slut who got caught.

I played Chopin on my Walkman and swore the baby

jumped every time he heard it. I spent one sleepless night after another trying to get into a comfortable position. I would be just about to nod off and the swine would start kicking. I sweated like a pig and ate in the same fashion.

I had cravings for Jaffa oranges, and could eat up to six a day. It's no wonder I had nightmares, and chronic indigestion. My doctor told me I was retaining fluid. It felt more like I was retaining the rainforests' tropical monsoons.

Towards the end of my pregnancy, haemorrhoids also became a problem. Still, there was one advantage. For the first time in my life, I had breasts. I had gone from a puny 32AA to a size 36AA. However, the joy was short-lived. Nobody got to touch them or see them, and when Baby finally did arrive they disappeared mysteriously overnight, never to be seen again. I had also lost contact with my vagina; it vanished around the sixth month when my stomach expanded. I thought my body would never be the same again. I was correct, of course.

I watched television a lot. I recall the incredible snooker final between Joe Johnson and Steve Davis. I also remember the heart-stopping Wimbledon tennis match between Connors and Pernsforth. Stephen Roche, of the cycling profession, paraded through the streets of Dublin, celebrating his success with thousands of delighted Irish men and women.

My mum and I amused ourselves in the evening watching *The Colbys* and tearing the characters to shreds. We watched the *Late Late 25th-Anniversary Show* and the 'Aids' special that was broadcast nationwide, bringing the much-needed information about the deadly virus into people's living rooms. I still kept in touch with Jill and Joe on the phone. I wrote many boring letters and Joe always replied. Jill was doing very well in her job.

Karen was delighted when she heard I was back in Dublin, and was extremely supportive of my predicament, making many phone-calls and house visits during my internment. Joe promised to make a visit as soon as he had the money for an aeroplane ticket. My parents were just as delighted to know he would return home soon. Secretly I suppose they were hoping that our relationship would develop. They had known Joe as long as I had, and had always liked him. I was too preoccupied with the baby and my future to contemplate romance. I needed friends and he was one of the best.

In early September, Karen and her boyfriend Mick and I took a Dart out to Howth. The heat was stifling and my ankles were swollen and sore. Climbing up Howth Head was almost impossible. Mick stood behind me and with both hands pushed me up the rest of the hill. It was a comical sight. An elderly couple passed and looked on us dotingly. I knew what they were thinking. Inwardly I screamed: *No! We are not a couple. No! He is not the father.*

The last few days of pregnancy were hell on earth. I hardly slept at night, and had to roll out of the bed.

I couldn't actually manage to sit upright. It took hours to get into a comfortable position, only to want to go to the toilet yet again. On 20 September I lay on the bed crying. I had been to see my doctor that day and he had told me that the baby's head was not even engaged; it would be at least another two weeks. Time for me was condensed into hours and minutes. I thought it would never end.

The house had become a battlefield. The happy times when I was a teenager and my brothers' friends gathered in the front room were long gone. The atmosphere was tense with apprehension and the endless waiting. I was cranky and miserable and frequently lost my temper when my father hid the butter, or the bathroom was occupied. Jason had taken to staying out most nights, claiming he couldn't bring friends home, because the 'dragon' was there. I had begun to sense that I was a burden on the family and I also knew that things would be even more difficult when the baby was born.

Then suddenly, as I mulled over all these gloomy things, I felt an incredible rush of water pour forth from between my legs. My waters had broken!

My father broke the lights all the way to the maternity hospital. I kept telling him it wasn't necessary, there wasn't a solitary sinner on the roads, only us.

At the reception desk, there was great confusion. It was hard to tell who needed the most attention, my dad or me. He was sweating profusely, and his breathing was erratic. Anyone would think *he* was the one in labour. I was surprisingly calm.

The nurses gave me an enema, which basically means they thrust a hose of warm soapy water up my arse in order to bring on a 'motion'. They told me to hold on for ten minutes. However, the 'motion' had a notion of its own. If you ever have to go through this humiliating experience, make certain that you have access to a nearby toilet. It is not fair to innocent bystanders.

The nurse kept asking me had I pains in my stomach, and I kept replying I hadn't. It was the truth. I only had pains in the base of my back, similar to a rhinoceros set-dancing on my spine. They were increasing in length and intensity but I didn't think they counted. Oh, what abysmal ignorance!

My mother arrived with my bags, which she had packed when I was six months pregnant. 'Be prepared,' she had said. I knew they wanted rid of me but the packed bag really took the biscuit. She fussed incessantly and harassed any doctor or nurse that would listen to her. Eventually the midwife arrived and convinced her that I was not even in labour yet. I was horrified when I heard this, imagining what the pain must be like when labour really started. I was already in agony.

'Mrs Joyce, I can assure you that your daughter has a long, long way to go. There really is no point in you hanging around. Why don't you and Mr Joyce go and have some breakfast? It will be at least six o'clock before this baby is ready to come out.'

I had to hand it to her. My mother stopped talking. I tried to help things along as my mother was making me feel worse, not better. After a while, my parents decided to go away for a few hours.

I stood at the window on the third floor of the hospital and saw them get into the car. My father stopped short, just before he got in, and looked up. I waved and blew him a kiss. He waved back. They drove off. I then burst into uncontrollable tears. I was alone. Completely alone.

Eventually I was in such pain that the nurses decided to examine me again. They discovered I was 8 cm dilated and almost ready to give birth. I was almost ready to inflict a heinous injury on someone too. I suddenly discovered some choice words that were definitely not in the *Oxford Dictionary*.

'Touch me again and I'll fucking kill you, you cunt,' I screamed at the midwife.

'Now dear, calm down. Breathe deeply . . . concentrate.'

'Fuck! Fuck! Jesus, I can't stand the pain! You bollox! You fucking bastard! Matt! Matt Howard, I hate you! You bastard!' I verbally abused everyone who came into my mind. Then I started yelling, 'I want my mam. I want my dad.' I was hysterical. They had gone away and it was all the midwife's fault. 'You fat bitch, you sent my parents away.'

'Now love, come on. Baby isn't quite ready yet. They'll be back in time, you'll see.'

I knew inside they wouldn't make it. I knew the baby was coming. I knew I was alone.

She rammed a needle into my thigh and the pain subsided a little. The gas mask was beside me and I wrenched it from the stand. *In, out. In, out. Breathe. Breathe.* I felt light-headed and giddy. A combination of the two drugs had me distracted. I was laughing one minute, and crying the next. I thought of Matt. I thought of Andrew. I thought of Joe. Then I thought of Sam. That made me worse than ever; I had forgotten to pack Sam. It's hard to believe, but I needed that stupid toy more than ever.

'I want Sam!' I cried. 'I want Sam, I want Sam, I want Sam!'

The midwife was losing patience. She turned to the assistant nurse. 'Who the hell is Sam – the father?' I heard her whisper.

'He's a chicken, actually.' When I heard Joe's voice, I thought I was imagining it. Then I saw him standing over me. It *was* him, wasn't it? The drugs had me raving. I didn't know if it was only a hallucination.

'A chicken?' I heard the midwife repeat.

'A chicken,' confirmed Joe with his wonderful smile.

'And who are you, Henny Penny?' the nurse turned around, unable to contain her aggravation any longer.

'I'm Joe.'

'Are you the father?'

'No.'

'Maybe it's Matt,' the younger assistant nurse interrupted.

'No. He's not the father,' Joe assured her. The assistant nurse nodded her head up and down.

The midwife exploded. 'Excuse me, what did you say your name was?'

'Joe.'

'Look – I don't care if you're Jack the Ripper, do you

understand? This is a labour ward and this girl is about to give birth. Only family are allowed in here. I must insist that you step outside at once.'

'Then you'll have to physically throw me out . . . Nurse Ratchet,' he added.

I let out a scream as a contraction ripped through my spine.

'I'm her family,' he finished, looking quite grim.

The midwife relented. 'Well, steer clear, Matt, Joe, whoever you are.'

The anaesthetist was turning me over on my side. An impossible position to get into as the rising and falling pain was continuous without any break.

He ordered me to stay still for sixty seconds. Somehow, I managed it. Joe knelt down beside me, his face directly before me. He took my hand and held it. Suddenly, I felt a cold numbness creep through my legs then into my hips then into my back. All of a sudden, the pain was gone. It was a miracle. Maybe my legs had fallen off?

'How do you feel now?' the midwife asked. 'We've just administered an epidural, you should begin to feel the pain subsiding.'

'Dear Jesus, Mary and Joseph. Thank you, thank you, thank you.' I sobbed pitifully. No more the brave strong woman, swimming around with the dolphins, and squatting for a brief moment, while Baby just slips out effortlessly. 'Pick that up, darling, would you?' If they had offered me morphine, I wouldn't have cared. I would have injected it myself.

I was exhausted, emotional and very frightened. I concentrated on Joe, who commanded me to look at him. I was a baby, having a baby. I had read the entire Mothercare books, seen all the videos, gone to all the ante-natal classes but nothing could have prepared me for this. I knew it was nearly over, and I knew that I could feel nothing. I pulled myself together. The midwife and assistant nurse propped me up with some pillows and I could see my reflection in the window in front of me. I saw the first sprouts of black hair protruding from my vagina. It was the most incredible sight.

Time stood still. I remember the total silence as, with one last push, my son David entered the world.

'It's a stubborn boy!' the doctor laughed.

They laid him across my belly; I picked him up and kissed him. I did not care that my face was covered in his blood. It felt like the most natural thing in the world. I was overwhelmed with pride. His soft skin felt beautiful against my cheek. *My baby, my baby, my beautiful baby boy.* I kissed him over and over, and over.

'Would you like to cut the cord, er . . . Joe?' the doctor asked.

The cord was cut and tied into a knot. The doctor secured it with a pin. Then the nurses insisted on taking my baby son away. I asked the doctor why he was blue. He assured me that it was normal. They removed him for a few minutes and when they returned him, he had changed colour and was wrapped in a blue blanket.

I stared down at the tiny hands and feet and counted his fingers and toes. They were all there. Ten fingers. Ten toes. On his left cheek, one simple, solitary dimple; and a massive pair of lungs that would put Pavarotti to shame.

Joe sat quietly. I could see the colour returning to his face. The whole ordeal had taken its toll. His courage and commands had pulled me through.

'You were brilliant,' I told him. 'Where did you learn all that? How did you know what to do?'

'I didn't. I hadn't a fucking clue what I was doing.' We both laughed till we cried.

During my stay at the hospital, I became full of maternal

aspirations. I would never allow my child to suck a soother. I would make sure that it was breastfed. It would sleep peacefully in its own cot, and I would not give in to its crying during the night, no matter what. By the end of the first week I had bought a collection of multi-coloured soothers, a sterilising kit, and a bottle warmer.

My son slept peacefully beside me in my bed after a marathon four-hour screaming session. I had abandoned the breastfeeding when my nipples began to crack and bleed. Besides, he was starving to death and I felt guilty. I had had sixteen stitches inside, and my breasts had swollen with unused milk. Coupled with the piles and enemas, I was confused as to which end to hold on to, when I went to the bathroom. (Jaysus my arse, oh my boobs, Christ my fanny.)

Jill sent a bouquet of flowers, and Karen came to visit. My family piled in every day. I was perched precariously on a rubber tyre, unable to sit any other way. They thought it was hysterical. I was depressed and tired, and really wasn't up to people peering in at me like some monkey in a cage. I just wanted them all to go away. I couldn't stand them picking up David, waking him, and then leaving me to settle him back down again. Visitors should be banned from maternity hospitals, I thought.

After a week, I was allowed go home. Home? I wondered where that was. My parents went out of their way to make David and me feel welcome.

They had made the box room into a nursery and bought a beautiful Moses basket for Baby to sleep in. They were trying their best but my depression was great, and I must have seemed very ungrateful.

The days rolled into nights, and the nights rolled into days. I slept when he slept, ate when he ate, shat when he shat and basically had no time or energy left for anything else. I spent the best part of six months in doctors' surgeries and hospital wards, worrying about his sleeping and eating patterns. I was still overweight and self-neglected, and hadn't had one night out since I had returned from hospital.

One Saturday evening, Joe and Karen called together. Joe was home on a weekend visit; it was a delight to see two adults call for me.

'We're taking you out,' they said matter-of-factly.

'Don't be ridiculous, you know I can't go anywhere. Besides, who'll mind Junior?'

'I will,' my mam said.

'Are you sure?' I was delighted but worried.

'He can't do much damage in a few hours, can he?' she asked innocently. Nobody in their right mind was going to answer.

I enjoyed getting ready to go out. It reminded me of the old times. The living situation in the house had been deteriorating rapidly. It was all very well in the beginning. My mother went out of her way to help, even taking over the midnight feeds, so I could get some sleep. David's crying frequently woke up my father and brother who had to go to work the next day. They were getting sick of tripping over shitty nappies, baby baths, finding rusks stuck down the couch, and not being able to hear the television. It wasn't their fault. I knew I would have to start looking for alternative accommodation soon. I tried to put it out of my mind and went to get dressed. To my horror, nothing in my wardrobe would fit me.

Karen could sense my frustration. She picked up a pair of jeans. 'Here. These will fit.'

'They're my maternity jeans.'

Silence.

'Look, it doesn't matter. C'mon, the night is nearly over

and we're only going up the road,' she tried to change the subject.

I slipped on the maternity jeans and put on some make-up. My hair was healthy-looking, at least. As we walked to the local pub in the cool evening twilight, Karen linked me affectionately. Joe ambled behind us singing, sporting a newly acquired haircut. What used to be long waves had now been transformed into a short back and sides with a little quiff in the front. We taunted him without let-up. I asked him about Jill. Had he seen her? How was she doing? He told me that he hardly ever saw her. Her work schedule kept her in the air most of the time. It was good to be out again, talking about this and that.

As soon as I got inside the lounge, I phoned home. My mother reassured me that David was still asleep. Thank God, I thought. We ordered some drinks and went and sat near the window. The place was packed. There were wide-screen TVs everywhere.

'What's going on?' I asked innocently. I had lost touch with the outside world.

'Barry McGuigan's first come-back fight,' Joe filled me in. 'Where have you been – on another planet?'

'More or less,' I replied and they both laughed. I sipped my first pint of Carlsberg. It was delicious and I ordered another. And another. I felt drunk after the third.

The crowds were going crazy. Barry McGuigan had won. I joined in on the cheering. I didn't want to go home now. Then I remembered David, and got up to make another phone-call.

'Leave it,' Karen urged. 'Leave well enough alone.'

I realised just how cocooned I had become. I loved David, I had no regrets, but I didn't really understand how difficult it would be to lead a single person's life again.

Sitting there with my friends, I knew that my life would somehow never be the same again. I suddenly felt very lonely. I was desperately in need of financial support. I also began to think back on my teenage years and realised how much I had taken my freedom for granted, and that I would not be able to do what I wanted any more.

David would have to come first. I loved him with a passion. I loved his smell, especially after a bath. The softness of his head, his pudgy fingers, his gurgling. He made me laugh when he spat his food right back at me, the way his face turned a bright orange as he did a pooh, and then how he heaved a sigh of relief. They were simple small things; they were the things that brought me closer to him. He was my son, and having him had changed everything.

I made my fourth trip to the bar. I was counting my pennies, when I became aware of a set of eyes boring into me. I tried hard not to look, but eventually curiosity got the better of me and I glanced to my left. At the end of the bar, Matt Howard was perched on a stool, nursing a pint of Guinness. He smiled. I smiled back.

Dirty bastard.

I grabbed my pint and spilt half the contents in the rush to get back to my seat. 'You'll never guess who I just saw,' I said to Karen, puffing and out of breath. 'Matt Howard. He's sitting at the bar, can you believe it, the great big fucking bastard,' I added.

'Well, did you say hello or what?' she asked. 'Wow – Matt Howard! Sorry, I just have to see him.' She pushed past me and made her way through the crowd.

I was sick with nerves. I wolfed down my pint, grabbed a passing bar boy and ordered three more. I tried to remind myself that I was all grown-up. I was being childish and silly. I should have gone over to talk to him. I felt like a right prick, sitting there all indignant and red-faced.

To my horror I saw the crowd parting as Karen returned with drinks. With Matt in tow. Joe tut-tutted.

'Ah Christ,' I whispered. I reefed my shirt down as far as I could to conceal my protruding spare tires. I felt like a fat tub of goo. *Not now! Not now!* I implored. *Come back when I've my figure back, when I feel confident. When I've got a job. Go away! This is so unfair. Jesus Christ, You'll have some explaining to do when I get up there.*

'Hi,' he grinned from ear to ear.

'Hi.' *Oh great response, interesting even.*

'I've been watching you for a while. I wasn't sure it was you,' he smiled again.

Oh yeah sure. You didn't recognise me with all the fat you mean, go on, and rub it in.

'It's me all right,' I said pleasantly, hating him. *You don't look exactly slim yourself, could do with a little toning up, you've a double chin as well.*

'Sit down, for God's sake,' Karen squealed. She pushed me up in the seat and I kicked her hard under the table. 'I can't believe it's you,' she gushed. 'God, you look exactly the same. It's incredible. Wow.'

She went on and on. I sat between them, sipping my pint as they talked backwards and forwards over me. I felt about as welcome as a fart in a spacesuit. Still, I was grateful in a way. It gave me a chance to observe what had once been the great love of my life.

How many years had it been? Nine, ten? He appeared exactly the same, as gorgeous as ever. And he was giving me that look – the one he always gave me. What is it about you that makes my heart thump and my stomach churn? I asked him silently. Did you know how much I adored you? Do you know how much you hurt me?

Look at you. Still the same. Black curls that we girls spend a fortune trying to copy. I loved to run my fingers through them, and feel them bounce back into place. Why have you cut them so short? Your eyes are still hypnotic, cat green, mysterious but always giving away your heart. You bastard. Christ, I hate you for being here, all fresh and alive and desirable. I suppose it's only because I haven't had sex in a long time. That's the only reason I am even contemplating sleeping with you.

They were discussing ex-girlfriends and boyfriends. I listened with amusement as they each revealed gossip to the other.

'Jesus, remember that one Margaret, the one with the long blond hair that was always hanging out with you. She was a right dog – whatever happened to her?' Karen queried.

'I married her.'

'God, sorry.' Karen tried not to laugh but Matt beat her to it. Pretty soon we were all rolling about the place roaring. I don't know why I found it so funny. I was in bits.

'Did you really marry Margaret?' Karen was trying to be serious.

'Who are you to talk, you're still with Mick,' I reminded her.

'You're not.' Matt stared at her.

We all started to laugh again. What a bunch of cowards. We had settled for the first thing that had come our way.

'I heard you had a baby, Jack,' Matt said flatly.

Jack. He called me Jack. He had a special way of saying it that I hadn't heard for so long. Jack was short for Jackie, which was short for Jacqueline, but only certain people were privileged to call me that. Somehow the years between us just rolled away there and then. I was flattered and a little angry that he knew about David.

'Yes, I have a son, his name is David, and he's the best thing that has ever happened to me. I never really loved his father anyway.' That's exactly how it came out, word for word. Absolute shite. There was no need at all to mention the biological sperm.

He smiled a knowing grin.

The swine.

'How old is he?'

'Almost six months.'

Pause.

'When did you get married?' I asked, almost shyly.

'Four years ago.'

An eerie silence followed.

'Any snappers?'

'One boy, one girl.'

'Wow, you've been busy.'

He obviously can't keep his hands off her.

'It's not easy.'

'Tell me about it.'

'How come I've never seen you around?'

'I was in London for two years.' *I'm travelled.*

'What was it like?'

'I hated it.'

'What was he like?'

Hey, watch it. 'An absolute bollox. Like yourself.'

'Thanks for the vote of confidence.'

'I can't understand it. Line up ten good men in front of me and one bollox. I'll pick the bollox.'

'There must have been something good about him?'

What do you care? You have the Princess Margaret. 'Well. Yes. Of course. Initially there were lots of good things about him. I just can't think of any of them right now.'

He laughed. I managed a sneaky snigger. I was enjoying this.

'How long were you together?' he asked.

'Four years.' Another lie.

'That's a long time. It's a pity.'

I'm not to be pitied. 'It's OK. Honestly, I'm very happy about it.' *Oh Jack!*

'Well, you ought to let your face show it.'

Mercifully, Karen interrupted. 'Hey, gang, it's last orders. Jack, your twist.'

Was she completely without brains? I glared at her.

'Eh, it's OK. Actually I'll get them.' She finally got the message.

Matt stayed put. 'Are you living back in your parents' house?' he started again.

'I haven't a choice at the moment, although I feel in the way. They've been really good to me, but I'm wearing out my welcome.'

'Why don't you start looking for a flat?'

'I have to look for a job first.' *Where's your wife?*

'What were you working at in London?'

'Just basic secretarial work. I hated it, I wish I could do something else.'

'Why don't you consider going back to school?'

'Get a grip. I have David now. I can't do anything.' Whoops. That was positively hostile.

'Of course you can. I'm studying at night and working during the day.'

Really? I suppose Margaret Smargaret makes it all possible. 'Well, that may suit you, but I wouldn't be able to do the two without help.'

'You would if you really wanted to.'

Who the fuck does he think he is? I try changing the subject. 'Where's Joe gone? I haven't seen him all evening.'

'He's with someone in the bar.'

'Oh.' Things were suddenly very tense. As per usual I had had too much to drink. I was becoming aggressive and was slurring my words. The barmen were shouting, 'Closing time, now, ladies and gents. Come along, please.'

I wanted to cry. I wanted to run. I wanted to be sixteen again. Take me down to the beach and we can get stoned and do it all over again, make everything all right. Somebody change my life. Why was I so angry? This was nobody else's fault. I had chosen my own road. I had nobody to blame. I just couldn't grow up. Matt had grown up. Jill had grown up and Karen was doing her level best. I was so confused.

The lights had been turned on and Karen was getting ready to go. Matt sighed heavily as if being in my company had drained him. I felt so stupid. I tried to save the evening by telling him meaningless bits of gossip. Suddenly, keeping him there seemed like the most important thing in my life. A loud voice came over the intercom. 'Telephone call for Ms Joyce. Telephone call for Ms Joyce.'

Not now! I ran to the phone and my mother was hysterical. David was screaming his head off and she could not calm him down. She ordered me to come home immediately. For a split second, I hated David.

In the foyer Karen was hugging Matt. I watched them from a distance before I approached.

'Jack. I'll walk you down if you like.'

Yes!

'Yeah, I'm getting a lift from Mick anyway, you two go on.' Karen winked at me.

Walking down Seafield Road was a very strange experience. All the time I was aware of David and my mother pacing up and down with him, but I just couldn't bring myself to rush. I was worried but torn two ways. My maternal instincts and my hormones were battling it out. I was enjoying all these new feelings. It was so long since I had felt like a woman, since a man had engaged in an intelligent conversation with me.

Matt seemed in no hurry. We chatted about this and that and I laughed, boy did I laugh.

'My son can't pronounce F, he uses R instead, so the phone is a rone and a foot is a rut. You get used to it after a while.'

'David's arse is red raw from nappy rash.'

'Sudocrem is the best.'

'You've lost a lot of weight,' I told him. My paranoia and defence mechanisms were beginning to loosen.

'Yeah. I lost about a stone over the last year.'

'You really know you've lost weight when you feel it in your trousers. Whoops. I mean . . .'

'Excuse me?'

We both burst out laughing. *Oh God get them off.*

We were nearing my house and I was sure I could hear David's screams. I was anxious to get away. I was anxious to stay. I was anxious.

'God, it was really something else meeting you again. I think of you often,' I confessed.

'Ditto.' He delved into his pocket and pulled out a joint. He lit it up and took a long drag out of it. I was horrified.

'You're not still doing that shit, Matt?'

'Ah, only now and then.'

Suddenly I was disappointed. I wondered what I was doing there. It also dawned on me that he was a married man. It also struck me that my mother was murdering my child at this very minute.

I came to my senses abruptly. I reached out and hugged him; he held on. 'It really was lovely to see you again,' I said.

'Maybe we can meet up again, sometime.' He left the words hanging.

'Maybe,' I whispered.

Chapter 6

I ran into the house and raced upstairs, taking two steps at a time. It was totally silent. My mother lay crossways on the bed, snoring loudly. David was tucked up comfortably in his cot. He was completely unconscious. Typical.

I sat in the kitchen alone for about two hours. I was tired, but could not bring myself to go upstairs, get into bed, and go to sleep. I stole the key for the drinks cabinet from my father's overcoat. The only thing that was in it was a small amount of Pernod dating back to the 1800s, but I didn't care. I mixed it in an enormous tumbler with orange juice, the only mineral left in the fridge. It was sickening, but I drank the lot.

The midnight courts had begun. Why hadn't I asked Matt where he lived? I fretted. Why should I have asked him that anyway? He was married! Oh, so what. That meant nothing these days. But who was I to presume that? He probably loved his wife very much. Margaret – that tart. I couldn't believe he had married *her*. She had no brains. He could have had his pick of women. He could have chosen anyone. *He could have chosen me*.

Still, the blonde bimbo with the big boobs was probably great in bed. I bet she gave him blowjobs, while she was hoovering and ironing at the same time. The kids were probably beautiful too. Little angels that floated around the house and had excellent manners when they were out with Mam and Dad.

Why are you so resentful, Jack? I asked myself. Can't you be happy for him? He's entitled to a little bit of happiness. You're always so envious and jealous of everybody else. Just because you made a mess of your life doesn't mean you have to tear everyone else's apart.

I decided to have a light snack. Two bowls of Crunchy Nut Cornflakes, a rasher sandwich, a cheeseburger, two Cadbury's Snacks and a Diet Coke, just to convince myself I was still trying to lose weight. *You pathetic, fat has-been. Oh leave me alone! No! Look at the state of you! A bear wouldn't give you a hug. What makes you think that he'd even be the least bit attracted to you? He was just passing time, that's all. It was a chance meeting. A mere coincidence. You're just trying to make something out of it. Go to bed. Go to bed. Go to bed!*

I crawled up the stairs, thinking I was being quiet. The steps creaked and I heard my father groan. I slipped under the duvet and peered into David's cot. More remorse. 'I'm sorry, darling,' I whispered. 'I'm really sorry. I didn't mean it when I said I hated you, earlier on.'

I kissed him gently on the cheek. My head lay level with his. I stuck my hand through the cot bars and gripped his tiny fist. The minute fingers immediately encircled mine.

I love you so much, little man. Mammy's going to change. I promise you, tomorrow. Tomorrow, I'm going to change my whole life. Everything is going to work out fine. You'll see. I'll get a job. We'll move into a flat and you can take Thomas the Tank Engine with you. Just you and me, we'll set up home together. You'll go to school. You'll go to college. You'll get a degree, and become a professor, or something really important. You'll be proud of your mother, and tell your friends what a wonderful parent I was. Yes. It will all change tomorrow.

*   *   *

The next day, I had a hangover and David was very cranky. Joe called round. He only had one more night before he returned to London.

'Where did you disappear to last night?' I asked curiously.

'I met some friends in the bar. Besides, I wanted to give you a little space, you know.'

'No. Actually, I don't know,' I said grumpily. I really wasn't in the mood for this.

'Well. Present company, et cetera.'

'You mean Matt?'

'You should have seen your face.' He chuckled and lit up a cigarette.

'What do you mean?'

'It was so obvious.'

'What was obvious?'

'You two.'

'Are you mad? He married someone else!'

'I know.'

'You knew? Why didn't you tell me then?'

'I didn't think you'd be interested.'

'I'm not!' I screeched.

'Hey, relax, will you? You overreact to everything these days.'

'Sorry.' I calmed down. 'I guess I was disappointed, that's all. How could he have married that slut?'

'How could you have gotten yourself pregnant by a Brit?'

'Well, at least I left.'

'He will too.'

'What makes you say that?'

'Something I heard at the bar . . .'

I was secretly thrilled. 'Don't be ridiculous, we haven't seen each other in nine years. We probably won't see each other again for another nine. It was just one of those things.' *What did his face look like?*

'What would you do, say, if he was single?'

I tried to appear to be thinking it through, but I already knew the answer.

'Nothing,' I lied. 'I have David to consider now. Besides, I saw him smoking a joint last night, and it really turned me off.' That part was true.

'I don't believe you,' he said seriously.

I looked at him. I had detected something. I couldn't put my finger on it. Was it jealousy? Never!

'Why are you so concerned?' I asked.

'I wouldn't like to see you get hurt,' he responded in a rush.

My mother entered the room. 'Look what I found.' She held David upside down, and he chuckled.

'Baby! You're awake!' I took him in my arms and kissed him.

'God. What are you feeding that child?' Joe exclaimed.

'Soya milk.'

'Soya milk?'

'He's thriving on it. Aren't you, you little monster!' I tickled him and he laughed. I passed him over to Joe. He was wonderful with children. A born natural. I could see clearly he would make a great father. My mother was cooing and gooing at them both. She loved to see David and Joe rolling around the floor together. I watched them, as they shouted and played hide and seek. David was a carbon copy of me, not at all like his father. I was so glad.

Joe was having a ball. He was a wonderful friend, but sometimes, like now, I wasn't sure what to make of him. I was glad my mother had interrupted. I didn't really want to continue the conversation, or have it go any further. Last night I had realised many things. Firstly, I had to get a job. Secondly, I had to start losing some weight. Thirdly, I was badly in need of some sex.

That afternoon, I took David for a walk in St Anne's Park, my favourite place. The weather was warm and sunny and I enjoyed the stroll and the chance to get out of the house. As I kept him occupied on the baby swings in the playground, I watched as other 'normal' couples pushed their children, or helped them down the slide. I longed to be 'normal' just like them. Families swamped the overcrowded green, eating their picnics on the grass, and scolding their children from time to time. I felt so different from them all. So out of place.

In the evening, when David was asleep, I rooted out my old CV and got to work on updating it. When that was done, I took the evening newspaper and scoured the *Situations Vacant* column. Then I wrote out several job applications. Mam asked me what I was doing and I told her I was looking for a job.

'That's good. Be positive,' she said, patting me on the head.

When she had left the room, I turned to the *Flats To Let* section. I was horrified to see the cost of rents. How would I ever be able to afford to move out? Even if I got a job, I would still have to pay childminding fees. That would leave practically nothing to live on, let alone pay the rent. It seemed impossible. It all seemed impossible.

'Joe's on the phone,' my mother interrupted.

'What's wrong?' he asked, immediately sensing my anxiety.

'Everything!' I burst out crying. 'Everything! I've made a fucking balls of it all!'

'Look, I'll be there in ten minutes,' he said.

I put down the phone and felt a certain amount of relief. At the same time I was sickened by my own weakness. I was tired of constantly complaining, and leaning on others, expecting them to sort out my problems.

My loneliness and frustration had reached fever pitch. I needed someone. *Anyone.*

Joe arrived with a bottle of wine. He went out again and bought two more.

My mother popped her head in the door. 'Are you OK?'

'Yeah, Mam. I'm just a bit fed up.'

'Why don't you go out with Joe for a little while? I don't mind looking after David. He's fast asleep.'

I knew she wanted me to go out with Joe. I knew exactly what she had in mind.

'It's very late, Ma.'

'Look, if it gets too late, stay in his house. Everything will be OK here.'

'Ma?'

'Oh, for God's sake. Are you blind or what? The man likes you. Better the divil you know than the divil you don't.'

'Don't be ridiculous, we're just friends.'

'You'd better get rid of those airs and graces, Jack. Mark my words, no man wants an unmarried mother.'

'I'm not an unmarried mother,' I corrected her. 'I'm a woman with a child.'

'Ah, sweet Jesus! What difference does it make?'

'Mam! There's nothing between us, can't you get that into your head?'

Joe burst in the door, drenched to the skin. 'It's pissing cats and dogs.'

I had my coat on.

'Are we going somewhere?' he said wearily.

'Mam said she'd mind David for a while, so how about going down to your pad for a few hours? Would your Mam mind? We could sit in the kitchen even.'

'Of course she wouldn't mind, you know that,' he said, a little annoyed.

'Right then. It's settled. Go on, the two of you. Have

fun. Remember, there's no need to hurry home, Jack.'

'Yeah, OK, Mam,' I interrupted before she suggested we buy some condoms in the garage, as well.

Joe looked delighted with himself.

Mrs Hayden, Joe's mother, was a kindly old woman. She greeted me with open arms, enquired after the family, and then promptly left the room.

'She always does that,' I remarked, taking off my wet shoes and opening a bottle of wine.

'She never interferes,' he smiled. How I wished I had a mother like that.

'How's your dad?' I asked.

'Same as ever. He mopes around and then goes to the pub. Then he goes to the bookies. Then he goes back to the pub. I can't stand the way he behaves towards her,' Joe added.

Joe's father had never worked again. Unemployment had had an adverse effect on him. He changed over the years, and for the worse. He had turned the house into a battlefield. He blamed Joe's mother for everything.

'It's the same shit every night. They argue. He walks out. She goes to bed. He rolls home. I don't know if I can ever live here again. Every time I come home, I can't wait to get away again,' he said. I empathised.

'I know what you mean,' I sighed. 'Joe, I really need to get a job and a place to live. Mam and Dad are doing their best, but I'm in the way. How am I going to manage working and looking after David at the same time?'

'You could always come back to London,' he said half-heartedly. 'You wouldn't be out on the street.'

But I couldn't bear the thought of London.

We discussed childminding options for David, the possibility of house-sharing, the Corporation housing list, and how to get on it, job-sharing, part-time hours. We covered everything. I was all talked through and we were opening the second bottle of wine. I still had no answers. Joe was reassuring. It would all happen eventually, he said. One thing at a time.

We put on some old music and began reminiscing about The Limit and the good old days. We played CD after CD of our favourite music, taking in the remastered tracks and reliving what each one meant to us. Pretty soon, we were in hysterics. Laughing, crying. I was getting very drunk.

I lifted the empty bottle and turned it upside down. 'Shit! We've run out of ammunition!'

'Never fear.' Joe leapt to his feet and opened a cabinet on the wall. It was crammed to capacity with bottles of every shape and size and description.

'What will we have? Let's see . . . lager, wine, vodka?'

I could have kissed him. In fact, I decided I would kiss him. It was a long, loving, gentle kiss. I had not meant it to be. I lay back on the floor, and let go. The last thing I could remember was imagining Matt Howard inside me.

I awoke with a shocking hangover. I thought that was the worst of it. Then I felt something hard needling into my back. I realised I was in someone's bed – a man's bed, and the man had an erection. I racked my brains. Then the light went on. There was a moment of horrific clarity. I was afraid to move. I felt physically sick. I wasn't sure if it was the alcohol I had consumed, or the fact that I knew I had slept with Joe. Certainly, one didn't complement the other. I heard him moan softly. He wrapped his arms around my waist and pulled me closer. *Oh sweet Jesus. I think I'm going to throw up.*

I threw back the covers and jumped out of bed. Horror of horrors, I was stark naked. Christ, where were my knickers? I grabbed a blanket and wrapped it around me.

Anyone would think I had just been raped. I just about made it to the toilet, where I was sick.

It's hard to vomit quietly. I heard movement from the bedroom next door. Mrs Hayden greeted me at the toilet door. She acted dumb.

'Everything OK, dearie?'

'Eh, fine, thanks. I mean, good morning. Sorry – good-bye.' I ran past her as fast as I could and slammed Joe's door behind me. Then I stood stupidly at the end of the bed, still wondering where my clothes were. Joe appeared behind me. I turned around.

'Your tit is hanging out.'

I looked down, my left breast was exposed. I pulled the blanket up.

He handed me my clothes and I was dressed in one minute flat. He lit a cigarette and pulled on it, calmly watching as I grappled with socks and zips.

'Jack,' he started.

'No,' I shouted at him.

'I didn't say anything, just . . .'

'No! No! No!' I repeated. I was out the door faster than a filly at the Curragh Races.

Luckily, Joe's house was not too far from my own. When I let myself in the front door, Mam was in the kitchen, feeding David some Weetabix. There was more on the floor than in his mouth.

'Have a nice night?' she enquired.

One look from me told it all. She knew to leave me alone and not pry any further. It must have taken several novenas to bite her tongue. I went upstairs and sat on my bed. What had I done? Had I gone the whole way? Or just done the bare essentials? I had to phone Karen.

'What the hell are you doing, ringing me at this hour of the morning on a Sunday? It's only nine o'clock?' I could hear the alarm clock fall to the floor.

'Wake up, Karen. I need to talk to you. Right now.'

'I'll ring you back in an hour,' she said sleepily.

'No! This is an emergency.'

'Jesus. Hold on to your knickers, will you? Just let me get a cup of tea, and a fag, and I'll call you back.'

'No. I'll wait right here.'

'Jesus Christ! OK.'

I waited, and chain-smoked.

'OK, I'm listening,' Karen came back to the phone. I could hear her slurping her tea.

'I slept with Joe.' I could hear her choking on the same tea.

'About fucking time,' she coughed.

'I can't remember anything.'

'You actually did it?'

'I had sex with my best friend.'

'You could have done worse.'

'Karen! I fucked Joe! What am I going to do?'

'Well, Jesus Christ, how am I supposed to know? What's the big deal anyway? Why all the panic?'

'It feels all wrong.'

'But presumably you wanted to sleep with him, Jack?'

'I don't know. I'm confused.'

'Well, why did you do it then?'

'I was drunk.'

'You're always drunk.'

'What's that supposed to mean?'

'Look, you discussed it?' Karen sounded serious.

'No.'

'Did you spend the night?'

'Yes.'

'What happened this morning?'

'I just got dressed and left.'

'Hang on a minute. You just got dressed and legged it?'

'Yes! Yes!'

'You sick bitch,' she sighed.

'Karen, what am I going to do?'

'Well, you're going to have to talk to him sooner or later. Christ, the poor bastard. You could have at least said something before you left. Sometimes I can't understand you.'

'I tried. I just didn't know how to handle it.'

'Jack, sometimes you don't have to handle things, they handle themselves, you know?'

'No, I *don't* know. That's my problem, isn't it?'

There was a slight pause as she sipped her tea and I smoked.

'Well, was he any good? Like, had he a big—'

'Karen, I told you – I can't remember anything. I swear. I don't know how far it went. All I know was I woke up naked with a huge horn prodding me in the back.'

Karen sniggered. 'Then it was big.'

'I couldn't care less if he was hung like a horse right now. I'm horrified. I don't even know what I was drinking.'

'You dirty slut.'

'What will I do?' I asked pleadingly.

'You'll have to contact him, and the sooner the better. The longer you leave it, the worse it's going to get.'

'You're right. I hate you!'

'Can I go back to sleep now? There's something prodding me and all.'

'Dirt bag.'

'Good luck, Jack.'

Thanks, buddy. I'm certainly going to need more than luck this time. I went back downstairs and took David from his highchair. I sat him on my lap. I was exhausted. Mam was still keeping her silence, thank God.

'I'm going to the supermarket to get something for

lunch. I'll take him with me for the walk, if you like?'
she said.

'OK. I've some more calls to make anyway.'

'I'll say,' she muttered under her breath.

'Joe?'

'Hi, stranger.'

'I'm really sorry I ran out like that.'

'It happens all the time.'

Thank God. He was playing with me. I was so grateful.
'Can we talk?'

'Do you really want to?' he replied softly.

'No.'

'Then let's not.'

'Joe, I can't remember . . .' *Help.*

'You're some tiger,' he said lightly. 'I got a bit worried
when you asked me to tie you up and pour yoghurt all
over you.'

'Joe, please.'

'I really panicked, though, when you started to bark.
That totally freaked me out.' He paused. 'But the worst
was yet to come. It's just as well I couldn't find any veg-
etables . . .' And then, when he heard my sob of anguish,
he said soothingly, 'It's OK, Jack. You fell asleep . . .
nothing happened.'

*Oh sweet Jesus, Mary and Saint Joseph and all the other
saints' names that I can't remember, I'll be lighting so many
candles for you, the churches will be burning down.*

'Pity,' he sighed.

'Yes,' I added, half-heartedly. Then: 'Didn't we even
kiss?' I was certain I remembered that.

'We sure did.'

'That was nice.'

'It sure was,' he said cosily.

'Then what happened?'

'We lay on the floor . . .'
'And then?'
'You called me Matt.'
Ah Christ.

Chapter 7

The next day, Joe returned to London. The damage had not been irreparable. In years to come, the incident would be remembered in a humorous context. In a way it only served to bring us closer.

My mother was silent and my father was brooding. It didn't take me long to figure out why. It was quite evident that they had hoped I would be returning to London with Joe – that they would finally be rid of me. The tension in the house was increasing, the arguments becoming more frequent – and David and I were the cause of them.

It wasn't that they didn't want us. My younger brother was now in college studying for his Master's degree in Art and History. The atmosphere and noise was hardly conducive to studying. Thank God my sister Rachel had married young and left home a few years ago. David had begun to crawl and everything in the house had to be moved upward about six feet. He pulled things down, climbed dangerously, destroyed the bathroom, broke the video – the list was endless. He wasn't a bold child, he was simply at the age when he couldn't help exploring and touching everything. I tried to reprimand him but two minutes later he would be at it again.

My mother was wearing herself out trying to keep everybody happy. My father went out more often and I knew she resented me for that. I felt guilty and desperate and ever more determined to find a job and get out of their hair altogether. I bought the paper every day, to let them see I was making an effort. I enlisted with all the employment agencies in the *Yellow Pages*. I signed up with FÁS and visited the Social Welfare office. I went to the Local Employment Service and had my CV professionally bound. I wrote to all the local businesses that I knew of. I tried hard not to think about the childminding situation. I had no one to mind David; I would cross that bridge when I came to it. I knew intuitively that Mam couldn't help.

She worked fulltime as a waitress in a hotel, usually the weekends, but still, it would have been unfair to put such pressure on her; she had spent her life raising us and was only beginning to reclaim her own life.

It was almost the end of 1989 when I finally secured a position working as a secretary. The company was called Brady Insurances. The place smelt like a toilet so I used to call it 'Brady Urinals' instead. I absolutely detested it.

Finding a suitable childminder was a nightmare. Eventually, through the help of a local Health Board official, David was offered a place in a Health Board crèche on the North Strand on account of my being a single mother with low earnings. The fees were inexpensive and it seemed to be professionally run. The staff were friendly. Despite my initial worries that it wouldn't 'be good enough' I began to relax when I collected him each evening at 5.30 pm and he was still smiling.

Brady's itself was like a morgue. The staff were detached and businesslike, and stared at you when you laughed. I was employed on a temporary contract basis, which suited me down to the ground. I had no intention of making a career out of my badly paid 'typing and filing' position. I arrived at nine each morning, hung up my coat, picked up the first folder on the desk and began to type. The work was so boring, it would have put a glass eye to sleep!

I tried hard to save money, but David's needs were neverending. Mam and Dad had been looking after me financially for so long, that I felt it was only right to offer them the biggest chunk of my wages. However, we all soon realised that if I continued to do that, I would never manage to save the deposit money needed to move into a flat. So I saved every last penny. I visited many flats and apartments in Clontarf, and other areas close by. To my despair, it soon became apparent that I would never be able to pay the rent. I had to start looking elsewhere. I simply couldn't afford to live in Clontarf.

In the summer of 1990, I packed my things and moved into a two-bedroom flat in the inner city. It was not my first choice, but I had to move somewhere. My parents complained that it wasn't 'suitable'; I already knew that, but pointed out to them that a 'suitable' place was out of my financial league. Eventually they came around to accepting my way of thinking. I had not planned to stay there indefinitely. It was only a temporary measure, until something better came along. In time, I told myself, I would get a better job, David would be older and go to school, and childminding fees would not have to be considered. That was the plan, anyway. I ended up staying in my two-bedroom apartment for six years. The best-made plans of men and single parents!

When I went to live in the Good Shepherd flats, there were so many chips on my shoulder I was lop-sided. Having come from Clontarf, the culture shock was immense. I still carried the 'airs and graces' that my mother talked about. In truth, I didn't really know what to expect from the people there. I was scared. I looked down on them. I was sure they would reject me, so I rejected them first.

A classic case of the 'kill it before it kills you' syndrome. I didn't really belong there – I convinced myself of this. I was determined to convince them too. In all my arrogance, born of fear, I made enemies immediately. I made things very difficult for myself.

I ignored them, mostly. I kept myself to myself. If I happened by chance to meet my neighbours in the shop, or on the street, I never acknowledged their presence. Frequently, I would cross the street to avoid them. I actively encouraged David to play indoors. It was cruel and unfair to him. He was now at an age when he needed as much interaction as possible with other children. It wouldn't be long before his schooling years were upon us, and I was determined that David would grow up with the best education money could buy. He would speak correctly and behave in a civilised manner. I clung to my illusions for as long as I could. I was living in a self-made prison. My neighbourhood was the enemy. Even the Alsatians went around in packs. My father had always said, 'When in Rome, do as the Romans do.' I had my own saying: 'When living in the inner city, do your best to stay alive.'

Of course, the reality was, it was no different from any other area in Dublin. There were good parts and bad parts. There were good people and bad people. I was completely unfamiliar with their ways. They spoke differently and dealt with things differently. I didn't know how to fit in. They had no interest in me whatsoever. They sensed my air of 'class differentiation'. They had no choice; I imposed it on them.

I was put straight some weeks after I had moved in. David had taken it upon himself to pick some flowers from a window box in a flat across the road. I watched from an open window, secretly delighted, as he went about destroying what was probably a lifetime's work. I was only short of putting my hands together and applauding him publicly. Then a big lump of shite fell neatly through the window into my lap. It wasn't too solid either. I heard the laughter from across the street.

A man's loud voice rung out. 'Hey, gee bag. Get your snot-gobbler out of my fucking garden or I'll break his bleeding legs.'

David came scrambling over the wall, his face ashen and a clump of flowers still trailing from his hand. The laughter could still be heard from all corners of the street. I had got what I justly deserved. This incident taught me a thing or two. From then on in it was out-and-out war. I would never want or need any of them – I would make sure of that.

The trip to and from the crèche every morning and evening was hard, especially after the day's work, but I was determined to manage things on my own. I wasn't doing too badly really. Then, one day around Easter-time in 1991, I returned from work exhausted and hungry. I collected David from the crèche and noticed that he looked rather pale. He was now a big, bold, burly boy heading towards the four-year mark. He wasn't the angel I had envisaged in earlier years.

This particular day, however, he just sat in his buggy staring blankly ahead. Normally there was the usual tantrum in the morning when the 'clothes battle' began, and then there was always the second tantrum when we passed the sweetshop on our way back from the crèche. I watched him closely as we walked along. There had been no morning or evening tantrums. Could it be a miracle? Could he have transformed overnight into the blessed little child I had hoped for?

On the way home, I stopped off at the shop anyway, and bought him an orange ice pop, his favourite. He just stared at it. I really began to worry then. The minute we got in the door, he vomited all over the carpet. I put my hand on his forehead and he was very hot. He had had temperatures before, but I just knew this was different; he was so quiet it frightened me.

I thought of ringing my parents, but they were too far away. I thought of ringing Karen, but it would take her just as long to get here. I thought of calling on a neighbour, and then my dilemma became painfully apparent. The day was destined to arrive at some stage. Now it was here. I needed help, and there was no one here I could run to.

Eventually I was forced to telephone a doctor, who took two hours to arrive. He examined David quickly.

'Call an ambulance immediately,' he said gravely.

'Jesus, what's wrong with him?' I was panicking.

'I'm suspecting meningitis. I can't be sure; you will have to go to a hospital to rule it out.'

I packed some things, stifling my sobs. I didn't want to upset David. He just lay there listless and white as a sheet. I was really sick with worry. I felt so alone again. Suddenly, it dawned on me *why* I was alone. I had made it that way! Now I wished more than ever that I had a neighbour to turn to. My predicament was completely self-inflicted. It was my fault.

The ambulance arrived quickly. A posse of kids had gathered outside to see what the commotion was, but not one adult came to the door to investigate. There were lots of single parents on my road – I had always behaved like I was the only one. I saw them peer though their curtains. I felt so humiliated as I climbed into the back of the ambulance.

David was strapped and secured into a mobile chair. They placed a basin beside him. I sat opposite him and held his hands. I started to pray.

Our father, Who art in heaven . . . What came next?

In the hospital the doctors and nurses ran a series of

tests. They eventually ruled out the meningitis scare. Instead, he had an acute ear infection. They put him on a drip and detained him overnight for observation. I was so relieved. I slept uncomfortably in a chair beside him. We returned a day later with David already feeling better. I was exhausted and worn out from the whole ordeal.

I had phoned into work to say I had to take the day off, and I knew that the company wasn't impressed. They weren't interested in whether my son was ill or not. That was my problem, not theirs. I strapped David in a chair and put him beside me in the kitchen. I couldn't bear to have him out of my sight. As he smiled up at me, I realised that he had become my world. If anything had happened to him, I would have been heartbroken. Whether I liked it or not, motherhood had taken over and grown. Despite resenting him, I could not help but love him too. Just then, he threw a cup of milk at the wall and it slowly dripped down on to the floor. I watched it with glee, for it told me he was alive and well. It was the only time I let him get away with it. I needed to see his boldness to feel safe.

I wasn't back in the flat long when there was a knock on the door. I opened it expecting to find my mother or father. My nextdoor neighbour was standing there.

'Are you all right, love?'

I wanted to tell her to rev up and fuck off. *You're about six months too late.* Before my anger took control, I reminded myself of the hospital saga. How much I had needed someone, how I had had no one to turn to. I bit my tongue and invited her in. I was never going to find myself in that position again. I set about making some tea for us and gave David a drink of orange juice in his special cup.

My visitor's name was Alice. She was a big fat woman with bleached yellow hair cut severely into the nape of her neck and a tattoo on her left arm that read *Johnny*. She wore it proudly. Her ears were pierced so many times they had vanished beneath the mountain of earrings. She had a big booming voice that could have travelled the length and breadth of O'Connell Street.

She picked David up by the scruff of the neck and held him under her arm like a pup. I bit my tongue. Again.

'There's nothing wrong with this young fella,' she said matter-of-factly. 'If you ask me, he's overfed. What did the doctors say?'

'They said it was an ear infection.'

'Ah, ear infection, was it? Ah, everything is a fucking ear infection these days. Or a fucking virus. Fucking virus this, virus that. It's all a load of bollox.'

'Well, I'm just glad it wasn't meningitis.'

'Melon what, love?'

'He's fine now. Nothing to worry about.'

'Johnny had a bad dose of the flu just before Christmas. You know my Johnny, the little baldy bastard who's always pulling the girls' knickers down? The doctor said it was a virus. Ask me arse, I told him. I know me own child. Sure he was back to his usual self on the Monday, the little bastard. What's the young fella's name?'

'David.'

'A right little fat fucker if you ask me, a fine pair of balls on him and all.' She whacked him across the backside and to my amazement, David smiled. 'There's nothing wrong with this child, missus.'

Six dirty-looking kids had gathered at the door.

'Get out the fuck!' she roared at them and they scattered like rats. 'If you want anything, love, just call in to me. You never have to be alone in this place, unless you want to carry on with your high and mighty shite. They'll fuck you from a height, love. You need your neighbours. We all need someone.'

Alice was right. From that day onwards things changed.

I was never alone again – I made sure of it. When kids called for David, I invited them in. Alice dropped in every day; if she didn't, I made a point of calling on her. Usually, after a trip to The Hill in the early morning we would have a cup of tea together. She picked up the oddest things at the market and always returned with something for David and myself.

She was extremely kind. One day, she brought in a huge side of lamb. We cut it up into smaller pieces and rammed it in our freezer compartments. We were eating it for months. Lamb kebabs. Lamb chops. Lamb casserole.

If I didn't fancy going shopping in the city, there was no problem. They came to my door. Groceries. Clothes. Tobacco. Alcohol. Even electrical goods. I knew they fell off the back of a lorry, but it didn't matter any more. I was now a pure-blooded Roman. I was just trying to make ends meet like everybody else.

I was never robbed. They never robbed their own. They went out to Clontarf to do that. I thought it was funny. I bought a small ghetto-blaster and a portable TV that looked exactly like my mother's. They only cost me £100 for the two. I was thrilled to bits.

David seemed OK. I tried to look for things wrong with him. It was pure habit. A part of me still refused to accept we were both doing well. He was doing just as well here as anywhere else. As the culture shock began to diminish, I realized I had an army of good neighbours and friends to call upon when needed. I began to change. I began to see that it was up to me to fit in, not them.

I wasn't exactly happy. I was prone to spells of great loneliness that no one could fill. I still carried an air of separateness, but as the years passed I could see that that was part of my nature, and not my circumstances. I had always felt different.

I qualified for the Unmarried Mothers' Allowance. I

christened it 'The Scarlet Harlot Allowance'. That, coupled with my wages from the job and the children's allowance payment every month, just about got me through. I didn't venture out much, though; finances and baby-sitters prevented it.

Instead, I joined the Annesley Bridge Library. It was free and easy to get to. I read novels by the score. In the evenings, I had a few cans of beer. Sometimes Alice and others would call in, when the kids were asleep. Sometimes they brought their children with them. They laid their pillows on the floor and nodded off eventually. Their children were so adaptable; they went everywhere with them. We drank cheap wine and sang songs. Sometimes we played cards but Alice always cheated and there would be a row. For the best part we were surviving. There were even moments of peace.

Joe kept in touch, making his usual monthly visits home to Dublin. He took my letters for Jill back to London. The neighbours loved him. Alice was in like a shot when she saw him coming.

'Here's your friend, love. The big ride.'

'Alice!' I'd reprimand her.

'Ah, why don't the two of you settle down, love?'

'You sound like my mother.'

'A fine thing like that. I'd eat chips out of his knickers, I would.'

'He's just a friend.'

'Ah, you're full of shite. A good seeing-to is what you need.'

Karen and Mick visited occasionally. It was difficult for people to get to me by bus or train and then make the long journey home. It wasn't exactly safe to walk around the streets after 10 o'clock. I often sat on the edge of my bed when David was asleep and just listened to the noise outside.

On New Year's Eve of 1991 when midnight struck, the road came alive with gangs of people. The neighbours burst out of their doors and banged pots and pans and blew whistles. The kids raced up and down the road with bells and screamed, 'Happy New Year!' They hugged and kissed, and embraced each other lovingly. It was beautiful. I felt safer there than I ever had at home. Come 2 am it was a different story. The same people came flying horizontally out of their front doors.

'You fucking cunt! I'll bleeding burst you if you ever mention that young one's name again!'

'Don't talk to me about our Joey – what about your child, the dirty pox-ridden spa! You couldn't raise a cat, you whore.'

Neighbours who two hours previously had been full of good cheer were now beating each other senseless. Empty beer cans rolled and bottles smashed. Doors slammed and ambulance sirens blared. Fire engines thundered past. It was the same scene every year.

As time passed, I realised there is no cut-off point in life where you 'arrive'. It is an endless journey. You have to take it day-by-day, sometimes hour-by-hour. Years passed quickly but the days were long.

I was kind of happy around that time. As happy as I could have been if you didn't count the loneliness. Everybody was lonely. David and I were healthy, we had a roof over our heads, and I had enough money to keep us going. Unfortunately, the next six months would prove to be the most difficult of my life.

It started on Mother's Day, 10 March 1992. I watched from the window as people crossed the street armed with flowers and chocolates. Alice called in with a bunch of dandelions, then Jill phoned to say Happy Mother's Day and my mam sent me some perfume. Despite all this, I had never been keen on these man-made family celebration

days, like New Year's Eve and Christmas and Easter,
when unhappy families are forced to come together, like
it or lump it. There should be a 'Dysfunctional and
Abnormal Families Day', I thought, grinning. There was
nothing I hated more than discrimination.

The phone rang abruptly, interrupting my thoughts. It
was Joe.

'Surprise, surprise!'

'Where are you?'

'I'm in Dublin Airport.'

'Great.' I tried to sound delighted.

'Hey, don't get too excited.' He sensed my low mood.
I felt guilty for not being more responsive.

'It's Mother's Day, I know,' he said understandingly.

'Why didn't you tell me you were coming home?' I
asked. Normally he told me well in advance.

'I have a surprise for you.'

I was beginning to feel the first flutters of interest. 'Oh?
What kind of surprise?'

'You'll see. Meet me in St Anne's, up by the pond – and
bring David. I can't wait to see him.'

Glad of the distraction, I dressed David up warmly.
There was a cold March breeze, and a chance it would
rain. I didn't care. Joe or no Joe, there was no way I was
going to stay in today. I hopped on the Dart and got off at
Raheny Station. I had to carry the buggy by myself across
the bridge. Old women impatiently sighed behind me, as
I struggled with the pram, but no one offered to help me.
Didn't they recall having children? I wondered. Why was
everybody so selfish?

I pushed David along Raheny village down to St Anne's
Park, and wedged myself through a break in the wall. When
I let David out, he ran around in circles delighting in the freedom. Eventually he realised he was not restricted to circles,
and I spent the next hour chasing him from field to field.

It was sunny but cold. We walked to the Old Pond and David went crazy when he saw the ducks. Fortunately, I had had the foresight to bring some broken-up bread. Together, we threw it in to the starved birds. We were walking back around the pond and along the mucky hills when I heard a commotion. I looked up over the river and saw a dirty child tumble dangerously down the side. Then a girl followed on a skateboard. I thought they were going to hurt themselves. Then a man came tumbling down after them.

The foolish prick, I thought. He straightened himself up and all three of them started to laugh. I recognised the sound. It was Joe.

'You're mad!' I said.

'Hi,' he replied breathlessly. The two children were obviously having a ball. 'This is Ronan and this is Katie.' They paid no attention to me. They were too busy scrambling back up the hill.

Then, just as gleefully and twice as loud, a dark-haired woman came skidding down the hill. The children were screaming after her. 'Look at Mum, look at Mum!'

Joe went to the woman's aid. He picked her up and dusted her off. 'And this,' he paused, 'is Juliet.'

'Hi,' she said, in an English accent.

I extended my hand. It was, after all, Joe's friend. 'Hi, Juliet.'

Joe curled her long black hair behind her ears. Only then did the penny drop. I could see it in her eyes. I could see it in his eyes. *Ah Christ.*

Ronan came tumbling down again. Screaming and shrieking like a lunatic. Katie stood nervously at the top.

'Come on, I'll catch you,' Joe encouraged her.

She closed her eyes and dived forward, landing at Joe's feet in convulsions of laughter. It was obvious he had gained her complete trust. How long had this been going on? How come he had not said anything on the phone? They were beautiful children. Ronan was a sturdy boy with a roundy, happy face, full of mischief. Katie was very pretty, but much more subdued. She looked like her mother.

'This is David.' I pointed to the sleeping body in the buggy. 'As you can see, he has already had his adventure for the day.'

Juliet peered into the buggy. 'He resembles you,' she commented.

'Yes. I'm afraid his mannerisms are all mine too.'

'Poor bastard,' Joe smirked. Then: 'Ronan, watch your sister,' he called. Katie was dangling from a tree and trying to scramble to the ground.

'Joe has told me so much about you that I feel I've known you for years.' Juliet smiled at me. It was a genuine smile. Yes. Just how long had this been going on? I liked Juliet immediately. I was annoyed that I liked her immediately.

'How are you?' Joe beamed. He was lit up like a Christmas tree, radiating supreme joy. The picture was perfect.

I felt like a spare prick. I was trying hard to adjust, that is, within the time-scale I had been given to adjust. I was angry with him for dumping me in at the deep end like this. I even wondered, had he done it deliberately? Then I was cross with myself for not being happy for them. It was a very strange contradiction.

We sat down by the pond as the children played with the ducks. David woke up and was delighted to have two new friends. Especially two new older friends. He loved older children. Juliet talked freely and openly. She treated me like her best friend. I wasn't sure who she was doing it for at first, but it seemed to be completely genuine. She loved to talk and was very down to earth. She and I had a lot in common. She had married, the marriage had failed, she had set up home in Finchley, North London, and had met Joe in the local bar, where he was playing music.

At this point she stopped talking for a brief moment and smiled at him. He smiled back. It was obvious they were in the first throes of love. There was a special something between them.

The whole thing felt bizarre. I guess I had always taken it for granted that Joe would remain a loner. Now, that notion seemed utterly absurd. Watching him with the children and his devotion to Juliet, it seemed quite crazy to imagine him being alone for ever. This new relationship was as natural as night and day. Why hadn't I thought about it before?

Joe was a loving, loyal and sensitive man and a wonderful father too. That was when I felt the first twinges of jealousy. I was absolutely sickened to my stomach. How could I feel something like that when it was plain to see he was happy? Juliet was the perfect partner for Joe. My depression increased tenfold.

'I'm taking the kids for an ice-cream down the road. Come with us, Jack, there's room for David in the back.'

'Where did you get the car?' I asked, looking at the black Mazda.

'It's Juliet's. We came over on the ferry – it was cheaper. Besides, we needed it for the kids. Right, gang. Pile in!'

We drove down the causeway on to the beach. I remembered being sixteen, and Matt Howard. I smiled to myself. Katie went off to collect shells. She returned with a bucket-full. I held the strange shapes in my palm.

'I used to paint these when I was a little girl like you. Why don't you ask your mammy to help you paint them? Then you can put them in your room and look at them.'

'Mummy hasn't any paints,' she replied solemnly.

I made a face at Juliet. She blushed a little. 'Maybe you can ask her to buy some when you go home.'

'My mummy kisses Joe,' she added without any warning whatsoever.

'Katie!' Juliet interrupted.

'I have paints.' I changed the subject quickly. 'You can borrow them if you like.'

'OK,' she smiled. Then did an about-turn and fled down the beach with her arms flapping in the wind like an aeroplane.

My face burned with jealousy. It was ridiculous. I couldn't understand my feelings – they made no sense. Joe was entitled to kiss whoever he wanted. I couldn't figure out why it mattered all of a sudden.

'My God, she's got some energy – how do you manage? I can barely cope with one child.' I tried hard to conceal my inner turmoil.

'It's a case of having to,' she answered in a perfectly spoken British accent. 'I can see you're confused,' she added.

Intuitive *and* perceptive. Joe had hit the jackpot.

'Well, to be honest,' I confessed, 'he never told me, I'm a little shocked, that's all. God, I'm delighted for you both, really.'

'You're his best friend, I know. I hope we can be friends too.'

She was doing her very best. She delved into her pocket and drew out a small parcel. 'We brought you something for Mother's Day. I hope you like it,' she smiled and handed it to me.

I opened the beautifully wrapped box and inside was a tiny gold charm. I could just about make out the engraving on the inside: *J.J.* I looked at it for a long time. I wished it had been from Joe alone. I wished *he* had chosen it, not her. I found myself surprisingly upset.

David was now insisting he needed to go to the toilet. 'Can I go with Joe?' he asked candidly. He had that look on his face, the one that said, 'That's a man. I know it's a man and I'd like to examine him.' The lack of a father figure in David's life had become more and more apparent. Especially now as he approached schooldays. I knew it would be difficult. Mammies and Daddies would collect their children from school. Pretty soon he would notice – no Daddy. Then the inevitable questions would begin. I dreaded it.

The sky had become overcast and grey. Time had gone by very quickly. We piled back into the car and headed up the causeway.

'I'll drive you home, Jack,' Joe offered.

'No, honestly, the bus is just here. We'll get out here.' I didn't want Juliet to see where I lived. Luckily a bus came driving up the road at that very moment.

'There's our bus,' I said, sighing. 'Better run or we'll miss it.'

'Hey. Mind yourself, Jack. It was great seeing you. I'll call you soon.'

Juliet waved and the children shouted from out of the back window. I jumped on the bus trying desperately not to look awkward. The buggy slid across the floor. The bus conductor stayed sitting, chewing moronically on a piece of gum. I grappled with the buggy, my bag and David and somehow managed to get the buggy stowed safely out of the way. Then I slipped back into the seat and hugged David.

The bus conductor continued to stare at me. I stared back. The ignorant prick.

Without warning, David stood up, yanked down his trousers and pissed all over the floor.

I was never so proud of him.

Chapter 8

What was left of the day was spent in a semi-coma. I was dazed and uninterested, found it hard to concentrate on anything. I couldn't bear to stay in the flat alone. For the first time in a long time, I took it upon myself to visit home at teatime.

As I walked down Vernon Avenue, everything felt strange and different. I had forgotten the beautiful greens and browns of Clontarf, the cherry blossoms lining Belgrove Lane. It was that time of year when the cherry blossoms were snowing heavily on the footpath. David waded through the sea of pink. Every now and then he'd kick his shoe high in the air and the confetti-like petals would swirl around us. I had walked that road millions of times. As a child I went to the shops daily for my mother. 'Ten of the cheapest cigarettes, please.' The shopkeeper would hand me back ten Richmond. I could still remember the blue box and my mother puffing furiously on them. They had cost 12 pence then. I knew every crack and hole in the road. We always tried so hard not to walk on the lines, as we thought it would rain if we did that.

Our house hadn't changed much down through the years. That is, on the outside. Come to think of it, the inside hadn't either, and I'm not talking about the décor.

'Mam?' I called, as I let myself in with an old key. 'Dad? Anyone home?'

I heard the breeze blow through the house and I knew the back door was open. That meant my father was here, in the back garden – his favourite haunt. David went straight to the video cabinet and put on *Willy Wonka's Chocolate Factory*. I knew that guaranteed total peace for at least ten minutes.

I found my father in the back garden, as predicted. Hunched over a vegetable plot, he was digging away furiously, and cursing at the same time. I smiled.

'Dad?'

'Move, you bastarding thing,' he muttered.

'Dad?'

'Ah, bollox on the cursed object!' He still hadn't heard me.

'*Dad!*' I yelled.

'Ah what!' he roared, turning around to see who had dared to speak. 'Oh, it's yourself, I see. Where's Dennis the Menace?'

'Inside, watching a video,' I replied.

'He'll get square eyes if he keeps that up. C'mon you stubborn swine, move!' He jabbed at the ground in a temper, his face red with rage.

'What in God's name are you trying to do?' I asked.

'Get these bastarding roots out. They won't . . . fucking . . . budge!' The roots suddenly came loose and he tumbled backwards, tripping over his feet, and landing arse upwards on the grass.

'Dad, why do you have to be so stubborn?' I pulled him up with both hands and he dusted himself down.

'It's her fault. She planted it, she did it deliberately. She hasn't a bull's notion about plants. Look at it!' He waved the giant roots in my face. 'It's a shagging palm tree! I ask you, it's not Buckingham Palace we're living in. The woman was born to torment me. She'll never be done making me suffer.'

'Now Dad, that's a load of rubbish, and you know it. Where is she?'

'Over at the Headquarters,' he mumbled.

The Headquarters was a term my father used for the neighbours. He swore they gathered with one single agenda in mind: to talk about him. 'Tearing strips off me, no doubt, babbling on with their mindless prittle prattle, while I'm out here breaking me arse . . .'

I left him to it and wandered back inside. Nothing had changed. Why did I always think it would? It had been like this for years. Most couples died fighting for each other. Mine would die fighting *with* each other.

My mother returned flushed and hassled. When she saw David, her expression changed to one of delight. He seemed to be the only thing on this earth that could do that.

'Where's my little soldier? Where is he?' She tickled him, prodded him, and poked him.

'Mam, what's wrong with Dad? He's like a bear with a sore head.'

'Ah, sure don't talk to me.' She waved her hand dismissively. 'He never stops – morning, noon and night. Saints preserve us, I'll be one myself when I pass on.' She blessed herself quickly and then kissed her fingers.

'Why does he have to complain so much?'

'Ah, nothing's good enough for him – he'll always find something wrong. You have to learn to ignore him, love.'

But I didn't want to ignore him.

Dad arrived at the back door, rubbing the small of his back. 'In the name of Jaysus where did you put me garden gloves?'

Mam turned around. 'They're where you left them, Will. I don't wear them. How the hell am I supposed to know where they are?'

Dad started to pull all the kitchen drawers out. He knew quite well they weren't in there. It was all a ploy to infuriate Mam.

The plot thickened.

'Well, you probably threw them out along with all me other stuff.'

'What other stuff?' Mam looked mystified.

If he didn't win the argument first time around, he reverted to Plan B. Fabricating lies, to add fuel to the fire. The fire was already blazing. I thought, If the house is on fire, do you run into it, or out of it?

Watching Mam now, I thought about her mothering ability. Now I was a mother myself, I wondered had I inherited her traits? I was often impatient and intolerant of David. I felt I needed eyes in the back of my head to keep a constant watch on him. I couldn't recall my mother ever losing her temper with us. She saved that for Dad. She had always referred to him as 'the extra child'. She loved the three of us children. We were her salvation.

Mam made David sit on a high stool. She took out her scissors and made a meal out of trimming what little hair he had. She cut the fringe too much on one side and had to even it up. Pretty soon, he looked like one of the Three Stooges. David squirmed and tugged at the towel she had tucked into his neckline. The falling downy hairs were making him itch. I looked at Mam's face. She was humming away, happy as the day is long.

'Do you ever think about him, Mam?' I asked suddenly.

'Think of who?' she answered, comb clenched between her teeth. Her eyes remained fixed on the job at hand. She pushed David's chin into his chest. He objected strenuously. He had inherited my defiance. I couldn't decide if it was a good thing or a bad thing. He looked so cute, I couldn't help smiling as he struggled to get free, lips pushed downward in a long-drawn-out sulk.

I waited for her to take up the opportunity. I wanted to push the question again, but something in her determined face told me to back off. I was a grown mother, but she still couldn't bring herself to treat me like one. I sensed her fear. Behind the fear was sorrow. Behind the sorrow was the truth. I realised Mam couldn't go there, not today. I loved her. I loved her for loving my son. It suddenly dawned on me whose hair she was really cutting, and I wanted her to have her illusion, however momentary. The ghosts of the past were still sleeping. Neither she nor I were ready to wake them up.

I sat with David watching TV. There was a wonderful documentary on about Philip Lynott's untimely death and the fate of Thin Lizzy. I loved hearing the old songs again. Recalling that my brother had purchased some of their CDs, I searched through his collection until I found the particular one I wanted. The ghetto-blaster was downstairs, in the kitchen. I noticed it was no longer there.

'Mam, where's the tape-recorder?'

She appeared at the door with a look of exasperation. 'Shhh!' she motioned to the back door. 'Robbed,' she whispered.

'When?'

'Months ago. And the portable TV.'

Ah Christ.

That night, I did the same thing I had been doing for years. As soon as David was asleep, I went to my favourite place – the place that only existed for me. The place where nobody could gain access. I emptied the fridge of all its delicious goodies and lined them up, like soldiers. Then I took my six cans of beer and hid them behind the couch. I made sure I had the large ashtray, and plenty of cigarettes. I put my feet up and turned on the television and started my little party for one.

The parties had become a habit. Born out of boredom, or so I thought. I very rarely ventured outdoors any more, only to visit the library, Alice or the supermarket. This was the highlight of the day. My time, my little piece of heaven. I savaged several packets of crisps, peanuts, and chocolate bars, and washed them down with my cans of Budweiser. I looked forward to this so much. I gorged and drank and smoked to my heart's content. Pretty soon, though, the cans were empty and it was still early. I called in to Alice and asked her to mind David while I nipped down to the off-licence.

On the way back I heard my own thoughts pleading to be let in, but I was determined to keep the little bastards at bay. I didn't want to reflect on today's events. I just wanted to vanish up my own arse. At the rate I was putting on weight, the odds of that happening were rising by the minute. I didn't want to think about that either.

For the first time ever, Joe had genuinely surprised me. After he had turned up at the birth, I felt a bond with him that was indescribable. In real life, he wasn't the father of my child, but in the Labour Ward, he had taken on that role. I never really asked him why he had done that, what had prompted him to make himself available for the most important moment of my life. It was a milestone, but it wasn't something I had dwelled on afterwards. I was always good with delayed reactions. I was having one now. Juliet's face kept peering into my subconscious.

The experience in the hospital naturally transformed my relationship with Joe. After that, I saw him with different eyes. I felt a certain 'ownership'. Joe had become a special person. Maybe I had taken our relationship for granted? I never dreamed that I would be assailed with these intense emotions on hearing of this new girlfriend. I laughed out loud at my own arrogance.

Opening another can I threw the empty one on top of the pile gathering in the corner. I flicked from station to station. Fifty-seven channels and nothing on. In desperation, I turned on the radio. A woman was talking about her mastectomy and how to cope. I switched it off. I picked up a book and started to read, but couldn't get past the second page. I threw it across the floor. I knew that Joe would be waiting for the obligatory phone-call but I couldn't bring myself to make it. I just couldn't. I could not rise above this strange new emotion. It was devouring me whole. Oh jealousy, most definitely the deadliest of sins!

'Fuck it! Fuck it!' I hissed into the empty room. I got up, stumbled over to the bedroom mirror, and slowly started to undress. I forced myself to look, really look, at my naked body. It was horrific.

The layers of fat overlapped one another. I looked like the Michelin man. There were nasty stretchmarks on the inside of both my thighs. They had taken on that 'cellulite' look, pinched and flabby. My legs had never, ever been this fat. I had always had beautiful legs. My mother claimed that I had inherited them from her. It was the only thing she and my father agreed on. I turned sideways. Jesus Christ, what a sight. I still looked about six months pregnant.

The fat hung disgustingly over my pubic hair. I could have been in training as a Sumo wrestler. But the worst part was to come. I held up the small hand mirror behind my back and gasped at the reflection. My arse had spread so much that it was no longer distinguishable from the rest of me. If there hadn't been that slit in the middle, I could have mistaken it for a second torso. Sweet Jesus, how did I get like this? How long had I looked like this? I was absolutely devastated. Putting my night-dress back on, I was tearful and filled with self-disgust. The sight of my naked body was so upsetting to *me*, I could hardly expect anyone else to look at it. My confidence plummeted. What really disturbed me most was the thought that I was powerless to do anything about it.

Every morning I awoke filled with determination and resilience, only to have scoffed my breakfast, lunch and dinner by 10 am. No matter how resolute I was, my will-power weakened at the mere sight of someone chewing. I was a glutton, a pig. A big fat ugly pig. I touched my face and peered into the hand mirror. I looked old, wizened and wrinkled. Why? It wasn't like I was out on the town every night! I only had a few cans of beer on my own. My cheeks were red, like a woman with hot flushes in the middle of her menopause. I knew it was all the excess food. Why else did I feel so sick in the mornings?

Those bloody take-aways. They often gave me food poisoning. How many times had I woken up sweating and shaking? I knew I had to stop ordering food from the Chinese. God knows what I was eating. I'd eat anything. It could have been shite on a stick, for all I cared. The overdose of food was responsible for my ill-health. It had to stop. The midnight promises were made again. *Never again. Never again.*

When I awoke the next morning, David was standing beside me. He was holding a can opener in one hand and a can of beans in the other. A dessert spoon peeped out of the top. I looked at the clock. It was after 11 am. I had slept it out again. I realised I was on the couch; my clothes lay strewn around me. I sat up straight and put my feet on the ground and stumbled on an empty bottle of wine. Where had that come from?

I grabbed the can off David and yelled at him. 'What the hell are you trying to do! You could cut your hand on this, you dope!' I was so angry I slapped him across the face.

'I was hungry!' He started to cry.

'Then why didn't you call me?' I screamed right into his face.

'I did! I did!' he screamed back at me.

I was shaking and sweating and feeling very unwell. I wasn't in the mood for this drama first thing in the morning. I pushed David out of the way and went to the toilet. My stomach was churning and my head was pounding. It felt like there was a bunch of screaming monkeys running wild in it. I probably had another dose of food poisoning. I took two Anadin Extra. Another day had begun. I called in to 'Brady's Urinals' and threw a sickie. I knew I was running out of sick leave. Fuck them anyway. I'd soon find a better job.

Late in the afternoon, I managed to call Joe. I knew they would be returning to London that night, so I left it as late as possible. It was a deliberate move.

'Well, what do you think?' he asked me.

'She's great,' I said, and I meant it. 'Why didn't you tell me you were seeing someone?'

'Ah, I just didn't. I don't know why. I'm just as surprised.'

'Joe, you're really fond of her, I can tell.'

'The feeling is mutual, I think. I hope.'

'Are you kidding? She practically drools every time you look at her. It's great. I really mean that.' I did. I really meant it.

'You don't sound as if you do,' he observed.

'Look, I had one too many last night, is all.'

'Too many what?' he joked.

'Too much to eat, as per usual, what's new?'

'Look, I'll have to fly, Jack. We're catching the evening ferry.'

'Joe. The kids are beautiful. I can see they trust you. I'm so happy for you. I wish all of you the very, very best.'

There was an uncomfortable silence, and I wasn't too sure who had caused it.

'You're still my best friend,' he said softly.

'I know.' I was hurting.

'Jack?'

'Yeah?'

'When are you going to start living again?'

'Just as soon as you hang up! OK?'

He hung up.

And I died.

Chapter 9

The business of life had me baffled. Day in, day out, I did what was expected of me, never really knowing why. It wasn't long before Christmas had come around again. It was now the end of 1992.

My phone-calls from Joe had become more and more sporadic. When he did phone, our conversations were strained and difficult, to say the least. I was happy for him, but I was also envious, although I had no right to be – I realised that. So I tried to be jolly. Often, when he phoned, I would talk more to Juliet. We chatted about our children, how they were growing up so quickly.

David liked to talk to them too. My son was now five years old. He had started school that September. It was one of those precious milestones. He mixed well with the other children and was already showing talent, particularly with art and music. He still maintained his cheeky personality, although I never thought of him as a cheeky child. It was more of an overt confidence. I was rather proud of it. I knew he would learn to stand on his own two feet.

That was all I had ever hoped for. If he was happy, I was happy. I didn't really care any more if he didn't go to college and become a professor. Strange, how children change your whole perspective on life. What seemed to matter years ago could hardly be remembered now. Life before David was dim and distant, a foggy dream. He was my life now. I was determined to concentrate on him fully.

This Christmas, I decided, he would take his first trip to see Santa Claus. I hadn't taken him in previous years, as it seemed a waste of money. How were little ones to understand what was going on? I had been looking forward to this for a long time. I even bought him some new clothes for the special occasion.

'What's he like?' he asked me, chewing on a biscuit.

'Don't speak with your mouth full, David.'

'Well?' He completely ignored me.

'He's big and fat, with a red roundy face and a white beard. He wears a lovely red outfit with fur, and he goes "Ho! Ho! Ho!"'

'Why?' he asked.

'Because he's happy,' I answered.

'Why?'

'Because he makes all the children happy. That's his job.'

'Why?'

'Oh David!' We were still only halfway into town and I was exhausted from the endless questioning. 'Just wait and see.'

He cuddled up to me and kissed my hand. I felt guilty. I had screamed at him that morning. That wasn't unusual. I just felt so bad about it. I wondered, did other mothers lose their tempers as often as I did? David was a handful. Still, that was no excuse for shouting at him, or hitting him.

When I recalled hitting him I felt even worse. And what made me feel extra guilty was the fact that he always, always, forgave me. It was as if nothing had happened. I now understood children of violent parents – why those children always remained loyal to them, no matter how cruel their parents were. The vulnerability of children was startling. It was a frightening realisation. I could do what I wanted – it was possible that nobody else would know. But I would know. The screaming monkeys always let me know. Like now. My head ached with remorse. I pulled David closer and kissed his forehead. He was still my baby boy.

In the city centre, the Christmas season was in full swing. The Christmas lights dazzled brightly, illuminating Henry Street. David leapt with glee when he saw the enormous tree in the centre of O'Connell Street.

'Can we buy one like that, Mammy?' His eyes were as big as saucers.

'No, darling. It wouldn't fit in the flat.'

'Aw,' he smiled.

Such complete acceptance. Such sweetness.

We passed the street traders. Voices competed for business, the racket was deafening. I loved it, the hustle and the bustle. Irate parents dragged toddlers from shop to shop. Bags entangled in black market cigarette trading. Lighters five for a pound. It was chilly cold with a sharp breeze, but the colours and energy of Christmas cheer surrounded us in a blanket of childlike charm. I felt I was going to see Santa myself for the first time. I was so excited for David.

We joined the long queue outside Clery's department store. As we moved forward, inch by inch, we took in the window displays – of Christmas scenes, accompanied by Bing Crosby. My eyes welled up. It happened every year.

Soon we were at the entrance to Santa's Cave. A bored-looking elf shuffled us along and we found ourselves in a dark winding tunnel. I could see it had been made out of cardboard and painted black. Lights flashed on and off. David was a little apprehensive. We passed more moving puppets. A particularly sad-looking snowman was having a hard time of it. Its mechanism had gone haywire. It jerked its head back and forth, completely out of sync with the rest. A group of children had congregated around the window causing a bit of a traffic jam. David thought it was hilarious and began mimicking. The elf was really pissed off and pushed us forward.

All of a sudden we were in Santa's Cave and standing in front of us was the big man himself, old St Nicholas. Only he wasn't very big at all. He was about average height. To David he was an ogre, a monster of a thing. He stared up at him wide-eyed.

The dozy elf yawned.

'Come here, son,' Santa boomed in a feigned voice.

David moved hesitantly, not surprisingly, for Santa wasn't exactly very merry. Or if he was, it certainly wasn't his personality that was making him so.

Santa patted his lap, indicating to David to sit there. I urged him forward and he climbed up.

'Now then.' Santa tugged at his beard, which had seen better days. His moustache was crooked and I could smell a hint of tobacco from his clothes.

'And what's this little boy's name?'

'David.'

'David, is it? And tell me this, David, where are you from?'

'I live in me Mammy's,' he said.

'And where might that be, son?'

'Down the road.'

'I see.' Santa smiled at me, then he gave me a cheeky wink. 'And Mammy, tell me something else, has David been a good boy this year?'

'Oh very good, Santa,' I played along, feeling like a complete prick.

'And David, has Mammy been a good mammy as well?'

Pardon?

David smiled. 'Yes,' he said finally.

I heaved a sigh of relief. The elf let out a second big yawn and threw a loud cough in for good measure.

'And what would you like for Christmas, David?'

David thought, as only David could. The elf was tapping her foot impatiently.

'A fire engine, a computer, a bike and a spud gun.'

'I see. And what would Mammy like, do you think? A bottle of vodka, perhaps?'

The bearded bollox! I glared at him.

'I think she'd like some beer,' David nodded.

'Well now. You stand aside and watch that chimney there and a present will come down the funnel just for you.'

David was so excited he held on to his penis and jumped up and down.

Santa gave a big 'Ho! Ho! Ho!' As the pathetically wrapped present plopped on to the ground, David grabbed it and tore it open. Then he ran around in circles for about five minutes. Santa was laughing his head off. There was something disconcerting about his laugh.

We stood huddled in the corner as the disinterested elf took our photograph. Santa stood behind me.

'Perhaps Mammy would like to be Santa's little helper someday,' he whispered into my ear. Then he pinched my arse.

I let out a scream. Enough was enough! I pushed my way through the heavy crowds and stormed up to the reception desk.

'I would like to see the manager, please,' I demanded in my best Clontarf accent.

'Certainly, madam. I am the manager, what seems to be the problem?'

I explained about the sexually molesting Santa and he

apologised profusely. I refused to accept his apology. I wanted to see Mr Arse Grabber personally.

The manager asked me to come into the office. I was creating a scene and he didn't want the fuss to be open to public view. I was extremely upset. This first visit had meant so much to me and it had been ruined.

The manager made me some tea. I would have preferred something stronger but it wasn't forthcoming. They offered me my money back and a voucher for £50. The assistant manager took David to the restaurant for some refreshments.

I was not leaving until I'd given that bastard a piece of my mind. The manager was whispering on the phone. Every now and then he glanced over the wire and smiled. I was furious. The whole event had been a complete fiasco. Suddenly, the door burst open and in came the Santa from Hell himself.

He stood grinning at me like I was some long-lost friend. I stared back indignant and full of pride. Then he pulled the bedraggled beard from off his face and removed his cap.

'Hello, Jack,' he grinned triumphantly.

'Matt Howard, you dirty bastard!'

My father always said, 'When the student is ready, the teacher appears.' But meeting Matt Howard under such cruelly embarrassing circumstances was the last thing I needed.

I had spent weeks, even months, fantasising how it should be. I would be slim. I would look beautiful. I would devastate him with my charm and wit. I would impress him with my achievements. Er, what achievements? Oh foolish, foolish girl! It always happens when you're least prepared. After the initial shock wore off I began to see the humorous side to it all. When I thought about it, it was obvious there had been something fishy about Mr Claus right from the start. Of all the Santas in Dublin, I had chosen for us to visit him. The irony was too much.

Sitting in the restaurant of Clery's, I tried hard not to stare at him. I ate cigarettes and would have killed for a strong drink. Matt looked older. Why was I surprised? Tiny crow's feet had appeared on the corner of his eyes, but they only enhanced his beauty. The years had been good to him. David had no idea who he was, and was still babbling away to himself. He had eaten at least four Club bars and drunk a hundred additive-ridden orange squashes. I could see he was entering a 'hyper' state of mind. I tried hard to calm him down, while selfishly wishing that he were not there at all. I wanted to savour every moment, and find out as much information as possible. I wasn't letting Matt slip through my fingers again.

'You snake in the grass.' I couldn't help smiling.

'I really had you going, hadn't I?' He poked me playfully with his finger. 'I spotted you immediately. All I had to do was look at David – he's a carbon copy of you. Jesus, you have no idea how much I enjoyed that.'

'I'll never forgive you.'

'You've no idea how boring it is. Three hundred children a day, same old, same old – I couldn't resist.' He gave me that broad beautiful grin.

We talked about everything, and frequently talked at the same time. It was rushed and intense. Despite our meeting five years before, I still had the guts of fifteen years to tell him about. I could have stayed there for ever, but David was getting more and more difficult. At this point the manager appeared by Matt's side. He gave me a wink, then he motioned to Matt that the queues were getting longer.

'How in God's name did you ever get involved in something like this?' I asked him.

'I need the money, plain and simple.'

'I can think of lots of nicer ways to earn money.'

'Well, I could always sell my body.' Hmm, I thought hungrily. 'Look, I'll have to get a move on.' He stood up and replaced the ridiculous red hat and beard.

Don't go, don't go, I thought wildly. I cannot bear for any more years to separate us.

'Yeah. I have to go myself,' I stuttered. David was tugging at my arm and beginning to whine. I hated it when he did that, especially in front of strangers – when he seemed to do it the most.

We reached the entrance of the tunnel.

'Well, my career beckons,' Matt joked.

Please ask me for my phone number, I begged silently.

'Guess I'll see you around, Jack.'

OK, ask me for my address, anything, just please hurry! I shrugged my shoulders, not knowing what else to say.

Just then, a little curly-headed girl spotted him and screeched at the top of her voice. 'Look! There's Santa. There's Santa!' She ran up to him and grabbed his hand and pulled him back into the tunnel. I wanted to strangle her lily-white neck. I was even prepared to pay the consequences.

I was losing him again. 'I'm in the book,' I croaked after him, but he had already been swept inside. I could have cried with disappointment. I took David by the hand, a little roughly.

'Ouch!' he squealed. I had had enough of him for one day. I watched the happy families shopping for presents, enjoying the seasonal entertainment and pushed through the crowds towards the front door, wanting desperately to be home all of a sudden.

I was just about to leave when the obnoxious elf grabbed me by the arm. 'Here – you forgot your photograph.' She thrust it into my hand.

I opened the cardboard folder. We looked sweet. Inscribed on the bottom were the words: *David, don't forget to leave something out for Rudolph on Christmas Eve.'*

I turned it over. *Jack, that job is still on offer. Call me at 5677897.*

The bastard.

It took me three months to pluck up the courage to contact Matt. I tried many times. I picked up the phone. Put down the phone. Picked up the phone. Put down the phone. I drove myself and everyone around me absolutely crazy. It wasn't as if he had asked me to marry him. I wanted to call him, but I was scared.

Was he still married? Did I want to get involved with a married man? Did I even care that he was married? Maybe he felt sorry for me. Maybe he was still taking drugs. Maybe this. Maybe that. It was insane. I was blowing the whole thing out of proportion. He was an old childhood sweetheart, that's all. Why was I carrying on like it was the most important thing in my life?

The phone rang for an eternity. I was just about to hang up when he answered.

'Hi, Matt? It's Jack.'

'Who?'

Great. Fucking great. He didn't even know who I was! 'Jack. Jack Joyce.' Then I heard him sniggering. 'You bastard!'

'Sorry, couldn't resist it. How could I forget you? It's only been a couple of months since you said you would phone.'

'Well, sorry, I was busy.'

'Look, can we meet up for coffee? How about I call over or something?'

'Eh, no. It's kind of hard to find my place. How about we meet in town?'

There was no way on this earth I was letting him see where I lived.

'OK, what about Bewley's in Grafton Street. When suits you?'

How about right now? I'll hire a helicopter. 'Tomorrow?' I asked. Let me consult my non-existent social calendar.

'Sure, tomorrow's fine,' he said breezily. 'See you then. 'Bye!'

For the rest of the day I was in a complete spin. I pulled my wardrobe apart for something to wear, but nothing fitted me, not even my old maternity clothes. I ran to Alice for help, which was a bit of a joke. She gave me a dress which my father would have aptly described as a 'frock'. I was big, but Alice was enormous, hence I was shocked when I couldn't get it past my hips. I was so ashamed. In the end I settled for a jazzy tracksuit. It was the best I could do.

The following morning I was awake at 7 am. I wasn't meeting Matt until 3 pm. In the meantime I tormented Alice.

'What's his name, love?'

'Matt.'

'Matt. Ah yes, puts me in mind of Matt Talbot. He was a bleeding alcoholic. Is he an alcoholic?'

'No, Alice. Then again . . .'

'My husband was an alcoholic. Fucked off with some young one. Gave me the pox as a going-away present and all, dirty bastard. They're all dirty bastards. Where's he taking you, anyway?'

'Bewley's coffee-shop.'

'Bewley's? Sure Bewley's is full of prostitutes, love. You know your one across the way? Bucket fanny, with the new car? Got that on her back, so she did. They're all at it. Is he a pimp, love?'

'No, Alice. He's nothing like that.'

'And check his pockets for betting slips, love. Me sister Mary married a gambler. Had her heart broke. Poxy waster. They're all poxy wasters.'

Eventually, I couldn't take any more of Alice's doom and gloom. I was still battling with my own confusion.

Three o'clock was an eternity coming. I walked into Bewley's with David and looked around. I saw Matt sitting at a table, a pile of books in front of him.

'You're looking well,' he commented, moving up to let us in.

'I look like shite,' I corrected him.

'You look like shite,' he agreed.

I took out a colouring book and markers and handed them to David.

'Clever thinking,' Matt nodded. 'How's it going?' he added.

'Fair to crap,' I answered. It wasn't too far from the truth.

'I can't get over the size of David. God, he's a big chap, isn't he?'

'How old are yours?' I enquired.

'Six and eight. Jeanie's six, Robert's eight.'

'Nice names.' Fuck it. It's now or never. 'How's Margaret?' I said carefully. *Margaret. Smargaret. The perfect cow.*

'Great. She works evenings – I mind the kids. It works out fine.'

On the game probably.

'She's a qualified nurse, now.'

'Oh.' That took the wind out of my sails. *A regular Florence Nightingale, no doubt.*

'Have you ever thought about what I said, the last time we met?'

'We said lots of things. Which thing in particular?'

'About night school.'

'You're amazing, you know. We haven't seen each other in years and you're still saying the same things.'

'That's because you need to hear the same things.'

'I don't need anything,' I remarked, quite pleased with myself.

'Of course you do. We all do.'

'Did you qualify as a psychologist in the last few years as well?'

'Well . . . yes. Actually, I did.'

Jaysus!

'But I don't need any qualifications when it comes to you, Jack. I always had you figured. Right from the start.'

This was very annoying, to say the least. This wasn't what I had planned at all.

'Such arrogance,' I noted. 'Is it also part of your psychology training to dress up as Santa Claus and pinch women's bottoms?'

'Oh no. That part's voluntary.'

I chuckled. He was doing it again. Making me laugh. 'So what's wrong with me, Dr Howard?' I asked.

'You mean to say you haven't figured it out yet?'

'No, Matt, I haven't. But you have, I suppose?'

'No, I'm not *that* arrogant. But I do know some things. Some things are very obvious to me now.'

He sipped his coffee. I was intrigued. I was also pissed off and didn't know why. He hadn't said or done anything to offend me.

Yet I felt small. Like I was an insect under his microscope.

'Like what?' I asked sharply.

'Jack. You'll know when you're ready.'

Hey. This isn't what I had expected. Didn't he know he was ruining my fantasy? Shattering my delusions? I didn't want a running commentary about my life, what I knew, or what I didn't know. This wasn't the dope head Matt I had had a crush on as a kid. I had been living in the past for so long I had forgotten we were older. Matt had taken a different road – that was apparent now. I wasn't sure how to behave. It was like meeting a new individual. I would have to start from scratch.

'I feel depressed a lot of the time. I feel . . . cheated.' I was surprised at my own honesty.

'In what way?' He seemed to be genuinely interested.

'Well, You Know Who, for instance.' I diverted my eyes towards David, who was happy munching on a muffin and colouring in his book.

'None of us were prepared for that,' he admitted. 'I can see you've done a great job.'

I burst out laughing. If only he knew the truth – the real truth. The rows, the stress, the loneliness. Maybe he did.

There was a lull in the conversation. I wished we were in a pub. 'Fancy a drink?' I found myself asking him.

'No, thanks. I don't drink.'

You wouldn't say no to a joint, though, would you? I thought.

'I don't do drugs either. I've been clean for four years,' he added, as if he had read my thoughts.

This was positively unacceptable. I looked over his shoulder.

'What?' he asked.

'Just checking for wings,' I nudged him.

We both started to laugh. We sat for at least two hours. I was completely mystified by Matt's transformation. He told me he had studied during the day for the last three years. He was in his final year and he hoped to set up a practice of his own.

'I'm surprised,' I admitted.

'Why, didn't think I would amount to much, did you?'

'No.' I wasn't going to lie. I felt a little disappointed

by my own honesty. Matt had been a wild thing, but one thing he had never been was stupid. He had brains to burn. I couldn't figure out what had happened to cause such a huge change in his character. It was attractive. Something I would have liked a piece of, for myself.

I was still grappling with my life. I didn't seem to plan anything, aspire to anything or have an innate sense of ambition about anything. I was a little jealous. I was still paying homage to my crappy job in Brady's Urinals. Overall, I admired him, especially as he was a father of two children. I was struggling daily with one.

I noticed that additional information about Margaret wasn't forthcoming. When he did mention her, it was censored and vague. This gave me hope. Before long, I found I had told him everything that had happened to me in the last few years. He just listened. It was so long since anyone had listened to me. It was wonderful. He was so easy to talk to. His chosen profession would suit him down to the ground. I decided he would do very well as a psychologist, and told him so.

'Hey, listen. I have an idea, something that just might interest you,' he said suddenly.

'Go on,' I said. 'I'm all ears.'

'Well, part of my psychology degree includes a course in family history.'

'Yeah?'

'It's a ten-week course.'

'So?'

'The title of it is "Discovering Your Family History".'

'What in God's name would I be interested in that for?'

'Trust me. I think it would be right up your street. There's a new course starting in September, one evening a week.'

'I couldn't afford it.'

'It's free.'

'I have no baby-sitter.'

'Jack, you can find one. Haven't you a neighbour you could ask?'

'I'm working all day.'

'I told you already, it's in the evenings.' He gave a great big smile.

'I don't know,' I prevaricated.

'What's there to lose?' He seemed determined.

'Why are you so keen to get me to do this?'

'Why are you so keen not to do it?'

He was good. Really good. 'I can't see how a course in family history could help me.'

'It helped *me*.'

'I'm not you,' I smiled at him. The real truth was, I had begun to feel uneasy at the thought of delving into such areas of my life. I was wondering why it made me so uncomfortable. The mere thought of my family made my stomach churn. I wasn't sure whether I was ready to open up such a can of worms. The worms might turn out to be snakes. I had never liked snakes.

'You've done this course?' I asked.

'Twice.'

'I see.' I was mulling it over.

'Look, I'm doing it again this time. C'mon, do it with me – what have you got to lose?'

My mind was made up – for all the wrong reasons. The fact that he was going to be there clinched it. At the end of the day, it didn't really matter. How was I to know it would change my life for ever?

I went home, as high as a kite. I stopped off at the off-licence on the way and bought myself a good few cans. Why not? I was celebrating! Things were looking up. He had shown a great interest in me. I was thrilled to bits.

When I had settled David in bed, I phoned Karen. 'Guess what,' I started.

'You're pregnant?'

'Not unless it's an immaculate conception.'

'You've won the lotto?'

'Karen! I met Matt Howard again.'

'Oh God.'

'You'll never believe this.' I told her word for word what had happened. Every tiny minute detail of it. 'Are you listening to me?' I finished excitedly

'Yeah, I'm listening.'

'Well, what do you think?'

'What do I think of what?'

'What the hell is wrong with you?'

'Jack, you're slurring your words.'

'I am not!' I threw the empty can of Budweiser towards the bin, and missed by a mile. 'Come on, Karen, seriously – what do you think? Should I do this course?'

'Yeah. Actually I think it's time you did something else, other than drinking.'

'What else is there to do, for Christ's sake!' I defended myself hotly. 'You're not the one stuck in every night with a child.'

'Jack, you don't have to be stuck in every night. Mick and I have offered to baby-sit loads of time, but you never want to go out.'

'Well, that's all going to change now. I'm going to do this course, Yep, I'm going to do it, and another thing – I'm going to make something of myself. If Matt can do it, I can,' I said with confidence.

'You shouldn't need Matt to make any decisions, Jack. I'm tired of you saying you'll do this and that. You never do it in the end.'

She was really annoying me. She didn't understand how difficult it was with David, being a single parent with all that entailed. Anyone in my position would have a few drinks at night, especially if they had to type insurance claims for a living. It was my little treat. I wished people would stop being so negative. I didn't want to talk about that, I wanted to talk about Matt. I'd had enough of Karen. It was all right for her. She had Mick, a great job, a lovely apartment and a car. I had none of those things. I was really angry with her.

'Look, why don't you two come over some day. I'll cook us a meal, how about it?' I tried to bridge the gap.

'The last time we arrived, you had forgotten – remember?'

I had forgotten. It was awful. 'Karen, I swear I won't forget this time. I had a dose of food poisoning, I remember now. Hey, do you think Matt fancies me?'

I heard Karen let out a loud sigh. 'Look, don't get your hopes up. Keep your options open and your legs closed.'

I laughed and spilled a little of the beer on my tracksuit. 'Shit. Must go, Karen. Tell Mick I send my love.'

'Sure.'

The next day I went to the library. My hangover was particularly bad. I asked the assistant to recommend three really well-known psychologists. I came home with Jung, Rogers and Freud. After two pages I was bored stiff. The text might as well have been in Swahili, for I couldn't understand any of it. It was what my father would have called 'Gobbledegook'. I tried to memorise their names – that would be a start. From now on I was going to educate myself. I was going to match Matt's conversation with delightful anecdotes and analogies – just as soon as I knew what they were. I pored over the books but my head was aching. David kept interrupting and kids kept knocking on the door. It was impossible to concentrate.

I was going to arrive at that course knowing something.

Anything. I could hardly wait for it to begin. I crossed off the days on the calendar and swore every day I was starting a diet. It didn't occur to me that I had been on a diet since 1987 and the only pounds I had lost were monetary.

When the big day finally arrived, I was sick with nerves. It was a mixture of the night before and the thought of seeing Matt again. I had shyly asked Alice would she mind David for the one evening a week. She agreed immediately. I was all set.

I had come to fear hope. Hope had the power to crush. Turning left into St Patrick's National School reminded me of this one truth, a truth I had clung to. A truth that was old and outdated – one last remaining vestige of the old me. I was clutching it possessively, like an armed terrorist. I blushed at my own stupidity.

What are you doing here? I asked myself. I quickened my pace before I answered myself truthfully. I'm trying to change, came the loud reply. I don't want to, came the other voice. The battle had commenced.

I was at the main entrance door. There was no turning back now. I paused outside, hoping to hear something, but the only sound was my thumping heart, and the two voices at war in my head.

'Shut the fuck up!' I told them.

The great 'I' had spoken.

Chapter 10

I found the classroom easily – I could hear the sound of voices from inside. I took a deep breath and walked in. Matt was there, engrossed in conversation. I had expected the room to be full, like a real class, but instead I counted only seven people in all. If Matt hadn't been present, I would have turned on my heel there and then. At that moment he spotted me and beckoned me to come over.

'You made it.' He seemed genuinely pleased.

The chairs were arranged in a semi-circle. I waited to see where everybody sat. There were pencils on each chair accompanied by paper and some handouts. I picked them up and started to read. Very soon, people began to take their seats. I felt extremely nervous, like I was back in school. Matt sat beside me and that helped. A Woody Allen lookalike, only twice his size, took his place at the centre of the room. He was a bit dishevelled, unshaven with a wild mop of knotty hair. The kind of person who deplored wasting time on such menial chores as personal hygiene. The kind of person who was so fascinated with life and figuring it out, that they frequently forgot to eat.

'You're most welcome, everybody,' he started. 'Thank you all for coming this evening. My name is Brian, and I am your facilitator. The course lasts for ten weeks, every Tuesday evening from 7 to 9 pm. It would be helpful at this stage if you would all oblige by wearing these nametags until I get to know you all. Just to make things a little bit more interesting, I would be grateful also if you would draw a little picture on your nametag, just to let us all know how you are feeling today. Don't worry, I am not expecting any great work of art.'

Get me out of here, I thought. Name tags? Jaysus, I really was back in school.

Matt handed the badges around.

'My assistant Matt is sitting in on the course as part of his study for a Master's degree in Psychology. He will not be participating. He will be more of an observer. If anyone has any objection to this, perhaps you might let your thoughts be known now . . . no? Wonderful! When you are finished with your badges, we can begin.'

I stared at the stupid badge. How was I feeling today? How the fuck should I know? I felt a series of different emotions, the most prominent one being confusion. I wanted to be here because of Matt. I knew that was the wrong reason, so I felt confused about the whole thing. I also wanted some answers. An answer to my ever-increasing lack of interest. My ongoing resentment over David. My struggle with parenthood. My eating problem. My lack of interest in sex. Yes, that was a good one. It was hardly likely that I would find answers to that one, on a course about family history.

It was so long since I had done anything that it felt good just to have made the effort. Just to be there. Especially with Matt beside me. I had felt the loss of Joe deeply. That was exactly what I had felt – a great loss. No matter how hard I tried, I couldn't think about him without pain. It was a horrible sensation. I knew we were still friends; I knew we always would be – but something had changed. It seemed everybody had changed, except me. *Why?*

The fact that Joe and I had never gotten involved sexually kept me dangling. Always wondering, always curious. For fifteen years, we had shared a platonic relationship. I was always afraid that if we crossed that line, that invisible line, we would lose each other. I felt I had lost him anyway. Most ironically, to another woman. When we met now, I wanted to tell him that. It was an effort to keep it inside. Keep my mouth shut. Juliet had turned out to be a great partner for him. I could not deny that. I just always wondered, what would have happened if? What if? My life was an endless string of 'what ifs'. Here I was, experiencing another. Although this 'what if' had far-reaching consequences. This one was dangerous. I was playing with fire, and I knew it. However, I enjoyed the sense of perilous excitement. My life was so boring.

I wrote my name on the white piece of card and drew my picture underneath.

Woody Allen stood up again. 'Now then. Please introduce yourself, and if you like you can tell us a little bit about your background. Let's start, from the left, please.'

The first participant on the left was a man.

'My name is Fr . . . Fra . . . Frank,' he stuttered. He had drawn a picture of some clouds. 'I don't have . . . have . . . have . . . much to say,' he finished.

Frank was a tiny man. Slight in build with the worst wig I had ever seen in my life. It perched on the top of his little head like a thatched roof. It was much too big and looked like something one would pick up in a car boot sale. The ends curled outwards leaving a gaping hole underneath. I found it really hard to refrain from getting up and fixing it myself. He sat on his hands and rocked backwards and forwards. His nervousness was evident. I felt sorry for him.

'What do your clouds represent, Frank?' Brian asked.

The little man was mortified. He didn't like being asked anything.

'I . . . I . . . I'm not sure,' he stammered. 'I think . . . I'd like . . . like . . . like . . . to use the toilet.'

'By all means.' Brian pointed to the door. Frank excused himself and we moved on.

The second person to speak was a woman.

'I'm Diane. I'm separated.' She breathed a sigh of relief as if to say, Thank God I got that out. Her badge depicted a clown, with the mouth turned downwards. 'I came because I . . . well, because I just can't figure things out any more. I know my family have a lot to do with why I am the way I am.'

Diane was immaculate. Beautifully groomed and wearing the very best of clothes. Her suit was perfectly pressed. Underneath she wore a crisp white blouse. Her make-up was flawless and her elegant shoes shone like diamonds. She constantly pinched the skin on the back of her hands. Her neck and wrists displayed a glittering array of gold jewellery. Each time she lifted her hand to her face, she would scratch the side of her nose with her perfectly polished nail, and her jewellery would clink, clank, clink, like a wind chime. I guessed she was probably in her fifties, but wanted to look like she was in her thirties. She had probably been extremely beautiful in better days. Life had dealt Diane some pretty rotten hands – any fool could have seen that.

'What does your badge say about you, Diane?' Brian probed.

Diane was pensive. 'I guess I feel pretty depressed,' she replied simply.

Here's your sister.

Next came another man, a younger one.

'I'm Bertie. Bertie O'Neill.' This one stood up, cleared

his throat and looked like he was going to be at it for quite some time.

His badge had a round face with a big bright smile on it.

'I'm a salesman. I'm forty years old. I'm a gambler. I started to gamble some years ago, when my marriage broke up, but that's another story. I'll save it for another day.'

Thank God for that.

He laughed loudly. Nobody found it amusing, but Bertie wasn't put off in the slightest. He was on a roll. He rubbed his hands together like he was addressing potential customers.

'I went to Gamblers Anonymous about three years ago, after the house was repossessed. It was a shocking time for all of us, especially the children. Thank God, I've been on the straight and narrow ever since. I came to do the course because I too realise my addiction was handed down to me by my father. You see, my father was a gambler and—'

'And what does your badge say, Bertie?' the facilitator interrupted him at last.

'I'm a happy man today, thank God. I hope to be able to help someone here in my turn. I happen to know a lot about—'

' Yes. Thank you, Bertie,' Brian interrupted him again, but ever so gently. He was good; I'll say that for him.

The next man, sitting beside me, took his turn.

'I'm Connor,' he whispered. His badge had nothing on it at all.

Connor was about sixty years old. He was probably the oldest of all the people in the room. Connor muttered and mumbled, and was barely audible. Everyone leaned forward to catch what he had to say.

'I'm here because my wife thought it might interest me.'

That was all we got from Connor.

'I notice you have left your badge blank, Connor. Any particular reason for that?'

Connor looked confused. Like he wasn't sure how to answer.

It's not a trick question, Connor. Any day now. We've all the time in the world.

'No. I just couldn't think of anything, sir.'

'That's fine, Connor,' Brian smiled at him. 'And you needn't call me sir. Brian will do just fine.'

'Sorry, Brian.' Connor seemed disturbed and shifted noisily in his chair. He blew into his handkerchief every couple of minutes. If he hadn't done that once in a while, we would have forgotten he was there at all.

It was me. I stayed sitting.

'I'm Jack,' I said. 'I'm a friend of Matt's. He suggested I do the course, that I might find it interesting. Here I am,' I finished.

'I must say, I am intrigued with your badge, Jack. Would you care to explain it to the rest of the group?'

My badge had a dirty big black scribble on it. Nothing more.

'Well, I'm confused about a lot of things. Especially my family,' I surprised myself by saying.

'Things are a bit messed up, I suppose.' Diane smiled at me knowingly.

With the introductions over, the Woody Allen clone stood up and started to talk. Much to my astonishment I found the whole thing fascinating. Matt winked at me. I smiled back. How had he known I would enjoy this so much? I tried hard to concentrate, to give the impression I was really interested – which wasn't hard after a while. It really *was* interesting.

However, Matt was a distraction. I found it difficult not to look at his hands. Perfectly soft downy hairs covered them. They were small and unblemished, sleek and slender. They didn't look at all like a man's hands. Matt's were soft, like he had never done a hard day's work in his life. I thought about holding them. What they would feel like to touch. What my own hand would feel like in his. I thought about us when we were kids, how he had escaped to our house. I thought about his own family history and marvelled at his success. He had survived, relatively unharmed.

The facilitator was animated and intense. He gave everybody plenty of room to breathe, frequently stopping to allow feedback and questions, before he went any further.

The time flew by. Soon it was 8 pm and Brian called a halt for a refreshment break. Matt disappeared and returned a few minutes later pushing a trolley loaded with pots of coffee and tea and plates of biscuits. I looked away from the biscuits. I wanted to eat all of them, but was determined not to let anyone see my weakness.

I watched Diane pick at one biscuit. She turned it into a meal; holding the crumbs in her delicate hand, she nibbled in a ladylike way, enjoying every last morsel. How I wished I could eat like that.

'I only ever have the one,' she confided.

'How do you do it?' I found myself asking her. 'I can't have just the one, I'm afraid. I've tried. Believe me, I've tried. I always seem to end up eating the whole packet, then I hate myself.'

'I know, dear. I know. I used to do that myself. When Rory, my ex-husband, left me, I ate my way through shopping bags of biscuits and cakes. I told myself I deserved them.'

I laughed. 'You're so thin, how did you manage not to put on weight?' I was really, really curious. Diane was like a stick insect. Where had she put the fat? On her big toe?

'Oh dear. That's a long, long story. The food never actually stayed in my stomach for long. I always made sure I vomited straight after the binges. I only recently realised I am bulimic.'

Just my fucking bad luck. Why couldn't that happen to me? If I had just visited my best friend who was dying of cancer, I'd still find room to pack in a few thousand calories.

I could never have made myself sick, I thought wryly, no matter how much I ate. The more I ate, the more room I seemed to be making. I had so many spare tyres, they did a lap all by themselves. Diane certainly didn't look too healthy close up. Despite the beautiful outward appearance, I noticed her teeth were discoloured. Her hair, although impeccably set, looked brittle and lifeless.

Matt joined us. Our first conversation of the day.

'Well, what do you think?' he asked me, sipping his cup of coffee.

'I hate to admit it, but I'm actually enjoying it.' I *was* enjoying it, but I wasn't exactly sure why. I guess the adult conversation that had been missing in my life was one part of it. Getting out of the flat for a break was nice too. It was good to have somewhere to go. I enjoyed hearing other people's point of view. I realised I wasn't the only one in the world who had questions.

'I told you so.' He tapped the side of his nose.

'Where do these people come from?' I asked him.

'Everywhere. This course is always full. People come in for all kinds of different reasons.'

Tell me about it.

'I always find it intriguing,' he told me. 'As the course goes on, people get to know each other a little bit better; it's great when that starts to happen. Secrets begin to come out. They confide things. They *see* things. I love it. I keep coming back for more.' Matt's eyes were wide with enthusiasm. His passion was making me blush.

Passion. I hated that word! Passion was something that had always seemed discordant and remote to me. I had never felt passionately about anything. Except him, of course.

Now, for the first time in years, I felt a tiny flicker – a mere flash of inspiration. A sense of being on the precipice of something great. Like I had been guided here. I wanted some more – of what, I couldn't tell. Just something slightly reminiscent of what I felt when I was younger. A barely tangible something. I could feel it inside me, warm and glowing. Then it dawned on me. Hope. It was hope. The thing I had learned to fear so much. I hadn't a notion what I was hoping *for* – that didn't matter. Matt had rekindled an old me. I felt alive, just for a split second. Fresh. Full of the certainty that anything was possible. That wonderful eternal confidence of adolescence, still unconditioned by life's experience. The experience of reality.

I looked around me and wondered what paths had led these characters to this room here today. Were they the same as me? I could empathise with Diane. I could understand Connor. I could even stretch as far as Bertie who couldn't shut up. Why should he? He probably hadn't been listened to for years.

Brian called us to regroup and I took my seat. He continued to talk and I listened. It was no longer an act. My concentration improved by the minute. I was drinking in every word and syllable. I was drunk with want. Wanting to know, to understand, to be me again. That is, until the end of the first session when Brian, alias Woody Allen, knocked me for six with his closing remarks.

'I hope you all enjoyed this first session.'

Everybody nodded their heads in agreement, including me.

'There are some things now that I wish to suggest to you all before I give you your first exercise. When initiating this course in the past, I have found it helpful to lay down some ground rules, so to speak, some little tips I have picked up along the way. There are no rules, of course, just suggestions. I feel obliged to pass them along to you. They have been formed with everyone's best intentions at heart. It is totally up to you to do what you want with them. I am simply handing them to you. After that, it is nobody's business but your own. Again, I remind you, they have come about through my own experience of what happens to individuals who have completed the course in the past.'

He took a deep breath, and continued. 'Because of the nature of these exercises, I recommend that those of you who are single – that is, not in any relationship at the moment – refrain, if at all possible, from getting involved emotionally until the course is completed.'

My mouth hit the deck.

'The reason I suggest this will become apparent as we go along. Discovering your family history may become quite upsetting for some and even more so for others. There are certain things about our childhoods and families that have perhaps remained a secret for years. Maybe there was a great deal of pain attached to your family of origin. These memories can at times become overwhelmingly distressing. I am here to help you through whatever might come up for you. That is why it is imperative that you do not make any new emotional attachments while participating in the course. Any questions?'

Yes. What's the minimum sentence for Grievous Bodily Harm in this country?

I looked at Matt. He smiled gently at me. The penny dropped. He knew this already. Of course he bloody knew it! He was no more interested in me than the Man in the

Moon. I wanted to stick a knife in his eye. I felt like a pathetic piece of shit. All this time, I had fooled myself into believing there was something between us. That he had asked me to do this course as an excuse to see me.

With increasing despondency I realised his true motive. I was a guinea pig. A case. An interesting specimen for him to study. The bastard. I was so humiliated I wanted the ground to open up and swallow me whole. I swung my leg back and forth, barely hearing anything else the facilitator was saying. He was still waffling on. I twirled my hair, a habit I had formed as a child. I twirled it and twirled it until a great big knot formed in the middle. If the facilitator didn't shut up soon I would die. Oh God, how could I have been so naive? I wanted to cry, but my anger was consuming me so much, it kept the tears at bay. Thank God for my rage. It kept my dignity intact.

I looked at my watch and noticed it was 9 pm. Time to go. Thank God for that. Brian shoved a piece of paper into my hand.

'Please will you read the instructions carefully. Take your time. This exercise will require patience and tolerance. I want you all to come back next week with your written work. I look forward to seeing you all then. And remember, have fun! It is most important that you enjoy what you are doing.'

Have fun? I'll give you something funny. Something to laugh about. How about me, sitting here with my delusional dreams?

Chairs moved noisily and people began to don their coats. They chatted loudly, exchanging views on what they thought about the first session. I was not of a mind to discuss any of it. I simply wanted to get out of there as fast as I could. I saw Matt approaching me. Diane intercepted him. She asked him a question. Oh, how I love you, Diane! I made a run for it. I was never going back there. No matter what.

At home, I hadn't the heart to phone Karen, or Joe, or my mother. I prayed to Jesus that Alice would leave me alone. I was so embarrassed. Every time I had tried to move out of myself, something like this happened. I thought about the logic of the facilitator's advice not to embark on new relationships at this time. I wasn't stupid. It was probably very appropriate advice indeed.

I certainly was aware of my own family history. Unfortunately. Unlike others, I would have no problem remembering any of it. I lived with it daily, and every time I went to visit Mam and Dad.

Things had not changed in our home, and never would. I just felt I needed some support to do this course, but I couldn't call on my family for help. I was alone. Anyway, it didn't matter now. I was not going back. Besides, I knew all about my family; what more could I want to know? What extra knowledge could enlighten me any more than I already was? The whole idea was absurd. I was just so hurt over Matt. I thought he had cared about me.

That was when the two voices started up again. I went through the following day, listening to them both. The screaming monkeys had taken up permanent residence in my brain. It was a never-ending barrage of thoughts and feelings. I carried on trying to ignore them. David kept me occupied most of the time. I helped him with his homework and made the dinner. I rambled down to Fairview Park and played with him in the playground. When I looked in my purse, I saw a paltry £10 note. It wasn't enough for what I wanted. What I needed.

When David had had his bedtime story and showed signs of falling asleep, I made my move. On his windowsill was his piggy bank. Jill had given it to him as a christening gift, and it had cost a fair few shillings. It was made of crystal and beautifully decorated. It even had his name and date of birth engraved at the bottom.

I bit my lip. I turned it upside down and then back up. There was no way of getting the money out. There must be! I shook it, I banged it, I tried slipping a knife in the tiny slit, but nothing came out. There was only one other course of action. I contemplated it. The two voices were competing for first place. I let them battle it out.

You absolutely cannot and will not break this precious object.

Break it. It's only a fucking savings box.

Jill gave it to him.

You can buy him another.

It's one of a kind and of sentimental value.

Ah crap! He doesn't even look at it, most days.

It's his money; it contains all the money his family has given him down the years. You can't.

You can. You can replace it, and the money, when you have it.

You have no conscience, girl. You're going to smash it open for the sake of a few drinks?

Anyone would want a drink after today.

Shame on you, you're despicable.

Ah fuck you! You don't know what it's like!

Go on then. Break it. Break it!

I smashed the crystal box against the kitchen wall. It broke easily, its tiny pieces spraying my hand. The coins rolled all over the floor. I picked them up quickly, before I started to think again. My fingers were bleeding and my hand was shaking. I grabbed some kitchen roll and wrapped it around them. Then I put on my coat and checked in on David before I left. I knew it was wrong to leave him alone, but he was fine, fast asleep. Nothing would happen. Besides, I would only be gone for a few minutes.

I ran to the off-licence and bought some cans. I had enough for some more so I threw in a bottle of Bacardi as well. Then I bought some Coke and cigarettes. I passed the Chinese take-away on the way back home. I was hungry but I was not going to give in. I was not going to go down that road tonight. I was tired of being fat. Besides, I had very little money left. I would need it for tomorrow night. I wouldn't drink so much if I weren't so depressed over my weight. I knew I had a problem with my weight. *That was my problem.* If I could address that, everything else would fall into place. Just for tonight, I was not giving in.

I arrived back at the flat, breathless and scrambling for my keys. As I let myself in, I could hear the telephone ringing. I rushed to answer it before it woke up David.

'Hello, Jack.' It was Matt.

Fuck. 'Hello,' I answered coolly. I grabbed a can from the brown paper bag and opened it while I held the phone under my chin.

'What happened, Jack?'

'What do you mean?' I was determined to play dumb.

'You know what I mean. Why did you leave so quickly last night? I went after you, but you had disappeared. Did I do something wrong?'

The smarmy fuck. He knew quite well what he had done wrong. Well, two could play at that game.

'Of course not, Matt. I just had to get back quickly, for David and all that.' I drank between talking.

'Wasn't he with a baby-sitter?'

Clever boy. 'Yes. Yes, he was, but I had to get back to prepare him for bed. If he doesn't get his night-time story, he becomes very cranky – won't go asleep without it, you know what they're like.' *Stick that in your Freudian cap, you pox.*

'Funny, you seemed distinctly upset about something.'

Long pause.

'You know, Matt, I've thought about it all day. I'm not sure I want to continue with the course.'

'Why not?' he said flatly.

'Ah, I've done it all before, really.'

'That's a pity. I really thought you'd enjoy it. You seemed to be enjoying it.'

Suddenly something dawned on me. Hey, wait a minute! If I don't continue with this course he'll know why I quit. That will only give him even more satisfaction. Then he'll really know how I feel about him. I'd be crazy to stop now. I'll show the bastard – I'll finish it. Yeah, just to spite him, I'll finish the fucking stupid bastarding thing. Why should I let him interfere? I *was* enjoying it, until Brian had made his remarks.

'Jack, are you still there?'

'Why did you ask me to do the course, Matt? I'm very interested to know.' My voice had gone up, without my permission. I was really angry and the alcohol was weakening my defences.

'Because I care about you, why else?' he said quietly.

I was gobsmacked. 'You care about me?'

'Sure I do. Don't you know that?'

'No, not really.' *Don't do this to me now. I am angry, do you hear me? I am fucking angry! You will not make me cry. God knows you did all those years ago. You bastard.*

I was fanning my rage deliberately; it always masked my hurt. I could recall all my feelings from when I was that innocent sixteen-year-old. I had never had a chance to tell him what I felt. I wanted to so much now. The cans of lager were strengthening my steely resolve.

'I always cared about you, Jack,' he said. 'Why else would I bother to be phoning you, even now?'

I hadn't thought about that. I was softening again. I had to get off the phone, before I said anything I would regret.

'Look, Matt, I appreciate you calling, but David is awake – I can hear him. Perhaps I'll give it one more shot, next week. I'll talk to you then, OK?'

He heaved a sigh of relief down the phone. I heaved a sigh of relief down the phone.

It was possible I had mistaken Matt after all.

The following morning, I awoke to the phone ringing. It was 8 am. Who the hell was calling me this early?

'Hello?' I answered, dehydrated and bleary-eyed.

'It's Jill.' I could barely hear her with the noise in the background.

'Jill? It's eight o'clock in the morning. What's wrong?' I asked. Just then, David came running in from the bedroom, clutching the remains of his savings box. My heart missed a beat. Slowly, the previous night's memories began to surface.

Jill was chattering away hurriedly. 'I'm on my way to San Francisco, and I'm passing through duty free. I thought you might want some cigarettes or stuff. I can get them for a steal.'

David offered me the broken piggy bank. A lone tear rolled down his cheek. Our eyes locked. *Can he see the truth?*

I held the phone under my chin and took the broken pieces solemnly. I heard my conscience trying to get through. *No. I can't go there.*

'What happened, David?' the liar asked.

'I don't know.' He looked at me, searching for some explanation. A lump was making its way towards my throat. *Let me out! Let me out!* I swallowed hard. *Go away. I refuse to listen.*

'It must have been the bogey man,' the liar answered.

David stared up at me with his big trusting eyes. 'The bogeyman?' he whispered. Now I had terrified him.

'I heard him last night, you know,' the liar continued. 'I got the brush in the kitchen and chased him all the way to Clontarf. Then I smacked his arse with it and he ran away begging for mercy.'

David's mouth turned upwards. A reluctant smile crept across his face.

He looked at the broken pieces. I looked at him looking at the broken pieces.

'*Jack?* Jack, are you listening to me?' Jill was yelling down the phone.

'I'll buy you another one, sweetie, OK?'

He nodded. I watched him turn on his soft soles and ramble out of the room.

'Yes, I'm listening,' I shouted back to Jill.

'I saw Joe yesterday,' she said matter-of-factly.

'Did he ask about me?' I asked.

'No. Why would he ask me about you?' she said. 'Are you OK? You sound a bit funny.'

'It's too early in the morning for this,' I said wearily. As soon as I got her off the phone I crawled back into bed. It was the only safe place. Sleep temporarily turned my brain off.

The little voice, too.

Chapter 11

In the days that followed, I studied the handout given to me at the course. I read the instructions: *Describe your parents' background, as much as you know. Give details of your earliest memories of your childhood.* It would take me for ever to do this, I thought, but I was determined to do it, now more than ever. I tried to put Matt out of my mind, but it was difficult. Everything was difficult. I desperately wanted to talk to Joe. I knew I could not keep turning to him like a lover. He was not my lover. I wasn't even sure if he was still my friend. He was certainly unavailable to me, no matter which way I looked at it. At the first opportunity, I took my notepad down to the local library, where I knew there would be little interference. Once I started, I could not stop.

Welcome to my past. A place so vivid that amnesia itself would be unable to erase it.

Pondering my parents' beginnings, I found it a good idea to start just there. My father, William Joyce, hailed from a small one-horse town called Ballincullen on the outskirts of Tipperary. It was a remote little place. The Joyces were staunch Republicans. My father's father delighted in telling them stories from the Brotherhood days. Dad passed them on to us. They lived in an old ex-British Army barracks, complete with courtyard in the back. My father kept us enraptured with yarns about the Black and

Tans, and the 'Flying Columns' hiding in the coal bunker. He left home at the age of sixteen to come and live in Dublin. Shortly afterwards, he went for his first and last interview for a job.

He 'worked the bricks' for *Córas Iompar Éireann* for a total of nineteen years. This was a polite made-up title for the cruder and more honest definition. What he really did was shovel shit from under the train carriages, after they had departed for their destination. Later on, in his mid-thirties, he was given a white-collar job in their offices, and had remained there ever since.

My mother, on the other hand, was a true blue Dub. She came from Church Street in Dublin city as had all her descendants before her. Unlike Dad, she had plans, ideals, dreams. She wanted to be something and was willing to go to any lengths to achieve it. Christened Margaret, the family soon shortened it to Meta. Meta O'Leary set out in life to be different and ended up the same as everybody else. The only difference with Meta was she did not accept her fate with humility. According to Mam's testimony, which we heard every Christmas around the dinner-table, the pair met at the Galway Races. Meta had been 'stepping out' with a local boy from the inner city. An engagement was on the cards, but nothing had been settled.

Dad was smitten from the word go. He boldly introduced himself, ignoring her current beau. Meta was flattered. She was delighted to be the centre of attention, the object of rivalry. She was enjoying the game. When they returned to Dublin, Dad pursued her like a bitch on heat. He contacted her again and they commenced a serious courtship. Meta was happy to play one suitor off against the other. Eventually, Dad won. Alas, it was a short-lived victory, for he had won her hand under dubious circumstances.

The happy couple had spent a night down at the canal, snogging. The snogging must have escalated into a full-scale romp, for some weeks later Meta discovered she had 'a bun in the oven'. Her predicament was evident. Her parents, on hearing the news, were disgusted and ordered William to do the right thing and marry her immediately. Three weeks later, the couple were married up a side altar, at nine o'clock in the morning.

They had a cup of tea and my dad went back to work. Mam was sixteen, Dad a year older. I was only a dot, so to speak. A twinkle in the milkman's eye.

The new Mr and Mrs Joyce bought a house in Clontarf, compliments of a wedding gift from William's parents. The house had cost a whopping £2,500 – an astronomical sum in the early 1960s. It was one of forty, tucked away in a small cul-de-sac and surrounded by nothing but wilderness. Had I been able to choose my own home, I would still have chosen Clontarf. I had access to the seafront and the beach, plus St Anne's Park with its miles of open space, ponds, hills, nooks and crannies. It was a child's heaven. A paradise in my own back yard.

Still, all was not well in the Joyce household. The stage had been set for discord and resentment. It was always a case of 'anger on ice'. Each parent trying their best to keep their broken dreams to themselves.

Mam had a pretty good singing voice. On the rare occasion when she forgot about herself she would let out a bar or two. Secretly she had wanted to sing in the big showbands that travelled Ireland. Dad had hoped to go back to school, and perhaps even go to college.

There was no way any of that was ever going to happen now. They had been plunged into parenthood way before their time. Still only teenagers, they were suddenly expected to cope alone, fulfil their marriage vows and take to their new posts like cats do to cream. Their dreams had been shattered beyond repair. My mother was to spend the whole of her life raising children. Sacrificing her every wish and want in order to keep the family going. In those days, mothers were expected to be mothers. Nothing else.

I was born in Holles Street Hospital. Had I known what lay in store for me, it might have been wiser to have crawled back in. God had other plans, however, and He decided that I should live. My mother coped as best she could. Within weeks she was pregnant again, only she miscarried. Three months later Jason was conceived. He arrived safely too but the reception was less rapturous. Then another miscarriage. Dad was giving her a good run for her money.

There wasn't any such thing as contraception and the Church denounced it always. The Church ruled, and that was that. They tried the 'Billings Method', she told me much later, but soon another pregnancy was announced. So much for methods. It was pretty obvious from very early on that she was carrying twins. They arrived, half alive, in the seventh month of my mother's pregnancy. Desmond was pipped at the post ten minutes previously by my sister Rachel. They were equally frail and struggling to hold on to life's breath. They weighed in at a paltry one pound each – together, the equivalent of a bag of sugar. Their sweetness, however, was erased in the following hours as doctors desperately attempted to keep them alive. Those must have been terrible days for poor Mum and Dad. Both babies were read their last rites shortly after the birth.

My parents kept a bedside vigil. Neither man nor medicine were expected to prolong those early hours of life. Thirty-six hours later, Desmond passed away. His tiny lungs were unable to sustain him. Rachel's survival, while miraculous, was hardly compensation. Mam and

Dad had created a No Man's Land between them. The house became a virtual prison. If I could only get out on parole now and again, I would survive, I kept thinking. There were silences that lasted for weeks. Then, like volcanoes, they would sporadically explode, each blaming the other and never actually discussing the real problem. The 'Desmond' word was forbidden.

In our house, everything had a purpose and function. Everything. Except feelings, of course. They were left outside along with the dustbins, for the dogs to piss on. My mother was on fire with resentment. She had not planned to be left alone with three small children. It must have been very difficult for her. She was expected to cope alone with her grief. She fulfilled her obligations in total isolation: asking anybody for help was a direct admission of helplessness – evidence to suggest weakness. So many women suffered like that, in silence. I couldn't fathom, now, how they did it.

Contemplating the tragedy I put my pen down. The story seemed like somebody else's; it was tinged with great sadness but also with misunderstanding. My family had been shrouded in unexpressed grief for years. Now I was feeling the sorrow all over again. The library was quiet and peaceful. As always in moments of peace I felt my old self resurface. I looked around me, hoping for a distraction. The library assistant was stamping returned books. People moved slowly along the aisles, pausing to browse through a book and then replace it on the shelf. I wanted to stop writing, put my coat on and head over to the chipper. Instead, my inner voice prompted me to continue.

Suddenly, Desmond hung about me like a damp night air. It was too sad to dwell on. I changed thought formation and went searching for some cheerful childhood memories. I racked my brains for lighter recollections.

They weren't long in coming back. I took up my pen again and reapplied myself to the task in hand.

We never had a single solitary carpet until 1978. We had lino, in our sitting room, hall, and in our kitchen. My siblings and I used to amuse ourselves by stripping down to our stockinged feet. One would stand at the front end of the hall, another at the far end. We would take a dive, run as fast as we could to pick up speed, and slide from one end of the hall to the other, frequently landing on our backsides. Our bedroom floors were covered in 'Tintawn' a cheap rough duplicate of the next best thing to real carpet. In our room we had a set of bunkbeds. There was a battle nightly between me and Jason over who got to sleep on the top. I always won, being the eldest. Our younger sister Rachel, the surviving twin, had a room of her own on the other side of my parents' bedroom. She seemed to cry incessantly. We hated her because she got so much attention.

Jason and I weren't particularly close. He had his friends and I had mine. We went to the local National School which was just a short walk from our house. I remember my first day, and standing in 'An Lína'. The mornings were dark and damp. I wore a bright orange armband and my uniform trailed along the ground. It was supposed to last for a number of years. I looked like a midget wearing a circus tent. I don't remember being scared, but I was excited. I saw my mother wave goodbye at the railings outside as I took my first steps into the grown-ups' world.

I would watch for her to reappear outside at going-home time. Her beautiful auburn hair was instantly recognisable. Sometimes she wore a scarf over it. That meant she had gone to the hairdresser's – a monthly treat which was a gift from my father. I would ask her to remove the scarf so I could smell the hairspray; she'd bend down to my level and I'd sniff the pungent aroma.

My teacher was a woman from Galway. She drank tea all day. Her only topic of conversation was the weather, and how cold it was. She wore a beaded hairnet on her head and refused to speak anything but pure Irish. She wasn't the worst of the teachers.

Mrs Crinnion, our headmistress, had no competition. She had the power to stop us breathing. When she walked in, we stood up like soldiers. The only other person we did that for was Father Sheehy, the local parish priest. 'Good morning, Father,' we'd chant in unison. It was always relaxed and informal.

When Mrs Crinnion entered the classroom, chairs screeched as they went backwards. Girls stood terrified and the obligatory piss was done on the floor. She terrorised us with her giant frame and equally large voice. She quizzed us with her fluent Irish. At that delicate age, we were hardly proficient, and she knew this yet derived great pleasure in asking us questions. She knew quite well we wouldn't be able to answer correctly. Then came the mandatory threat.

'I'll turn you inside out, and hang you on a rusty nail.'

One day, a wasp landed on my friend's neck. I watched in horror as it crept around her collar and made its way down the front of her shirt. She saw it. Her eyes opened wide with terror. Still she would not call out for fear of 'The Dragon'. When the wasp stung her, I could see the red mark swell and the tears cascade down her cheeks. Such was the fear instilled in us.

We weren't even children yet. We were aptly named low babies and high babies. That's exactly what we were. One day 'The Dragon' charged in and proceeded to recite the 'Hail Mary'. The class struggled to repeat it with her, none more so than myself. She was watching me intently and I didn't know why. She called me to the top of the class. I stood there, tiny and terrified.

'You are not listening, child. Repeat!'

Repeat what? What was I doing wrong?

'Hail Mary, full of grace, the Lord is with thee: Blessed art thou among women, and blessed is the fruit of thy womb, Jesus . . .'

'Wrong!' she bellowed into my face. 'Repeat from "Blessed art thou".'

I did. 'Blessed art thou among women, and blessed is the fruit of thy womb, Jesus . . .'

'Wrong!' she screamed at me. 'Hold out your hand, child.'

I held out my lily-white palm. She produced an enormous ruler – the kind you find on a building site, a foot long and half an inch thick. She whacked it across my hand.

I winced.

'Repeat!' she demanded.

I repeated. I was wrong again. Of course I was wrong again! How could I correct my error until she enlightened me? I had no choice but to repeat what I had said before.

Another lathering across my hand. I heard some muffled cries from the other girls. A slow trickling river of urine poured from under someone's desk.

My hand was swollen and it ached. The only thing that made it tolerable was that she would not be able to keep it up for ever. She was getting bored.

'Don't you know that when you take the Lord's name, you must bow your head immediately afterwards? 'Blessed is the fruit of thy womb, Jesus,' and she bowed her head like a donkey to demonstrate the point. I had not known that. How could I have?

Now that I had been put in the picture, I repeated the

words. Lowered my head when I said 'Jesus' and said I
was sorry. It was all over.

I went home that afternoon with a broken thumb. I
was only four years of age. I guess that was when I had
'conveniently' forgotten how to say my prayers.

My mother noticed my hand and my tear-soaked face.
She took my hand in hers and inspected the swelling.
'What in God's name did you do to deserve this?'

When I explained what had happened, my mother was
enraged. Mam enraged was a force to be reckoned with.
First, she took me to the family doctor, who swathed my
hand in linen and ointment, that wonderful red stuff we
got on our grazed knees when we fell in the school yard.
The following morning, I was frog-marched up to the
principal's office. My mother stood firm and dignified
while 'The Dragon' did a complete transformation of
character and suddenly became the perfect headmistress.

She greeted my mother with a smile as big as china, but
her beady eyes gave way to her fear. It was the only time
I ever saw her grovel. She went out of her way to tell my
mother what a wonderful child I was. Her apology was
stifled and lacked sincerity. Mam was no fool. She told
her that if she ever raised her hand to me again she
would report her to the police. In those days, of course,
it would not have been taken seriously. The threat did do
something, though. It worked some kind of magic. I never
had any more trouble with the 'The Dragon' ever again.
She was sickly sweet and nice to me from then on.

She still supervised our class when our teacher was ill,
or on holidays. She also gave me a part in the school play
in sixth class. It was about Oliver Plunkett. I rehearsed it
for weeks on end. 'The Dragon' coached me herself.

On the opening night, I stood in the wings, waiting
for my entrance. I knew my parents were in the audience.
'The Dragon' was behind me, counting down. Then it was

my turn. I walked out onto the stage. The spotlight turned on me. It was my moment of glory.

I cupped my hand around my ear and strained my neck outwards. 'The Dragon' was aping in the wings.

'*Eist* (long pause) *le fum an gcling!*' My lone voice rang out. That was it – I only had one line. My mother jumped to her feet and started clapping. My father joined in and together they gave me a standing ovation. Other parents shushed them and they eventually sat down. It was a wonderful moment. I felt loved, and very proud.

When I was older, my father decided I should have weekly pocket money; every Saturday, he would hand me a beautiful shiny threepenny bit. I loved its bockady shape and fiddled with it all the way to the shops. I could never make up my mind what to spend it on. Jelly snakes. Blackjacks. Lucky lumps. Delicious orange and spearmint bars from 'Joyce's of Cork' (no relation). Real orange ice pops. Fizzle sticks that you could suck into a spike. Liquorice pipes with those tiny pink seeds stuck on the bottom. Fizz bags. Gobstoppers that lasted for days.

I laughed out loud at the memory, and the assistant 'shushed' me. I had forgotten I was in the library.

I had finished anyway. I gathered my belongings and walked along the North Strand, where I saw an ad for Christmas trees. Christmas trees already? The festive season seemed to be arriving earlier and earlier each year. It put me in mind of Christmases past.

Unlike the other children in our road, we were never allowed our presents until we had had our breakfast, and had been to Mass. We prayed the priest's sermon wouldn't be as long as the one last year. My father spent an age on his knees after receiving. We amused ourselves at the back of the church watching the crib. It went from night to day in sixty seconds. Every year it was the same beautiful scene.

I had sent a hundred letters to Santa Claus, always asking for the same thing. The one thing I truly wanted as a child was a real doll's house. I could never understand why year after year it failed to materialise. In truth, we didn't care what we got for Christmas – the sight of the crisp bright paper was enough to send us into a spin – but still I hoped my doll's house would arrive. Every year, I hoped, I prayed, I crossed my fingers, but Santa always let me down. When we returned from church my dad would start 'The Game'. He had locked the sitting-room door the night before.

'Meta? Meta? Where did I put that bloody key?' He would rummage in his pockets, muttering and mumbling. 'Now, let me think – when did I have it last?' He would rub his chin, put his hands on his hips, until we could stand it no longer.

'Please, Daddy! Please, Daddy! Let us in. Let us in!' I think he loved this part more than us.

'Not until you've formed an orderly queue.' That was an impossible thing to ask of us.

The feigned searching would go on for a few more moments until, eventually, even he could not wait any longer. He would produce the key and hold it above our heads as we squealed and screeched and jumped to try and get it. He slowly opened the door, and we charged in like bulls. It was like Aladdin's cave . . .

I smiled to myself and pulled my coat collar up. The weather had turned nastily cold. I let myself into the flat and was greeted with warmth, for which I was grateful. I remembered cold nights when we huddled together under my dad's Crombie coat. It kept us warm but we still caught colds. 'Pipe down with that coughing!' my dad would yell at us. We couldn't help coughing. The cold was cruel and I lay awake watching my foggy breath go in and out in the dark.

I always had to have the door slightly ajar to let in some light. I could never just get into bed and fall asleep. I was convinced there were monsters under the bed with their hairy hands that would reach out and grab my legs. I usually made a run from the door and jumped straight on to the mattress. It was in bed that I did all my thinking and worrying, as children are apt to do. Secrets lurked, just like the monsters under my bed. The whispering wind outside spoke in foreign tongues. Just like my mam and dad in the next room.

As I got into bed tonight, warm and cosy, and not drunk for once, I thought what a strange day it had been. I was tired but quietly calm. I immediately drifted into a deep, dream-filled sleep.

Chapter 12

The last few weeks in work had been hell on earth. Today my manager Gerard Shannon had called me into his office for a 'little talk'. I knew what was coming but couldn't have cared less. I was only there to pay my bills and I knew I would eventually get a better job.

Gerard Shannon was the ugliest man I had ever laid eyes on. He had a mouth like a slit orange, crossed eyes and he spat when he talked. Being in his company made my stomach sick. In the poky little office he remarked that I had been on sick leave for an average of two days every month. It wouldn't do. He wanted an explanation.

'It's my periods.' I heard the words coming from my mouth but I hadn't planned they would come out so sweetly. 'I suffer terribly from PMT,' I told him, knowing full well he was squirming with embarrassment. I went on to inform him of the 'tablets' that I had to take before my period came, and how they affected me. They made me sleepy. You see, I was practically bedridden with the tiredness not to mention the pain. I had no plans to stop talking. Gerard Shannon, the lecherous ugly manager, finally interrupted.

'Yes, well, the point is, Ms Joyce, that we are concerned about your continuous absences and have decided that we may well have to deduct pay if you are seen to be constantly missing days at work.'

I tried to imagine his wife having sex with him and nearly heaved. I fobbed him off with promises that I would try to do better. Pressure was mounting daily. I didn't want to think about anything, anything at all.

I decided to go back to the course. I was not giving in, not by a long shot. I was also curious to know how everybody else had gotten on with their exercises. I was feeling strange, almost disconnected. Besides, I had nothing else to do. Nowhere else to go. I also wanted to see Matt. I wanted to prove something to him. I was driven by pure frustration, and loneliness.

Inside the classroom, everybody had gathered. Diane waved – I was glad to see her. Matt was handing out leaflets. Brian was reading something. I took my seat along with the others, refusing to look in Matt's direction. *Come to me, baby. Come to me.*

'Hi, Jack.' Matt appeared at my side.

'Hi there,' I said coolly.

I felt calm and collected. I had managed to keep my eating at a minimum, and was thrilled when I weighed myself that morning. I had lost three pounds. It spurred me on to persist. I had put on make-up, and had managed to squeeze into a pair of jeans.

'I'm glad you came back,' he said softly.

So am I. So am I.

'Jack, can you spare a half-hour or so after the course? Perhaps we can grab a cup of coffee. There's a little place across the road – how about it?'

I was surprised. 'OK.' I tried to sound uninterested, as if I was doing *him* a favour.

The second session started.

'Welcome back, everybody. I'm pleased to see you all returned. I hope you had fun doing your written work. Perhaps we'll have time to discuss that later. This evening, I want you all to pair off in groups of two. Take these handouts and complete the questions as briefly as possible – say in about ten minutes. Then we will regroup and have a discussion about it, OK?'

Brian was wasting no time. Thank God. I was like the White Rabbit in *Alice in Wonderland*. *No time to think. No time to think.*

Diane crossed over to me immediately. I was glad. I was going to go in her direction anyway. We read the questionnaire and I saw her frowning.

'What does it say?' I asked.

'Where in the family did you come? Oldest? Youngest? Middle child? Read the following family roles. Circle the one that you feel would most appropriately describe you:

Caretaker/Fixer

Lost Child

Scapegoat

Clown/Mascot

'I don't need to write any of this down. I know it off by heart. Do you understand this, dear?' She passed the piece of paper to me.

'I think so. Hey, what did you think of last week?'

'I must say, it brought up a lot of things I didn't really want to remember. I guess I found it painful. My childhood was a nightmare,' she answered.

'Yes. I found it difficult too,' I lied. 'I feel funny,' I added, trying to put some truth back in.

'Funny, dear?'

'Yes, strange. I can't describe it any other way.'

'Maybe it's been a long time since you thought about it all?' she remarked.

'Didn't you feel strange?' I asked her, like a child in need of confirmation.

'Not really, dear. I've done two years of counselling already. There's nothing new in what I'm doing here today.'

'I admire you,' I said genuinely.

'It's not easy, dear, believe me. It's not been easy, any of it.'

I didn't like her tone of voice. A warning tone of voice. It made me feel uncomfortable. I was almost getting used to the feeling of being uncomfortable. It was like my shadow, following me everywhere I went. My lifetime companion.

Brian called us all together again and collected the written pages. 'Now . . .' he started browsing through the papers. 'Yes, this is very interesting indeed. OK, let's see. Connor? Perhaps you'd like to tell us why you see yourself as the Lost Child.'

Connor blew his nose, and proceeded to talk.

'Well, it's quite simple, really. I was the middle child. One of three. While completing last week's exercise, I realised something quite startling. I was prompted to root out the old family snapshots. The photograph albums are packed solid with photos of the eldest. That would be my brother Luke. There are photos of him sitting, crawling, his first steps, his first day at school, et cetera. Then there was my youngest sister Peggy. There were plenty of her as well, though not as many. Then there was me, the middle child. There are two photographs of me in total. That epitomises my life, really. Not important, not ever. I seemed to go unnoticed most of the time.' He let out a big sigh, then trumpeted his nose.

'Well done, Connor.' Brian nodded his head up and down. 'OK, let's go to Diane. You have clearly marked the Scapegoat. Would you tell the group why?' He smiled encouragingly at her.

'Well, I chose the Scapegoat because I was always the centre of attention. I was a rebellious child. My parents were workaholics. They were never at home. I did every-thing in my power to get their attention. It always back-fired on me. They used my "always being trouble" as an excuse to avoid what was really happening. They were never there for me. Yes, I was the Scapegoat all right. As long as they could focus on me, they never had to focus on themselves. It's taken me years of counselling to forgive them. There really wasn't anything wrong with me at all, except that I wanted to be noticed too. I guess I might have qualified for the Lost Child as well. Sometimes I'm not sure,' she finished.

'I can see you've received some counselling, Diane. I can tell by the way you talk that you have already begun the healing process. Well done. Now, who's next? Yes. Let's go to Bertie. Bertie, you have yourself ringed as the Clown/Mascot. Care to elaborate?'

Bertie the talkative salesman took the stand. 'I am the eldest of three. I see myself as the Clown because I was always making them laugh, you know. It wasn't much fun being brought up in an orphanage. I was very funny. I was able to do these great impressions. Can I just say I was interested in what Connor said. I wouldn't agree that he was a Lost Child at all – a man able to stand up for himself and talk like that. Could I just say to Connor that I found it very helpful myself to—'

'Well, hold it there, Bertie.' Brian put up his hand. It was like trying to stop a runaway train. 'Stick to your own story for the minute. We shall invite input from everybody later. Fine. Go on, Bertie.'

'Oops. Sorry, everybody! I didn't mean to offend anyone. It's my nature, you see. I'm very perceptive. Always diving in to give advice. My wife said I drove her crazy doing it. I'm only trying to help where I can. I see something, I say it. Anyway, where was I? Yes. As you can see, I'm a kind of funny guy.' He laughed to himself.

You could have fooled me, I thought for everyone.

'Well, thank you, Bertie. That was very interesting. I'm sure the group will have their comments for you too.' Bertie sat down, looking a little miffed.

'Prick,' I muttered under my breath.

Diane heard me and leaned over. 'Don't call him that, dear. A prick is useful.'

'OK, that leaves us with Frank and Jack. Who would like to go next?'

I nodded at Frank to put him out of his misery; he had been rocking backwards and forwards quicker than my granny and was obviously agitated.

'Well, Frank, I see you have had some difficulty deciding. Perhaps you'd like to talk about it a little?'

'I . . . think . . . think . . . I'm . . . I'm . . . all of them.'

Bertie the blabbermouth started to laugh hysterically. Everybody glared at him and he stopped abruptly.

'That's a very interesting perspective, Frank. It is possible that at some stage in our lives, we have indeed been them all. I can identify very strongly with that. Anybody else feel the same?'

Brian looked around the room. Before I knew it, my hand raised itself and my mouth opened without permission.

'I do,' I whispered.

'That's perfectly OK, Jack.' Brian smiled at me. I liked him. He was very gentle and very encouraging.

'I think I've been all of them,' I continued in a stronger voice. 'At the moment, though, I don't play much of a part in the family any more. The one that stands out the most is the Scapegoat. I was always in trouble as a teenager. I'm a bit of a Lost Child now, even though I'm a grown woman. I don't know if that makes sense to anybody else.' I looked around and saw to my surprise all heads nodding in agreement. I heaved a sigh of relief.

Matt winked at me. I was proud of myself for speaking up.

We broke for coffee and I went outside for a cigarette. I wondered why Matt wanted to talk to me. I had been studying his hands again. It was so long since I had had sex with a man. Even 'Woody Allen' was beginning to look attractive. I wondered what Matt's game was. Maybe there was no game at all. I couldn't bear to think about that.

Back inside, the group had begun a debate about their written work from last week. I was quiet and opted to listen. Brian decided to take everyone's work and read passages. I hoped he would leave mine out.

I found all of it very interesting, especially Bertie's, which surprised me greatly. His father and mother had died in a car crash when he was seven years of age. He was left in the care of an orphanage with his two younger sisters. He had spent his life looking out for them, even paying their way for third-level education.

Poor Bertie had had a rotten life, after all. I felt sorry for him. Brian read extracts from Connor's childhood, most of which was vague and choppy; he seemed to find it difficult to recall any details. By far the best was Frank, who for once could relax, as someone else read out his history. His memoirs were wonderfully colourful and full of descriptive detail. Brian commented on what a wonderful writer he was.

Then it was my turn.

Brian read out portions of my essay. Everybody listened intently. It felt good to be noticed. Everything was fine until he opened the floor to questions. Bertie was up like a shot.

'I was very interested in Jack's writing,' he started, gesturing with his hands like he was the Pope addressing his flock. 'I couldn't help feeling it was a little too sweet, though. Now I know in my case, and I only know this from my own experience, that I tended to go into denial about certain aspects of my past. That went hand-in-hand with being the family clown. Sometimes, we do escape our pain through denial and I believe this,' he finished and sat down.

I was furious. Who did he think he was?

'Jack, would you like to respond to that?' Brian asked gently.

Respond? Yeah. How about I respond with my fist? 'Yes. Thank you. I do realise now, having heard all the other accounts, that I misunderstood the question a little.' It was a half-truth.

'There's no need to worry about that,' Brian reassured me. 'We will be going further into things as we move along. There will be plenty of opportunities for you all to dig deeper, even if you think you have gone as far as you can.' He smiled directly at Bertie.

I was relieved to hear this. I had written what I had written. I wasn't sure what else I was supposed to say. Besides, Bertie was the only one with a negative reaction. Everybody else commented on my attention to detail. I was pleased with my efforts.

Diane put her hand up.

'Yes?' Brian asked.

'I was very touched by Jack's account of the twins. It made me very sad. That couldn't have been easy. In fact, I think it may have made Jack feel the odd one out, just like me.'

It was nice to have someone acknowledge my past. The rest of the group commented too on the sadness of this episode. It felt good to hear the feedback. It had been the family secret for so long and carrying it had taken its toll on me. It was good to have fresh input. It was good to have permission to say what I felt. I thought about my family. They had only got my vote, not my voice.

'Before we finish up for this week, are there any other questions?' Brian asked.

Frank raised his hand.

'I . . . I . . . need . . . to go . . . to . . . the toilet.'

'We're finished now anyway, Frank. Thank you all for coming and I hope to see you all again next week.'

Brian handed out a fresh questionnaire. I put it in my bag and got ready to go. Diane stopped me at the door.

'I hope that idiot didn't put you off?' She looked over at Bertie.

'Not a bit,' I told her. It was true. Wild horses couldn't have kept me away now. What had started out as an act had turned into genuine interest. The course was fascinating. It broke the week, and took me away from the boredom of menial everyday tasks. Now I had the added pleasure of being able to talk to Matt alone.

We sat at a quiet table in the coffee-shop. It was perfect for our little romantic get-together. We ordered some coffee and scones. To my surprise I wasn't hungry; I was too excited to eat. Besides, I had a phobia about eating in front of other people.

Matt was looking particularly beautiful that day. He wore a big woolly jumper and pair of tatty jeans. Just the way I loved him. Rough and tumbled. Yet he was always spotlessly clean. I could smell a hint of Polo aftershave – my favourite. I hate nothing more than a man drowned in smelly perfume. The scent was making me ache with want. I tried hard to avoid looking at his hands.

'There's something I've been wanting to say to you,' he started. 'Something I've been wanting to say to you for a long time.'

I could hardly breathe with anticipation. He looked up at me sheepishly. I smiled. The moment had arrived. The perfect moment. He was going to tell me he was completely and utterly in love with me. That he dreamed of me night and day. That he was beside himself with desire every time he saw me. That he had concocted this whole 'course' thing as an excuse to get next to me. I leaned dreamily across the table and batted my eyelashes.

'I have a confession to make,' he said bluntly.

'Yes?' My voice was barely a whisper.

'That night, down the causeway, when we were kids?'

'Yeah?'

'When I told you I'd slept with someone else?'

'Yeah?'

'I hadn't.'

Was that it? He had just performed open-heart surgery on me, then left the cut wide open for all to see.

'Oh.' I looked at him. He was blushing. 'Well, in that case I have a confession to make as well.'

'Yeah?'

'Neither had I.'

'Oh,' he said.

Then we both burst out laughing.

'It's no wonder it was a disaster,' he said, nodding his head sideways.

'I can't say the earth moved for me either,' I admitted.

We laughed heartily. It was a warm moment.

'I thought you were going to say something else,' I blurted out.

He looked up at me and held my gaze for a minute. I could read something in his eyes. He twirled his cigarette around and around in the ashtray, making little patterns with the tip. He had gathered the ash into a pile in the corner. I realised he was nervous. He wanted me to continue for him.

'You really hurt me, you know,' I said suddenly. It was out. It had taken thirteen years. Now it was out. It seemed like the right moment. What had I got to lose? It was almost as if he was inviting me to help him. The great psychologist was asking *me* for help!

'I'm really sorry,' he said, breathing out and leaning back in his chair. Then he shrugged as if he couldn't think of anything else to add to that. 'It doesn't sound very good, does it? The word sorry, I mean. Love means never having to say you're sorry. Bollox to that!'

Love? Was he trying to tell me he loved me? What did he mean? I had an overwhelming urge to reach out and touch his face. Feel the curve of his chin, rub the back of my hand against his cheek. His green eyes were urging me on. I crushed my cigarette out in the ashtray. My finger brushed against his.

'There is one other thing, Jack. Something else . . .'

Just then, a woman appeared at the side of our table.

'We don't want any more coffee, thank you,' I said, without looking up.

Then Matt said. 'Margaret! Hi.'

Oh my God. Margaret Smargaret, the perfect cow, was standing over me.

'Jack!' she squealed, as if we were longlost friends. 'I'd hardly recognise you, only Matt told me you were doing the course. I would never have known it was you.' She gave me the whole works, starting at my toes then going all the way up to my red infuriated cheeks.

'Margaret!' I tried to look surprised and stood up. 'God, it's great to see you again – you look amazing!'

She did, the fucking bitch. Still exactly the same. Big breasts. Minuscule waist. Long blonde hair. The years had been good to her. She still looked sixteen.

Matt didn't seem perturbed by her presence.

'I'm sorry I'm late.' She bent down and kissed him on the cheek.

You'll never make a good 'Cartier', I thought. *Your timing is shit.*

Had he known she was coming? 'Look, I've got to be going anyway.' I gathered my things hurriedly. 'Matt, thanks for the advice.' I winked at him behind her back.

Back home, I couldn't get Matt out of my mind. I was confused. He was giving me mixed messages. Maybe I was just mixing them up myself?

It was all very confusing. That night I spent an age watching David while he slept. Alice had taken him out for the whole day. When he returned, it was way past his bedtime. He climbed up on to my lap, and fell asleep watching TV. I couldn't bring myself to move him. I studied his face, all stretched and distorted from the position he lay in. His mouth was wide open, and every now and then he groaned. He was so, so beautiful. I wiped the strands of hair from his mouth and put them behind his ears.

I loved his smell. It was David's own special smell, distinct and unique. My son's smell. It was a long time since I had felt such overwhelming love. I didn't understand why. I just always seemed to be lost in the daily living of things. My love for him had grown through the years. I wanted to be with him in his dream world. A world of fun, no rules, no responsibilities, no decisions, choices, or deep thinking.

I had just covered him up and tucked him in when I heard the telephone ring. I grabbed a can of beer and got to it just in time. It was Joe.

'Hello, stranger. To what honour do I owe this phone call?' I said breezily, feeling OK with Joe for the first time in ages.

'I've been trying to phone you all day.' He sounded a bit strained.

'You hardly ever ring me. Am I supposed to be sitting here just waiting for your call?' I said a bit harshly. It was said out of relief. Like when your child dashes across the street, almost gets killed and when you get to him you give him a wallop instead of a kiss. 'I'm not here on a Tuesday evening,' I told Joe, more calmly. 'You'll be glad to hear I have taken up my bed and started to walk. I have joined the living world again. I am doing a course in family history.'

'That's hardly joining the living, more like hanging out with the dead. What the hell's wrong with you? Can't you just have some fun?' he quipped.

'It is fun, I swear! Hey, you sound funny,' I said, a little softer now.

'I'm in a coin box. I hate these fucking things.'

'What's wrong with your phone? Forgot to pay the bill again?'

'No, actually I haven't been at home for the last while.'

'I see.' I felt the beer warm my stomach and I started to relax.

'What's this family history shit?' he asked.

'I bumped into Matt Howard at Christmas – you know he's studying to be a psychologist. Who would have believed it? Anyway, he got me on this course. It's the best thing I've done since . . . having David.'

'Jack, he's a clapped-out hippie, a junkie. It's more than psychology *he* needs to study,' Joe said abruptly.

'Ah come on, you wouldn't believe how much he has changed. He doesn't drink or do drugs any more. Christ, do you remember him doing handstands on the bull wall? What a crazy bastard. I admire what he's done,' I said.

'Jack, be careful,' he said solemnly.

'Be careful of what?' I asked, my voice rising.

'Just don't get carried away,' he said angrily. The line crackled and his voice came in and out.

'I'm not getting carried away. Aren't you happy that I'm doing something with myself?' I was annoyed at his lack of encouragement.

'Sure I am,' he said, without a hint of enthusiasm.

'Look, Joe, when are you coming home again? I'm dying to see you. I've so much to tell you, and I feel we haven't had a really good chinwag in ages.'

'Well, that's one of the reasons I'm phoning you. I'll be home Tuesday week.'

'Great! I can't wait to see you and Juliet and the kids. David's always asking when they're coming home again. How long will you be staying?'

'For good,' he said flatly.

'What?' I'd obviously misheard.

'For good, Jack. Juliet and I have split up.'

Ah Christ.

I sat with my cans, staring at the wall, opening one after the other, thinking, thinking. I was thrilled Joe was coming home. I was also ashamed at the little voice that went *Yippee!* every time I thought about them splitting up. What on earth had happened? Why hadn't he phoned me to say that things weren't going well? Much to my disgust, I found myself feeling ambivalent over his arrival. I was becoming close to Matt and I wanted it to come to its natural conclusion. I wanted to sleep with him. I wanted to have an affair. Joe's return would make this difficult. I would have to be careful with my words when I was around him. I couldn't understand his warnings about Matt. It wasn't any of his business. I hadn't interfered in his relationship with Juliet.

I tried to convince myself that this was the same, although I knew deep down it wasn't. Matt was married. Joe was looking out for me. I was pissed off that he was penetrating my conscience. I didn't want a conscience. I wanted my own way.

I fell asleep with the television still blaring and a mountain of cans beside me.

Chapter 13

The next morning, I woke up sober and started to think over what Joe had told me. I was totally shocked by his news. I had expected him to tell me that they were getting married, and that my invitation to the wedding was in the post. I had expected to hear that they were planning for a child, or that they had bought a house. The last thing I had anticipated was to hear that they had broken up. It was the one relationship I had watched, admired and even envied. Now it, too, had faltered. Did no one stay together any more?

In one way, I looked forward to seeing Joe. In another, I didn't. His timing was all wrong. I wanted to be free to pursue Matt. I was almost certain now that my interest was not unrequited. Now, more than ever, I was prepared to risk the consequences. I had gone past the 'good conscience' stage and was willing to pay the price. What kind of a relationship did he and Margaret have anyway? They never seemed to be together. When she had kissed him in the coffee shop it was a very sedate kiss. There was certainly no passion or spark between them. He hadn't batted an eyelid when she walked in. It was almost like they didn't really care. The only thing I could surmise from that was that the marriage was effectively dead. I convinced myself of this argument in order to follow through with my own selfish plan. I

was out to get Matt, at any cost, monetary or emotion-
aly.

As I waited at the airport arrival hall, I racked my
brains to come up with supportive and compassionate
words for Joe. I still half-expected to see Juliet and the
kids following behind him. I couldn't accept or find any
reasonable explanation for this bizarre turn of events.
Already I had learned one very important thing after
attending only two weeks of the course. I hadn't been
much of a real friend to Joe. I had been too engrossed
in my own problems, almost to the point of ignoring
everybody else's. I remembered now all the crises in my
life when Joe had been there, even when he hadn't been
asked. That was true friendship. I was determined to be
there for him this time.

I spotted the quiff of blonde hair bouncing behind the
surge of passengers and waved frantically. He saw me
and waved back. He looked tired and drained. It was
not the Joe I had known. In fact, when I thought about
it, I realised I had never ever seen him in a bad mood
before. Now I was looking at a man who had obviously
been through the mill.

I didn't waste any time giving him a pep talk on the
fine art of surviving a broken relationship. I didn't bother
pretending to be happy. I wasn't going to deny reality
by trying to cheer him up. I returned the fifteen years
of friendship he had honoured me with, in one brief
moment. I reached out and put my arms around him.
He took my head and cradled it and kissed my ear. I
could feel his body shuddering. My God, he was crying.
He was truly heartbroken.

I kissed the top of his head and held him as tight as I
could. I understood the irony of our situation. We were
standing in a crowded arrivals hall in Dublin Airport. It
could have been The Limit. Only this time, I was the

strong one. The roles had been reversed. I could not move. I could not speak. That would come later. For the moment, I was a shoulder to cry on. Just like he had been for me, at different intervals in my troubled life. I felt an overwhelming love for him.

'It's good to see you, Joe' was all I could manage. He nodded his head from side to side, desperately trying to hold on to his dignity. I wanted him to know he did not need to do that. It was me, Jack, his best friend. I would always be his best friend.

We took a taxi to his mother's house. She was absolutely thrilled to see us both. She, too, had obviously decided not to mention the estrangement just yet. We all knew that Joe would talk when he was ready. For the moment it was enough to let him know where he was and who he was with.

'I'm really tired,' he whispered.

'I know.' I rubbed his arm with my hand. 'I'm on the phone. All you have to do is pick it up, day or night.' He nodded in understanding.

Back home, I was doubly confused, and not a little bit surprised at my own reactions. I had not planned to reach out to him at the airport. Yet it seemed like the most natural thing in the world. It wasn't sexual, but intensely passionate. Are they the same thing? I wondered. I couldn't recall ever seeing him vulnerable or needy. I had always played that role. He had always been the strong one, the rescuer. His vulnerability forced me to look at my commitments. He was only a human being too. I felt I had drained every one of my friends. Jill and Karen hardly ever rang. I wanted it that way, yet I didn't. I couldn't fathom my own behaviour. I was forcing people to do exactly what I didn't want them to do.

I wanted to be there for Joe and realised with shock

that I didn't actually know how to do that. I felt ashamed. Always taking people for granted.

Always needing a crisis to wake me up. It annoyed me to see him this upset. This upset, over someone else. I wanted to be the heroine, without having done the work. Juliet was a good woman. Who did I think I was? How convenient for me to suddenly be all concerned. I sickened myself.

The following morning I took David to school and went to work as usual. When I came home I tidied up. I remembered Brian's handout at the course and rummaged through my bag until I found it.

I read the first question: *Describe in as much detail as you can an unhappy incident in your home.*

Well, well, well. That was a tough one. Which one to choose? My mind had been racing with unhappy incidents ever since I started the course. I had tried to push them to the back of my mind, but even while I slept they tormented me. Making themselves known in fragmented dreams and persistent nightmares. I frequently found myself waking up in the middle of the night, drenched in sweat and with tears rolling down my face. Then I realised I was dreaming again. I dreamt constantly of holidays.

Holidays. Holidays. Before and after holidays were probably the worst times ever in our home. I often wondered, did other families go through this traumatic experience? What should have been something anticipated with joy and excitement, became the annual dread for me and my siblings alike. It usually started about a week before we were due to set off. My mother would become increasingly agitated and the normal arguing would escalate to fever pitch. Dad would disappear more and more to escape Mam's wrath. That only increased her bad mood and that in turn only increased our misery.

I was about nine years old when we had the 'famous' holiday in Courtown.

Every year we went to a mobile home, usually in Kerry, Cork or Galway. This year it was Courtown, County Wexford. It was the best Mam and Dad could do by way of vacation. Some families only got as far as Donabate. The holidays themselves were nearly always a success.

I could never quite figure out what got my mother started. It was almost like she had no control over herself. A bout of madness would overtake her and she was powerless to stop it. She simmered under the surface like a volcano, slowly building up, day by day, finally exploding in a pyroclastic cloud that devastated everything within a mile radius. It would generally begin with the odd smart comment to my dad, who had become accustomed to the yearly onslaught. It was the day of our departure. We scurried around the house like lunatics looking for last-minute items.

'Mam, I can't find my sandals.'

'William, where's my comb?'

'Dad, have you got the camera?'

'I hope you paid the milkman on the double, William. I don't want to be facing into any bills when we get home.'

'Yes, I paid the milkman,' Dad would sigh.

'Did you ask Mrs McCarthy if she'll keep an eye on the house?'

'I asked Mrs McCarthy,' he said flatly and shook his newspaper vigorously. This was always a sign that he was losing his patience.

'Did you cancel the newspaper order at the shop?'

'Ah, for God's sake, woman, stop prattling on and on. Why don't you give your mouth a rest?' he'd snort loudly and Mam would start to slam the dishes on the table.

'I only asked you a question – no need to snap the head off me. Someone has to check these things.'

'Well, if you're such an expert, why don't you check them yourself, instead of hassling me while I'm trying to read the paper.'

'Oh, put the paper away, for goodness sake. Can't you see I'm trying to get things into the car?'

Rachel was pulling at Dad's trousers.

'Ah, what in the name of Jaysus do you want now?' he yelled at her.

'Don't shout at the child like that.' Mam's voice had gone up slightly. 'What is it, love?' Mam pulled her over.

'Are we going yet?' she asked. Too young to appreciate the tense atmosphere.

'We'll go when I'm ready, do you hear? Young pup! Get out from under me feet, go on, be off with you.' Dad shooed her away like a dog.

'Don't call her a pup!' Mam bellowed at the top of her voice, her hands on her hips.

Dad got up to leave the room.

'That's right, leave the room. Go on, insult the child and leave me to deal with it!'

'It's a bloody good kick in the arse she needs, then she'd be in the manure business, wouldn't you?'

Rachel's mouth had begun to turn downwards.

'She only asked a question. You treat her like she's an enemy. Get in the car, Rachel, there's a good girl. We're ready to go now.'

'I said I'm *not* ready! Do not contradict me in front of the child!' Dad was turning twenty shades of purple.

'The "child" has a name, or haven't you noticed?' Mam was right up into his face.

At that point, Dad lost it. He slammed his fist on the table, and the milk jug overturned. It spilled over the side making a perfect white waterfall.

Rachel started to cry.

'Now look what you've done, you big bully. You do it every year!'

Mam was screeching. Rachel had scampered under the table, whimpering.

Where was I? Behind the kitchen door. My refuge, when they went to war. I had my colouring book and crayons with me, the ones Dad had bought me for school that year. Big fat waxy ones in bright colours. I started to draw on the wall. I knew it was bold. I couldn't help myself.

'It's you! You started the whole thing, with your bloody whinging and moaning. It's you that has her acting like a baby, and her almost five years old. Shut up, you bloody whiner! I'll give you something to whine about!'

'You hate her! You hate her! You've always hated her!' Mam was hysterical. All semblance of sanity gone out of her face.

I was drawing a picture. A picture of the Archangel Gabriel. I looked over my shoulder. He wasn't there. Father Sheehy had said – Father Sheehy had *promised* – 'Your Guardian Angel is always watching over you.' I had started to cry now; the snot rolled down my nose and into my mouth. I daren't sniffle. I wiped it on my T-shirt.

'May God forgive you, woman. If I hate anyone, it's . . . it's . . .'

Mam whacked him across the face. I heard the impact and winced. I could almost feel the hot burning sting of it. They both stood staring at each other. The only sound was their rapid breathing, and Rachel still cowering under the table trying to stifle her sobs.

'You've always blamed Rachel. She's only a child. It wasn't her fault that Desmond died.' Mam was crying, her words tumbling out in rapid succession.

'Godammit, I forbid you to talk to me like that, woman! I forbid it! As God is my judge, I'll break every bone in your body if you open your mouth once more.' Dad's voice had cracked.

Mam made a maddened lunge for the back door. She was completely out of control. She pulled Rachel out from underneath the kitchen table.

'That's it,' she said, breathless. 'I'm leaving. I'm leaving and I'm taking her with me. I'm getting away from this fucking house and I'm never coming back.'

Rachel was screaming and kicking. 'No! No! I want my dad!'

Hail Mary, full of grace, the Lord is with thee . . .

'Let her go!' Dad ordered. Suddenly calm with fright. 'Let her go now, Meta. You don't know what you're saying. Come on now, get a hold of yourself . . .'

Blessed art thou among women, and blessed is the fruit of thy womb, Jesus. I bowed my head.

Dad reached out to grab a hold of her and she tore at the air with her arms. Her face was white with rage.

'Don't you fucking touch me,' she spat.

Where are you, Jack? *I'm here, behind the door.* I am crouched in a sitting position, hugging my knees close to my chest.

I have destroyed the wall and broken my crayons. I can't get past *thy womb, Jesus.* I remember the prayer that Father Sheehy had taught me.

> *Oh, angel of God, my guardian dear,*
> *To whom God's love commits me here,*
> *Ever this day be at my side,*
> *To light and guard,*
> *To rule and guide.*

Mam is still struggling with the back door. Eventually

she frees it by kicking it violently. She drags Rachel down the pathway. My sister is still screaming hysterically.

'Dad! Dad! I want my dad.'

I can't take any more. I can't. I can't. My dad is crying. I scramble to my feet, panic-stricken, and make a run for the back door. Mam has slammed it closed after her. I can't reach the handle. I try climbing up the glass panels.

Open the door! Open the door!

My fist smashes through the glass pane. I am bleeding but I can feel no pain. I am beside myself with fear and panic. I am running down the garden, tripping, slipping and sliding.

'Mam! Mam! Come back, Mam! Don't forget me! Don't leave me behind! Mam!'

The garden gate is swinging in the wind. Backwards and forwards it swings, banging against the wall every couple of seconds.

Mam is gone. Mam is gone for ever. She doesn't want me. She doesn't love me. She left me behind. She only took Rachel.

I can feel the warm blood trickling down my wrist. Dad is trying to pick me up. I can see his hand coming down to me. I am biting hard into his hand. I fucking hate him. I hate my mother. I hate Desmond. And there are definitely no such things as angels.

I woke up screaming for Mam. I was crying. Great big sobs, the kind that make your shoulders heave. I was in my flat, surrounded by empty cans and bottles. I looked around me for more. There was nothing left. I reached for the phone.

'Mam?'

'Jack? It's one-thirty in the morning. What's wrong? Don't tell me David's sick again. Or did someone die?'

'Mam, why did you leave me?'

'Jack, have you been drinking?'

'Mam, I just wanted to know. Why did you take Rachel, all those years ago? Remember that awful row with Dad? You left me behind.'

'Jack, for goodness sake, child, I don't know what you're talking about. Is anyone there with you? What's the matter?'

I gave a long, shuddering sigh. 'It's all right, Mam. Forget it. I just had a bad dream. I'll phone you tomorrow.' I hung up.

I sat for a long time. Smoking. Thinking. I had never forgiven my mother for that. I had never even tried. I really thought she didn't love me. Now I realised how much pain they must have been in. I had always thought it was my fault. Otherwise she wouldn't have left me behind.

I went back into David's room. He was snoring loudly, with his arse propped in the air and his arms bent under his chest. I laughed to myself, and thought about all the times I had resented him. All the times I had thought I wanted to be free. All the times I had held him responsible for the lack of love in my life. It wasn't his fault. It wasn't my parents' fault. It wasn't *anybody's* fault. It was life.

I was wide awake now and the memories were clear. I picked up Brian's paper and read the second question. It was easier. *Describe a happy incident in your childhood.*

Ironically, one of my fondest memories was the hours following the big showdown. I recalled being in a small room in the Mater Hospital. I had inflicted quite a nasty gash across the main vein on my wrist. Dad had rushed me to the hospital. I still had no pain because my fear had not abated, despite Mam returning. She had left home for an entire twenty minutes. She walked up the garden path, with Rachel in tow. Silently, she let herself in the back door. I never heard them discuss what had happened. She obviously realised there was a *new* crisis. I guess I became the focus of attention.

In the hospital room a nurse was about to stitch my wrist. My father sat in a chair opposite me and commanded that I look at him. I did what I was told. I focused on him and didn't feel the needle. As he smiled bravely at me, I thought of all the times he had sat me on his lap and cut my toenails. I loved it when he did that. It tickled. In the mornings I used to creep into their secret domain, and kiss him on the cheek. His face was always rough and unshaven. I used to complain about the 'arrows' scratching my face. What pain he must have been in, watching me being stitched up. What self-blame he must have been feeling. What remorse.

The nurse finished the job and my hand was bandaged. Dad led me through the long winding corridors of the hospital, and stopped at the exit. In the corner was a huge bulky machine. It had words on it, but I didn't understand them. I had never seen anything like it in my life.

'Watch this!' Dad said, like a child himself. He put some coins in the giant monster and it made a loud thumping noise. I thought it was going to take off. Then it did a big belch. There was a slit at the bottom. Dad put his hand in and I thought it would never come out again. He winced and twisted his hand around. He then put it behind his back.

'Close your eyes,' he said.

I did.

'Now hold out your hand.'

I did.

'Now open your eyes.'

I did.

And there was a Cadbury's Crunchie in the palm of my hand. A full one, in a glorious gold wrapper. All for me.

Just for me. I had never, ever had a whole chocolate bar
for myself. I looked at the magic machine, the chocolate
heaven.

'Thanks, Dad,' I said.

As he bent down and kissed me, I wondered was he
the Guardian Angel?

Just then I heard David cough from the other room. It
was late in the evening and the flat was still and quiet. I
sobbed quietly into a paper tissue, not wanting to wake
him up. I tried to remember the holiday itself. Details were
sketchy at first, but soon the memories were clear as a bell.
It was amazing that we still managed to go to Courtown,
Wexford. It turned out to be the best holiday we had ever
had. We set off in our dad's black Ford Anglia, all three
children's bodies wedged into the back seat.

Dad arose early every morning with his razor and toilet
bag and slung a towel over his arm. He greeted the other
dads as they made their way to the public washrooms.
They compared weather reports and local entertainment.
The women queued on the other side, forming an orderly
line, and washed their hair in freezing cold water. They
swapped tips about washing clothes, and what was cheap
in the local supermarket. On the odd night, Dad treated
us to 'real' chips from the chipper van. We would get the
scent and beg him, until he couldn't resist the wonderful
fatty aroma himself. They came wrapped in newspaper,
crisp and steaming hot. We blew on our fingers. We
smothered them in salt and vinegar. If we were lucky,
a dollop of tomato ketchup might be thrown in.

During the night, Dad would place our makeshift toilet
– a bucket – in the centre of the floor. Inevitably, somebody
got up to use it. A different body would be allocated the
dreadful chore of taking it out the next morning to dispose
of its vile contents. On one occasion, Dad was taking a leak
and dropped a shilling in it by mistake. I offered to do the

honours straight away. I took the bucket to the back of the mobile home, rolled up my sleeves, closed my eyes and plunged my hand into it. I swirled it around in the urine and faeces, until I felt the cold coin slip into my palm. I ran to the site pump and washed it under the running water, until it gleamed in the sun. Then I set off for the amusement arcade, stinking of shit and piss. I was delighted with life.

At night, the town centre came alive. Amusement arcades filled with 'bowsies'. Neon signs screeched through the dark. The combination of noise and flashing lights was magical. Coins clanked. Sirens wailed. Every now and then a Jackpot would ring out and screams of delight would echo. We would gather around the lucky winner, feigning our best 'urchin' look. We hoped the nice man or woman might toss us a coin.

We searched the slots for forgotten pennies. I spent hours rolling them on to the black and white lines. If they landed in the middle, you won, and six new pennies would come pumping down the glass panel.

It was the only time I remember the family being almost normal. Mam and Dad seemed content. I felt loved, happy. I thought it would last for ever. Within hours of returning to Dublin, the squabbling had started up again. It was a short reprieve. Thinking back, the house must have represented something ugly, something perverse. There was something at home that ignited their resent-ment. That awful word 'reality'.

I looked at my watch: it was 4 am. I yawned. I crept into David's room and crawled in beside him, gently nudging him to move over. He threw his arm over me, hitting me in the face. I smiled. It felt good to understand something of my life.

The first seeds of understanding had begun to sprout. I had taken a personal experience in my childhood right through into my adult life. I had blamed Mam and Dad for my sense of inadequacy, my sense of failure. I had blamed David for stopping me doing what I had always wanted to do. It was an excuse. An excuse to *not* change. This was another eye-opener. Another penny had dropped. I was the moulder of my own dreams. I could do it if I wanted to. Perhaps now, armed with all this new knowledge, I could try to take a new direction. I could try to change things, even if it was a little at a time. I did not want to end up like my parents, bitter and twisted. With that thought I fell into a peaceful deep sleep. The first in weeks. I didn't know it, but I had passed the halfway mark of my journey and was already on the home stretch.

Chapter 14

Many things were becoming apparent. The deeper I went into my recollections, the more I discovered. Things had not been good for me. I had weathered a few storms as a child, there was no doubt about it. What struck me the most was the similarity of experiences being shared in the group. The more people opened up, the more courage I found to do the same. It worked a bit like a baggage carousel. My luggage kept going round and round. Every now and then I would take something off it, look at it, and then put it back.

I was beginning to see that my early experiences had had a profound effect on my way of thinking. That, in turn, had affected my way of relating. My relationships had always been strained and difficult. I had always felt like I didn't exactly belong. Others seemed to find it extremely easy to be intimate. I had no idea what the word meant. I was constantly obsessed with 'coping' and nothing else had a chance to sink in.

Now I was being haunted nightly, by visions and voices of the past. No matter how hard I tried they just wouldn't go away. A smell, a song, a word, could trigger off a thousand memories. I began to experience cravings for chocolate and sweet things, which upset me greatly. I brought it up at the next session, and was relieved to hear the same thing being repeated all round.

Brian was encouraging and put my mind at ease. 'This is perfectly normal,' he explained. 'In fact, it's a very good sign. I urge you all to continue writing, no matter how bizarre or strange your thoughts. Write everything down. I mean *everything*. The voices you are hearing are "you". Do them the honour of listening to them. It is probable they have never had a chance to express themselves before. Now is "their" time. Don't be afraid. Go with it. They will take their own course. If you don't, you are running the risk of ignoring yourself – which is why you all came here in the first place. Trust me. You are all being wonderfully brave. It is worth it. *You* are worth it. Believe it and you will leave this course feeling like a new person.'

I hung on to every word he had to say. I took notes whenever possible. I was compelled to keep going, to continue. I did not know what it all meant. I had a gut feeling it meant something. That was enough to push me forward. I did exactly what he told me to do. I listened intently to the rest of the group, some of whom were completely lost.

Diane had remained one step ahead of me all the time. I had asked her for her phone number and I was delighted when she gave it to me. Now I could contact her whenever I wanted. I wanted to and did, daily. Brian had suggested we draw on every bit of support available to us.

'Do you mean our families?' Bertie jumped up.

'Not exactly.' Brian hesitated, searching for the correct reply. 'This may very well be the time to side-step your families, just for the duration of the course. What I mean by that is, if you are experiencing bad feelings towards your family of origin, it would be wise to put some space between you and them. If your family support you in what you are doing, by all means rally them around.'

Bertie didn't get it. 'My family do support me. I'm not

sure I should start dumping all this on them. My wife has had a hard enough time already.'

'I'm not telling you to dump on anyone, Bertie. I specifically suggested people who you know are supportive,' Brian tried again.

'Are you saying she isn't supportive, or what?' Now the fella was getting the hump.

Diane intervened. 'Bertie, I think Brian is trying to help you choose correctly.'

'I don't need any help choosing anything,' he said, obviously irritated at the suggestion.

'Don't you?' Connor piped up, with a little sarcasm in his voice.

'Now, let's not get off the really important stuff here.' Brian was quick to resume order.

Frank had had his hand up for an age.

'Yes, Frank?' Brian eventually asked him.

'I find . . . it . . . it . . . it helpful to paint too.' Frank had been coming along fine in the intervening weeks. I had even grown to welcome his comments. He was intuitive and intelligent. It was a shame about his speech impediment.

'That's an excellent idea,' Brian said and everybody nodded their heads in accord. 'As well as paints, you could use markers, crayons, anything that will express your feelings outwardly. Use anything at all. The more creative the better the results.'

'I use David's paintbox,' I said shyly, and held up a scrap of paper that I had spent ages doing.

'What is it?' Bertie asked.

'It's a butterfly,' Diane said.

'Nah. It's an aeroplane.' Connor held the page at an angle.

'It's Ja . . . Ja. . . Jack, just Jack,' Frank said quietly. I smiled at him. Everybody laughed; it was a nice moment.

We finished our fourth session with plenty of food for thought. When I got home, I heard Joe's familiar voice coming from the kitchen. I knew that meant David would still be up.

'Hi, stranger!' I was genuinely pleased to see he had made the effort to come all the way into the inner city from Clontarf. The flat was overrun with children and noise. Joe was on all fours, with David on his back. Alice was clearly in her element.

'Howya, love, have a good time?' she asked.

I couldn't exactly answer that. She didn't really understand the nature of what I was doing. It was hardly fun, even if it was very interesting.

'Yes, thanks,' I smiled, lifting David from Joe's back. He protested loudly. 'Time for bed, mister,' I said.

'Can Joe read me a story? Please? Please?' I looked to Joe, who was already choosing a storybook.

'I suppose so,' I yielded.

Once he learned that, he had his pyjamas on in seconds. He slipped his tiny hand in Joe's and off they trotted to the bedroom.

I set about making some tea. I was flat broke and had nothing to drink. It didn't matter, tomorrow was pay day. Besides, it was late by the time David fell asleep. The fact that he knew Joe was there made him delay bedtime as much as possible. Every couple of minutes he would peer in the door.

'Can I have a drink?'

'No, you just had one a minute ago. Go back to bed, David.'

Five minutes later: 'I need to go wee-wee.'

Five minutes later: 'I'm hungry.'

'You can't possibly be hungry, David. Now stop messing and go back to sleep!'

He just wanted to be in our company. A man and a

woman's company. A mammy and a daddy, as he saw it. A normal family. If there ever was such a thing. Joe had dialled for a taxi.

'How long will they be?' I enquired.

'About thirty minutes.' He picked up some of the pages on the kitchen table.

'Oh Christ, don't read them!' I swiped them off him as fast as I could.

'What's all this?' He picked up some more. The table was littered with bits of paper. Poster paints were strewn everywhere. Old newspapers were spread out, and water jugs with brushes sticking out from them. I hadn't had the time to clean it up.

'David was painting,' I tried.

He lifted one up to the light. 'David didn't do this, even though it is childish. It's yours – I can tell.'

I was silent, watching his face. Joe had been home two weeks and he still hadn't volunteered any information. He was quiet and distant. We hadn't had much of a chance to discuss his break-up with Juliet. I was waiting for the right time. The thing was, I wasn't sure when to mention it. When not to. I didn't know if he wanted me to start the ball rolling, or if he didn't want any mention of it at all.

'You know, she was always asking after you,' he sighed.

The ice was broken. Now was my chance. I had to take it sooner or later.

'Who?' I asked.

'Don't be stupid, Jack. You know quite well who I'm talking about. You don't have to go around in silence, I can talk about it. You know, it was me who left, after all.' He put the picture back down, careful not to spill anything.

'You did?' I hadn't thought it was that kind of break-up. I knew Juliet had been madly in love with Joe right from the start. She must have done something truly awful to make him leave.

'Look, can we talk about it?' I started, handing him some tea. 'If you don't want to, it's OK. I just can't understand what could have happened. Everything seemed to be going so well.'

Joe plonked himself down on the couch. Picking up one of David's toys, he fiddled with it for a while. Then he asked, 'Was there ever anything you always wanted, Jack? Something you had wanted since you were a kid?'

I thought about it and smiled. 'Yes, actually, there is. A doll's house. God knows I sent enough letters to Santa. I never got one, though. I can never resist looking at them at Christmas-time, in the toy shops. I'm drawn to them,' I remembered sadly.

'Well, I always wanted a train engine, just like this one.' Joe held up the bright blue Thomas the Tank Engine. 'This isn't a toy, it's the real thing. Look at the detail on it.' Joe was studying the undercarriage.

'Juliet is a very good woman, isn't she? You couldn't have asked for more, Joe. She has a great personality, she's intelligent, gentle, a lovely mother to her kids. Despite all that, you weren't happy,' I chanced. It didn't make sense. I decided to go for the jugular. 'What went wrong? Something awful must have happened to make you leave.'

He smiled at me and patted the couch, indicating for me to sit beside him.

I got up and snuggled into his big strong chest.

'The woman I want is already spoken for,' he whispered into my ear.

'What?! You sneaky bastard! I never knew! Have you been seeing someone else? That's it, isn't it? You met someone else, didn't you, crafty fucker. I never thought you'd be the unfaithful type. C'mon spill it – I want to know everything.' I was secretly delighted. Sometimes, Joe had appeared to me to be too much of a Goody Two

Shoes. Now I had found a chink in his armour and I was preparing to prise it open with my questions.

He was laughing openly at me. 'There's nothing to tell, I swear! No, I wasn't unfaithful. Well, not exactly. There *was* another woman. There I was, living with Juliet and constantly wanting someone else. I felt I was being unfaithful to her; just thinking about it was enough. My heart wasn't with her any more. It wasn't fair on her. Eventually, I knew I had to go. She didn't want me to.' His voice got lower. 'She begged me to stay. But it would only have been out of pity. Christ, it would have been the easiest thing in the world to stay. Any other guy would have,' he finished, sighing deeply.

'Not you,' I found myself saying. I knew him. It just wasn't Joe's style. 'I think I know how you feel,' I ventured. 'I mean, about wanting someone you can't have.' I looked downwards.

There was a slight pause.

'What's this course all about?' He changed the subject.

You're not getting off the hook that easily. 'Oh that! Its title is "Discovering Your Family History" and do you know, I can't wait to get there every week. I look forward to it so much. I couldn't begin to tell you what I'm learning. But why have you changed the subject? Who's the other woman?' I asked cheekily.

'I didn't change the subject – you did. Look, trust me. You don't want to know,' he said.

'I thought we were friends, Joe,' I said, a sick feeling rising up from the pit of my stomach. There was only one other woman I knew of in England, and that was Jill. My blood ran cold.

'Is Matt on the course?' He changed the subject again.

Oh God. 'Of course Matt's on the course. If it wasn't for him, I would never have had the guts to do it. I wish you could see how much it's helping me, Joe.' I was trying to avoid the subject of Matt; it always led to a stalemate, somehow.

'Be careful, Jack,' he warned.

There was an uncomfortable silence. Suddenly we both had secrets. It felt unnatural. Like there was a barrier between us.

'I really hope you'll stay in touch with Juliet. God, she was so fond of you, and David. You shouldn't cut her off either,' he added.

'Huh?'

'Juliet, I mean.'

'Of course,' I stared at him. *Who else were you thinking of? It's Jill isn't it? Fucking Jill. I should have known.*

'Yes, I agree – but it wouldn't feel right at the moment. Besides, she'd only want to know stuff about you. Maybe, I don't know. I'll give her a call sometime,' I replied.

'Do, Jack. She needs a friend. We all need our friends.'

'Too right,' I said snappily. *Who are mine?*

The taxi beeped outside.

I was desperate to know who the mystery woman was. I was curious and a bit disappointed too. For a brief moment I had heard my own heart thump in anticipation. Perhaps he had left Juliet for me? How ridiculous! I had gone through this conversation in my head for years. It was our platonic relationship that led me to think up all these crazy fantasies. The reality was, we would always be friends, and nothing more.

'Gotta go,' he said, pulling the curtain back. 'My chauffeur is here.'

'It's a pity you couldn't stay a little longer.' I hadn't really meant that, it just came out.

As Joe climbed in the minicab he turned and waved. I waved goodbye and closed the door. Thoughts of Jill and Joe together made me seethe with jealousy. I deliberately switched brain sides. I still had Matt lurking about on the other side. I concentrated fully on that instead. Now more than ever I wanted something to happen – and fast.

Things were definitely heating up between us. I could feel it in my bones, and between my legs. I was delighted he had apologised to me about our teenage philandering. It gave me hope. I was willing to give it a second chance, now that we were adults, experienced and adept at playing the game of love.

I wanted nothing more than to have one more night; whether he was married or not didn't matter any more. I wanted it. I wanted it with every passing minute. I wanted to make it right. To start again. To feel all those wonderful things a woman should feel. The climax of an orgasm. I wanted him to make it happen. He owed it to me! I deserved it!

I lay dreamily on the couch. How much more waiting? I listened to Steven Bishop, wooing me with his gentle songs. 'Looking for the Right One'. How ironic. I drifted in and out and became bored with my own thoughts.

Tomorrow was the sixth session of the course. I had worked hard all week, writing sometimes into the early hours of the morning. Some nights, I just had to get up and write. I went into the kitchen. The table was still in a mess from the night before. I gathered up all the pages I had written and carried them into bed, deciding to reread them, in preparation for tomorrow. I had begun to remember things in great detail. I no longer had to fight to get them to come to the surface. They made their own way up effortlessly. My pen danced over the pages and my hand ached with writer's cramp.

Not long after the Courtown incident, I changed. I changed greatly. Looking back now, the change was noticeable at least to me, although not, apparently, to my parents.

It had started one day on an ordinary shopping trip

to the little local supermarket. My mother sent me there daily for cigarettes and some provisions for the house. I took the shortcut, down Belgrove Lane, past the school, on to Seafield Road and out on to Vernon Avenue. Then I took another back lane, ending up in Moran's supermarket car park. In those days it was a tiny grocery shop, of course, with the barest essentials for sale. It was good enough for what my mother wanted, though – bread, tea, tomatoes and ten of the cheapest cigarettes.

I took the shopping basket and wandered up and down the small aisles. I got the things I had come for and went to pay for them at the counter. When I got outside, I realised I still had the tomatoes in my pocket. I had forgotten to put them in the basket because I went to weigh them first. I counted the change. Bingo!

A little devil appeared on my right shoulder. A little angel appeared on my left. I had at least 20p for myself. And I also had a choice – a difficult one. I could go back in and tell them about the mistake I had made, or I could pocket the 20p and spend it on myself. Nobody would ever know.

The devil won. I went into the sweetshop and spent my ill-gotten gains. Then I skipped up Belgrove Lane and sat on the school railings munching happily on my goodies. The next time I was sent to the shops, the little devil had appeared before I even went in. If I had got away with it once, I would get away with it twice. I plunged a packet of marshmallows into my brown anorak and walked out. Nothing happened.

Yippee! That was when my habit of throwing parties for one was born. I linked them up with my present bingeing and could see where it had all started. Then I remembered something else that had happened around the same time.

Dad often left loose change in his overcoat in the closet

downstairs. At night, when I was certain everyone was asleep, I would creep down and stick my little hand in the big pocket. The coins rattled in the dark. Too scared to awaken my parents by turning on the light, I took whatever fell into my hand. At first one coin, then two; soon I was taking handfuls and didn't know what to do with them.

I lifted a corner of tintawn in my bedroom and hoarded them there. Each morning I arose early, and would leave the house before schooltime and go to the sweetshop. I had the best lunchbox in school. It was a far cry from jam sandwiches and milk. I gorged on large Granny Smith apples. The girls in my class would compete for the 'butts' – the juicy core of the apple which I didn't eat. I soon came to see the advantages of being a robber. I had become very popular all of a sudden. I gave away sweets to anyone who asked me, and told lies about where the money had come from. One day, in the classroom, when everybody was out in the yard, I spied the 'Black Babies' money box. I reached up and dipped in. I grabbed a handful of coins and stuffed them in my pinafore pocket.

The little devil was winning hands down. My guardian angel had taken flight to greener fields. I was a thief and an over-eater at eight years of age.

The back of our house was a wild and unspoiled acre of land. It bore some of the best fruit going around – apples, pears, gooseberries. I planned 'The Great Orchard Robbery' while I did my homework, deciding I would use Jason, my younger brother, to assist in pulling the whole thing off.

I took an alarm clock and set it for 4 am, when I was certain everybody would be asleep. I was so excited that sleep evaded me. I arose at 4 am, being careful to turn the alarm off, and woke Jason. He got up sleepily, rubbing his eyes.

'Where are we going?' he asked, yawning and putting on his slippers.

'You'll see.' I placed my forefinger on his lips.

We crept down the stairs, making sure to avoid all the creaky ones. Jason followed like a lamb to the slaughter. Outside in the garden the birds were twittering sweetly. Everything was silent and the dew wet our feet as we ploughed through the field. The apples had already begun to fall and I gathered them quickly. I made a bag out of my night-dress and packed in as many as I could, scooping them towards me in great haste. I motioned at Jason to do the same. The apples were small, red and sweet. Delicious! I rammed as many as I could into my mouth.

Finally, I motioned to Jason to get moving. We made our journey back, through the field, up the lane, in through the garden, sliding silently in the back door. As quiet as mice, we stole upstairs and climbed into our beds. Nobody had budged. The operation had been a success!

I was alive with exhilaration. It was my first act of total defiance, and I had gotten away with it! Just to know that I had was enough. I vowed to do the same thing the next night, too. Feeling tired but happy, I snuggled up under the covers and fell into a deep, deep sleep.

The next morning at breakfast, Jason kept yawning. I kicked him under the table and he jumped to attention.

'What's up with the pair of them?' Dad roared, shaving cream dripping on the lino.

'Nothing,' I nodded.

'Not getting enough sleep. You're to be in your beds early tonight, do you hear?' He coughed loudly.

'Yes, Dad.' I winked at Jason.

I had pulled it off. The Great Orchard Robbery. It was my first taste of revenge, my first rebellion against my parents. And like the apples, it was sweet.

I stopped writing when a huge yawn came out of my

mouth. I rose to put on the kettle and helped myself to some cereal, then I checked on David to make sure he was OK. Then I returned to the kitchen table and continued my tale.

The following day I went to school as usual. I came home, had my dinner, did my homework and played out on the street. Dad was true to his word and had us tucked in with stories read by 8 pm. I was tired and feeling a bit off-colour so I didn't mind the early night. At about 1 am I awoke with vicious cramps in my lower abdomen. I tossed and turned for what seemed like an age but the rising and falling nausea only increased. Eventually I could stick it no longer and called out: 'Mam, Dad, I think I'm going to be sick!'

Dad appeared at the side of the bed, clutching his stripy pyjama bottoms with a bit of string. They always appeared to be falling down.

'Quit that shouting and roaring!' he bellowed at the top of his voice. 'What ails you, huh?'

'I feel sick,' I whimpered. No sooner had the words come out than I felt the bile rising into my mouth. I dashed to the toilet, just about making it on time, and threw up. My eyes watered with the retching. Oh God – I knew there was more to come.

'Were you out at that orchard? Answer me now!' Dad was hardly what you would call supportive, in my moment of need.

'I swear, Dad, I wasn't near it.' Another fountain of broken apples landed in the toilet. I felt a sharp smack across the back of my head.

'And what's all that then!' Dad was fuming. 'Bread and butter pudding, huh? *Huh?*'

I looked into the sea of sick. Chunks of apple swirled around before my eyes. I heaved again, but nothing came up this time. It went on all night. Every hour or so I would be doubled up with cramp. My little tummy had nothing left inside it.

Dad grounded me for a week. Jason got away scot free. I had been the 'ringleader' so to speak and had blackened his 'innocent soul'. He was not to blame. I had to take full responsibility for my actions.

To this day, I find it hard to keep apples in my belly. It's probably the only food I can't eat. It's a pity it wasn't chocolate or I'd be as skinny as a greyhound. My sweet tooth developed at an early age. I learned to stuff my feelings with sweet things, chocolate being the number-one offender. It made me feel better, or so I thought. That was all right when I was a child, but the bingeing continued when I grew up, and caused havoc with my figure. Each new faddy diet only resulted in a worse relapse. I wasn't sure in the end which was the addiction, the food or the dieting. I guess it was a bit of both.

To counteract my loss of dignity after 'The Great Orchard Robbery', I did the next wrong thing and introduced myself to another addiction. I robbed a cigarette out of my mother's bag when she wasn't looking. I puffed and puffed and wondered what all the fuss was about, until a local boy who was a year older than me – therefore deserving of the utmost respect – pointed out to me that I was not doing it right.

'Here,' said the expert. 'Watch me.' He put the cigarette in his mouth and drew the smoke in. Then he took a deep breath and pulled it all into the back of his throat. Then he worked a piece of magic that sold me once and for all. He spoke. No smoke came out of his mouth until a few seconds later. Then he did the same thing again. Only this time, the smoke came out of his nostrils.

'That's how you inhale properly,' he instructed me. 'That's how you really smoke.'

My back was against the wall. I had to be a real smoker,

like them. I drew in the putrid smoke and held it there. I
went green, then red, then white. I blew the smoke out.

There, shithead.

I was now also a drug addict, and I hadn't even had
my first period.

I put down the paper and laughed to myself. It was
funny, at times. I could see quite clearly what I had
been trying to achieve. I was trying to be noticed, but
I had learned to scream inside. Nowadays, with all the
information at our fingertips, any one of those incidents
would have alerted my parents to the fact that something
was wrong with me. I was acting out so much I could
have enrolled for Equity. They never took any notice of
my strange behaviour, though – even when they eventually found out about my stealing from the supermarket.
My dad had caught me eating sweets in the lane. He
challenged me about where I had gotten the money from
and I told him the truth. He scolded me and punished me
severely, but it had no effect and was useless as a means
of addressing the real problem.

I was an innocent child. I didn't want to be bad, but I
had begun to believe that I was. I had begun to internalise
the constant squabbling as being *my* fault. I had to do
something to convince myself it was my fault. So I robbed,
I cheated, I lied. The more I did these things, the more I
became the centre of attention. I certainly achieved that.
That was not what I was after, however. I wanted their
attention all right, but not this way. I was constantly in
trouble from then on. If only we had had even a little
family counselling. It might have done so much to stop
it all from snowballing. We never talked about things at
home, we just walked around the subject in our heads.
I thought about this and it made me very sad. *The real
reason for the family dysfunction was dead.* Yet he was still
living in our house.

Desmond Joyce, twin brother of Rachel, lurked behind the Venetian blinds, and in our suitcases. He hung out in the kitchen and was a fly on the wall. He was behind every argument, every slammed door and every turn of cheek. He had made our home into a bloody battlefield. The victims of war were my siblings and me. We were powerless to overcome something we could not see, hear, feel or talk to. If there was a survivor, it was Desmond himself, for he had escaped the living hell which his death had created.

We were a family searching for answers. Mam and Dad were filled with something they could not understand. Someone once said, 'You cannot change something, until it becomes what it is.' As Desmond was dead, he would never present an opportunity for them to resolve their conflict. As for me, I was destined to spin uncontrollably out of orbit and land somewhere on a distant planet. I would also be thrown there without any map. I, too, had experienced a 'little death' in myself. I hadn't stood a snowball's chance in hell.

This is the house that Jack built. A house made of cards. The faulty foundations had already been set. One strong puff of reality and it would all come tumbling down . . .

I was a little late for the next session of the course. As I sat down I realised that they had started without me. Frank had his head in his hands and looked clearly distressed. Not surprisingly. Bertie was being challenged at last.

'Ever since I started this course, things have been steadily going downhill at home. Rather than helping me, it is making matters worse. I really don't think it's for me any more. I made a mistake coming,' he complained.

'Let's see what the group has to say, Bertie. At least listen before you go.'

Bertie tut-tutted and sat down.

Connor raised his hand. 'I wonder if Bertie's wife resents his attendance here. After all, it was my wife who originally sent me here. Now she's acting very strange too. It's almost as if she doesn't really *want* me to change.'

'My wife only wants the best for me.' Bertie was indignant and red-faced. 'She doesn't think I need to dig up all this crap about my childhood.'

'What do you think, Bertie?' Diane was quick to reply.

Bertie sat silently staring at the floor. 'I gave her a dog's life, all her life. Why should I upset her any further? I owe my life to her. If she hadn't stayed – why, I would have no home today.' He looked defeated.

'What's her complaint, Bertie?' I found myself asking.

'She says I've changed. I'm not the same. I'm spending too much time writing this rubbish, thinking about myself all the time. I took away the best years of her life. I gambled it away.'

'So she doesn't want you gambling any more, but you can't step out of line, or want anything for yourself – is that it?' Brian got it in a nutshell.

'It's not as if you're out there gambling now, Bertie. It's only one night a week,' I reminded him.

Bertie put his head in his hands. 'I know I hurt her in the past,' he mumbled. 'Am I always going to pay for it? I have to do everything her way.'

'Perhaps the new you frightens her.' Frank spoke up without a stutter in sight.

Everybody went silent.

Yeah, he's right, I thought. Aloud, I said, 'Bertie, what's done is done. You're doing your best to make it up to her, but you also have to be yourself, and look after yourself. If you don't, who knows, you might end up gambling again.'

Everybody nodded in agreement.

'It would seem to me that your wife has the problem, but you feel responsible for everything,' Diane said.

'I think Diane is on the right track,' Brian said quietly. 'Bertie, what do you think?'

'It's no wonder I felt like the Lost Child.' He hung his head solemnly.

Diane continued: 'You may very well have been a lost child, all those years ago. I don't know about anyone else, but now I really feel you're the Caretaker, the Fixer, and you're trying to mend everything. It's not possible, Bertie, it just isn't.'

Bertie looked around. Everybody was agreeing with Diane. To my astonishment he stayed put and was exceptionally quiet for the rest of the class.

Connor related a similar story. 'I've been Mr Nice Guy for too long. "Yes, dear. No, dear." I lost my identity when I married Doreen. I always gave in, for the sake of peace and quiet, but I did myself a great injustice. Isn't it ironic that *she* suggested I participate in the course? Now she's behaving like I'm a selfish bastard. The truth is, I've been at her beck and call for twenty years. This is the first time I have ever completed anything in my life. I'm determined to finish it, if it's the last thing I do. This is for me.' He blew heavily into his handkerchief.

Frank had his hand up again.

Connor leaned over towards me. 'What's he do out there, anyway. Pull his wire?' I tried not to smile.

'You're excused, Frank,' Brian said automatically.

'But I wanted to say something,' Frank said, and we all giggled.

'Sorry, Frank. I thought . . . well, go on.'

'I've been getting h. . . h . . . help with my speech impediment.'

Bertie stood up and started clapping. We all joined in. There were a few war whoops thrown in.

Frank blushed and waved his hand for everyone to stop. 'I wouldn't have done it, only for the course. I didn't think I was worth it. All I ever wanted was to be noticed,' he said perfectly, without any mistakes. 'People automatically think I'm mentally deficient. I'm not – OK?'

Everybody was silent.

'There's nothing wrong with me. People have been treating me like a paraplegic all my life. They talk over me, pat me on the head like an imbecile. They avoid my eyes. I'm shy – that's all that's wrong with me! I guess I ended up believing them in the end.'

The silence continued. Frank rocked backwards and forwards, with his head down. His powerful words hung in the air. Nobody knew what to say. Diane was crying.

'Diane?' Brian gently urged her to speak.

'My husband left me for a younger woman,' she sniffled. 'I let the garbage build up for three weeks. I lined the black sacks up outside the garden gate. Hoping he would notice that no one had taken them out . . .' She broke down.

'They were there for weeks,' she continued, shuddering. 'It made no difference. Eventually the garbage men took them away. All I ever wanted was to be loved. To be me,' she sobbed into her tissues.

At that moment you could have heard a pin drop. We could all have been Diane. We had all played the 'garbage' game, and lost. It was a moment of complete understanding. A turning-point for the group.

Brian closed the session with a reminder that it was mid-term break in the school and that it would be closed next week. But it wouldn't put a stop to my writing. It was like a river: if you blocked the flow one way, it always found another way out.

Chapter 15

The break from the course was a welcome relief. I was tiring a little of the clashing personalities and my endless longing for something to happen with Matt. I had recently taken on board what the facilitator had suggested, about not getting involved. Obviously, Matt had too. He still phoned me the odd time and showed a great interest in my progress. That was enough to keep me hoping that, come the end of the course, we might get together finally.

In the meantime, I was still plagued with my childhood past. Now when I went to the shops with David I was besieged with cravings for childish sweets. I saw a fizz bag one day and went berserk. The shopkeeper stared at me.

'It's for my son,' I explained.

'Of course,' he smiled at me.

I bought ten of them, plus some cola bottles, marshmallows and milk teeth. There was a row outside the shop because David wanted them. I guarded them as if it were a matter of life and death.

I visited the family home a number of times. My behaviour was strange, to say the least. My parents finally started to ask questions when I arrived on their doorstep twice in one week. Mam hadn't forgotten the odd phone-call she had received in the middle of the night. I tried hard to explain my actions but it fell on deaf ears.

They thought I was reverting back to a second childhood and needed psychiatric help. They weren't too far off the mark either.

I asked Mam to pull out all the old family photograph albums and I pored over them with fascination. Upstairs in the attic conversion there was a secret door. I had hidden some things behind it before I left home. I was elated when I found that they were still there, especially my 'bottom drawer'. It was a term my father used to use for something special. It was in fact an old brown leather suitcase that had seen better days. The locks had long since been broken and it was closed tightly with the aid of an old scarf. It took some time to get it off.

I looked inside. It was a treasure trove of special memories. Some of the items made me laugh. I had held on to ridiculous things. A stud that had fallen off a boyfriend's shoe. Huge Valentine cards filled with scruffy verses and 3D *I love you*'s. Cinema and concert tickets. A tissue I had cried into when I broke up with Matt. A piece of chewing gum from a pen pal in Germany. St Patrick's Day Parade badges. My Communion rosette, and there, at the very bottom of the suitcase, was a diary. I took it out and examined the beautiful red hard cover. It was from 1974 – one of the worst years of my life. This was the biggie. I wriggled my hand into the inside pocket of the case and pulled out a tiny gold key. It slipped easily into the locked journal. Bingo! I had hit the jackpot.

Mam came in with some tea and biscuits. She was being extraordinarily kind of late.

'David's annoying your father again,' she told me. 'He won't rest until he lets him out to the pond.'

Dad had built a beautiful goldfish pond at the end of the garden. David had only one thing in mind: to get the goldfish and kill it. We knew that, because Dad was on his fifth fish. It was when the fourth one went missing that we copped on. Dad quizzed David about the disappearing fish.

'The cat got him,' he said innocently. 'I saw him with my own two eyes,' he reassured my dad. It was a very good explanation, except for the fact that they didn't have a cat. He was snared good and proper.

'There's some tea, love. Taking a trip down Memory Lane, are you?' she asked, peering over my shoulder.

'Just following up on stuff from the course,' I answered, ramming two biscuits in my mouth.

'Pity they don't teach you manners, dear.' She left me alone in the attic. I opened the diary and started to read.

I was eleven years old in 1974. I had made some new friends in Belgrove Secondary School. It was a year when all kinds of new and exciting opportunities were opening up to me – not least of all my emerging sexuality. I had begun to notice boys. My friends and I would peer over the wall that separated them from us at school. We often sent 'aeroplane' letters over it, hoping for a reply. One letter was returned – in a million tiny pieces. I could hear the laughter from the other side.

Among my new friends was a girl called Michelle. She had big red cheeks and a very jolly disposition. One day, she invited me to visit her house, which was on a new estate not far from my own house. A lot of new families had begun to move to Clontarf. Buildings were being erected overnight. The population was growing rapidly. I was delighted to be invited to one of the big new houses. My father had admired them in passing. They were very grand and expensive. The people who bought them were very rich, or so we thought.

I arrived at my new friend's house and knocked on the door. She came out to me and took me off to meet her other friends. There were a group of about ten. They had a large playing field in the estate and they gathered there daily. It didn't take long for me to notice there were plenty of boys around too. It was a bumbling eleven-year-old's heaven. The girls were immaculately dressed. I was envious when they appeared in pretty floral smocks, that summer's fashion rage. Some of them even had espadrilles that tied up to the knee. They looked smart and beautiful. I felt like a torn pocket. Still, it didn't seem to bother them.

Pretty soon, I was visiting the estate every day after school. It was a welcome break from the constant fighting at home. I was delighted with my new flock of friends. We shared a passion for Abba, who had recently burst on to the music scene, having won the Eurovision Song Contest with 'Waterloo'. We had never heard anything like it. Even our parents were bopping to their lively dance beats. We congregated daily at the wall – a meeting-place for all us kids. If nobody was there you didn't have to feel odd. You just sat there; eventually someone would come along. In the summer of that year there could have been up to twenty or thirty kids. Sometimes we spilled out on to the main road and walked into St Anne's. We played great games of rounders.

The boys were all members of the local Catholic Boy Scouts. To encourage the girls to have fun too, The Ventures were born. We would camp in Larch Hill. The girls would cook, the boys collected wood and did manly stuff. They were wonderful days filled with fun and excitement and the chance that someone might want you for their girlfriend. To make this possible, we realised we needed some privacy. Frequently parents would watch from their doors, wise to the sexual revolution taking place in our bodies. To escape them we constructed our very own 'den' in the back of an empty workers' yard not too far from the estate.

There we smoked cigarettes and swapped dirty jokes

which none of us understood. Most of us would have had our first innocent brush with sexual contact then. I kissed a boy for the first time after losing in a game of 'Truth or a Lie'. A piece of paper was folded up into a box-like construction and twisted backwards and forwards. When it stopped, you had to choose a particular flap and when that was lifted, you had to obey the instructions written underneath. Mine was to kiss a local boy. The kissing was not done in the den, of course. I walked down a lane and sat on an old water tank. The boy, Patrick, followed me down. He leaned forward and kissed me on the lips. Just a peck. It felt nice and warm. I was almost levitating from the thrill.

In the group, we decided to go and see *Jaws* in the Savoy cinema. I had nobody to accompany me until the day before the show, I was walking home from school when Patrick came running up behind me.

'Will you go with me?' he yelled into my face.

'OK,' I answered.

That was that. I was officially betrothed. We went to the cinema with the gang and he tried to put his hand up my skirt. I told him to get lost. The relationship ended two days and three hours later, when he ran up to me again in the same fashion after school.

'It's all off,' he yelled at me.

I was heartbroken for at least twenty minutes, until another fat little boy called Sean ran up behind me and shouted, 'Eh, will you go with me?'

'OK,' I said.

I was going with him for three weeks, although I never actually had a conversation with him in all that time. But I was going with him! I had a boyfriend! That was all that mattered. One thing was for sure; these strange specimens called 'boys' behaved very oddly indeed. My confusion lasted for some time. Twenty-nine years to be exact.

Around August of 1974, my mother called me into her bedroom and handed me a small booklet.

'Read that,' she said.

'What is it?' I asked, turning it over from back to front.

'It's about the birds and the bees,' she said.

'Oh,' I said. I went and sat on the stairs. *Girls' Talk* it was called. Published by the wonderful Catholic Association of Ireland.

'Don't read it there.' My mother whooshed me into the bedroom.

This must be interesting, I thought. I opened it up and began to read, but I couldn't make head or tail of it. I remember it saying something like God would bring the man and woman together, and through God's love and the Holy Spirit a child would be conceived. It would have been handy if it had explained exactly how the child was conceived. It omitted to tell me that. I went to ask my mam.

'Mam, what does it mean . . .'

'Read the book, love. All your questions are answered in there.'

It seemed to me that she was as confused as I was. One thing was for sure; she didn't want to enter into any long debate about it. I threw the book under the bed. That was the end of my sexual education. The rest of my knowledge was picked up under the clock-tower in St Anne's Park and the double-seaters in dark cinemas like 'The Green'.

It was unfortunate because around this time I began to feel quite 'strange'; an uncomfortable feeling had come with my changing body. Outwardly I looked like a kid but inwardly Mother Nature was a busy bee.

One day, I was sitting in class when I felt a dull ache between my legs. I shuffled and twisted but the dull ache moved on to my back and around into my tummy. I asked if I could be excused to go to 'An Leithris'. When I got there, I pulled down my pants to find a dark brown stain. I thought I had shat myself and I was embarrassed. Too embarrassed to tell my teacher. I bravely sat out the rest of the school day in my dirty pants. At home I went to the toilet again. The dark brown spot had turned into a bright red bloodstain. Christ! I thought I was dying. I was bleeding to death and didn't know what to do. I grabbed some toilet tissue and rammed it into my knickers. I was very upset. Perhaps I had cancer or something?

I decided I would have to confide in my new friend Michelle. I mounted my bike and headed for her house. The pain was still niggling me and I could feel with each movement of the bike the trickling blood oozing out of me. Michelle's mother eyed me up and down as I hobbled into their porchway. We climbed the stairs to her bedroom.

'I think I have leukaemia,' I started.

'What?' Her eyes were wide at the prospect of knowing someone who was fatally ill. 'My cousin's friend has leukaemia. She gets nosebleeds. My sister said she would bleed to death. That's what happens.' She only managed to increase my panic.

'I'm bleeding!' I burst into tears.

'I don't see any blood. Where is it?' She peered up my nostrils.

I was going to have to tell her. 'I'm bleeding down there,' I whispered, pointing between my legs.

'Out your front or your bum?' she asked.

'My front!' I blubbered.

'Sounds like leprosy to me.'

I howled even more.

At that point Michelle decided to consult her mam. She didn't want any 'bits' falling off on to the new Curragh carpet. She was gone for ages. I was sure I could hear the wail of an ambulance siren heading in this direction.

I was glad I hadn't told Mam. She would have had a heart attack. My dad would be beside himself with grief, and take his own life. Three deaths in one family were enough. I didn't want to be responsible for his as well. I was wearing my shorts and the blood had begun to seep through. If they didn't come quickly, I'd have to swim for it.

Michelle's mother burst through the door. 'What's your mother's phone number, dear?' she asked in a snotty voice.

I gave her the number.

'You have the the "monthlies", dear. Here, put this in your pants.' She dangled a Southalls Sanitary Pad in front of me, making sure not to cross the invisible line in case she got it herself.

What was it I had? Was it like the mumps or something? I went to the bathroom and put the big wedge of cottonwool into my pants. Everything was destroyed. I wanted my mam.

Ten minutes later I heard her knock at the door. I longed to run down the stairs and bury myself in her strong arms. Instead I wobbled down the staircase, unused to having something stuck between my legs. Mam was quiet. She smiled at me. I noticed she didn't have much to say to Michelle's mother. The latter didn't seem to have anything to say to either of us. I didn't care. Mam was here now and she was going to explain all of it. We walked a little down the road and then she bent down on her hunkers so she was eye-to-eye with me.

'Well, Jacqueline. I understand you became a woman today.' And she kissed me on the cheek. That was it. That was all she said. I bled for eleven days, nonstop. Mam went and bought a big packet of the nappy things. They had big loops at either end of them. I didn't ask what they were for. I just shoved them in there every few hours. When they were used, Mam instructed me to wrap them up in toilet roll, and hide them in a plastic bag in the wardrobe. When the bleeding had finally stopped, she took me and the bag into the garden. She lit a fire at the end wall. I was certain I was going to be burned at the stake like St Joan of Arc. I was a witch. I was diseased. I had some terrible affliction that had to be kept a secret. Even Dad didn't know I was sick. In reality, I was about to turn twelve years of age and I had just experienced my first period. Perhaps if Mam had taken the time to explain the facts of life to me, the whole ordeal might have been less traumatic. I needed to know the hardcore details. I needed to know I was normal. I had already accumulated enough strange feelings to isolate me from others.

The last thing I needed was to feel even more different. Now I had a bleeding 'front'. A right weirdo altogether. I never mentioned the incident to any of my friends, but from that day onwards things changed on the new estate. The girls began to treat me like an outsider. They were treating me appropriately, or so I thought. I was convinced it was because of the 'leprosy'.

I continued to call for Michelle, although her attitude was anything but friendly. I got the distinct impression it wasn't an attitude of her own making. In school, she played with me constantly. In contrast, when I called at her house, she was cool with me, and always seemed to be doing her homework. Being the young idiot that I was, I simply did not cop on. The coolness soon extended around the estate. I was finding myself sitting on the wall alone, more and more. They gathered at the other end, chatting and playing. I couldn't comprehend what was happening. The only people who seemed to show any interest in me were the boys. I didn't want the boys. I wanted to be with the girls. This went on for some weeks . . .

I put the diary down for a moment and went to the

attic window. In the back garden I could clearly see David standing close to the goldfish pond. My dad sat in supervision on the other side of the pond. I knew David's tactics. They eyeballed each other like John Wayne in the westerns. Who would crack first? Mam came in again with some strawberries and left them beside the diary. I munched a few and went back to reading.

One day, I decided to call for Michelle one last time. When I knocked at the door, I saw her mother peep from behind the curtains. Michelle came to the door, opening it only a little and jutting her nose out through the gap.

'Are you coming out, Michelle?' I asked, my voice filled with hope.

'Look, I'm sorry. My mam said I'm not allowed to play with you any more.'

I stood there. 'Oh,' was all I could manage.

She shut the door in my face.

I cried all the way down Vernon Avenue. I let myself in the back way and sat at the kitchen table crying.

'What's up with her?' Dad asked Mam. Why didn't he ask *me*?

My Mam had a silent conversation with him behind my back. You know the ones that are 'mouthed' with a few hand gestures. I distinctly saw her pointing 'down there'.

Dad cleared his throat. 'I see,' he said flatly. He opened his newspaper and started to read. I went upstairs and lay on my bed. I was extremely upset. I couldn't understand what had gone wrong. I knew Michelle liked me and I had always been polite around her mother.

I desperately wanted Mam or Dad to ask me what was wrong. I needed their help more than ever, at that delicate age. I hadn't got the sense to walk away. The rejection only spurred me on to try harder. I now sat daily at the end of the wall while the abandonment spread from family to family. Soon, I was not welcome at any of their houses, but I was not put off. I found out from the boys where they were all going each day.

They frequently went to the CRC swimming pool. I followed them alone and jumped into the pool. They ignored me and left me at the shallow end to talk to myself while they dived and splashed and played. Even in the changing rooms they left me at the other end. I stubbornly persisted. I had to. I had no explanation. I had to find one.

Through the grapevine I heard that Liz, one of the girls, was having a birthday party in her house. I was cute enough to know that if I just turned up they wouldn't send me away. So that's exactly what I did. I knocked at the door of the house that displayed balloons on its knocker. Her father answered. He greeted me coldly but invited me in. It had worked. My second real stab at defiance! It was even sweeter than the first!

Inside the house, the other kids had all arrived. I handed Liz a small present that my mother had paid for. They all looked at it as if it contained something contagious. She put it with the others. The food on the table was a glorious spread of homemade goodies. Her mam had done a fine job, making a tortoise out of rolled-up tinfoil and its spikes held cocktail sausages on the end. I was afraid to help myself. Nobody was offering me a seat, let alone anything to eat. It only occurred to me a few minutes later that I did not want to stay. I had made my point. I took my coat and left.

Thinking back on it, I was proud of myself at such a tender young age, for having the balls to do it. 'Well done, Jack!' I said to myself out loud.

Some weeks later I also invited myself to another girl's 'home disco'. It was held in their garage. I arrived clad in my tartan gear, for I had jumped on the Bay City Roller bandwagon. I wore my leather wristband that came all the way from London. It had *Eric* inscribed on it, for I was his number-one fan.

The garage had been beautifully transformed with a flashing spotlight system. The girls gathered in one corner, the boys in the other. I stood awkwardly in between them both, a place as neutral as I could find. I was duly ignored at that gathering. I wondered now where I had got the confidence from to behave so boldly. It was my old friend defiance, I suppose. I spent most of my waking hours trying to figure out what I had done to cause this latest disaster. As with every other problem in my life, it never occurred to me that I had in actual fact done nothing wrong at all!

I handled it the exact same way as I had handled all the other 'situations'. I invented something bad about myself to justify others' rotten behaviour. After all, it must have been me. It seemed I was cursed – I could do nothing right. I couldn't even make a friend. This time I decided I was very little fun to be with. That was the problem. I would have to be funnier from now on. I was too quiet, too reserved, and too damn plain. With that decision made I went about redoubling my efforts. Alas, it was all in vain. I was on a collision course with myself and had set standards that I would find impossible to meet.

Rereading this old diary, I realised with increasing alarm what I had done to myself. Once again, I had internalised others' behaviour as being my fault. This thread of self-blame ran through my entire childhood. I felt so sorry for eleven-year-old Jack, and what she had suffered. I closed the diary – I couldn't bear to read any more. I never *had* found out what had happened to cause such revulsion towards this young girl. Looking back at it now, I couldn't accept that it had anything to do with having my first period. It seemed so ridiculous now, although at the time it appeared to be the logical explanation. It was a mystery that had never been solved. However, there was someone who might be able to throw some light on it . . .

I closed the suitcase and tied it up with the scarf. I went downstairs. Mam was sitting at the kitchen table reading a knitting pattern. David was out the back with Dad. Every now and then I could hear Dad roar at him.

'Mam, can I ask you something?' I sat down and lit up a cigarette.

'Go on,' she said, a note of hesitancy in her voice that warned: *Don't ask me something that might upset us all.*

'Do you remember the new estate up the road? I used to hang out there when I was eleven or twelve.'

'I remember it well. How can I ever forget it?' she said with anger. This surprised me.

'How come you remember it well?' I was intrigued.

'Oh, that bloody bitch Mrs What-was-her-name. You know, Michelle's mother.'

'Mrs Hand?' I offered.

'That's the one. A right fucking bitch. God forgive me!' she blessed herself quickly. 'Don't you remember she forbade her daughter to play with you?' Mam looked at me like I had three heads.

'Of course I do. I just wondered, do you know why? Why did she do that? That whole experience destroyed me,' I said, a tear forming in my eye.

'I know very well how it affected you, love. Don't you remember your father going up to see her?' she asked.

'He did?' I was shocked.

'Oh yes, indeed, he did. I ordered him to go, when we saw you traipsing around after them like a lost sheep. We knew something had gone wrong. Your dad asked you what the matter was and you told him what that bitch had said.'

'I did?'

'Fucking cow, God forgive me. Do you know what she said in her defence? It was a private estate! Only for the boys and girls that lived there! You know what she really meant, though?' Mam looked at me, fire in her eyes. 'My daughter wasn't good enough to play with her daughter. That's what she was really trying to say. In other words, we weren't as well off as them. Well! Your father gave it to her right between the eyes. "My daughter will go where she pleases. She has as much right to play here as anywhere else," he said to her. The old bitch nearly fell in her standing,' she finished.

I was absolutely flabbergasted. 'I never knew he did that.' I wiped the tear from my cheek.

'Oh, he did. To be sure, to be sure. And he said a lot more besides. She was always polite to him after that. "Hello, Mr Joyce. How are you, Mr Joyce?" Your father never forgot it; he taught her a thing or two in manners. All the money in the world they had, but no manners.'

I went to the back window. Dad was holding a pitchfork in his hand and threatening to poke David up the arse with it. I smiled to myself. I remembered what Brian had said at the last session.

'What's Beirut for one child could be *The Little House on the Prairie* for another.'

Now I understood what he meant. Every child is different. Children perceive their surroundings differently. I had lived in Beirut for so long that *The Little House on the Prairie* was still only a television programme.

Mam and Dad *had* cared about me, *had* loved me – despite all I had thought and felt as a child. I was now willing to admit that I had not been able to see that. I had come to some pretty lousy conclusions as a child. I was wrong about them. I could see it now, and that was all that mattered.

Chapter 16

It was late November in 1993. It had been a very eventful year so far. I had just completed my seventh session of the course. Matt and I had taken to having coffee afterwards almost every week. He still maintained enough distance to keep me dangling. I didn't mind. It was only a matter of time.

I was completely immersed in the course. The group had opened up as Matt had predicted. We had even had moments of rapturous laughter. The mid-term break had served us all well. I was busy preparing for Christmas and felt almost contented with life.

Karen and Michael agreed to call over for an evening, along with Joe, who was home again on a weekend cheapie. There was no mention of Jill. I was looking forward to seeing them. I tried my best to clean the flat up and enlisted Alice's help. Before she came, though, I gathered all the empty cans and bottles and filled three black sacks. I didn't want her to see them so I crept out at night and dumped them outside the gate. Alice had become very fond of 'the little fat fucker' and had begun to call him 'Spud'. I didn't like nicknames at the best of times, but in this case I was prepared to make an exception.

She arrived at the door laden down with Jif and Mr Sheen. 'Who's coming, love – the fucking Pope?'

'Don't be silly. Come in. You know there's no need for you to do any of this.'

'Ah, fuck off, will you? The place is like a kip. You're a dirty bitch, do you know that?' She barged into the bathroom. 'Holy Jaysus, a nacker wouldn't live here.' She bent down and started to scrub.

I joined in, feeling embarrassed. Even by Alice's standards I had let the place go to pot. I continued turning up empty bottles and cans. I gathered everything I could see and began assigning things to certain places. The walls had become yellowed from cigarette smoke, especially in my bedroom. I vowed to have the whole place painted, as soon as I had the money. I was excited and in good form. I had planned to cook for us all. I decided to ask Alice for a good recipe.

'Is the ride coming?' she asked.

'Yes. What do you think he would like to eat?'

'Ah, you're not falling for that shite, are you? The way to a man's heart is through his stomach? Bolloxology. The way to a man's heart is through his Mickey, love. God knows, haven't I been on me knees often enough to prove it?'

'Alice!' I couldn't help laughing. 'I am not trying to win Joe's heart. We're friends, that's all. I'm having all my friends over for dinner.'

'Could have fooled me, love. All this fucking carry-on. For friends now, is it? Why don't you just shag the bastard and be done with it? A fine young fella like that going to waste.'

'Alice! He is not going to waste. He has just broken up with his girlfriend in London. The last thing he needs is casual sex. Besides, I think those particular needs are being met elsewhere,' I said angrily. I wasn't going to let my emotions get in the way. I wanted Joe's friendship in whatever context that meant.

'Bollox!' she shouted. 'A good ride is what he wants. Gets the tension out of them. Take my Eddie, for instance. Lost his job. Banged the arse off me for weeks. I couldn't bend over and he was on top of me.'

'Alice, can we change the subject, please?'

She continued working, scrubbing the walls, the floors, whistling away to herself. Even the children joined in. David got a toothbrush and scrubbed the taps. Other children gathered in the kitchen and swept the floors. They only succeeded in making things worse. Soon there was hardly room to move around.

Alice put them straight. 'Here! What in the name of Jaysus are you's doing? Get the fuck out and clean your own homes! And clean yourselves while you're at it. The smell of shite of you's is cruel! Go on – scarper!'

The children giggled and made a run for it. Alice chased them with the brush. David thought the word 'shite' was hilarious. He walked around and around in circles, repeating, 'Shite! Shite! Shite!'

By early evening the flat resembled something like a home. I had bought some flowers and a tablecloth. There was a nice chicken casserole in the oven. The smell drifted through the rooms. I had wine cooling in the fridge and David had just nodded off. I had dressed up nicely, and put on some make-up. I was determined to make the evening a success. When a knock came at the door, I ran out. It was Alice. I could see the others getting out of a taxi.

Ah Christ. Not now, Alice.

'Listen love,' the big woman told me, 'if you need anything, I'm only next door, if you want to go down to the local, like.'

'Eh, thanks, Alice, but I don't think we'll have the time.'

Too late, they were at the door. I saw a fourth person

trailing up behind. For a moment I thought it might
be Juliet. I was delighted to see it wasn't. Then the
familiar silhouette of Jill came into view. My delight
plummeted. My stomach churned. It was my worst nightmare come true.

'It's you,' I said stunned.

The others let out a yahoo. I had to act fast. *No problem.
I can handle it. I can handle it.*

'The bastards! They didn't tell me you were coming.
Are you home for long? Oh Christ, it's so good to see
you!' I squeezed her until she could hardly breathe.

'Hold it! Hold it! I wanted to surprise you,' she splut-
tered, trying to loosen my grip.

*Surprise me? Well, you've certainly done that. How all per-
fectly convenient, convivial and fucking fantastic.* I looked at
Joe from over her shoulder. He was smiling stupidly from
ear to ear. *You must think I was born yesterday, you bastard!*

I had completely forgotten about Alice. I decided it
would be better to introduce her, rather than leave her
on the doorstep.

'This is Alice,' I told them all. 'She's my neighbour and
my friend. Alice, you already know Joe.'

'Howya, love.' She winked at him.

'And this is Jill, another friend of mine. Jill lives in
England. We haven't seen each other for quite some time.
We have a lot of catching up to do, haven't we, Jill?' My
voice quivered with repressed anger.

They all shook hands. That only left us to go indoors.
Alice stood standing, grinning from ear to ear and chewing mechanically on her cigarette.

'Well, let's go inside,' I said. Hoping she would get the
hint. She didn't.

'Hey, why don't you join us for a drink?' Karen suggested. I could have strangled her. She didn't understand.
Alice wasn't like us.

'Ah thanks, love!' Alice was absolutely thrilled.

Joe was hiding a smirk behind his hand. It was a long time since he had smirked. I was grateful for that, but was still grappling with the thoughts of who had put it there. Perhaps Alice being there wasn't such a bad idea after all?

Inside, I poured everyone drinks.

'What's that smell?' Karen asked.

'What smell?' I shouted in from the kitchen. 'A bleachy smell?' Jill nodded in agreement. 'I was cleaning!' I replied, topping up my glass again.

I returned with drinks for everybody. 'Alice, what would you like? Wine, vodka? The wine is nice. It's a rounded full-bodied red.'

'Ah, not for me, love. Sounds like something you'd stick up your hole. A can of beer will do. Where did you say you were from, love?'

Jill was trying hard not to choke on her drink.

'Em, I'm from Dublin.' Karen was in agony trying to keep a straight face.

Joe had to leave the room.

I was furious. I didn't mind her crude banter, but not in front of my friends.

'I've been living in the South of England for the last few years.'

'Lovely, lovely, and what do you do there?'

'Oh. I'm an air hostess,' Jill answered in her extra-polite voice.

Oh, look at *me*! I parroted angrily. I'm an *air hostess*! I'm so fucking dazzling, doesn't it hurt your eyes just to look at me?

'An air hostess, is it? And sure haven't you got the looks and all to go with it? Sure 'tis only another name for a glorified waitress, isn't it, love?'

I drained my glass and refilled it in horror. I went to

check on the casserole. It was well done. Now what? I supposed I'd have to feed her too. Fuck it! Fuck it!

To my amazement the gang didn't seem in the least bit perturbed by Alice's comments. She had settled in. The slippers were off and she was yapping away to Jill. This only fuelled my anger.

Joe appeared at the kitchen door. 'Need any help?' he asked.

'Which kind?' I remarked snidely.

'Ah, don't panic, Jack. She's not doing any harm to anyone. Here, give me the carving knife before you do any damage.'

I was trying to slice up some garlic bread but kept burning my hands. I went to refill their glasses but they hadn't even finished their first. I was on my fourth. I set the table for six places. I had to take David's baby chair from his room. I would sit on that. Dinner was served and I could hardly swallow a mouthful.

'This is lovely,' Mick said. That meant it was really good. Mick hardly ever made a comment about anything.

'Yes, it is lovely,' Jill agreed.

Joe was shovelling it into his mouth. No need to ask what he thought.

'Massive,' Alice said, with her mouth full.

After dinner I poured some more wine. I had already drunk a bottle myself.

I put on some music. Alice was really getting into the swing of it while I was becoming more and more sullen. I wanted to be alone with 'my' friends. I especially wanted to kill Jill.

But Alice wasn't budging. The night was ruined.

'Now tell me this, love,' she addressed Mick. 'These antibiotics you were talking about, Arguementan.'

'Augmenten,' Joe corrected her.

Sweet Jesus. I went back into the kitchen and opened the

bottle of vodka. Nobody had wanted any. Well, I wasn't going to let it go to waste. There were plenty of cans too, in the fridge. I had a quick straight vodka and opened another can of beer. I drank half it and topped up the rest with vodka. When I checked on David, he was fast asleep. I heard peals of laughter coming from the sitting room. It made me angry. Everybody was having a good time, at my expense.

I couldn't think of a good excuse to get rid of Alice. Couldn't she take a hint? I knew they were only being polite for my sake. I was certain of it. They were probably completely browned off with her. They'd never come back again, not after tonight. I was ashamed of Alice. Shitehawk! It was all right to have her around when I needed her. I had wanted tonight to be special. When I saw Jill it was the straw that broke the camel's back. Now Alice was in there with her, taking over. I was determined to get Alice out of the flat. I had the courage now. I was going to put Joe and Jill on the spot. I had a right to know what was going on. I marched back in, a little tipsy and the door slammed off the wall. There was a lull in the conversation, but then they started up again.

'Jack. Sit down, for God's sake.' Jill motioned me to come and join her. She was sitting on the floor with her glass half-empty. It was the same glass of wine I had given her when she arrived.

'I'll just top up your drink first.' I tried to take her glass.

She covered it with her hand. 'No thanks, Jack. I'm OK.'

I was annoyed. The least she could do was appreciate my hospitality. 'Anyone else ready for a top up?' I looked around the room.

Alice held out her glass.

I snatched it angrily from her hand and stormed out. In the kitchen I fixed myself another handmade cocktail. Joe appeared at the door again.

'What the hell is wrong with you?' he asked.

'Nothing!' I said. My voice was high-pitched. A dead giveaway.

'Jack, what's wrong. You're like a bull in a chinashop!' He reached out to me and I pushed his hand away.

'I just wanted to spend some time with my friends, that's all. I can't even get that right.' I slammed the bottle down on the counter.

'What are you on about? We're all here. Why don't you stop running in and out of the kitchen and come and spend some time with us?'

'I can't!' I snarled. 'Lady Muck has taken over. Jesus, does she not know when she's not wanted?' I heard some footsteps.

'I'll be off now.' It was Alice. She stood at the door awkwardly.

'OK,' I said coolly, leaving her to find her own way out. I heard the door slam.

'For Christ's sake, Jack. Could you not at least have seen her to the door?'

Now Joe was getting on my wick. I stormed into the other room, where Mick, Karen and Jill were sitting silently. They looked at me like I had two heads. I couldn't stand it any more.

'What? *What?*' I roared at them.

Joe followed me back in.

'That's it. That's it, Jack. Enough is enough,' Jill said as Karen gathered their coats.

'What's fucking wrong with everyone?' I shouted.

Mick tut tutted.

'Jack, your behaviour is disgraceful. That poor woman. You made her feel so unwelcome,' Jill said coldly. She was zipping up her jacket.

'What!' I threw my hands in the air in disbelief. 'Look, she wasn't invited. I wanted to have a quiet night – just

us. For God's sake! She embarrassed the hell out of me!'
I tried to defend myself.

'She didn't embarrass us,' Mick put in.

I was really surprised at him.

'Karen!' I turned to Karen for support.

'Sorry, Jack. I'm out of here. I can't take any more of
this shit. It's the same thing every time. You do it *every
time*. I'm sick of it!'

She was getting angry now, I could sense it.

'What the fuck are you talking about? Sick of what? You
know, you all come over here and behave like fucking
saints, then you leave. None of you gives a fucking damn
about me and David, what we have to cope with!' I was
shouting at the top of my voice now.

'Shut up, for Christ's sake. You'll wake David.' Joe
glared at me.

I walked right up to his face. 'Since when did you give a
fuck about me or David? You're not his father or anything
and you've no right to speak to me like that in my own
house!'

Joe had gone beyond the point of reasoning. He pushed
me away from him. I lost my footing and fell backwards
on to the floor.

'Look at yourself, Jack. You're drunk again,' Jill put in
for good measure. Karen and Mick nodded their heads.
Now they were all ganging up on me.

'Oh, put a fucking sock in it, Jill. Do you think I'm a
complete idiot? The two of you marching in here, like
we're all good buddies. Do you think I'm blind and deaf
and dumb too?' I screamed.

Joe, Karen, Mick and Jill all stared at each other, looking
for an explanation.

'What the fuck are you on about?' Joe asked. Now he
was getting red in the face.

'You and Jill!' I screeched.

Karen threw her hands up in the air. 'Huh?'

Then Joe proceeded with his devastating words. 'I don't know what you're thinking about, but let me say something now. So I don't care, is that right, Jack? I'm not his father, is that right? You fucked-up little bitch. Who was the one who stayed with you all through the birth, who was the one who talked to you, and helped you through your pregnancy? Was there someone else there that I don't know about? You're so self-centred. Always thinking of yourself! You're not the only one who's struggling, you know. What makes *you* so fucking special?' He threw his hands up in exasperation, and for a moment I thought he was going to punch me right in the face. 'If anybody cared about you,' he raved on, 'it's me! Do you think anyone else would tolerate your sad little life this long – huh? You're sick, Jack. You're sick, and you need help and until you get it, lose my phone number. I'm washing my hands of you from now on.' He grabbed his coat and made for the door.

'You're jealous!' I lunged at him. 'You've always been jealous – because you couldn't have me for yourself. You're jealous because I'm seeing Matt, because I'm getting my life together. You've always resented my feelings for Matt. You can't handle it, so you had to strike back like a rattlesnake, dirty and low, and get together with Jill.'

Joe started to laugh at me. 'Is that right? You selfish little moron! I've always tried to protect you from Matt. You're such a stubborn self-righteous know-it-all that you won't listen. You won't heed your own friends' good advice!'

Karen was nodding in agreement. Jill lunged forward and lashed her hand out at me. Mick stood between us to try and intervene. I struggled to get free of his grip. I would have torn her hair out.

'C'mon, you're wasting your time. I think it's time to go.' Mick took charge.

Jill was out of breath but pulled back. Joe opened the front door. I wasn't letting them go. I had never heard Joe speak to me that way before. Not ever. It frightened me.

I had to stop him from leaving. I *had* to.

'I know I have a problem,' I cried out.

Joe stopped and turned around.

'I know I have a problem,' I repeated, more quietly. 'I intend to do something about it.'

Joe was still furious, his eyes flashing with anger. The others were urging him to move on. He desperately needed to hear me say something that would fix this.

'I'm joining Weight Watchers,' I lied. 'I'll do it on Monday. I know I have an eating disorder. I've known it for some time. That's what makes me drink so much. I wouldn't drink so much if I could get a handle on my weight.' There that ought to do it.

'*What*?' they all said in disgusted unison.

'This is fucking unreal!' Karen started to laugh hysterically.

Joe's expression was indescribable. His eyes welled with tears. It was clearly obvious he was extremely upset.

'You do that, Jack,' he sighed. 'You do that. Join Weight Watchers. If that's what your problem is, then go ahead and solve it. If it's as simple as all that, then go for it.'

I hadn't lost a single pound for weeks. I had no intention of ever going to Weight Watchers. It was the only thing I could think of to stop this horrible nightmare. Jill was crying openly. Mick was trying to remove Joe from the flat.

Joe paused in the doorway. 'By the way, what's there to be jealous of – this stinking existence you call your life? Nothing was ever good enough for you. Stay the drunken bum that you are, Jack. I don't give a fiddler's fuck if you drink yourself to death. Just don't involve me any more,' he spat. Then he walked down the steps.

'Shame on you, Jack.' Jill was weeping. 'Shame on you.'

I saw Alice's curtain draw back slightly. It was all *her* fault, I thought savagely. If she hadn't stuck her big fucking nose into my personal life, none of this would be happening. I wanted to knock on her door and tell her exactly what I thought of her.

I hated this godforsaken place. I hated Alice. I hated David. I hated Joe.

How dare he speak to me like that? After all the time and effort I had put into our friendship in the last few weeks. Just because his relationship had fallen apart, that didn't give him an excuse to take it out on me. I went back inside and fixed myself a drink, at the same time turning the music up to full volume. I didn't care if it woke David or any of the neighbours. God knows, I had to listen to their fucking parties, night after night.

Typical Jill. Only home three seconds and straight in with her 'holier than thou' bullshit. She made me sick. Miss fucking Prim and Proper. Her life was so simple. No kids. No bills. No housework. What the fuck would she know about anything? They had probably been talking about me behind my back. As for Karen and Michael, they lived in the twilight zone. They had each other. They were cute whores too. No children or mortgages. They didn't know what it was like to be alone, night after night, when the only conversation available was with a five-year-old kid and the forty-year-old illiterate twat next door. How could they be so cruel?

'Fuck them! Fuck 'em all!' I ranted. 'I don't have any reason to feel ashamed. They are the ones who should be ashamed!' Destroying the night like that, after all the trouble I had gone to. Jesus Christ! The fucking nerve of Joe, speaking to me like that about Matt. It was obvious that he was bitter. He was always trying to fill my head with stories about Matt. Trying to put me off. It wasn't out of friendly concern, either. Jesus, I wouldn't like to be in his shoes now.

'I'm not doing anything about this situation,' I said loudly to the room. 'I'm just going to sit pretty and they'll all be begging my forgiveness in the morning. When they do, I'm not going to give in, either.'

As soon as I could manage it, I was going to get as far away from this place as I could. I had never belonged there. It was all right to talk to Alice once in a while. After all, she was my neighbour – I had to be polite. But I shouldn't have let her into my life. I had invited her in for a cup of tea and now she was living in my ear!

I wished I'd never had David. I wouldn't be living in this godforsaken kip if it wasn't for him. Now my two best friends had gotten together behind my back and abandoned me into the bargain. I was filled with an overwhelming rage. It surged through me like an overdose of cocaine. I got all my CDs and records and laid them out on the floor. Then I went to the kitchen drawer and drew out the largest, sharpest knife I could find – the bread knife.

Yes. This will do the job nicely.

One by one, I slowly carved into the CDs, drawing circles, squares. Then lunging at them like a madwoman, tearing into them as deeply as I could. I ripped. I hacked. I stabbed. I stood up and threw them all about the room. I picked up the leftover glasses and smashed them at the wall. It felt great. The noise was deafening. The music blared. The hatred spilled. I was running out of objects to destroy.

As I stood in the centre of the room looking around me, I was like a wild woman scanning the place for new objects on which to unleash my wrath. My breathing was rapid and my body shook from head to toe. Suddenly, I heard loud thumping on the walls from the flat on my other side.

'Go fuck yourself!' I screamed, picking up the table. I smashed it against the wall and the broken fragments flew through the air. I was completely out of control. I heard the bedroom door creak. Who was that? A neighbour? The bastards were after getting in. I picked up a broken leg of the table and burst out into the hall.

David was standing in his pyjamas tearfully clutching his Action Man. 'I want my granny,' he whispered, tears cascading down his cheeks.

I stared at him, wondering who he was. *Who is this child?* Then it stopped. Just as suddenly as it had started, the hurricane abated.

'David,' I said calmly. He stood motionless, his face white with fear. He was trembling from head to foot. His pyjamas were soaking wet. He had pissed in them. A pool was forming beneath his feet. He stood in it shaking and crying.

'I want my granny,' he whispered again.

Slowly, I began to return. I could feel my body return into itself, as if it had been astral travelling. As if it had taken flight. It had visited Hell and was slowly slipping back into my skin. Suddenly, my limbs felt sore, my arms ached. I looked at my hands. They were cut and bleeding.

What the fuck happened? Were we mugged?

I stood there amidst the destruction. The broken table, the smashed glasses, the CDs scattered everywhere. Even the cushions had been lacerated, their downy feathers still fluttering in the air. Somebody had gone crazy. Somebody had destroyed my home.

Some madman had run amok and wrecked our flat. I picked up the CDs and looked at them. They were mine: I had spent a lifetime collecting them. Splinters of glass lay sprinkled on the carpet; now and again, big chunks of it came into view. I collected a few in my hand and looked at them. Then I carefully placed them in the kitchen bin. It would take me for ever to clean all this up. What had happened? Where had I been?

I suddenly felt so, so tired. I sat on the edge of the broken table and I looked at the boy. He was my child, wasn't he? Perhaps he was hungry, or thirsty.

He stood there staring at me.

'David, what on earth are you doing out of bed?' I asked him.

He turned on his heel and walked back into his room. I laid my head on the floor. I was so, so tired. Just then, I spotted a yellow object, stuck down beside the heater. I reached over and pulled it out. It was Sam.

Joe, don't leave me. Don't leave me like this.

I squeezed his hand. 'Old MacDonald had a farm, ee-i, ee-i, o. And on that farm he had some . . .

Chapter 17

I am thirty years old and have just graduated with Honours in my chosen subject of 'Escapology'. I am convinced that I am right and the whole world is wrong. There are no exceptions, grey areas, maybes, ifs, buts or anything else.

I awoke the morning after with the worst hangover of my life. My eyes were glued together. When I did manage to open them, my vision was blurred and limited. I wanted to die there and then. At that stage, I had only taken in the horrors of my hangover. In the minutes that followed, my brain launched a further invective, bombarding me with the details of the terrible night before.

I cursed loudly, trying to pull the non-existent covers over my head. That's when I realised I was sleeping on the kitchen table. Then I remembered I had a son. I pulled my body up and tried to stand on my two feet. A sharp pain shot through both legs and my hands felt swollen and sore. I looked at them in shock. They were bandaged, very badly, with bits of toilet roll that had hardened with blood and adhered to my fingers.

My legs were black and blue from bruising, as if someone had spent the night kicking me. I was terrified to look in the mirror, but I knew I had to.

It wasn't my face, or anything like it. What had happened? I could remember the argument with Joe, and I vaguely recollected them leaving. I couldn't remember anything else after that. It frightened me. The absence of David's voice only fuelled my anxiety.

I walked to his room. His bed was empty and a pair of soggy pyjamas lay in a heap on the floor. My stomach began to rise with fright. I fled to the toilet and puked into it. Nothing came up, but the dry retching continued. I tried to light a cigarette but it only made me want to vomit again.

Jesus Christ. David, where are you? Sweet Jesus, please fill me in, because I think I am losing my mind. Please tell me what has happened? Where the fuck is David?

Confusion and terror had come at me with a terrible force. Shaking and weeping, I searched each room thoroughly, calling out for him.

'David? David! Where are you? For Christ's sake answer me!'

The doorbell rang and I raced to open it.

'Registered letter, Mam.' The postman thrust a large clipboard under my nose. I signed it just to get rid of him. Then I threw the brown envelope on the ground.

The doorbell rang again. I ran at it like an animal, tripping over some of David's toys. I opened the door and there stood Alice, with David. He was washed and dressed, and stood holding her hand.

'David!' I squealed, pulling him to me. He didn't react the way he usually did. No hugs. No kisses. He maintained a blank expression and an even less emotive response. 'What the hell is going on?' I turned on Alice.

'You weren't in the best, love,' the big woman tried to explain. 'David knocked at the door so I took him inside and I . . .'

'Who the fuck do you think you are!' I screamed at her, grabbing David's arm. 'Get in here this minute!' I told him.

'Listen, love—' Alice tried to intervene but I slammed the door shut in her face. David stood in the hall staring at me, then he turned on his heel and went inside.

I looked at my watch. It was 10.30 am. Too late to send him to school. I knew from my earlier look in the mirror that I couldn't have gone out the door anyway. I phoned my job and told them I had a sore throat. I did a very good impression of a hoarse voice, all thanks to my yelling and the forty cigarettes I had smoked the night before. Then I went inside to David, who was sitting on the couch watching *Sesame Street*, clutching his Thomas the Tank Engine.

I was in no mood for humouring him. Besides, if I started to get into all that guilt, I was as good as dead. One small chink in the armour could have sent me reeling with remorse and regret. I couldn't remember half the details of the previous night and this frightened me. No, there was no room for any of that. Anyway, any minute now, the phone was going to start ringing. They would all be on their knees. I had already made the decision that I would not accept the first apology. Perhaps not even the second. It all depended on how good the grovelling was.

I made some tea and toast for David. He accepted it calmly, still not speaking to me. Fuck you, you little bastard, I thought. See if I care. Fuck all of you!

I had a small shot of vodka and managed to keep it down. I didn't really want a drink, but I knew it would ease the horrific hangover. I then took two Anadin Extra. About a half hour later I was beginning to feel slightly human again. I made some coffee and lit a cigarette. Then I sat down beside the phone, and waited.

That was Tuesday morning. By Friday night, the Ice Queen had begun to thaw. I had gone through every emotion known to mankind. Rage would overwhelm me. When it had run its course, it would slowly begin to dissipate. Then I would plunge into a terrible depression and sob for hours into my pillow. Then the justifying would start again and the rage would follow. I was up and down like a whore's knickers. Going around and around in circles. Poring over every detail until I had myself completely insane. I found it almost impossible to sleep at night. As time passed, I realised very slowly that nobody was going to call. As with all these situations, when the shock began to wear off, I wondered how I had ever thought they would.

I was completely stunned at their behaviour, never mind my own. What had happened to cause such an exaggerated response from them all? We had had our tiffs in the past, but this was completely beyond the beyonds. Had they all been drinking on the sly themselves? I could excuse Jill. She was away most of the time and didn't really know what she was talking about. She was always anti-drugs and drink. Her outburst came as no surprise. She was responsible at least in part for my return to Ireland.

Nobody could have listened to her day in, day out, complaining. All I was doing was having a good time. There was absolutely nothing wrong with that! I still couldn't prove that she and Joe were having a fling. The mere thought of this justified everything I had done. I was entitled to be angry! It was *me* who had been hurt!

As for Karen and Mick, their behaviour was outrageous. They hardly ever called to see me any more. I decided that wasn't my fault either. They never bothered to keep in touch with me. They were happy being together, made a point of rubbing it in. However, it was Joe's words that ricocheted around my brain late at night. How could he be so cruel? How could he have called me those things?

I was anything but selfish. I was raising David alone. It was very difficult. Sure, he had been there for me as

a friend, but not all the time. I was doing most of the
hard work. He had called me a 'fucked-up little bitch'.
I couldn't erase the words from my mind, no matter how
hard I tried. They hurt so much I thought I would die
from the pain.

Fucked up little bitch.
Fucked up little bitch.
Fucked up little bitch.

To make matters worse, he had left it like that. I was
certain that he would phone soon; he just needed time to
see how wrong he was.

Another seven days passed. I was desperate. I had
picked up the phone several times to call Joe. When I
heard the dial tone, I would quickly put the phone down.
I had now come to the conclusion that it was a conspiracy.
They had all gotten together and made a pact. Then I came
up with an even better theory. They had all been killed in
a car crash on the way home. There had to be some logical
explanation for this unbearable silence. I spent the days
in a drunken fog. Not caring to stop, not daring to try. If I
was a drunk, then I was going to do the job properly. I was
going to be a spectacular drunk. A drunk with character,
with finesse! I'd give 'em something to talk about!

I wandered around the flat during the day, hovering
about the telephone. It only rang three times in the two
weeks. The first time it was Mam, wanting to know would
I come over for tea. She sounded a bit worried about me. I
couldn't face her or Dad or anything remotely connected
to the family. When I had run out of reasons to blame my
friends for my predicament, I turned back to the original
source, my family. A little voice tried to tell me that it
wasn't their fault, either, but I quickly dealt with it by
drinking some more.

The second phone-call was from Alice. She didn't get
past saying, 'Hello.' If she hadn't the nerve to knock on

my door, then I wouldn't tolerate her on the phone. The third call was from the job. It was the union shop steward informing me that Gerard Shannon was issuing me with a written warning. A second one, and I was sure to be suspended without pay. I hardly batted an eyelid. I didn't care if I never worked again.

I tried to busy myself fixing up the flat. I gathered the debris and broken items and placed them all in a big black sack. I managed to fix the table by sticking the legs together with masking tape. It looked ridiculous but it had to do. I warded off the nagging voice that asked: *What happened?* Don't think about it, I told myself. It will go away if I don't think about it. I attended to David's needs. The bare essentials. He didn't seem to give a shit whether I was there or not. The feeling was mutual. I went through the motions, I was on autopilot. Days turned into nights, nights turned into days. I had no sense of time any more, what day it was, what week it was. I was living in a suspended time capsule, where nothing could be measured in terms of reality. A fog had descended and dulled my senses. I was very contented with that. Sooner or later, someone had to come and get me, didn't they?

Nearly two weeks after the big confrontation, my phone rang again. I answered it in my perfected helpless victim voice. It was Matt Howard.

'Jack? Is that you?' he asked.

'Yes,' I said pitifully.

'Where have you been? There's only two sessions of the course left,' he said, genuine concern in his voice.

'I don't care about the course, Matt.' I really *didn't* care about anything. It was the truth.

'What's wrong, Jack? You were doing so well.'

Was I? Was I really?

'Let me come over and talk to you.'

Oh God. Don't do that. I won't be responsible for my actions.

'I don't think that would be a good idea.' *Please come over. I would love nothing more.*

'Look, I'm worried about you. I promise I won't try to persuade you to come back to the course or anything. Just let me come over and sit with you for a while. C'mon, what do you say?'

'OK,' I said finally. I gave him the address. I was disappointed to learn I had missed a session. It all seemed so hazy, like something I had participated in years ago. All I wanted was to end my confusion, put a stop to my restlessness. I wanted my friends back, but I wasn't going to degrade myself any further. Matt's phone-call was like a shining beacon in a stormy sea. I got myself ready. I was cheeky enough to shave my legs. Then I shaved my bikini line. Just in case. Then I shaved under my arms. What was I thinking of? I was deliberately setting out to seduce him. He was in Rome now. He would have to do as the Romans did. I had watched *I, Claudius*. I was no fool.

Around 9 pm Matt arrived at the door looking stupendous. I was startled at his fresh complexion and jovial mood as he stepped inside. I offered him a drink, which I knew he would refuse.

'No, thanks,' he said, almost revelling in the opportunity to say no.

I poured myself a large vodka and coloured it with orange.

'Thanks for letting me come over,' he started.

'I'm OK. As you can see.' I gave him my best smile ever.

He was looking around him and rubbing his chin. 'What happened here? A hurricane?' He was pointing to the broken table.

I was hoping the expensive make-up was adequately

covering my burning cheeks. 'Oh that!' I exclaimed, over-doing it a little. 'It was David! You know yourself, they break everything!'

He smiled. 'He did a good job all the same. A hammer couldn't have done it better.'

I detected a slight grain of sarcasm. 'Well, it's had a few accidents actually.' I tried to cover up. I was searching desperately for some decent music to play. The best CDs had been destroyed. I pushed the on-going question to the back of my mind, the question that kept waking me up in the middle of the night. The same question that remained unanswered. *What had happened that night after the gang had left?* It gnawed at me like a caged hamster. Most of it was blacked out. I just couldn't remember what I had done or said after they had left.

'What are you thinking?' Matt interrupted my thoughts.

'Oh nothing, it's nothing.' I waved my hand. I eventu-ally had to settle for Dean Martin. I put the CD in and turned it on. It sounded stupid. It was a Christmas present that Mam had given me last year. This was probably its début performance.

'Since when did you like Dean Martin?' Matt asked in disbelief.

'I've found that when I'm writing for the course, or painting you know, that I like this kind of background music,' I lied through my teeth. He seemed to buy it. I sat down beside him and looked him straight in the eye. 'Well, have I missed anything interesting on the course?'

'Yes. Actually, last week's session was very interesting. Poor Bertie got another going-over – it was from Frank this time.'

'He needs it. Every bit of it.' I sounded like a profes-sionally trained counsellor. 'A Fixer, if ever I laid eyes on one. Fair fucks to Frank. God, he's really doing well, isn't he?'

'He certainly is. It's amazing to see how fast he is coming on.' Matt sipped his orange. I lowered my drink in one gulp.

'Matt, when we were in the coffee shop that time, and Margaret walked in, do you remember?'

'Yes. I remember.' He gave me a dazzling smile.

I found it hard to stop myself from diving on him there and then, but thought, *Wait for it, girl. Mohammed has come to the mountain. He is in my home, on my territory. There is no need to rush. I have waited so long for this moment. I am going to enjoy every single bit of it.*

I sidled up beside him on the floor. He was sitting on the couch, his legs slightly apart. I casually laid my elbow on his knee.

'For so long I've wanted to tell you how I felt all those years ago when we were down on the beach.'

'Now's your chance,' he said, lifting his hand to push my hair behind my ear. My whole face tingled with his soft touch.

'You know, I was expecting something different,' I told him.

He smiled knowingly. 'So did I. God, what a pair of idiots! We really didn't know what we were doing, did we?'

I laughed. 'Well, you were the man. I expected you to know everything.'

We were both laughing. I was loving every single second of it. I wanted it to last for ever and ever. I wanted another drink, too, but no way was I going to ruin this opportunity. We were very close now. A few inches were all that separated us.

'You know, I'm very grateful to you, Jack. It was you who taught me to face up to what I really am.'

I was flattered to say the least. 'I did?' I looked up into his eyes. His lips were inviting me, wide and beautiful. I wanted so much to just reach up and kiss him gently.

'Yes,' he whispered into my ear. 'If it wasn't for you, and that whole experience down on the beach, I would probably have been another ten years finding out the truth.'

He's in love with me. I knew it! He has always been in love with me!

'Go on,' I urged him, placing my hand on his.

'I tried so hard to hide it, to pretend, always hoping it would go away. I dated so many other women. How naive of me! Looking back now, it was so obvious. I had always been gay.'

Excuse me? I stared at him. 'What?'

'Jack! Don't tell me you didn't know I'm gay!'

I was paralysed from the neck down. 'Jesus Christ almighty,' was all I could manage.

Matt reached out to me and put his arms around me. I was frozen solid with shock.

'But . . . but . . . you're married!'

'Lots of gay people are married.'

'You have children.'

'Lots of gay people have children.'

'They do?' I asked innocently.

'Margaret and I decided very early on that we would stay together for the sake of the children.'

I kept staring at him. 'Matt, don't you know that I have spent the best part of my life in love with you?'

'You only think you are in love with me. You are in love with a memory, that's all, Jack. You are in love with being in love.'

'You led me on, Matt. You must have known!' I was starting to cry now.

'Jack, I swear I thought you knew. Everybody knows I'm gay!'

'You mean, everybody except me,' I sobbed. Then I remembered Joe's cautioning. He had known all along. He had tried to protect me after all.

Ah Christ.

'I can't handle this,' I said, grappling with the couch to get up off the floor. 'I can't handle this, I fucking can't!' I ran into the kitchen and took the bottle of vodka. My hand shook. I poured some into a glass, spilling most of it on to the table.

Matt appeared at the door. 'It's not the end of the world,' he said gently.

I stared at him like he was a total stranger. Who was this guy? I didn't know him? He wasn't my Matt. Surely, any minute now he was going to burst out laughing and the joke would be on me. Yes, any minute now he's going to tell me that he's back on drugs and he was hallucinating.

He tried to touch me and I pulled away.

'I haven't got Aids, just in case that's what you're thinking,' he said rather coldly.

'Oh Matt, I can't believe it, you of all people. I can't accept it.' He came over to me and put his arms around me. This time I gave in. I had no strength to resist him. I felt I had lost them all – all my friends, my family, and now the greatest love of my life. I had lost Matt. He held me there for an age. Every now and then I peered up into his face, still not wanting to believe it. Matt was gay. Matt was gay. I had always thought of gay men as poncy feminine cross-dressers who talked in funny voices and walked peculiarly. Matt was nothing like that. He was a big strong masculine type. Ruggedly handsome, bursting with testosterone! I would never have guessed in a million years that he was gay.

I could hardly bring myself to look at him. I felt like such an idiot. My portfolio in stupidity was complete. I was the greatest gobshite on earth. Who else knew? Jill? Karen? Why didn't they tell me if they knew! The bastards! And Joe – *why did you leave me to find out like this? Did you do it deliberately? Did you want to teach me a lesson?*

'What about Margaret?' I asked him finally. My head was crammed with questions. New ones were popping in every second.

'Margaret and I have been together for eleven years. She knew almost from the beginning. We did everything we could. You know, for years I tried so hard to be straight. I went to counselling with her. For her sake, for the kids' sake. We have an understanding now. We live in the same house, but she has her own life. We're the best of friends. She's also a great mother. I was very, very lucky.'

I thought about Margaret, all the rotten things I had said about her. She must have had a really hard time of it. Now I realised what she had sacrificed in her own life, for the sake of her children. I also realised that I lacked that kind of vocation towards David. I sank lower and lower as I thought about it.

It was beyond self-hatred. I loved him so much, but something was stopping that love from taking its natural course. My anger kept getting in the way. Why did I hate everyone that I loved? It didn't make sense. I knew somewhere deep inside that it wasn't true. My anger was only a momentary thing. The remorse and regret for hating everybody made me feel so ashamed of myself. I was a bad person. A bad mother. A bad friend. *I am bad. I am bad. I am bad.*

'What did you mean when you said that I helped you?' I asked, confused.

'That night, on the beach, I learned the truth. It always came back to haunt me. You haunted me. You represented the truth,' he said sadly. 'I just couldn't face it until I had gone down every avenue. Sadly, I hurt a lot of people through not accepting that truth.'

Matt was wonderful. He stayed with me until the

early hours of the morning answering all my questions.

By the time he was getting ready to leave, I had changed my attitude towards him. I understood things a little bit better. There was only one more question that really needed to be answered.

'Matt, why did you want me to do the course?'

'Still haven't figured it out, Jack? I care about you. Don't you believe that?'

I nodded my head. Now I knew he had no ulterior motive. I just found it almost impossible to believe that anyone cared about me at all.

'You will understand soon,' he said, buttoning up his coat. 'I know I said I wouldn't do this, but I have to. I want you to promise me one thing.'

I already knew what he was going to ask me.

'Please, please, finish the course. You have come this far. Please? I ask you as a friend. I know you can't see how it is helping you at the moment, but I swear, Jack, it will all make sense in the end.'

I promised. I hadn't any reason not to believe him. Besides, he was the only friend I had left. And I had enjoyed the course. It had already helped me. It had brought a lot of unwanted pain, but an awareness too. I trusted that Matt was in my corner and I owed it to myself and him to see it through. What else could happen to me?

As I walked out on to the steps of the flat with him, the morning light was beginning to emerge. He walked to the bottom of the steps, and then turned abruptly.

'You know, there is a man out there for you,' he said quietly, and blew on his cold fingers. 'It's up to you now, Jack. Only you can make it happen.'

I knew who the man was. I had always known who the man was. It was too simple. Too uncomplicated. Too fucking easy. It had been right under my nose, but

I couldn't accept it. I was like Matt in many ways – disregarding the obvious. My feelings for Joe had always been strong: I had just never given them any credit. How convenient for me to decide I wanted him now, just because Matt had trusted me with his secrets and rejected me. *You don't deserve him. Who do you think you are? Think you can just change your mind? Just walk back and say, Here I am, I understand now? Can we get together? You're bad! Bad!*

It was too late. It was hopeless. I didn't deserve him. And I could never tell him now. It would be weak and selfish. Besides, if Joe was with Jill, I couldn't interfere. They would make an excellent couple. I had realised too late, that was all. I was the White Rabbit, complete with pocket watch and glasses. *I'm late! I'm late! For a very important date!*

He would never have me now.

I crawled into bed with Sam and cuddled him against my chest. I felt empty. So empty that my tears dried up and my mind was stilled. A strange silence came over me. My mind had become a complete blank. I couldn't think of anyone who had made a worse mess of their lives than me. I had had so many wires crossed; I had electrocuted my very soul.

I no longer knew who I was. It was the first time in twenty years that suicide seemed optional, but I didn't have the energy or the will to carry it through.

I lay there praying that God would take me. It seemed like the most logical solution. Everybody would be much better off if I wasn't here.

I fell asleep and dreamt of a little girl. She had a freckled face and her eyes crinkled up when she smiled. She was playing in the middle of a field and calling me to join her. On closer inspection the little girl began to change. Her smile was wilting and being replaced by a sad expression. Then she began to cry, but no noise came out of her mouth. The closer I got to her, the more she deteriorated. Her clothes became tatty and ragged. Her face became dirty and her hair was matted and uncombed. She was shrinking before my very eyes, growing smaller and smaller, until she vanished into an insignificant dot. I woke up screaming and flailing my arms about the place. My night-dress was drenched in sweat.

I went into David's room and sat on the edge of the bed watching his chest rise and fall as he slept. How many times had I sat here before? The only time we seemed to get on well was when he was asleep. I was able to communicate my feelings to him then. I was able to kiss him, touch him, hold him and talk to him – when he was unconscious! I realised what a terrible mother I had become. What was my excuse? What use was I, sitting on the edge of his bed, proclaiming my devotion while he snored? How incredibly convenient for me to choose the middle of the night to share my love with him.

What about the daytime, Jack? Why don't you attend to his emotional needs? Why don't you spend happy times with him? Why do you have to sit here every night feeling sorry for yourself? He is none the wiser.

I let the voice speak. I let it fill my head, which was at long last empty. The screaming monkeys had all left, and there was an enormous void. I allowed the new voice ample room, not really caring what it said, or what it meant. I simply let it be. I was no longer at war with anyone, anything, or any place in the past, present or future. I was silently resigned to not knowing anything.

I understood that I didn't know.

I was standing in the eye of the storm. A place so tranquil and peaceful, I wanted to stay there for ever. Sitting on the edge of the bed, my life drifted before me like a streaky black and white movie. I was no longer in it. I was watching. A spectator, viewing from the sidelines. I had disconnected, come out of myself. I saw the girl in my dream, the torn tatty child, neglected, rejected and lost, and realised, with terror, that it was me. *I was the little girl in the dream.*

Sleep overcame me eventually. When I woke up the numbness was still there. I was grateful for it. No rage. No fight. No will. I went about the day quietly, allowing my thoughts to come and go freely. It amazed me. The more I let go, the calmer I became. The calmer I became, the more I learned.

I had given myself permission to be wrong. To be so wrong about everything that it was almost humorous. With it came a tremendous sense of relief, a softness I hadn't felt before.

David must have sensed something, for while I sat sipping a cup of tea, he came over and hugged me without warning, without words, without reason. He put his little boy's arms around my legs and stayed there for a moment. My eyes welled up. I hadn't anything to say either. Words evaded me for hours. It was good not to have to say anything or do anything. I patted him on the head. No great show of emotion. No irritation. No nothing.

Tears fell constantly. I washed the dishes and cried. I took the dinner out of the freezer and cried. I ironed my clothes, and cried. I watched *Thomas the Tank Engine* and cried. The dam burst. Just when I thought I had cried a river of tears, a fresh bout would begin. I didn't need any particular thing to start me off. I was like a tap. On, off. On, off.

Fortunately, David did not seem perturbed by his mother's odd behaviour. Anything was better than my wrath, I suppose. I could not bring myself to say what I wanted to say, *I am sorry David. I love you so much. I do not hate you. I never did. I hate myself. That's what's wrong with me. I hate myself.*

Words would not do any more. I knew I needed to show him these truths through my actions.

I was happy to work through this new phase, whatever it was. I knew intuitively not to do anything at all, except go with it, wait and see what would happen next.

I was preparing to take a shower when the phone rang. I let it ring for an age.

The sound of it ringing made me cry. Somebody was thinking about me. I wanted to appreciate it. I listened to the format. Two rings. Stop. Two rings. Stop. Then it stopped ringing altogether.

When it started to ring again, my heart soared. Somebody really, really wanted to talk to me. For a brief second I allowed myself the luxury of hoping it was Joe. Then I answered it.

'Hello?'

'Hello, Jack?'

'Yes?'

'Jack Joyce?'

'Yes? Who is this?'

'It's Andrew Fenton. David's father.'

My journey had become a bottomless pit, with no beginning, no middle and no end.

Chapter 18

Isn't it strange. Just when you think things can't possibly get any worse, they do. There is a certain inevitability about it. You think, Well one more disaster won't kill me.

Instead of being enraged with Andrew, my English lover, I had murderous thoughts towards Jill. How else would he have gotten my phone number? I certainly hadn't given it to him. I was more alarmed at his choice of introduction. I had never heard the term 'David's father'; it seemed all wrong. David didn't have a father.

'How did you get my phone number?' I demanded.

'Your mother gave it to me,' he answered.

'Did you tell her who you were?' I asked.

'No. I didn't think it would be wise,' he said.

'You got that one right. How did you find out?'

There was a long pause. 'I'm afraid your friend Jill let it slip.'

Of course.

'Well, whatever you have to say, you had better say it now.' I couldn't believe I was encouraging him. I really thought he had just contacted me out of curiosity. I wasn't taking any of it seriously. The sooner I got him off the phone, the quicker this whole damn thing would be over. I had enough on my plate as it was.

'Have you consulted a solicitor yet?' he said calmly.

'Pardon?'

'Well, have you decided what you are going to do?'

'Do about what?' I said impatiently. I was getting a bit pissed off with this jerk that I hadn't seen in five years.

'Jack, didn't you receive the letter?'

'What letter?'

'Christ,' I heard him mutter under his breath.

Then I remembered the registered brown envelope. 'Wait – I did get a letter, but I didn't open it,' I said.

'I suggest you do so now,' he said steadily. 'If you wish, you can phone me back afterwards.'

I was beginning to feel somewhat uncomfortable with this whole scenario. Putting the phone down, I went in search of the misplaced brown envelope. I found it in the bread bin; it was smeared with tomato ketchup. As I lit a cigarette and studied it, an awful feeling came over me. It occurred to me it was hardly a friendly line or two from my distant lover.

I slid the bread knife through the sealed opening. It was a court summons. I tried to read the small print but could not understand the technical jargon. I could only surmise from the heading what I thought it was. The panic waves had begun to rise and fall as it slowly dawned on me that it was an application from Andrew seeking access rights to David. I was being summonsed to appear in court. It was the last straw.

I went back to the phone and dialled the number which he had conveniently printed at the top of the letter.

'Hello?'

'It's Jack,' I said hoarsely.

'Hi. Listen, can we—'

I stopped him right there. 'No. You listen to me, you fucking prick. You are never *ever* going to get access to my son. You may very well be his biological father, but that is all you are. He knows nothing of you, does not *want* to know anything about you, and he does not need you. I have raised that child single-handedly from the day he was born. What makes you think you can just walk into his life and suddenly start to play Happy Families? You have no idea what you are getting yourself into. I'll never agree to access. *Never*. Do you understand?'

I was surprised at my own anger. A fierce protectiveness had come to the surface. I was the last person on earth I would have expected this reaction from. They were not taking David away from me as well.

'What you agree or disagree with is none of my concern. I am David's father and therefore obliged to provide for him in whatever way the courts see fit. I have not just casually walked into his life either. I would have been there right from the start, had I known he existed. From what I hear, it will not be a difficult decision for the judge to come to. If I didn't live in England and had known about your negligence before, I would have applied for custody long ago.'

Negligence? What the fuck is he on about?

'I don't know what you're talking about, but I do know this. You will never lay your dirty British hands on my child. Over my dead body!' I said and hung up.

While I sounded powerfully strong, my legs had begun to wobble beneath me. I sat down and lit a cigarette. I spied a can of Carlsberg under the couch and pulled it out. It was empty. Fuck it! Fuck it! The thoughts were lunging at me now. The fear running rampant through every bone and sinew. I never thought this day would arrive, yet here it was. It was all upon me now. What was I going to do?

I ought to have known Jill was behind this. The fucking bad bitch. How dare she take it upon herself to inform Andrew of anything? First to betray me by telling him I had had his child, then to go and inform him that I was a negligent parent! To round it off neatly, she then had to go and steal Joe right from under my nose!

All of a sudden the reality of it all shot through me like a gun explosion.

I ran to the telephone and took out my little black address book. It took ages for her to answer.

'Hello?' she answered sleepily.

'Guess who, Jill?' I said calmly. 'It's your old friend, Jack. The one who is the negligent mother, right? You must be able to remember me? I'm the one who had the baby and raised him on my own, only now I'm a negligent mother who is being taken to court by a man who has never seen his child, or even known of his existence until a really good friend of mine informed him of all this. I believe that's you, Jill. Anything to say?'

'Jack, I did it for David's sake. He needs a father, now more than ever. One of these days that child is going to get hurt. It is my responsibility as your friend to . . .'

'Save it, Jill. David could have had a father, until you fucked it up,' I interrupted her. 'Your kind of friendship, I can do without. If I lose my child over you, I'll fucking kill you. Do you understand me?'

'That's right, Jack. Go ahead and abuse me too. It's because I love you that I have acted, out of concern.'

'Love me! You stole Joe from me, now you want to rub salt in the wounds by taking David away too. What's in it for you? You could have had anybody, but you had to choose Joe, didn't you. Fuck you, you dumb bitch! You haven't a fucking clue about anything!'

'You need help with your drinking, Jack. Listen to me . . .'

But I couldn't listen any more. I slammed the phone down. My body was shaking. I was so angry I thought I would kill someone. It only spurred me on to get to the bottom of this problem as quickly as possible. I made a list of people I had to call. That bastard was not going to see my child, no matter what happened. I would fight him tooth and nail.

I would go all the way. I didn't care what it took. He was not getting near my son. David was mine. He would always be mine!

My first call was to my solicitor. I had discovered her through my father when I had first had David. Social Welfare had advised me to make a will and appoint a guardian for him, should anything happen to me. It had cost me a hefty sum to have it drawn up. Now I was glad I had gone ahead with it. It could very well come in handy in the next few weeks, I thought.

I asked her could I visit her as soon as possible and she made an appointment for me to come in the following day. Thank God I was still off work. I had a doctor's certificate for two weeks. I tried to phone Karen a number of times. After leaving a third message, I realised she wasn't returning the call. Then I rang Matt and explained it all to him. He was kind and listened, but there wasn't much advice he could give me. Then I phoned Mam and Dad, who jumped to my defence immediately. I had expected this. It was not out of compassion for me, but for David. They had grown to love him and could not bear the thought of sharing him with anyone else. The more calls I made, the more despondent I became, until I could not stand the overwhelming fear any longer. I dialled Joe's number.

'Hello,' I said shyly.

'Yes?' he answered coolly.

'Look, I know what happened the other night has really upset you, but I need your help,' I said, shivering with the fear of rejection.

'I already told you, Jack. I'm not available. You must

help yourself.' His voice was harsh. Then he put the phone down.

I burst into tears. Things had suddenly taken on a very serious overtone. Surely they were all aware of the gravity of my situation? Why were they ganging up on me like this? I was desperately lonely, not knowing where to turn next. I kept glancing at the court summons. I had four weeks to prepare. I had not dreamed of taking Andrew seriously, now I had begun to wake up. I was alone, completely alone. This was one fight I was going to have to deal with by myself. I was ready to face it but I needed support. Just then, David poked his head around the kitchen door.

'Mam, can I go in to Alice?'

I had forgotten about Alice. Now I missed her more than ever. I needed her more than ever, but I couldn't bridge the gap. I was sinking further and further into a place of retreat.

'You can go, if she doesn't mind,' I said to the hopeful little face.

'Thanks, Mam,' he smiled.

Despite everything that was going on, David and I were very close and getting along better than we ever had in the past. I had begun to recognise that he was an innocent party. The thought of having to share him made my stomach churn. I had never prepared for that.

I realised the simplest of things were what made him happy. Breakfast, dinner and tea made him happy, walks in the park made him happy. Me watching a movie with him made him happy. Why had it taken me so long to learn that his needs were simple? All he wanted was my time. Just like I had needed that attention when I was a kid. It wasn't about toys, holidays, money. All he wanted was me, to know I was there and that I cared.

I was shocked that Andrew was even interested in

seeing him. After all, surely he had considered that he would have to pay maintenance? What about the distance that separated them? What about the fact that David didn't even know him? I tried to persuade myself that everything would be OK on the day. A judge would surely consider all aspects of David's wellbeing.

In the morning I was awake early and heard the soft thud as the postman dropped something in the letter box. I picked it up – it had an English postmark and stamp. I opened it.

The letter was from Andrew's solicitor. This was a man who had obviously done his homework well. The contents of the letter made me laugh out loud. It was such rubbish! Poor Andrew. He was trying to scare me. It had the desired effect, though. My laughter was a cover for fear. By the time I reached my own solicitor's office my nerve had begun to weaken.

'Hello, Jacqueline,' she said calmly.

Greta Leahy was a tough cookie. She had been working as a solicitor for many years and specialised in family law. I couldn't have chosen a more appropriate representative. A bit of a private book in her personal life, Greta had defended the Joyces on more than one occasion. I needed a strong individual this morning – she was just the ticket. I handed her the court summons and the letter. The offices were cramped and stuffy but had just been freshly painted. The crisp smell assailed my nostrils. I sat in front of her while she fiddled with her glasses. She proceeded to read each letter slowly, making no comment. Then she read them again. After this she put her head on one side. I didn't like the look of that. I chewed my nails furiously. Then I sat on my hands to stop myself.

'I'm afraid that this is very, very serious.' She removed her glasses and wiped the inside corners of them with the sleeve of her blouse.

She picked up the summons first. 'You must appear for the court summons. If you don't, a warrant for your arrest could be issued.'

Huh?

'I presume you were hoping you could avoid appearing and that he would eventually lose interest?' I nodded my head.

She picked up the second letter. 'There are some extremely grave allegations in this letter, Jack.'

I stared at the ground. Much to my disappointment, it didn't open up. I looked all around me instead. 'I know,' I said softly.

'Before we can go any further I shall have to question you about this. If there is even a grain of truth to the accusations, I'm afraid we are in for a bumpy ride, not to mention a costly one.' She paused and then began to read extracts.

'My client has been informed that your client has a serious drinking problem. Our client fears for the future safety of his son, and is willing to apply to the said court for full custody of the said child David, if he sees fit.'

I stared at the wall, on which hung a beautifully framed copy of van Gogh's *Sunflowers*. I had always loved van Gogh with his vibrant yellows and oranges splattered passionately across the canvas.

'Well, Jacqueline?' Greta leaned over her desk. 'What have you got to say in response to this? I have to know if there is any truth in it.' She was becoming impatient.

'It's complete and utter rubbish,' I said. 'He's only trying to scare me. He can't go accusing me of these things. He hasn't even seen me for five years. It's all a load of crap!' I laughed gaily, as if it were a game of Snakes and Ladders.

Greta began tidying up the files, attaching the letters inside and sighing loudly. 'I'm afraid I can't represent you, dear. I must know what I am dealing with. Frankly, you haven't a hope of winning if you don't come clean with me.'

'What?' I replied in disbelief, thinking: Don't you fucking start as well! 'I already told you, it's all rubbish! I swear it is! Besides, he can't prove anything. It's just scare-mongering, that's all.' I had not prepared myself to be rejected by a middle-aged battleaxe barrister.

'I'm sorry, Jacqueline. I've been in practice for a long time, and one thing I am not is stupid.' She peered down her nose at me. 'I have seen this thing time and time again. I am not prepared to fight your case unless you are willing to work with me.'

I had had enough of her riddles and philosophical scorning. I donned my coat and walked out. She was my last ally. Not to worry, there were a million other solicitors to choose from. Besides, I was a single parent. I could apply for free Legal Aid.

I found the phone number listed in the telephone directory and rang it. I was refused immediately. There was a waiting list, and the average waiting period was six to eight months. I hadn't got six to eight months. I hadn't even got six to eight weeks! The whole telephone conversation had been about as useful as a kick-start for a racing pigeon.

I wandered home. David was still in Alice's. I passed her flat and blinked back the tears. I wanted to call in, just to speak to another human being who wasn't going to jump on the 'Get Jack!' bandwagon.

The Good Shepherd flats had become my home. I looked around me. The dirty Venetian blinds and smell of urine on the steps was almost welcoming. I let myself in and closed the door behind me, then I searched through my purse to check out my financial standing. I had exactly four pounds. Not enough for even two cans. I had to get money somewhere. Just then, I heard a knock on the door. It was David, clutching a beautiful bunch of carnations.

'Where did you get those? I hope you weren't stealing again.' I sniffed and admired the beautiful pale pink flowers.

'They're from Alice,' he smiled proudly.

'For you?' I asked.

'No, Mammy, don't be silly. They're for you!' He thrust them in my face. I wasn't getting too excited, just in case he had made a mistake. The way things were going, I expected them to be snatched back off me in seconds.

I took the flowers and put them in my one and only vase. This too was a gift from Alice; she had purchased it on 'The Hill' some months back. It had a small chip on the lip but was otherwise perfect. I arranged the flowers carefully. Then I walked out the front door and up the familiar steps to Alice's flat. I knocked at the door. I had hardly finished the second knock when she opened it.

'Hi. Thanks for the flowers, Alice,' I sniffed, awkwardly shifting from one foot to the other.

'C'mon in, love,' she motioned kindly.

Why was she being so kind to me? Why you, Alice? Why you of all people?

My behaviour towards her had been the very worst. She had never judged me, not once. I soon realised why. When I thought about it, the answer was obvious. Alice had been judged all her life. She knew what it was like to be constantly criticised, scrutinised and made a fool of. She knew the pain of being ostracised. She knew all about class distinctions. She knew her place in this world. At least someone did! I was still trying to find mine.

At this moment in time, Alice was all I had. She was the one I least expected to have anything to do with me. I felt guilty sitting in her kitchen, sipping her tea that she paid for by cleaning houses from 6 am to 10 am every single day. Her larger-than-life presence eased my racing mind. I could have sat there all day. It didn't matter whether we had any conversation or not.

Jimmy, the youngest of her children, wandered in. 'Ma, can I have a biscuit?' A clever boy, he knew his chances were increased when a visitor was about. She raised her hand to him and he legged it out the front.

'That poxy child will be the death of me. Never plays with the other kids, can't get them to play with him. A right fucking oddball altogether. We had to tie a bone around his neck so the dog would play with him.'

I laughed. It was the first time I had laughed in two weeks.

'Can't get him to eat anything either. Biscuits and tea – that's the fucking lot. Has to run around the shower to get wet.' I was really laughing now.

'When we took him swimming, had to throw him in the pool twice before he made a splash, fucking useless skinny bastard, takes after his oul fella,' she added.

Alice prattled on like only Alice could. I sat there drinking tea and chuckling, and for a whole hour I forgot. I forgot about Matt being gay. I forgot about Andrew Fenton and the court summons. I forgot about my guilt and confusion. I forgot about my anger towards Jill and Karen and Mick, but I still couldn't forget about Joe. His face swam before me like a vision. His words of condemnation remained locked inside, piercing my heart every hour or so. I couldn't bear to think about him. I never thought I'd see the day when he would reject me so cruelly. The first glimpses of my true feelings towards him had begun to surface. It was a frightening revelation, one I could do without. It seemed there would be plenty of time to grieve over his loss. I didn't hope for a reconciliation.

During all the years I had known him, he had never done anything like this. I respected the seriousness of it.

I respected his decision to cut me off. It was a strange and wonderful feeling. I acknowledged for the first time ever that I had hurt someone. Even if it was only acknowledged within. I knew what was happening, I just refused to let it out. This was not the time. If I let my feelings become real, I might have to face the fact that I had lost him, which would be too much for me to bear.

Contrary to my outward composure, I was dying inside. I was lonely and lost and hurt. I loved my friends and I loved David more than anything else in the world. I had begun to see, ever so slightly, that I had taken them for granted. Even so, I could not trust myself to change. My only glimmer of hope lay in the two course sessions that were left. Why they had become a matter of life or death for me, is uncertain. I should have been obsessed with the ever-increasing difficulties.

I had been living my childhood for weeks now, and something was happening. It would have been wrong for me to stop going when I needed something 'completed' in my life. I had never completed anything before. I started many projects, dreamt many dreams, planned many plots and failed to get even some of them off the ground. The course was currently keeping me afloat. Even though it had been a painful experience, I wanted more than ever now to see it through. It was the only thing I was doing right. The only thing that seemed to be fruitful.

Without hesitation, I asked Alice to listen to me. I asked her to help me with the course questions. She was delighted that I could trust her with such personal stuff. To me, nothing seemed private any more. My secrets were out.

I picked up my last couple of pages of work and began to recap. Alice barred the kids from the kitchen, opened the fridge and took out some cheap cider. I had come as far as eleven years of age. Strangely enough, the next couple of years were vague, to say the least. I put this down to the fact that I had had my first drink when I was twelve.

My accomplice in crime was none other than Joe himself. We had become buddies overnight when I found his missing Labrador wandering in the back lane. I advertised in the local supermarket and Joe appeared at my door to take the dog home. Her name was Sandy; she was a beautiful Golden Labrador with floppy ears and drooling tongue. Not much of a guard dog, I imagined, as she waddled home with me without any protest.

I had liked Joe from the start. He made me laugh. Unlike other boys, he didn't try to put his hand up my skirt and he was a year older. That counted for everything. He introduced me to his friends, who came from a different part of Clontarf. Unlike my 'anti-menstruation' estate friends, Joe's mates were ordinary down-to-earth kids. They welcomed me into their little gang immediately.

We gathered at the church grounds and often sheltered under the large pyramid roof, taking refuge from the insufferable rain. Smoking was already part of the gang philosophy. It wasn't long before alcohol was introduced. My only experience of alcohol had been a sip of wine from my dad's glass when he had his back turned. I thought it tasted like vinegar and I spat it out.

Now I was sitting under the church walls as I lifted a bottle of Smithwicks beer to my lips for the first time. It was Hallowe'en night and Joe and I had met as soon as darkness had fallen. We walked together and talked together. He had a plastic bag with him. I was certain it was filled with popcorn, apples and monkey nuts, but he pulled out a six-pack. I looked at him disconcertedly. I was a little bit afraid. Then I gave myself a pep-talk. *C'mon. You're twelve now. Time to grow up.* I watched Joe drink the Smithwicks. He slurped at the rim of it like a real man. I was impressed. Then it was my turn. It tasted disgusting but I sure as hell wasn't going to let him know.

'What do virgins eat for breakfast?' he asked me, draining the remains of his beer. I was still trying to get past the frothy bit.

'I don't know, what do virgins eat for breakfast?' I hadn't a clue. What was a virgin anyway?

'Cornflakes!' he laughed loudly. I laughed loudly. I hadn't a bull's notion what any of it meant but it didn't matter. The small portion of alcohol I had managed to drink was taking effect.

We began to knick-knack on people's doors. I would camouflage myself in a bush and Joe would innocently ask, 'Eh, would you like to help the Hallowe'en Party?'

'Get your fucking cheeky little arse out of here before I call the guards!' would come the reply, and on we would go to the next house and to the next. At the last house, a kindly old woman with white hair asked him to open the plastic bag. Then she threw a beautifully handmade toffee apple inside it.

'There you go, son,' she smiled at him and closed the door. We burst out laughing and ran down the road.

Fireworks exploded in the black moonlit sky. Children clad in white sheets wobbled from house to house. Green-faced witches with brooms scurried along the footpath. There was a run on the old lady with the toffee apples when word got out. Sparklers crackled and bangers exploded noisily on doorsteps. Bonfires were under way. Children worked relentlessly, dragging anything flammable to the roaring infernos. Aerosol cans imploded with force and parents guarded the younger ones, who watched from a distance.

I was reeling from excitement and the one and a half bottles of Smithwicks.

Joe had kindly left me half of one. I drank it slowly now,

savouring the warm glow in my bones and wishing there was more. We joined up with the rest of the gang and sat around the bonfire, warm as toast. We exchanged ghost stories and Joe decided to paint my face black from the ashes. I had been told to come home at 9 pm. It was now about 11 pm and I didn't care. I felt so grown-up. I felt I could do anything. I felt I could take on the world.

We danced around the fire, whooping and yahooing like Indians. Free, wild, innocent and pure. I could see Joe holding my hand tightly as we danced around and around until I lost my balance and fell over, laughing hysterically. I lay there staring up at the yellow moon, the stars twinkling in the clear night sky. I was so happy, as happy as I would ever be. I had found a way to live in the world. A way to cope, to fit in. A way to make the madness go away. I had found a way to be me.

That night, I said a little prayer to my guardian angel. I thanked her for introducing me to this wonderful thing called alcohol. It had given me a new lease of life. It soared through my veins like an electric volt and filled me with confidence.

My ever-churning stomach had stopped rotating the wrong way. I had a smile on my face. I was able to make conversation with the other boys. It was all so easy. I leaned over on my elbow. Joe was blowing smoke up into the air. He was making perfectly rounded circles. I mooched on over to him and laid my head on his chest. I cuddled into him. I was safe and happy. It would always be like this from now on. I never had to worry again. I had found my two best friends. Joe, and alcohol. As long as I had them, life was a cinch.

I stopped reading and wiped the tears from my face. My loneliness consumed me. Alice was crying too. The clock was ticking quietly and the sound of a passing car faded in the distance. I was no longer twelve. Life was not a cinch any more. Joe had deserted me.

'Alice, I've lost him, do you hear me? I've lost him.'

She poured another drink, wiping her eyes on the back of her sleeve. I took a long swig out of my glass. It did nothing. I was stone cold sober. Even alcohol had given up on me. So now I had lost my two best friends.

I didn't know that I was about to step forward into a new awakening, a new life. Honesty, the murderer of souls, the spirit taker, had come to get me. Like a thief in the night it would steal my pride. It would free me of me. So I could learn to live again.

Chapter 19

Everybody gets their moment of truth. Some see it for what it is, a revelation. They grab at it eagerly, recognising its worth. Others ignore it, hoping their gut instinct was wrong, and patiently wait for the next one to come along. Only it doesn't. It is true to say, some people do get two moments of truth, but it is a rare phenomenon. I only got one. And it hit me over the head like a mallet in a dingy classroom at a course called Discovering Your Family History.

It was the eighth session. God only knows how or why I had decided to return. My personal life was like a black hole that I kept staring into, like the Dublin Corporation workmen stare into their prospective holes, breastfeeding their shovels. The course was the only thing that was going right for me, and while it didn't seem like the most important issue that I should have been addressing, I was determined to see it through to the end.

I was delighted to see everybody again. To my surprise they were equally delighted to see me. This was a first. Everybody else connected to me was running as fast as they could in the opposite direction, including me.

Matt, too, greeted me with open arms. It was strange to be in them, the way I had always dreamed. Now they felt beautifully strong, with the strength of someone who really loved me, not the fickle 'in love' type. I had begun to discern the difference and had learned one great lesson. That I was not looking for romance at all. *I was looking for love. The real thing.* I looked around me and surmised that every single individual in the group was doing the exact same thing. I had confused sex with love and vice versa.

'I suppose a ride is out of the question?' I whispered in his ear. He burst out laughing.

Frank and Connor and Bertie were exchanging family photographs. Periodically they roared with laughter as someone recognised the other. Diane was scribbling away on the back of a book.

'What is it?' I peered over her shoulder.

'Jack, dear!' She swung around and hugged me hard. 'I didn't think you were coming back. You missed it last week.' She looked positively radiant.

'You've changed your hair,' I commented, touching the beautiful blonde-tinted strands.

'What do you think?' She patted the back of her head childishly.

'You look beautiful no matter what colour your hair is.' My eyes had begun to well up already.

'Are you all right, dear? Did something happen last week?'

Jesus. What an understatement. Have you got ten years? 'I just can't stop crying,' I explained in a choked voice. 'All the time. I walk down the street and I start crying. It's really embarrassing. Actually, your hair reminded me of Mam.' I decided to be honest.

'Did your Mam pass away, dear? I'm so sorry. It's hard to know. I don't like asking,' she said.

'No! Mam is alive and well. I guess you can say there *has* been a death in the family, but not of a physical kind.' I winked at her and she smiled back. I knew she thought I'd completely lost it. She was probably right.

'I can see you two are getting along fine.' She nodded

at Matt. Nothing like the old change of subject. It works wonders.

'Yes. We're old friends. We grew up together.'

'Any chance of, you know – you two getting together?' she asked.

'He's spoken for,' I answered, amused by my own irony. Then I went and took my seat and the session began.

Brian was his usual self, welcoming everybody and answering questions. From the content of the conversation, I surmised that I had indeed missed a great deal. The group were discussing things much more freely. This evening's topic of sexual memories had sparked off a vibrant and energetic debate. Everybody was complaining about the lack of sex education in their childhood and the consequent fumbling through teenage years. We had all shared a common bond. We were hopelessly sexually inadequate. After Matt's confession I felt like I was a virgin again. I was relieved to discover that it had not been all my fault. Perhaps if I had had another suitor, the experience wouldn't have been so traumatic.

The real beauty of it was I could start all over again. At thirty years of age I could call myself a virgin and apply for a second licence. Mind you, this time I was going to be more careful about my choice of partner. I would also make sure that he was a homeowner. I wasn't going down any lanes, or back seats of cars even if he drove a Mercedes. This lady was going to do things in style – and preferably with a heterosexual like myself.

Bertie was enlightening us all with a tale of woe about having warts as a kid. Then he graduated to his piles. I wasn't exactly in the mood for hearing about his arse but he seemed to think it was all connected sexually. That he had acquired these 'physical' symptoms as a result of his 'inner' sexual inadequacies. Now we had two Woody Allens in the group.

'For the first two years of my marriage, I went to bed with my T-shirt on,' Diane confided. 'I was too embarrassed to let my husband see me naked. I was always obsessed with my outer image. If I had been taking more of an interest in our relationship, I don't think he would have run off with a younger woman.'

Connor disagreed. 'Don't you think he was a bit of a bollox really? If he was that type he would have run off anyway. He should have been paying attention to you, not elsewhere as he was obviously doing. I can assure you, T-shirt or no T-shirt, I personally would find it difficult to take my eyes off you for a second. No offence meant, of course.' Frank and Bertie nodded in agreement.

Diane blushed. I was pleased.

'Jack, you're very quiet.' Brian turned the group's attention on me. 'We missed you last week.'

Everybody nodded.

'Things have been very difficult. If you don't mind I'll just listen for the moment. Every time I try to talk lately, I start to cry. I'm quite embarrassed about it.' I lowered my head, suddenly feeling very ashamed and stupid.

'I think you'll find the group understands. We had a few crying sessions here last week, didn't we, people?'

They all nodded.

'On the subject of last week,' he went on, 'I found it interesting that three of you expressed almost identical stories. It would seem that alcoholism was a common factor and had a profound effect on all of you. I would like to extend that discussion a little bit more this week. I've taken the liberty of asking Matt to kindly share with us his story. I think you might find it of interest.'

Brian went to sit on another chair. Matt, declining to take the chair himself, stood up and leaned against the table and folded his arms. My moment of truth was upon me.

'Thanks, Brian. Right – I've been asked to share a little bit about my own family background. I hope I don't bore you all. This is my third time doing this particular course. I initially participated because it was part of the curriculum of my psychology degree. I have since completed the course twice over because basically I have an interest in alcoholism and drug addiction.'

This was news to me. He continued.

'On all three courses, I discovered alcoholism coming up again and again as a recurring theme. It is a family disease, now recognised by the World Health Organisation. It's not surprising, then, when I hear account after account of alcoholism doing its worst in families throughout Ireland. I am a recovering alcoholic and drug addict myself.

'I went to a treatment centre four years ago after my wife threatened to take herself and the children as far away from me as possible. Like most alcoholics, I could not see that I was in trouble. I was a classic case of denial. It's only when the shit hits the fan that an alcoholic might make a move, or perhaps when they are faced with an actual life or death sentence, such as a failed liver, or institutionalisation. Let me tell you about my parents. I come from Clontarf.'

He took a deep breath and smiled at me.

'Long before I was ever introduced to alcohol I was introduced to drugs. My parents were too busy getting drunk themselves to notice. Besides, I was not falling around the place. I seemed happy all the time, so they assumed everything was OK. In hindsight, of course, I realise they wanted to assume that everything was OK so they could get on with their all-night parties. Dad was a silent drunk, the type that goes to the pub very early in the morning, drinks all day, then returns in the early hours, frequently falling asleep on the couch, or on the odd occasion on the kitchen table.'

I swallowed hard.

'Mam was left at home to supposedly mind the kids. She believes to this day that she drinks to cope with her loneliness, her frustration and boredom. She really believes that it is perfectly normal for her to be as drunk as a skunk. If anyone else had to live with my dad, she reckons they would drink just as much too!'

Everybody laughed, except me.

'As a child, I often came home to find her asleep on the floor, still in the same clothes as the night before. My younger sister would be trying to put the dinner together. We would pick her up and dump her on the bed and get on with things ourselves. I did all the shopping, housework, and often helped the younger ones with their homework. I often had to ward off debt-collectors from the hall door. One day they even came to take out our furniture.

'No extra points for figuring out that I was The Caretaker, The Fixer in our home. Being the eldest it was expected of me: I expected it of myself. I thought everybody lived like that. Anyway, there were times when we had nothing to eat at all. Mam would buy her cans and we would have to starve. We would wait up for Dad to come rolling home, as he sometimes brought the odd bag of chips and we would descend upon him like vultures. Then he would attack Mam for not feeding us and she in turn would attack him for not feeding us. One blamed the other and so on. Life continued as normal in between.

'I suffered in school, of course, often being exhausted from the previous night's rows and arguments. I failed every exam. I took my first drugs when I was thirteen. I graduated to hard drugs when I was fourteen. By the time I was seventeen I was dealing drugs in the neighbourhood. I thought I was cool and I had a plethora of friends.

I didn't realise how quickly they would disappear when I changed. They were only fair-weather friends. They were no loss.'

I had begun to sit on my hands.

'I remember one morning, my younger sister was hungry and went to climb up on to a high shelf where she believed there was a can of something to eat. She slipped and fell and broke her leg. My mother beat her for not asking her first. My father beat my mother for beating her. They had a very colourful marriage. Mam was black and blue most of the time. I escaped into drugs. It was a wonderful time. I lived to escape. Had I not had access to something mood-altering I'm not sure I would still be here today. I had to survive it some way.

'But drugs alone were not enough any more. They weren't doing what they used to do so I began to drink as well. I started to experience blackouts. Which, by the way, is not the same thing as passing out. A blackout is a period of time for which you can't remember anything. At first it would be an hour, maybe two. In the end it was full days. I was sick in the morning – often nothing would come up. I would be sweating and shaking. Almost like I had the flu. I didn't realise I was suffering from withdrawals. I was bloated and pale and constantly tired and depressed,' Matt continued.

As he spoke, I felt the words pass through my skin and into my blood. They side-stepped my mind and entered my heart. I felt a physical piercing. A pain so great and heavy I thought I would be immobilised for ever. As I sat there in frozen attention, the truth enveloped me. He was talking about little old me. I wasn't sure if he had gone and written out an account of me deliberately. Was it possible that two stories could be so identical? I thought of David, the can of food, the sweating, the sickness. With each passing second a new set of feelings attacked my being.

Each word thumped me right between the eyes, kicked me between the legs. The truth was being spelled out to me. I was at its mercy and couldn't move. The picture was crystal clear, almost as if someone had turned on the TV and I was watching a movie about me. The reception had a clarity never experienced before or since.

Matt continued. 'Of course, by the time I was twenty I had another problem. A much bigger one. I hadn't enough money to support my drug and drink habits, so I had to take to criminal activities to keep afloat. I started with small things – house break-ins, car theft. It escalated along with my addiction. My younger sister had a small savings account. I got my mother to sign a withdrawal slip while she was drunk. Then I drank it all, every penny of it.'

I winced with pain, remembering David's beautiful money box. I was not aware of anyone else in the room now. My tears were running freely and quickly. I jumped when I felt someone's hand slip into mine and squeeze it hard. I looked up – it was Matt's. He was sitting beside me and continued to talk.

'Nobody understands the alcoholic like the alcoholic does himself. And yet the alcoholic is the last person in the world to understand what is actually *happening* to him. People do not realise that an alcoholic is suffering too. All anybody sees is the destruction and pain that they are causing to those around them. The alcoholic is not a bad person. He is a sick individual who needs to be treated for his illness, like any other illness. You can't treat a broken leg with a Band Aid, can you? Once I understood what was wrong with me, I was able to come to terms with it, and then set about changing it. Not without a great deal of hard work, time and excruciating pain.'

Someone handed me a piece of tissue. I realised my whole body had begun to shake and shudder. No matter how much I wanted to stop crying, the tears just kept right on coming. I had gone past caring. It was the first time ever that I caught a glimpse of myself through someone else's eyes. I was grieving a thousand deaths. I was feeling twenty years of loss. I was experiencing the slap of rejection. I was understanding compassion. I was in the midst of humility. The presence of God. I stood in the centre of my own being, as the life I had led swirled around me like a tornado.

Every pore, blood vessel and hair strand felt vulnerable to the touch. I was exposed and naked. The storm kept battering away, until the house that Jack built was blown to bits and dispersed in the wind. All that remained was an empty space, a drenched tissue and Matt's hand.

I felt someone playing with my hair. My head was turned sideways, inwards. I could smell my mother's cooking, taste the sea in Courtown. I could feel the wet of David's tears. I could see the expression in his china-blue eyes. The hurt and pain I had caused him. The blaming and hatred and bitterness I had unleashed upon him just for being alive. I could see the can with the spoon sticking out of it and it twisted like a knife in my stomach. I could see Desmond, cold and waxen, lying on a slab. A dead child with a living spirit that had haunted our home for thirty years. I could hear Jill's words. *'You have a drinking problem.'* They repeated themselves over and over and over until my head ached with their persistent echo. I felt my lips move as the words tumbled out without any sound.

I'm an alcoholic.
I'm an alcoholic.
I'm an alcoholic.

My guardian angel kissed me gently on the back of the neck. I felt its protective warm glow envelop me completely. When I opened my eyes it was Matt's arms that were around me. The group had gathered too. Diane was weeping uncontrollably, Connor was sniffing loudly into his handkerchief. Frank was smiling at me. Bertie, who would normally give an aspro a headache, was shoving a cup of tea beneath my nose. What was very strange was the ongoing devastation inside. I could not connect with anything outside that. I was surrounded by people but they were so far away. I was inside, looking out, instead of outside looking in. I must have stayed there for an age, without moving, feeling the fury. I felt like the inside of an empty tumble dryer. Swirling around and around, no definite shape or form, yet knowing it was a beginning. An atom, a particle of what was to be.

As the fear and terror began to subside, my tears were less violent, the shuddering eased off and the winds abated. A calm descended on me. A beautiful clean, white calmness surged through my heart. I recognised it for what it was. My moment of truth. My guardian angel. My higher self. The real me. Jack. Jacqueline Joyce, as she really was.

I sipped my cup of tea, aware of the muffled whispers from the other members of the group. Brian had taken his seat and was trying to condense whatever lessons had occurred that evening. I did not hear a single word that he said. I didn't need to.

I looked at my watch. Strangely enough it had stopped – at exactly the moment Matt had begun to talk: 7.32 pm. I laughed out loud. Everybody stared at me. I laughed again. I would never have the watch fixed, never. I showed it to Matt, who smiled and hugged me. Perhaps there were such things as celestial beings. Feathered friends who worked behind the scenes. Matt pointed out that I had been crying and leaning on the watch at an angle. It was possible that my tears had run into the works, causing it to shut down. I chose instead to believe it was a sign. Something wonderful had happened to me. The truth of my twenty years of hiding had unleashed itself with a terrible wrath.

While my crying subsided for a while, it was not long before it started again. This time I expected it, hence it did not cause me much concern any more. I was getting used to it and let it happen. Sooner or later it would stop, when it was ready to stop. I did not know it but I had acknowledged my own worthiness. I had allowed myself to be hurt and to feel it. It was my first experience of self-love, self-respect and self-protection, all of which were inexplicably alien to me.

Matt took me to the coffee-shop. I was overcome with an exhaustion so profound I could have put my head on the table and fallen asleep right there and then. I swirled my coffee around and around still trying to take in the assailing revelations. They were still knocking on my door. I was still opening it.

I had nothing to say really. I noticed a flower in a vase on the table. It was a single pink rose. I picked it up and smelt it. The scent was sweet and tangible.

'How are you feeling now?' Matt asked.

'I can't put it into words,' I answered truthfully.

'Jack, you're going to be OK.' Matt leaned across and put his hand in mine. My hand suddenly felt tiny and soft, like a child's. I started to cry again. Would it ever, ever stop?

'What am I going to do, Matt? My life is in shite.' I couldn't believe my own words.

'You'll do what I do,' he said, sipping his coffee with his free hand.

'I really am an alcoholic, aren't I?' As I said the words, they sounded familiar, not nearly as shocking as I thought they would.

'What do you think?' he said.

I nodded dolefully. 'Why didn't you tell me? Why didn't you challenge me before?' I asked.

'Because you weren't ready,' he told me. 'There would have been no point. I could have ruined a unique opportunity if I pushed it. It's best that you see it yourself: you're a chronic alcoholic.'

I didn't like the 'chronic' bit but found myself unable to argue the point.

'And all this time, I really thought I had a problem with food,' I said wryly.

'You *do* have a problem with food,' Matt put in. 'But only because you are an alcoholic, not vice versa. One will cross out the other, you'll see. It's all the same. You're suffering from an emotional illness.'

I sat and drank coffee and listened to Matt, hanging on every word. He explained to me slowly the workings of alcoholism. The theory that it was in fact a disease. It helped greatly to know that I was sick, and not bad, as I had thought. I was dubious about the fact that not everyone would share that view.

'It doesn't matter what they think. Jack, it's not going to be easy, I assure you. It's tough. I'll help you if you want my help.'

'You knew right from the beginning, didn't you?'

'Of course. I've always known you were an alcoholic.' He patted my hand and laughed. I couldn't see the humour of it.

'I guess everyone else does too, huh?'

Bit by bit, the picture was becoming clearer. I explained to him the fight that had taken place in the flat with Joe Hayden and my friends. I told him about Alice and about the court summons. Suddenly my head was racing at a million miles an hour. How was I ever going to sort out the mess I had made? If I lost David my life would not be worth living.

'You're not going to lose David.' Matt waved his hand. It was easy for him to be so flippant. It was my life. David was my life. I couldn't bear to think of sharing him with anyone else. Matt pointed out to me that Andrew was not looking for custody, he just wanted to see David and get to know him.

'Who are you to have the monopoly on that child? Just because you're his mother doesn't make you his owner. You *don't* own him, you know. Don't you think he needs a lot more people than you in his life? My kids need all their grannies, granddads, neighbours and friends. They need every single one of them. Jack, you're so self-centred and selfish, you *have* to change your attitude. We don't always know what's best for our children.'

That hurt terribly, deep down to the bone but he was right and I knew it. It wasn't as grave a situation as I was making it out to be. What was really bothering me was stuck in my gullet unable to go down or up. It was like a piece of bone wedged in my throat.

'One thing's for sure,' Matt went on. 'Keep drinking the way you are and David's going to suffer. He may very well end up in England with Andrew. To be honest, if you continue down the road you are going, I'd be *glad* to see him off.'

I thought about it and tried to be honest. I didn't want to do David any more harm.

'What's really hurting you?' Matt had read my mind.

My eyes were welling up again. I shook my head from side to side, unable to get the words out.

'It's Joe, isn't it?'

This time, I nodded my head up and down. I smiled at the mention of his name.

'Oh Jack. No one fucked it up more than you have where that's concerned.'

'I know.' I admitted it, at long last.

'I'll sponsor you,' he said matter-of-factly.

'What does that mean?'

'It means I'll guide you, so to speak. Are you willing to come to AA with me?'

'AA?'

'Yes, Jack. Do you want to or not?'

I didn't need to think about it. 'I'll go.'

'Good. Now I have a few rules. You must do exactly what I tell you to do – understand?'

'Yes.'

'OK. First you must not try to contact Joe.'

'What?'

'You mustn't under any circumstances try to contact him. You have a lot of work to do on yourself first.'

'I can't agree to that! I've *got* to contact him. I've got to make it up to him. I have to apologise. What will he think of me if I don't do it straight away?'

'Trust me on this one, Jack. If you move too hastily he won't believe a word you say. A simple apology is not going to fix this one. You have to show him you're sorry. Show him you mean business. You can make amends to him by staying away, for the time being anyway. Do you understand?'

'No! I have to stop them now!' I shouted angrily.

'Stop who?' he asked.

'Joe and Jill. I think they're . . . an item. Christ, I can't even bring myself to say it,' I blubbered.

'You contact either of them, and I walk.'

I looked at him stonily. I had no choice but to believe him. I was determined to get it right.

'How do you know you're right about this anyway?' I asked. 'What makes you the expert?'

'I'm sober four years. You're not. Therefore, I know. You don't.'

I wanted to smash his head in. I hadn't changed at all.

I was seething with anger. I wanted to bang Joe's door down and tell him I knew I was an alcoholic and that it would be OK now. As if that would be enough to convince anyone.

'Your main objective now is to get sober. Other people and relationships do not come into it.'

'But they do,' I argued.

'Jack, you're either with me or you're not. Do you want to stop drinking or not?' he said impatiently.

'I want to stop,' I said half-heartedly. I did want to stop but my fear was dictating that I wouldn't be able to.

'We start tonight,' he said, getting up from the table.

'Huh?'

'The first thing you need is a baby-sitter. You will have to go to a meeting every day.'

'But!'

'You also need to go to your doctor at once. You may need medical treatment of some kind. When did you have your last drink?'

'Last night,' I lied.

'You're lying.'

'I had a can this morning when I woke up. Look, I feel fine. Just tired.'

'Here is a directory of meetings in Dublin. You have to come with me for the first couple of months. You'll also need to find yourself a good counsellor.'

'Hey! How long is all this going to take? I have to be back in work next week. How many meetings do you think I will need?'

Matt laughed. 'One a day, three months minimum. Then you'll only have to go for the rest of your life!'

'Where am I going to get a baby-sitter?'

'I don't know, Jack. I'm not responsible for that. If you want this you'll find one.'

'Well, thanks. But it's not that easy.'

'It was easy enough to find a bottle of vodka, wasn't it?'

I glared at him. I wanted one right there and then. I was beginning to feel uncomfortable and irritable. I couldn't understand how I could still want a drink after everything that had happened that evening. I presumed it was wrong so I didn't mention it.

'It's simple really, Jack,' Matt said gently. 'No tricks. You go to a meeting, and don't drink in between.'

I hadn't the foggiest notion what the fuck he was talking about. I felt confused and overwhelmed by the whole thing.

'You need help, girl. Lots of it. I told you – it's going to be a very hard struggle. You're going to need all the strength you can muster and a lot more. You must concentrate on this alone and nothing else. Even David will have to take a backseat. Do you understand me?'

'Not really.'

'It's OK if you don't. You will.'

'You said that before,' I reminded him.

'Was I right?'

'Yes, you were. You fucking bastard.'

'Trust me.'

'Do I have any choice?'

'Yes. Your misery is refundable at any stage.'

'Har, har,' I said.

He left me at the bus stop and I made my journey home. I almost fell asleep on the bus. On the way to the flat I ran past the off-licence, terrified that if I looked in, it would engulf me whole. When I reached Alice's flat I knocked on the door. 'Alice, I really need to talk to you.'

She invited me in. I explained everything. Every tiny detail. It poured out of me at a hundred miles an hour. When I had finished Alice just stared at me.

'I haven't a fucking breeze what you're on about, love, but if you need a drink I have one in the fridge.'

'No, Alice! Look, I really need your help with David. I'm going to be out most nights. I'll pay you, say, £5 per hour? Would you mind him, please?' I begged her.

'Ah Jaysus love, no need to beg. Course I'll mind him. Hope it's not one a those religious cults you're getting yourself messed up with. Fucking mental, them lot. Sure, you're not an alcoholic, love. I should know. That fucking swine what called himself a husband – now *he's* an alcoholic. Poxy waster. You're not one of them, love. I've never seen you piss in your pants.' *Please, dear Jesus, shut her up.* This was not what I wanted or needed to hear. One slight turn to the right and I was out of there. Up to the off-licence. Matt or no Matt.

'Thanks, Alice!' I cut her off and left immediately. Back in the safety of my own flat I heaved a sigh of relief. But the relief was short-lived. An ominous brown envelope beckoned me to open it. I knew as soon as I did that it was from Brady Insurances. I was temporarily suspended without pay until further notice, they informed me.

I had enough to cope with right now. Sod the lot of them.

I took out all the literature Matt had given me and began to read. I read and read until my eyes were heavy, and eventually I fell asleep. An elephant shouldn't have been able to wake me after the day I had had.

However, I slept fitfully, waking up with horrific nightmares and sweating and shaking. I searched the flat for something to drink. There was nothing alcoholic in sight. I drank at least a gallon of orange juice. I awoke around 7 am glad that there had been nothing to drink.

Once David was in school I phoned Matt and arranged to meet him in the city centre that evening. As we climbed a winding staircase in an old dilapidated building, I could hear voices and chairs being scraped along the floor. A big sign hung on the door. *AA meeting in progress.*

I stepped inside and the door closed behind me.

Chapter 20

In early December 1993 the new Jack was launched. Icy winds had arrived without warning and the dark evenings were with us once again. I had just survived my first seven days without a drink. It had been incredibly difficult. I had attached myself like glue to Matt. I followed his instructions to the letter and had expected to feel better. If anything, I felt worse.

Now, without my crutch, my anaesthetic, every feeling, emotion and thought that I had buried in a bottle surged forwards in a volcanic eruption. I was a walking Montserrat. It was like waking up in the middle of a nightmare. Then realising the nightmare was real. My mood swings went up, down. Up, down. I hardly knew what to do with all of it.

If it hadn't been for Matt who was readily accessible by phone, I would never have made it. He ordered me to call, no matter what time it was. I guess he was sorry he had done that when I rang him for the fourth time after midnight. The nights were the worst. I tossed and turned, fraught with worry about everything. The court case. My job. David. I laid my head down on the pillow, exhausted, revelling at the thought of soon being asleep. Then the buggers would invade my mind, like enemy troops marching to the front line. My head was a padded room of shame and guilt. I was in the no man's land of 'early recovery'. Very early recovery. Every minute and every second seemed like an eternity.

I had my list of tasks, constructed with the help of Matt. Each time I did one of them, I crossed it off with a sense of satisfaction. It was all I could do. Follow instructions, and hope for the best. I put my trust in Matt and got on with the chores of the day and a lot more besides.

My first stop was to make a call to my doctor. He examined me thoroughly from head to toe and gave me a clean bill of health. I explained the recent developments and still found it strange to hear myself using the term 'alcoholic'. After all, my definition of an alcoholic was a tramp-type wino staggering wildly across traffic-laden streets. He would be wearing an old torn overcoat, held together with a piece of string, and have a bottle of cheap port peeping out of a brown bag. His hair would be shoulder-length, wild and matted from living outdoors, and he would shout obscenities and talk to himself. I didn't look anything like that.

My doctor asked me, had I experienced any withdrawal symptoms. I told him I hadn't. I then asked him, did that mean I wasn't an alcoholic? He told me it meant nothing of the sort. I was sorely disappointed. Secretly, I still clung to the last remaining illusion that perhaps I had escaped this wretched affliction. I was quick to point out that I very rarely drank during the day. That I was never hospitalised. That I mostly drank beer, not spirits. That I didn't drink anything like two bottles of vodka a day. That I had only had one blackout. That I wasn't in debt.

Each illusion was gradually eradicated as I went to my meetings and listened to others' experiences. I realised Ireland was rampant with alcoholism. One man described it as 'three and a half million alcoholics clinging to a rock'. It got a great laugh. Most of the people who attended AA meetings were ordinary types, just like me. In fact, the vast majority of them could have been me. The Skid Row bum was virtually non-existent. I was reluctant to accept that these people were suffering from alcoholism. They looked jolly and laughed a lot of the time.

Anyway, my doctor wrote an explanatory note to my employers, saying that I was being treated for alcoholism. He also prescribed some mild medication to tide me over the first few weeks. I was certain there was no need for the pills. By the fourth day, I had taken them all. I had not expected my nerves to be in such a bad state. Doors banged and cups slammed as if they had loudspeakers attached to them. Large crowds and voices terrified me. I heard a chainsaw serial killer trying to break into my flat, and dreamt the Nazis were following me. But I didn't have any real withdrawal symptoms. No rodents or spiders or anything like that. Just Nazis. I got away lightly.

When I shamefacedly explained to my doctor that I had been temporarily suspended from work, he told me the company would take a sympathetic view, if I was willing to accept appropriate treatment and own up to my problem. He advised me to wait until they had received his note before contacting them. I agreed. It was the best I could do for the moment.

One day, while following my new regime of housework in the flat, I opened David's schoolbag, for the first time since he had started school in September. Inside it were four unopened letters addressed to me, several news-letters, memos and a mashed pear stuck to the bottom. The bag reeked of old sandwiches and leather and I had to wash his books down with a damp cloth. I opened the letters and read in shame. The school principal had been concerned about his absences. She was also concerned about the poor quality of his homework. In addition, she expressed dissatisfaction with David's attire. It was not right, she wrote, to send a child to school without a full uniform.

Full of guilt, I walked straight over to the school, which wasn't more than five minutes away. I put my hands over my ears to protect them from the biting cold and the screech of oncoming traffic. I was a nervous wreck by the time I reached the principal's office.

The woman greeted me kindly and asked would I like a cup of tea. I was expecting to get a good lecture on the finer points of parenting but came away pleasantly surprised. I realised, all I had to do was tell the truth. The more I did it, the more I got used to hearing it. Nobody had turned me away so far. The principal showed great compassion and interest as I relayed again my story and what I was trying to do. She offered to work with me and suggested a few small things that would help. I took them on board and put a plan of action into practice immediately. I left the school and returned home to consult my list again.

I found it extremely difficult to venture outdoors at all. It wasn't the weather that was putting me off. Every corner that I turned beseeched me to *Drink this! Drink that! Eat this! Eat that!* Billboards on the street. Posters in the train station. There was no escaping it. *Drink me! Eat me!* I felt like Alice in Wonderland and wanted to put a plastic bag over my head. I had even had to leave the cinema on my one and only trip out with David. I counted seven ads for alcoholic drinks and then promptly got up and left. I took David to Burger King instead, but even there I could not escape the constant barrage of lunchtime drinkers exhaling their alcohol-scented breath all over me. I had taken to unplugging the television after 6 pm. It, too, was an endless provocation. How was I going to stay sober in this alcohol-soaked culture?

While David was at school, I attended to the flat, and the million boring jobs that I had omitted to do in the last two years. Every day I recovered more and more evidence of my drinking habit. I found two small baby vodkas stuffed inside David's Barney pyjama bag. I ran screeching to the sink, holding the offending articles out from me like they were dead vermin I had found in a trap. I emptied them down the sink and threw in a good measure of Parazone to drown out the smell. The flat had begun to stink like a swimming pool. I tidied, I swept, I mopped, I washed, I polished.

Everything was filthy. The lace curtains had turned brownish-yellow in colour. I watched them spin in the washing machine and the dirty grey water gather at the bottom. Then I prepared a proper dinner for David. I had forgotten how to cook. We had been living out of the local Chinese take-away for months. I put a nice tablecloth on the table and set two places. It looked pretty, almost normal. Knives and forks and glasses. I stared at it for a long time and forgot what I was doing. I wondered, had I been abducted by aliens, returned to earth and suffered loss of memory in the intervening lapse of time?

At 1.25 pm I left the flat again for a second journey up to the school. David was ecstatic at the sight of his mam waiting outside. It filled me with joy. I had never collected him from school. Only once, and then I was late. All the other kids had gone home at 12 pm, I remembered sadly, as I had scolded him outside the gates for not telling me. He pointed to the unopened letter in his schoolbag. I hadn't even apologised.

Now he ran out with his arms waving. He lost his balance and fell over in the excitement. 'There's my mam!' he shouted to anyone who would listen. Collecting a child from school. It was such a simple thing that I had taken for granted. I remembered seeing my own mother outside the school and how good it had made me feel.

I had forgotten the simple things in life, and their

importance. David straightened himself out and charged into my knees like a bull. I grabbed him and kissed him, feeling like a proper mam. It felt good. I looked around at all the other mams. I was going to be like them from now on. Back at home, David turned his nose up at my culinary efforts. I didn't mind. I had made the effort. I was doing everything Matt had told me to do. He said it would take time, that routine was very important, to establish it as soon as possible and to keep doing it. When dinner was through I sat down to tackle David's homework. That was a nerve-racking experience. His homework was simple and uncomplicated but David's attention wandered and his concentration was poor.

How long had he been like that?

I knew he was not a stupid child. He just hadn't had any assistance. By the end of the first week he had started to write a little bit better. I wrote notes at the bottom of his homework and the teacher responded the next day. It was a wonderful scheme. We kept in touch daily and both recognised his progress, no matter how small. She informed me of his conduct in class and any improvements. She turned out to be a great ally and friend.

In the afternoon, I made an appointment to join an Easy-Slim club. I had continued to lose weight ever so slowly, but I was bingeing on chocolate all the time and was concerned that I would put on even more weight now that I had quit drinking. I went to my first class on a Monday evening and weighed in. The instructor talked with me and we set a goal. I found it helpful and useful. My admission and action had shown determination. I was not going to tackle one thing. I was going to tackle them all, one day at a time.

I went to an AA meeting every evening as agreed. I argued with Alice that it was too much to ask her to baby-sit every night, so she introduced me to a young teenager who lived three doors down and between them they shared the workload. Alice refused to accept any payment. The teenager was delighted with a packet of cigarettes. Everybody mucked in to help as best they could. I realised I was very lucky.

As the days passed, I could see what a bitch I had been. I knew I didn't deserve the help I was getting, but that only spurred me on to take full advantage of any that was offered. It was the only way I could repay people – by showing them that the effort on my part was at least sincere.

Matt had made an arrangement for me to see an alcoholic counsellor once a week. The counsellor was kind and informative. She encouraged all my other activities. I discussed the course I was attending and she was fascinated with the resulting changes that were taking place in me. She was a very important and much-needed part of my recovery. In the confines of her private room, I was able to express my fears and anxiety and troubled heart. I was still devastated over the loss of Joe and my other friends. She insisted that I continue with my work and routines. The right time would come along, she promised, and warned me that it would be unwise to do anything just yet. I used up ample boxes of Kleenex and drove her insane with the same whining Matt refused to indulge.

In the late evenings, I read recovery books and literature. When my mind wouldn't be still, and when I couldn't concentrate, I listened to light music or nature tapes. I once played a tape with the sound of dolphins splashing in and out of water. It didn't do me any good but it sent David off to Noddy Noddy Land in seconds.

I invested in a new personal stereo and walked for at least half an hour every day. Matt had said it would help me. It certainly did. I complained and whinged down the phone for as long as he would let me. Especially about

David and the hardships of trying to get sober and mind him at the same time. He then told me about a woman who had six children, no husband and no job and who was sober for sixteen years. I never mentioned it again.

After two weeks, I contacted Greta Leahy for the second time and asked her to see me again. To my surprise she agreed. I told her my story as honestly as I could and she was agreeable and responsive. She gave me a notepad and asked me to keep a daily record of my activities. She also decided to reply to Andrew's letter to explain the situation in the hope that the whole thing would be settled out of court. There was only one week left to negotiate. I couldn't believe it was only three weeks ago when my life had been changed so dramatically. It felt like three months.

I brought up the question of fees with Greta and asked what I would be expected to pay for her services.

'Nothing for the moment,' she replied.

I was surprised and didn't know what to say. I thought it was probably a favour she was doing me because she knew my father so well. I went to let myself out and was about to close the door behind me when she raised her head for a moment. She assured me that all would turn out well on the day. I had no choice but to believe her and start praying. I was too focused on staying sober to think about it in great depth.

'By the way, Jack,' she said, scribbling in her file, her glasses perched on the end of her legal eagle nose, 'my son is in AA. Sober many years now.'

I smiled at her and she smiled back. Outside I marvelled at the coincidence.

When I visited the local Community Welfare officer, they allocated a social worker to my case. She was a warm-hearted and compassionate individual who offered her support and assistance. She informed me of all my entitlements – medical, social, tax, employment, and so on. I realised there were a lot of services I was not availing myself of, and they were all free. There had been a great deal of change in the social welfare system. I was not claiming half my entitlements.

The people at the office helped me fill out the necessary forms and they were duly posted on the way home. Two days later I received a cheque from the Tax Office for £200. It threw me into a complete spin. There is only one thing worse for an alcoholic than bad luck, and that's good luck. I rang Matt immediately.

'I just got a cheque for £200 from the Tax Office. What am I going to do with it? I have to get rid of it – I'm afraid I'll drink it.'

'Calm down,' Matt laughed. 'Give it to your solicitor,' he said calmly.

'What? But she doesn't want any money from me,' I explained.

'Give it to her,' he ordered.

'OK!' I said and slammed the phone down. I put the cheque in an envelope and posted it to Greta immediately. I rued the day I laid eyes on Matt. Then I visited the local Interflora shop and sent Mam a beautiful bouquet of flowers. The message was simple. *I love you, from Jack.*

After that, I sat down and wrote two letters: one to Jill in England and one to Karen and Mick, although it was really for Karen. They were short and sweet and I purposely didn't ramble on. Just like Matt had told me, I simply explained what I was trying to do and I hoped they would believe me. I deliberately worded Jill's letter so that there was no reference to Joe. I waited for a phone-call but nothing came. Matt had prepared me for that too.

By the end of the first couple of weeks, nobody could say I wasn't trying. I had done everything Matt had told me to do. Everything except for one small item. I couldn't pray. No matter how hard I tried to get on my knees, I

could not do it. Matt said not to worry about it. I would
be able to when I was ready.

I didn't question him. I waited and waited. I waited for
all the madness to go away. I waited for the nightmares
to end. I waited for David to bound home from school and
have scored a perfect 10 out of 10 in all his homework.
I waited for Jill and Karen and Mick to ring at the door
and shout, 'Hip! Hip! Hooray!' I still hadn't won the
Lotto, or even a car, or a holiday. I secretly waited for
Joe too. He would phone me, I fantasised. He would
start crying. We would meet and fall into each other's
arms. He would forgive me and get down on bended
knee and propose marriage to me. Now that he knew
my exceptional qualities, he would beg forgiveness for
his heartless rejection, and we would all live happily
ever after.

Yeah, yeah. Of course, none of that happened. I just put
on my coat and went to another bloody AA meeting. The
people there laughed and smiled and welcomed me and
shared their wonderful lives. They were filled with happiness and hope. I wanted to kill them all. I had begun to
pretend again. It kept Matt off my case and gave me some
peace. Inside I was a wobbling mass of jelly, ready to top-
ple over with the slightest provocation. I was not happy.

Where was the pay-off?

I had just received an invitation to the annual Christmas
party at work. It was being held in a local hotel. Like
all the previous ones, it was bound to be an all-nighter,
sodden with drunken groping managers, just like Gerard
Shannon, appalling food and crap entertainment. Just my
kind of thing. I knew I would have to decline. At least I
had a good excuse. I was sick. It was the truth. I sat looking
at the invitation for a long time. I thought it ironic that they
had invited me, when they had practically fired me at the
same time.

I had been consumed with compulsions all day long. This was turning out to be the hardest day to date. I physically shook with the desire to drink, and tried everything to take my mind off it. I had some meditation tapes in my bag and played them over and over and over. Nothing worked. I phoned Matt but he was in college and I knew he wouldn't be home until late. I had a £20 note in my purse. I had planned to use it to pay it off my ESB bill in the post office the following morning. I played with it for ages. Twisting it and turning it, making it into different shapes. A fan, an aeroplane. I bent it and folded it and looked at it. I suddenly wished I hadn't got it, then the decision-making would have been out of my hands. No mon, no fun.

I was quietly going insane. It had been an absolutely horrible day. The rain had thundered down relentlessly without any let-up. I had spent an hour with David at the kitchen table trying to do four simple sums. My patience and tolerance levels were at an all-time low.

He slept now in his comfortable bed with his side lamp on low, and the door ajar. I envied his childhood. I wandered from room to room sighing, chewing my nails, drinking endless cups of coffee and tea. I ate two bars of chocolate and tried the phone again. Matt still wasn't home. Then I picked up the phone again and rang Mam.

'Mam, did you get the flowers?' I asked.

'I did, pet. What a thoughtful gesture. Of course, I didn't tell your father. I can't believe you remembered. It meant so much to me,' she said tearfully.

'Remember what, Mam?' I asked, puzzled.

'Desmond's anniversary. They arrived on his anniversary. Isn't that why you sent them, love?'

I hadn't got the heart to disillusion her. My higher power was having a field day. If I had been lacking in faith I was now certain that something much more powerful was working through me. I had had no idea it was Desmond's anniversary. I heard the emotion in my mother's voice. It was filled with relief. Someone in the family had remembered, had acknowledged her pain. She needed to hear a lie. I was not going to spoil her momentary peace. I had given her some joy. I didn't want to take anything away from her any more.

'Of course that's why I sent them,' I said gently, still reeling at the coincidence. 'I love you, Mam,' I told her.

'I love you too, Jacqueline. It was such a lovely thought. It made me so happy that somebody did something,' she said.

I hung up feeling humbled and grateful and wondered, was Desmond my guardian angel? Maybe I had a few.

Despite all this, I was still desperate for a drink. The devil had joined forces with the compulsion and was urging me to act on his prompts.

I tried to think what I was trying to achieve. What would happen if I had a drink? What would be the big deal? Just a couple of cans – I wasn't going to burn the house down! Anyway, nobody would know. Not even David. Only I would. Look – I couldn't do much damage with £20, could I? I would start again tomorrow. My need for a drink overrode the concerns of court cases, pending job termination and everything resembling responsibility.

Before I knew it, I had my coat on.

The off-licence wasn't far. I hurried, not because David was alone but because it was 10.55 pm, five minutes to closing time. I cursed myself for having waited so long, and quickened my step. It was still raining and I was soaking wet through to the bone. I arrived at the off-licence with one minute to spare.

The shop keeper was releasing the shutters. They were already at half-mast and I dived under them just in time to find myself standing in the middle of Aladdin's cave. I wasn't fussy. I grabbed the first set of cans I could see and then I took a bottle of white wine from a pyramid at the front door. I didn't know what it was, nor did I care. It was cheap – that was all that mattered. I put them beside the cash register while the owner finished closing the shutters. There was a mirror before me and I caught a glimpse of my reflection while I stood there waiting to pay for my goods. I looked like a deranged mountain woman. If you're wondering what a deranged mountain woman looks like, imagine, if you would, a banshee who has been caught in a thunderstorm. A few loud 'keening' sounds would have made me picture perfect. I ignored the woman in the mirror and got back to the one who was impatiently rapping her fingers on the counter. What was that fucker doing outside? Building an extension? He eventually returned inside.

'Nasty night,' he commented.

'Indeed,' I answered.

He carefully placed the six cans in a brown bag and then in another plastic carrier bag. Then he took the bottle of white wine and wrapped it gently in pink tissue, twisting the top and Sellotaping it down. Then he put that in a separate plastic carrier bag. I wasn't Christmas shopping, I thought furiously. Just put the fucking things in a bag so I can get the fuck out of this place.

'Looks like it's going to be down for the night.' He rambled on about the weather as he started to add up the amounts on a small yellow pad of paper at the till. *For fuck's sake! Why can't you just ring it up like any other normal shop keeper?*

'Sorry about this, love,' he said comfortably, 'but the till is done for the night. Have to do it manually.'

I couldn't fucking care less if he'd been mugged, beaten, or if his wife had been raped in between. I could almost taste the cans and the beautiful warm feeling surging through my veins. I was drunk already with anticipation!

'Now, let's see. That's £8.99 for the beer and £3.99 for the wine – that makes . . . £12.98 altogether, love.'

Thank Christ I wasn't having a New Year's Eve party or anything like that. I made a mental note to order at Easter-time if I ever got around to organising one.

I sighed with relief and stuck my hand in the back pocket of my jeans. I fiddled around with my fingers. No sign of the £20 note. It must have been in the other pocket. I lifted my wet coat again and slipped my hand into the other pocket. It wasn't in there either. I moved to the two front pockets. Nothing. I checked the two coat pockets, even though I knew I wouldn't have put it in there. I opened my bag and ransacked my purse. Nope. *Fuck it! Fuck it!*

I looked all around me. Just in case I had accidentally tossed it out while my hands were searching, I got down on my knees and crawled, retracing my steps over every inch to the door. The shopkeeper was becoming increasingly impatient with me. Besides, he was locked in a room with a mad witch, dripping wet and crawling all over the floor, shouting loud obscenities to herself.

'I'm sorry, love, but you'll have to move along. I'm afraid you'll have to leave if you can't pay.'

I looked at him with fire in my eyes. 'I swear I had a £20 note. Just here.' I pointed to my backside. By the expression on his face, I could tell that he would have preferred to see the £20 note. 'Where's the nearest cash machine?' I asked him, panic rising in my voice as the minutes ticked by.

'There isn't one for miles, love.' He began to unwrap the drink as slowly and methodically as he had wrapped it.

'Look, I swear to you, I have the money. I must have

left it at home. I can give you my address, and I'll bring it down first thing in the morning. Hey, look – you know me, I've been in here before.' I was desperate. My voice had transformed. It had a sad pleading essence. It was genuine too.

'I'm sorry, love. No credit.' He put the bottle of wine back in place. The cans went back on the shelf as well.

I was broken-hearted. I tried to calculate in my head if I got a bus to town and found a cash machine, I would have to go to a night-club, which would be the only thing open by that time. Then I would be OK. The man ushered me out of the shop. As I stood outside in the rain, it intermingled with my tears, which were coming down just as fast. I felt a desperate crushing of spirit. My mouth was dry. My clothes were stuck to me and my shoes sloshed noisily as I headed for home.

What the fuck am I doing? What in the name of Jesus am I doing? I said it out loud. A car fled past at great speed and drowned me in a fountain of muddy silt that had gathered like a pond at the edge of the road. I walked home slowly, shivering with cold and shock. What had come over me? This was useless! I'd never be able to stay sober if I was going to react like that every time I wanted a drink. For the first time, I saw the power I was up against and appreciated the need for a power greater than myself. I began to ponder it. I quickened my step as the reality began to seep through my rainsodden clothes. I had left David alone, in the flat. I began to run.

My old friends were back – guilt and shame, the only visitors I had these days. I charged through the front door and ran to David's room. Thank God! He was wrapped around his Barney pyjama bag, still fast asleep. I was out of breath, and as I stood there looking down on him, my wet clothes dripped on to the carpet.

I went to my bedroom, turned on the heaters and

stripped. I put on some warm night-clothes and dried my hair with a towel. After placing my jeans and jumper, which were heavy with wet, on the heater, I saw a piece of paper slowly descend. Like a feather in the air, it swayed backwards and forwards, finally coming to rest in the inside of my sneaker, which I had placed under the radiator. I picked it up. It was the £20 note – still folded in the shape of a fan.

I tried to figure out where it had come from. Perhaps it had got caught in my jumper or my sock? Only God knew. Hang on – *maybe God did know?* I was overwhelmed with a strange sense of coincidence again. Or was it? Could I make the necessary leap of faith? Could I perhaps believe that somebody, something, somewhere, had been looking out for me? That it had not been a coincidence at all, but divine intervention? I acknowledged the uncanny number of coincidences that had been occurring. Then I did something that I hadn't done since I had made my Holy Communion.

I knelt down and blessed myself. I stayed there for a moment and tried to remember some prayers I had learned at school. I remembered the Hail Mary only because 'The Dragon' in junior school had made sure I would for the rest of my life. I was loath to say it, because of the memories it invoked. I still couldn't recall the full 'Our Father'. So I opted for a short one-way conversation with this strange thing they called a higher power.

'Dear Whoever You Are. Thank you. PS: Please help me.'

Then I blessed myself again and got up. There were no choirs of angels or flashes of light or the sound of flapping wings. I didn't feel any different. I still wanted to drink.

However, I felt an enormous relief that I hadn't. I was very grateful. I also had digested a big chunk of truth about this disease called alcoholism. It wasn't going to go away, not ever. I lay on my bed, munching biscuits and listening to music. I thought back over my life, only this time I added alcohol to each circumstance and the picture revealed a startling common thread. Any event had always been followed by a drunken spree. I had put my bad luck down to circumstances in my life. I could see clearly that I myself had created most of the circumstances and then made them worse by adding alcohol to them. It was a bit like putting a match to paraffin.

I tried to accept responsibility for my actions, and then quickly discerned that if I was going to do that, I would also have to own up to the consequences. I shivered at the thought of what the consequences might have been, had I got my own way in the off-licence that night. The madness had begun to wear off now, and while the gnawing was still there, a clarity of mind was too.

There wasn't an ongoing battle between them. They were both there in my mind but quite separate. Standing side by side. I realised I had a choice. I could get drunk if I wanted to. I could stay sober if I wanted to. Which set of thoughts was I going to choose?

That was going to be my dilemma.

I went searching for Sam and found him at the end of David's bed. He had been neglected and looked dirty. A blob of jam had hardened on his left ear and I picked it off. I squeezed his hand and 'Old MacDonald' started off all right but then slowed down to a deep drawling sound. The battery had died. How ironic. A bit like our relationship. I thought about Joe. Allowed myself the luxury of a short fantasy. Just for a minute. It was a fatal mistake.

I had known for some time that I had begun to miss Joe in a way that was shockingly different. I was not just missing a friend. I was missing *him*. It had begun to sink in some weeks back when I heard Diane talk at the course about her husband. I was identifying with her feelings. It didn't take a genius to figure out that she was talking about a lover. Joe was not my lover. Then I asked myself that awful question. Why? Why did I feel so differently about him? Did I want him as a lover? As sure as day follows night the answer came at me screaming wildly into my ears. Yes! Yes! Yes! I dismissed it, of course. I knew full well that that would have been a convenient decision to come to.

After all, I had just been rejected by a gay man, found out I was alcoholic, had the threat of a court case hanging over me, and hadn't had sex for two years. Even with that clarity and vision the thoughts persisted. I had spent the best part of twenty years with Joe. It hadn't mattered that we had not had sex. We had had everything else. We had weathered many storms together. Of all my friends, I would have described him as my best.

What was a lover anyway, if not a best friend? Then what is love? I found myself dreaming about him but not in a romantic sense. It was a curiously straightforward desire to extend what was already a good relationship, beyond the realms of friendship. Of all the people in the world, I couldn't think of one with whom I would like to spend the rest of my life, except him.

He was already a huge part of my life. Now I didn't even know if friendship was still possible. I had taken it for granted for so long. I had destroyed it with my own two hands. And now I couldn't bear to think of the future without him.

Why had I avoided my real feelings all this time? All these years, carefully tiptoeing around what was under my nose all along?

The answer was that I was afraid. I was terrified of trusting myself. It wasn't Joe I had doubted. It was me. If the relationship had failed, I would have lost his friendship. Now I had lost the chance of both, and hated myself for it.

*Look at you! You're pathetic. You're snuggling up to a yellow
chicken. Aren't you concerned? Are you proud of who you've
become?* No!

*Well, an hour ago you were prepared to throw it all away
again.* I wasn't really.

You think you're in love with Joe, don't you? I know I am.

What makes you think he'll entertain you after all this? I
don't think he will. Fuck off, will you?

*Not much work in loving a man you don't have to see or
speak to!* There's more work in it than you'll ever know!

Perhaps you are in love with him, but is he in love with you?
Go away!

When I got up to go to the toilet, the telephone beckoned
me. Willed me to use it. I picked it up. I dialled the number
slowly. Heard it ring. My heart thumped. Then I put it
back down. I picked it up again and dialled a different
number.

'Hello?' Juliet's British voice answered.

'Juliet, it's Jack. I know it's late.'

'Oh – Jack.' She didn't sound exactly thrilled to hear
from me.

'I'm really sorry I haven't contacted you before now. I
wanted to. To be honest, I didn't want it to seem like I
was interfering,' I finished.

She laughed hysterically.

'Are you OK, Juliet? How are the kids, I mean?' I lit a
cigarette and took a deep drag.

'The kids are fine. I'm fine too, I suppose. I just have
to get on with it.'

'Look, for what it's worth, I don't know what happened
with you and Joe and I don't expect you to tell me either.
But I know this much. He loved you.'

'I know he did, but he loved someone else much more.
I just couldn't compete,' she said sadly.

'Juliet, there was no competition,' I reassured her.

She laughed again, a touch bitterly. 'Of course, you would see it that way, wouldn't you. After all, you had his heart right from the beginning. You had a head-start of twenty years. How could I have competed with that?'

'Excuse me?' I was completely at sea.

'Jack – c'mon. Any fool could see that you were the one, even when he couldn't have you. He obviously hoped he could settle for something else, but it didn't work out. He was true to himself in the end. His heart was with you, even when he was with me. He just decided it would be better for him to be alone than live a lie.'

'Juliet, this is Jack, not Jill. I think you've got your wires crossed,' I said nervously.

She sighed heavily. '*You're* the other woman, Jack. Believe it.'

'No, I can't be! No, it's Jill – I'm certain of it.' I sounded like a complete and utter moron.

'You know, he always said that you were an intelligent being. I'm beginning to wonder. Can't you see that he has been in love with you all this time?'

I swallowed hard, not knowing whether to celebrate or start crying. I was speechless. 'I can't think right now,' I told her, my voice trembling. 'Oh my God. Juliet, I'm sorry. I didn't know that. Oh my God.'

'Jack, take my advice. Stop looking for Mr Right in the wrong places. It's like searching for jewels in the mud. Joe was made for you and you for him.'

Brave words from a woman he had just ditched. I was amazed at her acceptance.

'I think I'll have to go and lie down,' I said rather stupidly. 'I'm sorry if I've upset you. I really had no idea. Juliet – I'm so, so sorry.'

'I like you, Jack, always did. I wish you both the very best.'

I put down the phone, went into my bedroom and lay down. I stared at the ceiling all night, and wondered, had God deliberately omitted to dole out 'cop on' the day He made me?

Chapter 21

Alice and I sat in the front row of the hard-backed seats. We were in the school auditorium awaiting the glorious opening of a nativity play. The participants backstage were all between four and eight years of age. Their excitement could be heard all over the hall. They thumped and banged and shouted loudly. Elbows and knees occasionally burst through the slit in the middle of the curtains, and frightened faces peeped out from the wings. I couldn't see David, which was just as well. It would only have increased his pre-performance nerves. The parents were just as noisy, exchanging pride-filled comments about their own children.

'My Deirdre's a cow,' one whispered in Alice's ear.

'Go on?' she said. 'Must run in the fucking family, love.' The parent turned away in disgust.

I was at my son's first nativity play. I was twenty-one days sober. I was still alive. Amazingly, so was everyone else.

The curtains jerked back, making an ugly squeaking noise. There stood the cast, all giggly and silly. The parents erupted into a loud cheer. Some could hardly contain themselves and jumped up and down in the seats.

'Jaysus, will you's shut the fuck up!' Alice yelled and everybody went silent.

I could just about catch a glimpse of David. He was

tucked away at the back, where I knew he was happy to
be. He held tight to his staff with one hand, and scratched
his balls irritably with the other. The tablecloth on his head
was held on by a piece of string and he tugged at it every
couple of seconds. Soon the whole thing was lopsided and
he stared out at us like a one-eyed Cyclops.

Jesus and Mary were very professional, remembering
their lines perfectly, but the younger ones were restless
and wandered off the stage shouting and waving.

'There's my mam! Howya, Mam!'

The audience laughed hysterically when one of them
obviously had had enough and lay down in the crib for
a kip. Joseph and Mary were disgusted and started to
cry. A shepherd boy decided he needed to piss and
began to strip without any modesty whatsoever. A teacher
appeared and rescued him just in time.

David made his one and only appearance when he
brought forward what was supposed to be frankincense
as a gift for the Baby Jesus. He dumped the heavy weight
in Mary's lap. She let out a yelp and didn't look happy at
all. The fright made her forget her lines. There was a long
difficult pause where Mary looked from side to side for a
prompt. Eventually she was forced to ad lib.

'Jaysus, thanks, mister. It's massive.'

She brought the house down. David scampered to the
back to take up his manly stance again. Then another
shepherd let out a rip-roaring fart. The whole thing was a
disaster from start to finish. Teachers ran about frantically
trying to save the day. The play concluded after four
minutes. The applause was deafening. It was the most
beautiful thing I had ever seen. It wasn't the first time
I had laughed that week, either. I had forgotten the
simple therapy of laughter and was beginning to feel
its benefits.

Things had improved. They had definitely improved.

After the phone-call with Juliet, I clung to the belief that Joe still had my best intentions at heart. Even Jill had had my best intentions at heart. The shame made me want to curl up and die. Perhaps they had felt forced to confront me for once and for all. I tried to see it as an act of love and not the rejection I had thought initially. I made myself believe it, because *not* to believe it would make none of it worthwhile.

I was working very hard on my recovery, day and night. I had a routine going and stuck to it rigidly. In the mornings when I awoke, I knelt down and said what is probably the best prayer ever thought of. 'God help me.'

I was still marvelling at the beauty of waking up. The wonder of having slept peacefully for seven hours. The delight of not feeling sick. No headaches, no sweating, no nightmares. Everything was still in the same place as I had left it the night before. My clothes were neatly folded away, the dishes were washed and still in the cupboard. No open phonebook, to remind me I couldn't remember who I had rung. No overspilling ashtrays with mountains of half-smoked cigarettes. No cans, or bottles, or empty purses. It was complete bliss, just to start the day with no worries about yesterday.

After taking David to school, I usually popped into the school oratory. I sat there for about fifteen minutes, watching the candles flicker. Sometimes I lit one for Joe and me. I wasn't sure if I was supposed to pray for a reconciliation: I did anyway. Over the weeks I lit candles for everybody I knew. It cost a small fortune, but the statues were happy. After that I visited the post office. I had recently learned that I could pay my bills by the week. I made a point of dropping in and paying off a small amount on every bill. It was the first time I had ever received a gas bill that was in credit. *Yippee!*

I even had some spare money, which I put by in a special

savings account for David. It was strange to have extra
money. It frightened me still.

On returning home, I ran a long hot bath, something
that I had not indulged in for months. I filled it to the brim
and added lots of nice-smelling oils and perfumes. Then I
lit candles all around it, turned on a meditation tape and
lay there, trying to be peaceful and serene. I was trying.
I really was.

After my bath, I put on my make-up. It didn't matter
if I wasn't going anywhere, I put it on regardless. I had
invested in some good make-up and experimented with
different kinds of shades and textures. It was fun. I had
cut my hair short. It was manageable and made me look
younger. At one o'clock I turned on the lunchtime news.
I had made a point of learning something new every
day. I had no idea who was running the country and
wasn't really interested. I just knew it would be helpful
to tune in to the living world. At 1.25 pm I donned my
coat again and walked back up to the school to collect
David. I didn't have to bow my head, cross the street, or
run past everybody. I forced myself to say hello to everyone that I passed. To my surprise some said hello back.
It felt great to be free of shame, if only briefly. But
there was always something just around the corner to
remind me.

At home after school, David once came running in
to me complaining that the television wasn't working. When I went to investigate, I found that he had
accidentally hit the remote. I raised my arm jokingly,
feigning that I was about to strike him. It was all in jest.
David didn't think it was funny at all and immediately
guarded himself by raising his elbow to his face and
turning his back to me. I was shocked and upset, and
realised that, no matter how much I thought things
had improved, it would take a long time for David

to recover from the effects of my drinking and bad temper.

In the afternoons, I re-rented all the videos I thought I had seen. It was interesting to watch them again sober. There were whole scenes I could not remember. In between the videos I had accumulated a whole new bunch of friends. AA members dominated the phone day and night. I was never alone. I had an army of people to turn to at any time. I could no longer use loneliness as an excuse for drinking.

My weekly visits to the alcoholic counsellor continued. I told her about the telephone conversation with Juliet. She showed no excessive emotion and I felt deflated. If I had to eat any more humble pie I would vomit, I thought rebelliously. She instructed me to send myself a Christmas card. I felt a right twit, sitting at the kitchen table writing this ridiculous verse to myself. In the end I wrote *Happy Christmas Jack, from me*. Then I sealed the envelope and posted it quickly while no one was looking.

She also encouraged me to write down my feelings about Joe in letter form. She was quick to add that they were not meant for sending, simply for therapy. I wrote volumes furiously. Some were horrible character assassinations filled with bitterness and hate and resentment; others gushed with loving words and romantic soliloquies. I kept them all at the top of my wardrobe. Within a few hours I would wonder how I had written such drivel. Then I would remember the wise advice, and appreciate the fact that I hadn't sent any of them.

My Christmas card arrived safely the next day. I opened it, read it, and then threw it in the bin. A mountain of other cards arrived from well-meaning AA members. Some I had not brushed shoulders with, yet they had found the time to send me a card. It warmed me. I felt like I had a second family. Every day, I would quickly check to see if there was anything from Joe, despite knowing in my heart I was only fooling myself.

I arrived promptly for the last session of the course. The gang were there, dressed up to the nines. Matt had put on a bit of a spread for afterwards. Spirits were high and voices equally so.

I hugged everybody and was delighted with all the comments about my weight loss. I had managed to maintain it, by counteracting my chocolate binges with good brisk walks. I felt good and looked good and I knew it.

Brian stood in the centre of the floor and began to speak. 'Well, I'm glad you all turned up for the final session. I have to say I have enjoyed working with all of you immensely. You were a particularly interesting group and participated and contributed greatly.'

He cleared his throat. 'I would like to thank each and every one of you with a small presentation. These are completion certificates. As you can see, I have your name and date inscribed on them and I hope you like them.'

He called us one by one and we accepted our little gift. It was a nice touch and something I would treasure for ever. When that was completed we arranged a chair and desk in the middle of the floor.

'I hope you all remembered to bring in your defining object?' Brian asked. Everybody nodded. 'OK, then let's get the ball rolling. Who wants to go first?' Bertie had his hand up. 'Right – Bertie.'

Brian sat down on the edge of the seat and Bertie stood erect and proud. Then he reached into his little briefcase and pulled out a hammer. Everybody started to laugh, including Bertie.

'As well you may laugh. This will need very little explaining indeed. I happened to be reading a lovely little quotation book the other day and I read this: "If the only tool you have in life is a hammer, then you tend to see every problem as a nail." No extra marks for figuring out what that means in my life. Hence the hammer. It represents my way of relating to people. I fix things. That's what I've always done. I thought that was what I was supposed to do. The course has helped me to see that I can actually hinder things by trying to do that all the time. It's time for me to change my set of tools, I guess.' He stepped down and we gave him a round of applause.

Next up was Connor. He blew heavily into his handkerchief before starting, then he reached in his breast pocket and pulled out a birth certificate.

'This is my birth certificate,' he announced. 'Damn well took me five weeks to find it. It was carefully tucked away in the attic, out of sight – just like me.' He paused for a moment, thinking about what he had just said, then put on his reading glasses and opened the document.

'According to this here document, I am Connor Joseph Costigan. I forgot who I was. I lost my identity. I don't want to forget who I am again. The course has helped me reclaim me. I am very happy to say who I am today.'

We clapped loudly for Connor. His genuine sense of achievement was shared by all of us.

Diane got up next, looking distinctly different from the woman who had first attended. She wore a pair of trendy jeans and a loose-fitting jacket. Her hair was free, glossy and decidedly untidy. She looked natural. She reached into her bag and laughingly drew out a Barbie Doll.

We all fell about the place roaring. It took a few minutes for the mirth to die down. Diane herself was finding it hard to stop sniggering. It was lovely to see her laughing at herself.

'Well, you don't have to be a genius to figure out why I brought this baby. It's actually a Sleeping Beauty Barbie. An exact replica of me. Always waiting for the prince in shining armour to come along and kiss me and then I could start living. I'm not waiting any more. I'm starting my life *now*. There's so much I haven't done! I don't want to be a doll any more. I'd much rather just be me.'

We clapped long and hard as Diane sat down. That only left poor old Frank. He remained sitting and Brian got up instead.

'Frank has asked me to read you something for him. His defining object is a poem that he wrote, and it's entitled "Life":

> *You can't hide shame with a Band Aid,*
> *You cannot treat guilt with a pill,*
> *You cannot mend a heart with Sellotape,*
> *You cannot fill a hole with a drill.*
>
> *You can't travel light with an elephant,*
> *You cannot feel joy without pain,*
> *You can't make a fool intelligent,*
> *You cannot make a cripple lame.*
>
> *You cannot end wars without bleeding,*
> *You cannot use Braille without words,*
> *You can't forgive without healing,*
> *You cannot ignore what hurts.*
>
> *You can't really love without hating,*
> *You cannot feel love with your head.*
> *You can't become whole without breaking,*
> *You cannot kill what's dead.*
>
> *You can't have a soul without spirit,*
> *You cannot change what is,*
> *You can't fail without merit,*
> *Because you cannot kill what lives.*

There was an eerie silence for a moment. Then Connor

started to clap slowly and we all joined in. I had always known Frank was talented. His poem had drawn us all into our individual journeys, and brought tears to our eyes.

Frank stood up, bowed and sat down again. He rocked backwards and forwards, blushing profusely. That only left little old me. I stood up.

'I have in my hand what's called a "death pass". It's a piece of paper that granted twenty-four hour visiting access to parents of dying children. Mam and Dad were holders, because my brother was very weak and frail when he was born. Unfortunately he didn't make it. He died within thirty-six hours of his birth. I brought it here today because it represents the dysfunction in our home when I was a child. Although Desmond died, Mam and Dad never dealt with it. It was the family curse, the family secret. Desmond was the Scapegoat, if you like. Because of his death, I suffered, we all suffered. I don't want to carry his death any more. I just want to be me. I realise I drank to cope with Mam and Dad. They argued to cope with Desmond. As for Desmond himself, he had a lucky escape. I'm putting him where he belongs. In the past.'

I folded the yellowed and torn document and put it in my pocket. Nobody clapped. It would have been inappropriate. I understood.

After that, we gathered around the big old table and ate sandwiches and cakes and drank tea. We exchanged phone numbers and vowed to stay in touch. It was sad saying goodbye. I felt I had known everyone there a lifetime and yet it had only been ten weeks.

I promised Diane to stay in contact and thanked Brian for all his help. Then Matt and I went to have a cup of coffee. It was strange, but now I had begun to notice his gay side, I couldn't understand how I had never noticed it before. He was so tidy and particular, folding his sugar

bag neatly and sipping the tea daintily. His hair was
perfectly in place and his clothes were immaculate. Matt
had a feminine side that made women fall head over heels
in love with him. He was easy to talk to, easy to approach,
and easy to trust. No wonder I was so attracted to him. He
was the perfect partner!

He pushed a small parcel across the table.

'What's this?' I asked him.

'Open it and see,' he grinned.

I opened the miniature packet and inside was a keyring.
On the back of it was engraved the Serenity Prayer.

> *God grant me the serenity to accept the things I cannot*
>   *change,*
> *Courage to change the things I can,*
> *And the wisdom to know the difference.*

I held it in my palm, savouring the words. 'Thanks, Matt.
That's really thoughtful of you. Just one thing. When do
I get the wisdom bit?'

'When you die,' he replied flatly.

We both had a good laugh. I hugged it close to my
chest. It was the nicest thing anyone had given me, apart
from 'Sam'. No one could top that.

Inside, I was dreading Christmas. I had always secretly
detested it. It was the Happy Families syndrome again.
It made me sick to my stomach. I tried hard to ignore
the silly season gags, the monotonous advertising, the
jingle-bell junkies and David's endless demands for every
toy he set eyes on. I wanted to buy him everything, to
make up for all the rotten thoughts I had had about
him. I wanted everything to be OK. I felt such remorse
over my failed mothering skills. Matt warned me about
this 'overspending'. He reminded me that it wasn't what
David really needed, no matter what he said. He needed

to know I was there in the full sense of being a human being, not just physically but emotionally.

Most of all I tried to avoid happy couples strolling hand in hand, as much as I avoided the lethal buzz of a busy pub. I made an extra effort to visit Mam and Dad. To my surprise Rachel and Jason were there too. We sat together on the floor and watched the Christmas tree being erected. Dad hovered unsteadily on the edge of a stepladder, not sure if he wanted to put his full weight on it.

'Ah, for goodness sake, William, will you stand on the thing properly.' Mam stood beside him holding the trunk and becoming more and more impatient as he dithered around. One step up. One step down.

'Quit whining and give me the damn lights,' he ordered.

Mam did as she was told. I could tell by her face that she thought she could do a quicker job. I tried telepathy to persuade her not to nag, but her mouth beat me to it.

'William, you need your glasses – that's what's wrong. If you had your glasses on, the job would be well done by now.' And she marched off in search of them.

'Bollox,' he said, under his breath.

'No worries, Pops, we'll have it up before the next millennium,' Jason joked.

'With a bit of luck, they'll be out of fashion,' I added.

'I couldn't give a monkey's,' Dad hissed through clenched teeth, 'I'll be dead and buried by then, and so will she, God willing.'

We all laughed and Mam returned with his glasses in hand.

'No need for them now,' he said triumphantly. 'Jason, switch them on there, son.'

Jason plugged the lights in and they went on. And off. And on.

'Ah, what's wrong with them now?' Mam asked crossly.

'They're supposed to do that, you thick.' Dad stepped down, breathing a sigh of relief.

For once Mam's tongue was silenced.

They invited me to come for Christmas dinner, insisting that it was not right for David and me to be alone on Christmas Day. I complained bitterly about the falseness of it all. It only made them plead more. In the end I agreed. Dad gave Mam a satisfied nod. They were obviously very pleased. I chatted with Rachel, my younger married sister whom I hardly ever saw. She had wisely made plans to be elsewhere on the big day. No wonder Mam and Dad were delighted to have me aboard. I began to shake with the thought of being alone with them for three full hours. There was no way out of it. Besides, I didn't want to be alone with David. Especially that day. I wanted to stay sober, no matter what. Mam and Dad's was probably the safest place to be, all things considered.

I watched them in the living room, busying themselves with this and that. They suddenly looked older. They appeared to have aged about ten years – I hadn't noticed it before. Then I realised they *were* older. It wasn't my imagination. They were reaching their half-century soon.

With that thought, I settled my indecision. I was grateful for the invitation and even looked forward to it.

Mam appeared with a cup of tea, and sat beside me. 'When is the court case, love?' she asked.

I didn't really want to think about it. 'Friday. Three days,' I answered.

'What's happening then, do you know?' She seemed concerned.

'No, I don't, Mam. I won't until the day arrives. I'm leaving it all in Greta's capable hands. We've discussed it at length.'

'Are you going to agree to access?' she asked carefully.

'I probably will, Mam. It's about time David saw his real father. Who am I to deprive him of that?'

'I guess you're right. It won't be easy, though. Your father will have his nose out of joint,' she added.

I sat silently looking out the window.

'I've been meaning to ask you, love.'

I prepared myself.

'Have you seen poor Karen lately?' She referred to her like she was a homeless refugee.

'No. Why?' I asked.

'Ah, just wondering how she is – with the break-up and all.' She blessed herself.

'What break-up?'

'Ah, now surely you know herself and Michael broke up? Sure didn't I meet her mam in the dry-cleaners, and she's back home. Poor thing is broken-hearted. Have you not been in touch with her?' she asked innocently.

'No, I haven't.' I sipped my tea, trying to disguise my shock.

'Well, that's what I heard,' she sighed. 'By the way, if you don't mind me asking, have you seen Joe at all?'

'Mam, I've been very busy lately, running here and there, what with the course and everything. I'm sure he will be home for Christmas as usual.'

I didn't want to hear his name. And I was secretly fuming. I couldn't believe Karen hadn't contacted me. That she was at home, nursing a broken heart and that she didn't want to discuss it with me. Then I thought about my own sense of self-importance. I reminded myself that I wasn't as important as I'd like to think I was. It was hard and it hurt.

I had hoped to tell Mam about my decision to stop drinking, but Matt had advised me to keep it to myself, especially as it was Christmas-time. I couldn't understand his motives. I thought my parents would delight in my good news and see it as a positive step. He didn't share my confidence. Now I was glad I hadn't told them anything. I was so angry I wanted to kill. Just when I thought I was the walking epitome of serenity, my rage would surface again.

I left the house distressed and confused. When the anger abated, I started to cry. I was really hurt. We had been friends since early childhood. I had known Mick and Karen for fifteen years. Now they had split up. Neither of them had contacted me. Jill had not even phoned to let me know. Neither of them needed me. Neither of them wanted me. I was feeling really sorry for myself and was set to indulge in one gigantic pity party.

I struggled all evening, wallowing in anger and sadness. I had just about had enough of everything. Outside I could hear the Christmas spirit in full swing. The flats were writhing with mini-parties. Everybody was getting drunk, except me.

I thumped the pillows on my bed and cursed Matt. I wished I had never met him. I wished I could unlearn what I had learned. I wished I could unlearn it all. I didn't want to be aware. I didn't want to be an alcoholic. I didn't want to be dysfunctional. I didn't want to be different. *I just wanted to be like everyone else. Normal!* Only I didn't know what normal was. If only I could take a sleeping tablet, preferably one that lasted until New Year's Day. I didn't want to go through this charade. I wanted the whole thing to be over.

I turned on the television in time to catch the end of *It's a Wonderful Life*. Jimmy Stewart was returning to his family, desolate and broke. The house was alive with townsfolk. His children had collected money to make up for his £8,000 loss. There was a Christmas tree erected and a bell was placed on the top. The bell tinkled. His child turned to him and said, 'Remember, every time a bell rings, an angel gets his wings.'

Jimmy smiled, remembering Clarence the angel, who had saved him from certain death when he attempted suicide, earlier on in the story. He picked up a book and opened it. Clarence had inscribed something on the inside leaf: *No man is a failure, who has friends*.

I cried myself to sleep.

The following day, I confronted the job situation. I walked from my flat to Brady Insurance's and arrived unexpectedly at the office. The dreariness of it reminded me that sobriety had also heightened my senses. In the reception area, two girls were sipping coffee and stopped their conversation abruptly when they saw me. I was inwardly terrified but reckoned Christmas week was as good a time as any to approach the manager. Besides, he should have received the doctor's note by now, and I was relying on his compassion to see me through. Much as I hated the job, I needed to keep it now more than ever. With the court case the following day, I had to have something substantial to give the judge in my defence. I knew that to turn up jobless would go against me. Things were bad enough as they were.

I passed the line of covered Olympic typewriters; nobody was working. For the first time, I heard laughter coming from the canteen. A scrawny two-foot Christmas tree with three red baubles had been erected and stood at the side of the manager's door. There were lights on the tree but I noticed they weren't working. I changed the company's name from 'Brady Urinals' to 'Scrooge & Sons'.

Inside his office, an unusually relaxed-looking Gerard Shannon was having a tipple with the assistant manager. They almost choked on their drinks when I rapped lightly on the open door. The assistant manager smiled weakly at me and exited like a bullet.

'Jacqueline! What a surprise. Come on in.' Gerald smiled at me, revealing his hideously discoloured teeth. I smiled back with a Colgate sparkle.

'Please – sit down. I wasn't expecting you, or was I?' he said slowly. I detected a slight slur in the words and my eyes went to the open bottle of whiskey on the table. His eyes wandered in the same direction. We both stared at it. Then he whipped it off the table and put it down on the floor beside him. What did he think I was going to do? Grab it and run down the road swigging out of it like a madwoman?

'I received the letter from your doctor, Jacqueline,' he said pompously, and my heart sank. Then: 'I want you to know that we will support you and help you in any way possible. I am sorry for your . . . em . . . trouble,' he said.

'Thank you,' I replied, genuinely surprised.

'If you need any financial assistance for treatment et cetera, we will oblige, of course. In the meantime, we would just like to see you get well. Don't worry yourself about the job – come back when you're ready. Perhaps part-time to start with. Would that be a good idea?'

I was stuck for words. 'That would be great. I appreciate all your help, Mr Shannon.'

'Not at all, Jacqueline, not at all. Anything to help.'

I left the office quite stunned. Honesty had paid off as Matt had promised it would. I prayed tomorrow would show the same results.

Chapter 22

I had never been inside a courtroom before. Standing in the foyer, I felt as if I was waiting to be sentenced to life imprisonment. My solicitor, Greta Leahy, was struggling with files and folders and briefcases. She dropped the files on the floor and they landed with a heavy thud. Judging by their weight, anyone would think I had a long criminal history. It didn't look good. I was extremely nervous and unsure of how to behave. Did you genuflect in front of the judge? Did you salute them? I looked around me and was horrified by the total lack of privacy.

The foyer was like an open barn. Groups huddled in corners discussing private affairs, whispering back and forth. I couldn't understand it. After all, this was the family courts. People were here because of domestic difficulties. It seemed unfair to expect them to gather in this great big hall and stand beside the very person they were prosecuting. There were even children running up and down, taking advantage of the polished floor and turning it into a skating rink. It all seemed terribly wrong.

One woman stood crying, as she spoke to her barrister. Her private life echoed around the hall. It was obvious she was applying for a barring order. Her husband leaned against the wall not two feet from where she stood and mockingly tried to interrogate her. No wonder women gave up. From now on, I would appreciate the guts and courage it took to get this far.

Just then I spotted Andrew Fenton, splendid in suit and tie. I nodded at him. He nodded back. He was still devastatingly attractive. I could see some similarity between him and David, although ultimately David looked like me. Watching him now, it was obvious he was his father. They shared the same expressions; even when he smiled the likeness was uncanny.

I had taken particular care with my make-up today. I had worn my good suit too. I was thrilled to bits when the zip went up nice and easy. I had even recovered my waistline and proudly surveyed my reflection in the mirror. I looked smart. I needed to. Solicitors walked briskly to and fro, consulting with their clients. Greta was doing the same. I saw her talking with Andrew's. They were laughing together. I wasn't sure whether I should take that as a good sign or a bad sign. She returned, still smiling, took me by the arm and backed me into a corner.

'OK, here's the deal,' she started.

'Hold on a minute,' I interrupted. 'Do you know him?'

'Yes, actually I do. He's good – very good. A real clever clogs, but he can be a right bully too,' she said.

'Well, you looked like you were old buddies to me,' I commented.

'Oh that! That's all part of the act, dear. In the courts, they're all the same. Wall-to-wall bastards. Don't be fooled.' She tapped the side of her nose.

'What does he want?' I asked.

'Not much. One Saturday every month. He'll fly over. He's also consented to financially maintain David – £80 per week. If I were you, I'd concur,' she finished.

'If I don't?' I asked.

'He'll fight you with whatever he's got. Trust me, Jack,

you don't want to see what he's got. He's sure to bring up your drinking.' She paused.

'I see,' I said. I thought about it. I certainly needed the money for David. His expenses had been rising ever since he started school, and I knew they would continue increasing in the coming years. One Saturday a month didn't sound too bad. Besides, I could do with the day off. Most importantly, I knew I couldn't hold on to David for my own selfish reasons. He needed a father now more than ever.

'OK,' I finally agreed. 'Let's go for it.'

'We'll still have to go before the judge,' she said.

'Why?' I asked.

'The access order still has to be signed and witnessed. It won't take long. We'll be in and out in a jiffy. Don't worry.' She patted my arm with her hand.

It was another hour before our case was called. As I walked into Court Number 47 behind Greta, I suddenly felt very nervous. Greta motioned to me to zip my mouth. I didn't know whether to sit or stand. The District Court clerk hollered, 'All stand, please.'

We all stood, and the judge entered. It was a woman. *Yes!* She was very young, which surprised me. For some reason I had expected her to be in her late eighties, I don't know why. I thought judges had to be old to be wise, I suppose. Greta motioned me to sit down. I did. As I pulled the chair closer to the table, it made a horrible screeching noise. The judge looked up over her glasses and down at me. I was terrified, so I played with my lucky charm – the keyring Matt had given me. I pressed it against my palms and repeated the Serenity Prayer.

Greta approached the bench. 'Your Honour, our respective clients have agreed on terms of access by mutual consent.'

The judge was taking her time reading the details. 'Ms

Joyce, you are happy to consent to access? One Saturday, every month?'

'Stand up!' Greta hissed at me. I stood up.

'Yes, Your Honour. I am happy to do that.' Was I suppose to sit down again?

'Excellent. Excellent. Take note, Clerk. One Saturday every month by consent.'

I was still standing.

'You may sit down, Ms Joyce.' She peered down her nose at me.

'Thank you, Your Honour.'

I heard the door open behind me. Greta looked round; I was afraid to. The court clerk was busy scribbling out the access order. I noticed the judge was humming. Unless I was going completely insane, it sounded very much like 'Santa Claus Is Coming to Town'. I looked at Greta. She was smirking and trying to wipe it off her face. I nearly burst out laughing myself.

The clerk handed the piece of paper to the judge. She handed it to Greta. Greta handed it to me. I handed it to Andrew who handed it to his solicitor. Then the clerk wrote out a second access form and repeated the whole thing again. Even Andrew was trying to stop laughing. I thought I would never get out of there. Then the clerk shouted again, 'All rise.'

We all stood up.

'Merry Christmas to you all,' the judge said and exited the room.

I heaved a sigh of relief. The two solicitors were chuckling together. It was probably the easiest few bob they had ever earned. I didn't care. It was over, and I hadn't been found guilty. We turned to walk out of the courtroom. Sitting in the back were Mam and Dad, Alice and Karen. They had all turned up, all except Joe. No matter. Karen was there. I threw myself at her when we got outside.

'You came, you came!' I shouted, squeezing the life out of her.

She laughed out loud and tried to get me off her. A very strait-laced barrister was eyeing me up and down like I was the scum of the earth.

'We won!' I shouted in his face. 'We no longer have to live in hiding, do we, darling?' I kissed Karen right on the lips. The barrister rattled his newspaper and marched off in the other direction. Mam blessed herself. Greta broke down laughing.

Alice slapped Dad across the back. 'Some fucking fruit and nut, your daughter.'

'Fruit and nut?'

'Nutcase, fruit and nut? Someone fill him in.' Alice looked around.

Dad was bewildered. 'William, it's a joke,' Mam put in.

'Ask me arse,' he sneered.

We all stood there laughing and hugging. It was a wonderful special moment. I had my family and friends back. I couldn't have been happier. As I was about to leave, Greta called me outside the main door. She handed me an envelope. I looked inside. It contained £200.

'Keep it, Jack,' she said kindly. 'I thought you might need it for Christmas, with David and all the other expenses. It cost nothing this morning, honestly.'

This was the icing on the cake. I was speechless.

'I don't know what to say. Except that I'll spend it well. Thanks for everything.' I hugged her, feeling emotional and unworthy.

'You're welcome,' she said blithely and made off down the road towards the car park.

The others came out and we shared cigarettes. I looked sheepishly at Karen, who had made a great effort to support me. I didn't know how to put into words my gratitude for her appearance at the court, especially considering her own difficulties. She had turned up despite all that.

'I heard about you and Mick,' I said to Karen. 'You know I would have called you, but I wasn't sure you wanted me to.'

'I needed some time. It wasn't your fault. I just wasn't ready to face anyone.'

'I'm so glad you came. I appreciate it so much. Look, why don't we have a cup of coffee somewhere and we can talk about it in private?' I suggested.

'Sorry, but I have to get back to work. No worries. I'll call over Christmas and we can have a good chinwag.' She hugged me again.

'I'll look forward to that,' I finished.

'Jack, you're doing really well. We're all proud of you,' she said.

We're all proud of you? Who's we?

Mam and Dad offered me a lift home but I declined. I had decided to do some extra Christmas shopping. I didn't want £200 hanging about my person. I walked from Dolphin House on the Quays past the Halfpenny Bridge. Buskers huddled together in the chilly December wind. They were singing carols and doing it rather badly. Nonetheless, I stopped to listen and enjoyed it immensely. A cap was on the ground, held down by a large stone, to stop the wind from taking it away. I threw in my small change. They thanked me. It felt good to be alive.

I walked down the Quays, until I reached O'Connell Street, alive with street-traders competing for customers. The crowds moved like swarms of bees. I allowed them to carry me down Henry Street. The lights flashed on and off and overloaded shoppers jostled to get past me. I made my way slowly down the street. I was in no hurry. I was enjoying the atmosphere and tightly clutched the brown envelope as I strolled up Moore Street.

I veered left into the Ilac Centre, went straight to Roches department store and headed for the Household Section. I searched high and low until I found what I was looking for: a beautiful crystal savings box, just like the one I had broken. I picked it up and felt its dead weight. It was almost identical. I went to the checkout and asked could I have it engraved. I was sent to a private booth and I instructed them to inscribe: *David, 20 September 1987*. It wasn't the best job in the world – I'd seen better engravings on wet cement. Still, I wasn't prepared to wait for a professional to do it. And it was the thought that counted. They gift-wrapped it for me and I put it in a large carrier bag.

Then I headed for the butchers on Moore Street and bought the biggest turkey and joint of ham that I could see. Alice would appreciate that. It was the least I could do to repay her for all the nights she was minding David. After that I wandered around the shops looking at clothes. I had a really hard time buying a pair of trousers and a sweater for myself. They cost £50 altogether. I didn't feel I was worth £50 and crept out of the shop like a thief. I stopped in a small coffee-shop and bought myself something to eat. Then I set off back to Roches Stores for the last leg of my shopping trip.

The toy department there was a wonderland. Hysterical children were being dragged by the earlobe by over-wrought adults along the toy-laden aisles. Dolls walked and talked. Computer games played noisily. A fire engine shot through my feet at an alarming speed, its siren wailing as it fled past. A little boy came charging after it and was promptly walloped across the backside by an irate mam. I smiled to myself. Then I had a thought. I searched along the shelves and picked up a beautiful brand new Thomas the Tank Engine, its newly painted blue and black engine shining in the fluorescent light. I tucked it under my arm. Then I stumbled on a large brown teddy bear, pretty much like the one I had had as a kid. I bought that too. I was just about to leave the store when I caught sight of something in the corner of my eye. I turned back slowly and stood staring. It was the most beautiful tiny doll's house I had ever seen.

I knelt down to examine the miniature furniture and petite rooms. It even had a library, complete with minuscule books. The walls were papered and displayed framed paintings. I gently lifted one off just to see that they weren't stickers. Everything was real. Even the chandeliers worked. I turned the light switch on and off in silent amusement.

An assistant appeared at my side and bent down. 'It's a beauty, isn't it?' she remarked.

'I don't think I've ever seen anything as beautiful in my life.' I couldn't take my eyes off it.

'Had you got it in mind for a little girl, perhaps?'

I looked at the assistant. 'Eh. Yes. I suppose so.'

'How old is the little one?' she enquired.

'Thirty – sorry, I meant nine. She's nine years old!' I blushed.

'Oh, she'd simply love this.' The assistant had me eating out of her hand.

'Do you really think so?' I played along.

'Oh yes! This particular house has sold out. In fact, it's the only one left, I think.'

That did it. 'What's the damage?' I asked.

'One hundred pounds.'

'Jaysus.'

'Think of her little face on Christmas morning.'

I thought of my little face. 'I'll take it,' I said.

Having spent the entire £200, I headed for home. I was broke and I was delighted.

The following day was Christmas Eve. The last time I

was sober on Christmas Eve was when I was thirteen. This year, to my delight, I really got into the swing of things. Mam and Dad had passed on their old Christmas tree in lieu of the new one they had just put up. It was a bit bockady and I had to fill a bucket and surround the base with stones to keep it steady. David was in his element, jumping up and down. I decorated the tree with some cheap bells and tinsel that I had picked up on Henry Street. It was bright and cheerful, just the ticket. I twisted the lights around the branches and plugged them in. Hey presto! They actually worked!

That night, it took for ever to get David to sleep. I read him Mr Men books until his eyes – and mine – started to droop. Just as I was about to sneak out the door, he would pipe up again, and demand to hear a Christmas story. I would have to relay the whole Santa thing again. Eventually, matchsticks couldn't have kept his eyes open. He turned over and snored happily in his teddy bear pyjamas. On his bedside locker sat a sandwich and a glass of milk for Father Christmas. I took a bite of the sandwich and sipped the milk. I removed the large red stocking that hung on the drawer knob and took it away to fill. As I did so, I put on Bing Crosby. It was the only time his singing seemed appropriate. Now his soft crooning was lulling me into a deeply peaceful state of mind. I was definitely getting older.

Taking all the gifts I had purchased, I arranged them on the floor, then carefully wrapped each one in expensive velvety paper. I reached for some gift tags and wrote their names in my best handwriting, then attached them to their relevant parcels. The dolls house, to me, from me. The fire engine for Joe. The brown teddy for Desmond. I arranged them neatly under the Christmas tree along with David's gifts.

I looked at them for ages and then realised how stupid I

was. I cried hard. I was still living in an illusion. However, it wasn't a fatal one. It kept me going. No way was I going to surrender this particular illusion. There was too much to lose. I wiped my tears and sat on the floor, smoking a cigarette. It then occurred to me that I hadn't once thought about a drink. I was dead chuffed.

Christmas Day came and went. Having dinner in Mam and Dad's didn't turn out to be as difficult as I thought it would be. There was a card from Jill on the mantelpiece. She had forgotten my address and sent it c/o Mam and Dad. I was really pleased.

David was hyper from an overdose of presents and chocolate. When we left, I filled two black sacks full of toys and piled them into the back of Dad's car. Back home, Alice called in with two plates of turkey and ham. She was delighted with the present but insisted that we ate some of it.

In the early evening, I took a stroll with David along Fairview Park. Children, dressed in their new Christmas clothes, raced up and down on new bicycles and roller blades. Little girls pushed new buggies and carried new dolls. We walked along the playground and watched them happily scurrying around. I was enjoying myself. I inhaled the clear pine-scented air, ran my hand along the bushes and felt a rush of childhood innocence. I used to do that when I was a kid. I'd skip along the road, coming home from school, and run my hand through the thick leaves. It felt wonderful. I was reclaiming the simplicity of being able to feel.

When David and I got back home, I opened my Christmas presents. There was some money from Mam and Dad. A packet of Rolo's from David (Alice's idea) and the doll's house. David immediately wanted to play with it. I had a hard time explaining it was not a toy. However, I let him at it, knowing he would soon tire of it. A clatter of kids sat around the room eating popcorn and watching television. I was glad of the company and was quite enjoying the telly myself for once.

When the doorbell rang, little Johnny, Alice's son, went out to answer it. I thought it was funny. They could have all been my children.

'Missus, there's an oul fella at the door,' he said.

'Tell him I've no money. I can hardly feed the eleven I already have.'

I heard him repeat word for word what I had said and laughed to myself. He returned breathless and confused. 'Missus, he won't go away.'

'Ask who it is,' I instructed him, getting a bit annoyed. It was probably one of the parents looking for their mislaid child.

Johnny returned again, obviously pissed off. 'Says he's a friend of yours. His name is Sam.'

Ah Christ.

I went out closing the living-room door behind me.

A quiff of blond hair perched against the porch door. 'Are you coming out to play?' Joe said.

'You've grown a beard.' I couldn't think of anything else to say.

'All the rage, this time of year,' he smiled.

'Where's your sleigh?' I giggled.

'Refuelling.' He motioned to a banjaxed car parked at the kerb.

'I guess you'd better come in, then.' Joe stepped into the hall. No sooner had he put his foot in the door than David had twigged it. He came running up the hall without so much as a hint of shyness.

'Joe! Joe!' He threw himself at him and Joe lifted him up. It was useless to try not to cry. 'We have a Christmas present for you!' He jumped up and down excitedly.

'We?' Joe looked at me. I blushed.

David dragged him by the arm. 'C'mon! C'mon!' He pulled him into the other room and ran to the tree, hauling out the present. Then he proceeded to open it himself.

'David!' I yelled. 'Let Joe open it himself.'

The other kids clamoured around in a circle.

'I'm afraid you've got an audience,' I smiled. I folded my arms and stared at him.

He removed the paper carefully and took out the engine. 'Ah ha!' he said. Then: 'I have something for you two as well.' He handed David an envelope. He tore it open. There was a £20 note inside.

'What's this?' David asked, looking disappointed.

'It's for your savings box,' I said.

'Boring!' he sighed. The little bugger.

Joe told me to close my eyes and hold out my hand. I stood there, arm outstretched, hoping he would plonk a great big kiss on my lips. Instead I felt a cold object being placed in my hand.

'Open your eyes,' he said eventually.

I looked down. 'What is it?' I asked stupidly.

'It's a war medal, read it.'

It was a Maltese cross. I flipped it over and it read: *Jack. For bravery and courage. Love, Joe.*

I put my arms around him, not caring that the children were watching, not caring that David was watching, not caring if my guardian angel himself was watching. I kissed his ear and felt the roughness of his beard scratch me.

'I thought I'd lost you,' I whispered.

'You'll never lose me – you know that. I just had to do what I had to do.' He pulled me closer.

'I know,' I said. 'Thank you. Thank you for loving me.'

I lost my virginity again on 31 December 1993.

Joe suggested a drive along Dollymount Beach. 'C'mon, it'll be fun. We can count the condoms together.'

I could hardly resist. I didn't lose my knickers because I wasn't wearing any. I didn't hear any choirs of angels either, but I was certain I could hear Bing Crosby. Still, Bing Crosby is all right by me.

My journey was complete.